MURDERER OF THE GODS?

After a failed coup attempt, the dark lord Lucian was exiled from the Golden City of the gods and has dwelt for centuries among the worlds of Man.

During that time he carved out a star empire of his own, in competition with the great Terran Alliance that dominated most of human-occupied space.

Now the Power has returned—the Power that fuels the immortality and astounding abilities of the gods—and Lucian has resolved to cast aside his ties to humanity, end his exile and make his way back to his beloved celestial city.

But what he finds when he arrives there is not what he expected: Mysterious beings all in black roam the cosmic pathways, most of the gods have somehow vanished, and those who remain look upon him with unadulterated suspicion and hate.

Now he must clear his own name and find the true culprit even as his brother and sister gods do everything in their power to capture and destroy him.

No one ever said it was easy to be the god of evil...

"Plexico is master of Space Opera."
–Pulp Fiction Reviews

The Shattering/Legions Saga
by Van Allen Plexico

The Above:

   Lucian: Dark God's Homecoming

   Baranak: Storming the Gates

Shattered Galaxy:

   Hawk: Hand of the Machine

   Falcon: Revolt Against the Machine*

The Shattering/Legions Trilogy:

   Legion I: Lords of Fire

   Legion II: Sons of Terra

   Legion III: Kings of Oblivion

The Legion Chronicles:

   1: Cold Lightning

   2: Red Colossus*

  * forthcoming

LUCIAN

DARK GOD'S HOMECOMING

A Novel of *The Above*

———

VAN ALLEN PLEXICO

Ethriel!
"Not Guilty!!"
-Van Allen
Plexico

WHITE ROCKET BOOKS

*In memory of Katherine G. Plexico
and Roger Zelazny.*

*A stand-alone novel, this book is also the first volume in the
"Above" series and is a part of the "Shattering" saga.*

This book was originally published in 2009 by Airship 27 Productions.
It is also available as a limited edition hardcover and as an eBook from White
Rocket Books.

This is a work of fiction. All the characters and events portrayed in
this book are either products of the author's imagination or are used
fictitiously.

LUCIAN: DARK GOD'S HOMECOMING (THE SHATTERING)
Copyright 2009, 2015 by Van Allen Plexico
Cover art by Mark Williams
Cover design by Van Allen Plexico

A White Rocket Book
www.whiterocketbooks.com
ISBN-13: 978-0615606422
ISBN-10: 0615606423

First White Rocket paperback printing: February 2012
First hardcover printing: July 2015
New paperback printing: July 2015

0 9 8 7 6 5 4 3 2

The Above
(higher energy; slower movement)
Realm of the gods of the Golden City

- Our Universe -

The Below
(lower energy; faster movement)
Realm of demons; the underverse

THE ERAS OF THE SHATTERING UNIVERSE

First Pax Machina

First Terran Empire

First Dark Age

Second Terran Empire

Terran Alliance

Second Dark Age

The Young Empires

Second Pax Machina

Shattered Galaxy

The battle line between good and evil runs through the heart of every man.
—Aleksandr Solzhenitsyn

ONE

Down rained the night, cloaked all in fire and brimstone. Surely the dark forces of Hell were conspiring to bring me down. Me—doubtlessly the darkest of them all!

A faceless figure in black pursuing me, I raced through twisted vistas and realms shot from strange, demented nightmares.

Please do not think less of me for fleeing. Were I a warrior god, I would have squared off against this creature and battled him to the bloody end. Being something else entirely, I did the only thing I could: I fled.

And the Dark Man pursued. Relentlessly, tirelessly, he pursued.

Lungs burning and legs aching, I sprinted the final miles toward the gates of the Golden City.

My adversary struck at me with gouts of flame and fingers of lightning, searing my flesh and dazzling my eyes. I retaliated as best I could, sometimes opening pits of molten lava in his path, other times raining down burning meteors upon his head. Our running battle must have razed portions of a dozen worlds and more, and still the pursuit went on.

Not wishing to abandon all hope entirely, I gave it everything I had. But even the gods tire after a while. I was nearing my physical and metaphysical limits, and I knew it.

And then I topped a rise and saw the City.

My city. The Golden City. Its domes and spires sparkled in the sun of a perfect, cloudless sky. Upon seeing it my heart leapt, as it hadn't in all the thousand years of my exile.

So close! Almost home!

But then—*pain.*

Ragged claws raked through my tattered cloak and across my back as I surged toward the gates. Dark energies besieged me every step of the way.

My heart about to burst, I poured the last of my strength into this mad dash.

Furious, my adversary lashed out at me with all his might. Tendrils of fire ensnared me and surged over my chest and arms, then flowed toward my legs, seeking to bring me down.

My sweat flowed in rivulets along my face and neck as I swept the flames aside and ran for the gates. Disoriented himself for a moment, the Dark Man fell a few steps behind me. I didn't bother to look back; I lunged for those cold, gold surfaces and laid my hands, and my fondest wishes, upon them. The fire again swirled around me, singeing my hair, but I gritted my teeth and heaved against them with all my strength and all my force of will.

The great gilded doors resisted, and I was not surprised: many of the gods had wanted me gone from the City, and they had laid their own wishes in that regard upon the gates.

An eternity that in reality could not have lasted more than two seconds passed. The gates felt the force of my personality, and knew me, and had no recourse but to yield. I slipped through the narrow opening, the Dark Man mere inches behind me now. His black robes flared around him as he lunged after me, talons slashing.

I delivered the strongest punch I could muster to that featureless face, staggering him. As he stumbled back, I raised my stinging hand and made one last satisfying and defiant gesture before shoving the gates closed and slumping against them, gasping.

The gates would not know him. They would not open for him. I was safe.

Safe in the heart of my true enemy's stronghold, I realized with a groan.

One issue at a time, Lucian.

Allowing myself a few breaths and some measure of self-congratulation for having gotten this far, I stood and gazed at the vista laid out before me. In its spectacle and its grandeur, it represented everything I had missed for the thousand years of my exile. No matter who controlled it at the moment, it was and always would be my city. The city of my dreams.

My eyes drank in the glorious sights that never failed to stir me, no matter how cynical and jaded I grew: a city wrought all in gold and silver and jewels beyond counting. A realm that reflected in its appearance the esteem its inhabitants held for it.

Know simply that the City is the center of the gods' existence and the focus of our hearts' desires. At its center flows the Fountain that pushes the not-quite-metaphorical current through the circuits of our bodies and our lives. Once, it had been my home. It remained my dream and my utter ambition. I believed with complete conviction that, upon reclaiming it, I would not willingly surrender it again.

That was when it hit me. No, not the massive, golden-armored fist. That came a few seconds later. What hit me first was the shocking realization that the inhabitants were nowhere to be seen. I was alone in the main thoroughfare of the City. Alone, in an immortal city usually teeming with gods and goddesses, their retainers and favorites, and a multitude of assorted other hangers-on.

Amend that thought. Not totally alone, as the voice that boomed and echoed throughout the city revealed.

"What supreme arrogance!"

Inside, I felt my stomach sink, along with my slender hopes of being warmly welcomed back into the fold.

"You dare to come here? To show your face at the site of your unforgivable, unimaginable crimes?"

"Surely it was not as bad as all that," I called back. "And don't you suppose I've more than served my time?"

Golden lights flared about me then. I knew them all too well. Collectively known as the Hosts of Baranak, they were half-sentient, ephemeral servants and heralds of our own great god of battle. Ghostlike, they flitted about me, their sparkling majesty filling my vision momentarily. When they withdrew, I blinked and beheld a sight I'd hoped to avoid: the golden god himself, grand and awful and full of wrath, standing before me in all his polished glory and muscular power. Intense blue eyes glared at me from above a blunted nose and thick blond beard. Golden armor covered him from neck to toe. A huge, golden-hilted sword hung at his side, and I remembered that it was strong and swift and terrible.

"Baranak," I said, brushing my long, dark hair back out of my eyes and greeting him with the closest thing to a smile I could manage.

"Lucian." His voice was deep and rumbling, his face cold and expressionless. "I cannot imagine your plan, or what you hoped to gain by all of this. But you should have remained in hiding." His fists knotted. "For now you must be punished. And with the Fountain flowing once more, you can be punished."

This was surely the most I'd ever heard him utter at one time, and I frowned, trying to make sense of his words.

"My plan? But the insurrection was so long ago—"

"So many of us dead!" he bellowed. His fist swung out in a golden flash, sending me sprawling. "So many!"

Ages had passed since I'd last met that fist, and I would have been quite pleased never to encounter its like again. As I pulled myself up, shaking my head to clear it, he advanced, his face still somewhat calm but his eyes burning brighter with controlled fury. The massive fists lashed out again.

"Dead?"

I tried to ask him just what the hell he was talking about, in between blows, but to no avail. The brutality of the beating I absorbed was matched only by its thoroughness. As we are unable to create portals within the confines of the city, I could not make my own exit and flee. There was absolutely nothing I could do but take the beating.

What you have to understand is that Baranak is supposed to be able to kick my ass. That doesn't mean I won't do my best to resist, it simply means I will fail. I am not, after all, the god of battle. Unfortunately, he is.

As oblivion descended, his words echoed through my mind once more. The other gods—dead? Was that what he had meant? How could that be?

Any further consideration had to be deferred, as I was busy lapsing into unconsciousness.

In sleep's cold embrace I dreamed, and in dreams I saw again the events that had started me on my journey back to the City.

On a day like so many before it, running back endlessly across the centuries, I awoke with the Mysentian dawn and climbed out of bed, gazing out of the broad palace windows overlooking my capital city, gingerly stretching my aged body, my withered muscles, my brittle bones.

Instantly I sensed it. Something felt different that morning, both within my flesh and in the very air surrounding me. Before I could pause to consider it, though, the serving girls entered, carrying trays of fruits and bread.

The resounding crash of their trays hitting the marble floor caused me to look up in surprise, only to witness the girls fleeing my bedchamber, shouts of alarm on their lips.

Startled, looking about for signs of intruders, I pulled my robe tighter about myself and rushed after them. Tyren, the captain of my guards, met me at the door. Having served me for many years, he had earned my implicit trust, and I waited for him to explain this strange turn of events.

It was not to be. Gawking, eyes wide, he stumbled back a few steps, then called for his men. They rushed up behind him, resplendent in their white uniforms, weapons at the ready, even as I attempted to ask what was happening.

"Who are you?" Tyren demanded. "Where is my lord Markos?"

Frowning, utterly bewildered, I searched the faces of the guards, these men and women who had been in my employ for much of their lives. None of them exhibited the slightest signs of recognition. Shocked and rapidly growing fearful as well, I whirled about, casting my gaze across the furnishings of the room, seeking a mirror. I desired above all else at that moment to see what my guards were seeing. It was not to be, of course. I had banned all mirrors from my presence years earlier, when my aging had grown so pronounced that I could no longer bear to look upon myself.

At last I brought my hands up to my face, and then I began to understand. My shock, profound after so many decades of helpless wasting away, must have been obvious. My skin felt smooth, my hair thick and strong. Looking at my hands, I saw they belonged to a young man, not to the ancient figure I had become.

Staggering back, I slipped and fell to the cold floor, and fears immediately rushed through me. Had I broken a bone? No! I had hardly felt the impact. I was whole again. I was young!

Springing to my feet, I faced my guards and laughed maniacally, practically bouncing in the air. Confused, they hesitated in moving to apprehend what they surely took to be an intruder in the palace. One of them recognized something about my features then, minus the wrinkles and spots, and gasped in awe. Others quickly followed suit, and then the captain, Tyren, knelt on one knee, his mouth working soundlessly for a second.

"My lord Markos," he whispered finally, using the name I had adopted on this world. Awe filled his voice. "How can this be?"

I could feel it then. In truth, I had felt it from the moment I had awakened, but its long absence had dulled my sensitivity to it. A low, soft buzzing, growing steadily stronger. Not a sound; a sensation, a feeling, as of a current, long absent, now flowing once more through the firmament, through the fabric of the universe itself.

A sense of awesome, nearly limitless power, once again at my disposal.

The Power! After long decades, it had returned. During the night it had swept over me, carrying away the effects of age and restoring my appearance and condition to that of a man of thirty. It had made me a god once more!

Scarcely acknowledging my guards and the advisors who had rushed up as word of an intruder had spread through the palace, I turned the entirety of my attention instead to a goal I had believed forever denied me.

What would become of Mysentia, this world upon which I had dwelt in exile for ten centuries, and over which I had reigned for much of that time? What of the war I had been fomenting subtly against the mighty Terran Alliance? To what fate was I abandoning the Mysentians, and the other inhabitants of the Outer Worlds?

At that moment, I did not know and scarcely cared at all. For me, a destiny far greater awaited. The Golden City, so long denied me, beckoned.

Thus did I take my leave of the mortal realm and set my foot upon the Road once more, the Road leading home.

My faceless acquaintance with the excessively somber sartorial preferences had been lurking along the way. Who was he? No way to know, and he had not seemed the talkative sort. Had he been lying in wait for me? Someone in my line of work cannot afford to believe in coincidences.

The dream images faded then, and I drifted in peaceful blackness for a time. It could not last, of course, though I clung to that great oblivion with all of my unconscious willpower for as long as I could. Some small part of me, you see, knew where I would find myself upon awakening, and wished to delay that bitter revelation for as long as possible. Soon enough, though, reality reasserted itself and my worst fears were dreadfully, depressingly confirmed.

I awoke to a cold floor beneath my prone body and a throbbing in my skull. My muscles ached, my spirits flagged, and depression overwhelmed me, to the point that I scarcely felt any desire to move. Though there was scarcely a reason to do so, I opened my eyes, and was greeted with the sights I had expected. Black marble tile beneath me stretched endlessly into darkness in every direction; immense stone columns soared into nothingness above. No visible walls. No furnishings whatsoever. All just as I remembered it from my last stay here, a thousand years ago. Any remaining hopes I might have entertained evaporated.

At that moment the sound of hushed words from nearby reached my ears, and I became aware that I was not alone. My eyes, peering through the gloom, focused on three individuals who sat huddled against a nearby column. They were clad in what appeared to be military flight suits, dark blue with gold insignias. The look seemed somehow familiar to me. Alliance? That could scarcely be possible, here. Yet, as their faces resolved to me, I knew they were no gods. Humans? Apparently. But—here? How?

"—told you already," one of them was saying, "there was no malfunction. All the systems showed green. It just powered down. I don't know what we could have done differently." The voice was male, high-pitched and filled with anxiety. "Everything checked out right up until the end."

"If that's so," came a deeper, rougher voice, "then you must have screwed things up even worse than I thought."

"That's enough," a third voice stated firmly. "Whatever happened, we're here now, and our only priority is to get back home. And we will." This one was female, firm, and confident. The leader?

"We don't even know where 'here' is," the first voice complained.

"Then we have to find out."

A pause, then the second, rougher voice growled, "Maybe our friend over there knows. Maybe we should try to wake him up again."

"Leave him alone," the woman said. "He looks to be in worse shape than we are."

One of the figures was staring at me.

"No, I think he's already awake." It was the first guy, the nervous one.

I sighed softly, wanting to roll over and go back to sleep. But some small degree of curiosity about these people, I had to admit, tugged at my mind. Reluctantly, and with some effort, I pulled myself up to a seated position and faced the others, waiting.

They all stood then and made their way over to stand in front of me in a semicircle.

"Hello," the woman said. "Can you understand me?"

Their uniforms were definitely Terran Alliance issue, I could see now. Could they actually be Alliance officers? Or was this some joke of Baranak's?

Not meeting their eyes, I nodded once.

"Good," she said. "Are you all right?" A pause, then, "Can you tell us where we are?"

This woman surprised me. Her voice was strong and even, lacking the fear and desperation I would have expected from any mortal confined in this place—the fear already detectable in at least one of the others. Perhaps she simply knew too little to fully appreciate her plight, I thought to myself. Drowning in self-pity and horrified at the thought of revealing that fact to mere humans, I resolved to ignore them.

"Can you tell us where we are?" she said again. "Can you help us?"

I emitted one sharp laugh before rolling onto my side, my back to them.

"Hey!" shouted the rougher voice. "What's that all about? You can understand us—why don't you answer the captain's questions?"

Seconds ticked by. I was in no hurry. Where else would any of us go? But they were all standing there, waiting, hoping I could tell them something that would explain their bizarre predicament. At last, I turned back to them.

"Who," I asked, "are you?"

They all seemed shocked that I had actually spoken.

Regaining her composure quickly, the woman said, "I'm Captain Evelyn Colicos. Terran Alliance Navy."

The Terran Alliance. So it was true. Only a day earlier, still powerless and trapped in exile, I had believed the Alliance represented my mortal enemy—mortal in every sense of the word. Now, a god again and removed entirely from that existence, I cared nothing for that government or its people, save a lingering sense of resentment and animosity.

The woman gestured at the two men, gruff one first.

"Lieutenants Frank Cassidy and Tony Kim. And we..." Her voice lowered, and she all but whispered, "...We would appreciate your help."

I took a deep breath, pursed my lips, and looked them over carefully, taking the opportunity to appraise them. All three were what one would expect of naval officers. They were fit to the point of being athletic. The captain had short but full blonde hair and piercing blue eyes so vivid they struck me as belonging more on one of my kind than hers. Behind her, the rough-sounding guy, Cassidy, was tall, though not so much as me, and an imposing specimen, blunt of nose and ruddy of cheeks. He kept his head shaved and his muscles filled out his flight suit. The other man, Kim, possessed hair even darker than mine, worn in a crew cut, and was the shortest of the three, though wiry.

Perhaps realizing after a few moments that I was in no hurry to speak, the captain addressed me again.

"We—" She hesitated, frowning, then, "I'm sorry if this doesn't make sense to you, but it doesn't to me, either. We were aboard a long-range spacecraft, and something happened—"

"The *Copernicus*," I said. I remembered hearing about its disappearance on the news, days ago, just before I'd taken my leave of Mysentia and started for home.

"Yes! Yes, that's right."

Emboldened perhaps that she had gotten a word or two out of me, she pressed on.

"We had just jumped, and something must have gone wrong. When we emerged into what should have been subspace, the engines shut down…"

"Yours was an experimental ship," I said.

"How did you know that?" the smaller man, Kim, demanded. It seemed to me he hovered perpetually on the verge of hysteria.

"I think I know," Cassidy said. "I think he's from the Outer Worlds."

"A spy, maybe?" Kim asked, looking from Cassidy back to me.

"He does look familiar, now that I think about it."

The captain silenced them both with a look, then turned back to me, her brow furrowed.

"What else do you know about our situation?"

"You sought to improve jump technology. You jumped farther than you know." I grinned. "Much farther."

"The stars disappeared," Kim said quietly, his voice shaking.

Ignoring him, the captain continued.

"The next thing we knew, we were attacked by these bright lights."

"The Hosts of Baranak."

"I—all right, sure. And they nearly tore our ship apart before bringing us here. Wherever here is. And a man—a huge man, in gold armor—threw us into this—" she looked around at the infinite-seeming depths of blackness around us, "—this place, whatever it is."

"We didn't do anything to him," Cassidy interjected angrily.

"You scarcely could have," I replied, a slight smile playing about the corner of my mouth. "And he was no 'man.'"

The captain looked back at the others. Each of them shared a confused expression. Shaking her head as if to clear it, as if this could all make sense to her somehow if she could just sort out the pieces, she turned back to me.

"We're lost," she said flatly. "We're out of our depths. Anything you could tell us would be welcome."

I met her eyes. "Are you so sure of that?"

She shrugged. When she spoke again, her voice was softer.

"At least tell us *something*…"

I considered her request for a long moment.

"My advice to you: Abandon all hope," I said, and turned my back once more.

Silence for perhaps two seconds, and then, "Son of a bitch! Who do you think you are?" Cassidy grabbed my shoulder roughly. "You'll answer our questions, or—"

His voice trailed off as my dark eyes met his. He felt something of the Power then, and faltered, staggering back a step. My wrath aroused at last, I made as if to rise, but stopped myself as the woman interposed herself between us.

"Frank, that isn't helping," the woman said. "Step back."

Somewhat reluctantly, Cassidy moved away, smoothing out his flight suit as he went, his face still revealing his anger.

"We don't even know this person," the captain said. "Maybe we should start over." She bent down over me, extending a hand. "My name is Evelyn. What's yours?"

She startled me with her composure, and, though my anger dissipated almost instantly, I determined to shake her up. Considering the truth I was about to reveal, I couldn't help but laugh. I took her hand and shook it.

"Pleased to meet you. I am Lucian, considered in these parts to be the devil himself. And as to where we are," I gestured broadly with both hands, "welcome to the dungeon of Heaven."

Their faces registered no expression. Unfortunate—I'd hoped at least for shock or fear or something to indicate they appreciated the seriousness of their situation. But they truly had no clue.

"Now if you will excuse me," I said in as friendly a manner as I could muster, "I have to be thinking of a way out of this most inescapable of prisons, before Baranak surely returns to execute us all." I turned away, and this time they respected my wishes.

Perhaps, during my time among their kind, I would have been more patient with them, more willing to help. But those days were now over. And thus I found I had little interest in their plight. And I had not, I reminded myself, not precisely been among their kind—the Alliance—but among their enemies, the Outer Worlds. I had fought their kind for centuries. Help them now? Hardly, I thought. Let them rot.

Whether they believed me insane or simply decided to abide by my request, the humans left me alone after that exchange, and didn't speak to me again for some time. They retreated a few feet away, huddled together, and spoke in hushed but intense whispers. Try as I might, though, I found myself quite unable to ignore them.

The captain, Evelyn Colicos—I surprised myself with how easily that name came back to me—carried herself as a leader should, despite being well out of her depths. She kept her cool, for the most part, and directed their discussion, as they walked through the series of events that had led them here.

After a time, the debate grew heated along some finer point Cassidy was pressing. Kim took issue and their voices raised. Just as they seemed ready to come to blows, the captain stepped between them.

At that moment, I found my mind spinning backwards through the centuries, to the days prior to my failed revolt. Memories long suppressed flooded forth, sweeping me along helpless in their path.

My Halaini. My lady of poise and strength and grace. My goddess, my muse, my inspiration, and my conscience. She who had encouraged me to strive beyond the limitations of my Aspect, then consoled me when I'd invariably failed. She who had argued so strongly against my secret plans to overthrow Baranak's ruling circle and install myself as ruler of the City. She who had watched in sorrow as my plans were exposed and an army of gods marched out to meet my followers and me before we were fully ready to strike.

She had stood there, in the main square of the City, her hands raised between both armies, appealing for peace and restraint. She had faced even mighty Baranak down with the sheer force of her will and the purity of her intent. She had been determined to stop my war before it got going, and she had said--

"There's nothing to be gained from this, can't you see?"

My mind snapped instantly back to the present.

Those words. Had Evelyn actually spoken them, just then? Or had they merely floated up to me, from out of the depths of time, echoes and memories of my long-lost love? I wasn't sure.

I looked at the humans again and saw that their captain had indeed spoken them. She had stopped the fight with those words.

Thus did the mortal woman Evelyn Colicos, with her poise and her strength and her grace, inscribe the first cracks in the wall surrounding my black heart, and summon ghosts from ten centuries in the past to torment me. That was the moment when all my plans and dreams came to naught, though I scarcely suspected the truth until much, much later.

At about that time the door opened, shattering my reverie.

The "door" was in actuality a portal, a breach in the fabric of reality that could only be opened from the outside. It shimmered into existence a few feet from us, blindingly bright golden lights flooding through. I raised a hand to shade my eyes, and saw the humans behind me cringing.

"Could you turn it down a bit, perhaps?" I called into the light, my voice tinged with sarcasm. "I don't think the humans are equipped to tolerate your glorious radiance."

The two of Baranak's Host who had entered flared in indignation before settling into a more torch-like blaze. They moved to each side of the portal as their lord and master—and our captor—stepped through. Behind him came two others, whom I did not recognize at first.

"The dark god himself. So. This one is the cause of all our pain and woe," said the figure to Baranak's right. I knew him then: Vorthan, the self-styled god of the forge. Our engineer and builder. His mottled bald scalp reflected the Host's golden light; above his black goatee, two red-tinged eyes seemed to bore through me. His muscular arms were crossed over his chest, and contempt dripped from his every word. "My compliments, Baranak, on his swift capture."

"Indeed, you acted swiftly," came a female voice to Baranak's left, "but are you certain you acted properly?"

Alaria, of course. Tall she was, and curvy, fitted within a tight, black dress that shone of intricate patterns in the flickering light, iridescent and shifting and almost snakeskin-like. Her eyes, rimmed in black, sparkled with many colors; her thick, pouty lips shone with the color of wine. Her narrow face, pale to nearly white, lay within a sea of hair so deeply red as to appear almost black, shot through with shades of burgundy and magenta where the light struck it. Two long braids trailed down her left shoulder and over her breast. In all, her Aspect caused me to ponder anew the concepts of beauty and love and desire. What else would you expect? As with all of us, she lived up to the part she desired to play.

"Is this then the guilty party?" she asked, gazing at me where I sat.

"Who else?" Baranak growled.

"And there is no doubt?" she continued.

The big, blond god seemed momentarily troubled by her question, but swept it aside.

"Can there be any?" he said by way of answer.

"None of the other few who remain has a motive," Vorthan added.

Baranak nodded.

"And Lucian's past deeds are well known," he said. "He conspired to overthrow this realm once before, and was exiled. From there, he doubtless plotted any number of schemes to bring us to ruin. And he has nearly succeeded."

"Is there even any point to me saying that I don't know what you're talking about?"

Sullenly I stared back at them, growing more resigned to my fate by the moment.

"You feign both innocence and ignorance," stated Baranak. "Very well. We shall convene a trial to prove your guilt. And then you will be executed."

"You will be consigned to the Fountain," Vorthan added, "where your form and energies will disperse..." He smiled. "And you will cease... to be."

Nothing unexpected there. I nodded impatiently.

"Right, right—but what exactly am I accused of? Can you at least tell me that much?"

Baranak glared at me, full of righteous fury.

"Mass murder," he hissed.

"Excuse me?"

"You are charged with the murder of seventy-two gods," he said coldly. "Nearly three quarters of our number are gone forever. And for that…" His eyes burned into mine. "…You will pay."

I absorbed this news with a degree of shock. So many of our kind—-dead? It was no easy trick to kill just one of us, but *seventy-two*? My stomach twisted and my heart quaked at the mere thought. Then I remembered that the Fountain had not flowed for years, and had started up again only recently. The Power had been denied us for so long. Of course, I had thought only of my own loss during that time—-what else would you expect? But during that period, we had all been vulnerable…

Baranak whirled and stalked toward the portal even as I fought to regain my wits.

"You do realize," I called after him, "that at least one homicidal figure in black is patrolling the main path to Earth's plane, right? You do not suppose he might have anything to do with this?"

"This one will stop at nothing," Vorthan muttered. "The master of lies, indeed."

Wordlessly, Baranak stomped back through the portal. Vorthan followed without so much as a backward glance, but Alaria remained another moment, her eyes meeting my own, her expression unreadable.

"Alaria!" came the booming voice.

Casting her eyes down, her black dress flaring at the bottom as she turned about, she followed the other two out of the dungeon. The Hosts closed the portal behind them and darkness descended once more.

I stared at the point where the opening had been, my eyes readjusting to the lighting, and contemplated what I had been told. I was being framed, obviously. And who better to frame?

Anger and depression settled over my spirit, and I sat in solitude for a while, considering my situation. The humans must have been impressed by the visit of our captors, for they kept to themselves during that time and I all but forgot them.

After the passing of perhaps an hour, they must have worked up their courage once more, for I heard one of them approaching. It was the captain, Evelyn. She knelt beside me, and I saw that her expression was pained.

"If you're suffering from delusions," she said, "clearly you're not the only one."

I shrugged, my mind still occupied with Baranak's words.

"I am innocent, of course," I said.

She nodded earnestly.

"Innocent. Yes. The devil himself. Of course."

Despite my frustration, I couldn't resist a laugh, and she joined me. I found my depression lifting somewhat, much to my surprise.

"I apologize for our presumptions earlier," she said after a pause. "We had no right to assume you'd wish to help us— especially if you do have some connection to the rebellious worlds."

"I—" Words failed me. Indeed, I found myself quite unsure of how to respond.

"I disagree with their positions, of course," she continued, apparently oblivious to my discomfort, "but certainly you wouldn't feel any compunction to aid those whom you might view as the enemy."

"I—" I did not know what to say. Speechless? Ridiculous! My thrashing at Baranak's hands must have caused some sort of brain damage.

"You do view us that way, right? As your enemies?" She frowned. "I can tell."

Was the woman sincere? I felt adrift, uncertain of my actions and my feelings—not a sensation I to which I was accustomed. Was she intentionally shaming me? Or could she possibly be as open, as sincere, as she seemed? I could not get a read on her, and it galled me.

Leaning forward, she rested a hand on my shoulder, and met my eyes.

"We won't make any further demands of you," she said. "If you should find some way to assist us, and feel willing to do so, we'll be grateful."

I may have nodded once, my throat dry.

At that moment I had one of those out-of-body experiences, where you see yourself from high above. And I saw myself conversing with this mortal woman, as if she were one of us. And I was amazed. Certainly, in the thousand years of my recently ended exile on her plane of existence, I'd been forced to deal with humans, to interact with them. But always I had occupied the highest reaches of power, where I was removed from contact with all but the elites. I'd slain dukes and princes in my day, as well as generals and admirals and enlisted men by the bushels. By the end I had built my own power base among the Outer Worlds and had them on the brink of a war of liberation from the old Terrans. In all that time, though, only a very few mortal women had known my attentions, and none of them for long, even as the mortals measured time. My regard for most of them had been slight, indeed. None compared to what I had known in the eternal realm, to goddesses such as Halaini or Alaria. A thousand years had not been enough to make me forget what I had been forced to leave behind, nor to make me accept what I had deemed sub-standard replacements.

Yet here I sat, an inexplicable and undeniable interest in this mortal woman growing within me. Once I realized it, it struck me as quite ludicrous; no mortal woman—no mortal at all—could evoke such a reaction from in me in so short a time. No, this had to be something unrelated to any specific woman. Something that had been building within me for quite a while. I could see it now. This woman, Evelyn Colicos, was the catalyst of the moment, but the root cause was ten centuries spent in exile among their kind. It had softened me. That simply could not be.

While my own mind had been in turmoil, the captain apparently had been doing some thinking of her own. Standing, she walked a few steps away, then turned back, gazing down at me.

"I do have one question, though," she said.

I sighed. I had known it was too good to be true. Her mind was always active, always thinking. Good traits in a captain, but not in a cellmate.

I looked up at her, waiting.

"So you're a god." She shrugged. "Okay. We'll take that as a given, for now."

One of the others snorted; we both ignored him.

"But, if so," she continued, "why can't you simply walk out of here?"

Grinding the balls of my hands into my tired eyes, I replied, "A portal into here has to be opened from outside. Our powers are negated within the dungeon. It is actually a walled-off pocket universe, a step below the City, and the Power scarcely trickles into this space."

Lieutenant Kim had been approaching, and he scoffed at my words.

"I'm not buying any of this," he said.

I shrugged.

"Lieutenant," Evelyn said to him, softly but tersely, "I was just apologizing…"

Kim ignored her.

"That big guy seemed awfully sure you were guilty of something," he said.

"Occupational hazard of being the 'dark god,'" I replied. "Of course, I am indeed guilty of… much."

He looked down at me, shaking his head in wonder.

"I'm supposed to believe there's really some kind of 'dark lord?' And he's you?"

"You can believe what you like," I replied sharply. "I seek no followers among your kind. Not any longer."

"Our kind?"

"Humans. The Terran Alliance."

"Who would ever follow you?" Kim growled.

I shrugged. "I had supporters aplenty among the Outer Worlds. Soon enough, we would have been standing triumphant on your Earth, your old order swept away."

And then I cursed soundlessly. I had given in to anger, and given away something I had wished to keep hidden. Who was the god, here? How could I have allowed these mortals to push me so, and cause me to slip?

The third human, Cassidy, approached then, eyes wide.

"I do know this guy!" he said. "I recognize him now!"

The captain and Kim turned, regarding him with questioning expressions.

"We've believed for years," he began, "that a family out among the Outer Worlds was building a coalition against us, either through intimidation or outright conquest of their neighbors. They've always kept a low profile, working through intermediaries and puppet rulers, so not much has been said about them publicly within the Alliance. Their current head is supposedly called Markos, probably named after the original one, years ago—who probably didn't even exist, anyway."

My dark eyes studied Cassidy carefully, but I said nothing.

He snorted a laugh.

"We've only been able to acquire a few pictures of him or the other leaders, over the years, and a bunch of us in the Directorate had begun to think maybe it was all a myth—something the Outies cooked up to scare our security forces out along the frontier. But—I've seen what few pictures we do have, and this guy has to be a part of that family. Maybe a son or a nephew—though he looks just like the guy from a generation ago." Cassidy paused and nodded slowly, his eyes drilling back into mine. "The secret leader of the Outer Worlds. I'm sure of it."

"Well, well," I breathed. "An intelligence man." Something from my dim, distant past reacted to that thought, but I quickly, reflexively suppressed it before it could fully register.

"Though not a particularly discreet one," Evelyn noted. She looked at me, waiting.

"Guilty as charged," I said then.

Cassidy nodded again, his jaw setting, his mouth curling into a self-satisfied smile. "You're the son?"

"I am Markos. The only Markos there has ever been."

Cassidy frowned. "That's impossible. You'd have to be…"

"Immortal?" I laughed. "What part of 'god' don't you understand?"

Cassidy grew visibly angry again, but held his tongue.

"I was Markos, rather," I said finally. "But no longer. All of that has turned out to be only a momentary diversion. A sideshow."

"Why?" Evelyn asked.

How much to tell them? I inhaled deeply, considered for a few seconds, then decided that recounting a bit of the story might actually do me some good.

Sitting back, I spread my hands before me and began. "A thousand years ago… well, let us say that I objected—strenuously—to the prevailing power structure in this City. For my troubles I was exiled to your mortal realm."

"They kicked you out," Cassidy said.

I ignored him and continued. "After a brief time of casting about for something to occupy me there, I seized control of the planet Mysentia in the Outer Worlds. It was not difficult for one with my knowledge, my abilities. And there, under the name Markos, I ruled, subduing your fellow humans to my will." I smiled. "For a time, life was at least tolerable.

Security and safety I possessed there in full measure, along with control over the destinies of millions. Leading a world in rebellion against your Alliance was nothing to me—a entertaining diversion, at best."

Even as I said those last words, though, I knew them to be false.

Evelyn frowned.

"Why 'Markos?'" she asked, after a moment.

"I—because—" A veil of fog descended over my mind as I pondered that simple question. "It seemed—"

She stared at me, waiting.

I felt that an answer—a good answer—hovered out there, somewhere just beyond my reach. The fog...

"This is all preposterous," Cassidy growled.

I was grateful for the interruption. My mind cleared at once, as I set Evelyn's question aside and faced Cassidy.

"Look around you," I said. "How did you come to be here? Are you so sure your understanding of the universe is the only possible one?"

Cassidy looked away, unsettled.

"This is just ridiculous," Kim said. "Bad enough he's an Outie rabble-rouser, but one with delusions of godhood, to boot."

I glared back at him.

"Delusions? You fool. You insect. You have no idea." Despite my determination to ignore these creatures, they had succeeded in raising my ire—a fact that further angered me and spurred me to react.

Kim shoved past Cassidy, fists raised.

And again Evelyn was there, between us, voice gentle but firm and eyes unwavering as they met my own.

"Enough!" she said. "We're all equals now in our imprisonment, and the rebellion is very far away from all of us at the moment."

Calming myself, I executed a small bow to her and reseated myself on the cold floor, drawing my long coat about me again, turning away from the others.

Evelyn would not be deterred. After a few moments, she spoke again.

"Please—let's put the accusations and innuendo aside. I genuinely want to understand," she said. "I want to know who you really are... and where we are. But I don't know how we're supposed to believe you, especially when you actually claim to be... *evil*."

I sighed, then looked up at her again. Her eyes sparkled in the dim light, betraying no deceptions. I found, unexpectedly, that I, too, wanted her to understand.

"Evil is my Aspect as a god, but not necessarily my nature," I said, for perhaps the thousandth time in my long existence. I paused, considering the strange sense of sincerity I felt behind the phrase this time. "At least, perhaps not my nature any longer."

I considered my own words, and then laughed humorlessly.

"Not that it matters," I said. "Baranak has already made his decision, and found me guilty. His one-track mind will not entertain any other possibilities."

I steepled my fingers in front of my chin, my mind sifting through the strange series of events that had brought me to this point.

"Understand one thing, though," I told her. "I was a god long before I found myself involved in the affairs of your worlds."

"And before that?"

"Before... that?"

I looked at her, then looked away and said nothing.

Cassidy and Kim, still lurking nearby, frowning, shook their heads and retreated some distance away. Soon enough, it sounded as though they had set the issue of my presence and identity aside for the moment and were resuming an earlier argument over engineering problems with their ship.

The captain, however, remained. She sat across from me, her eyes penetrating, never leaving mine.

"So," she said, finally, "you and your people are gods. But what does that mean, really?"

I tried to ignore her, but found I could not.

"We are who we are," I finally said, by way of answer. "Our origins are lost in the mists of time."

"Mm hmm."

She pursed her lips in a way I could not help but find most attractive.

"I can explain no better than that," I finally said. "Why do you care?"

"Because, if we truly are in some other universe, and you've been to mine, I want to know how you got there, and how you got back again. It might help us to get home."

I sighed.

"It is not that you are in an entirely different universe," I said, "it is merely that you are... well... a level up from your own plane, so to speak. Whereas subspace, which I imagine you were attempting to penetrate, is a level down."

I smiled, sitting back.

"One might say that, in your nice, new, experimental ship, you simply lacked for a decent roadmap."

Evelyn attempted to question me further, but, despite any personal feelings on my part, I studiously ignored her. After a brief while, she gave up and returned to the others.

An uneventful few hours followed, during which Kim cast occasional unsavory glances my way. Eventually the three humans slept, and I sat there in the near-darkness with my mood grown black as my prison and my soul.

I do not know how much time I spent in bleak introspection before being roused back into attentiveness by the flaring of a portal opening. This time I stood, determined to face Baranak down—but it was not our glorious golden god of battle who passed through. Alaria instead emerged from the flaming circle and stood before us, now wearing diaphanous robes, backlit and glowing, leaving her curvaceous silhouette an interplay of shadow and fire.

"Lucian," she whispered, "whether you are guilty or innocent of these crimes, we both know you will receive no fair hearing from Baranak. He is convinced of your guilt and means to see you consumed by the Fountain immediately."

"He made that abundantly clear, yes."

"You deserve the opportunity to prove yourself."

She gestured toward the blazing portal, and the freedom beyond.

I blinked.

"You mean…"

"Go!" She waved again at the glowing exit. "Find your evidence. Find the murderer. But do it quickly!"

I looked at the portal, then back at her. It didn't quite add up. I hesitated.

At that moment the human captain pushed past me, the other two in tow.

"If you're not going, we are," she said.

I scoffed.

"Going where? You have no idea what horrors await you out there."

"It can't be any worse than staying here, at that guy's mercy."

"You don't even know where 'here' is," I replied.

The captain moved very close, gazing up at me. Her eyes sparkled, there in the dungeon of my City.

"You know the way back to Earth," she whispered. "Or at least to the Outer Worlds. Take us home."

"I thought you were not going to make any further demands upon me."

"I take it back," she said quickly. "Just this one thing."

I shook my head.

"That path is not safe for any of us."

She looked past me at the glare of the open portal.

"Then at least show us the way." Her voice was now louder, and very firm. "We'll go by ourselves."

I snorted.

"Indeed?"

Rising to my feet, I made my decision and started past her.

"Without a guide you would scarcely get a mile from the city," I said.

"What do we have to lose?"

"You have no idea," I repeated quietly.

"Lucian," Alaria hissed, "you must come now!"

"We need your help," Evelyn said. "Please."

For a long while afterward I attempted to rationalize my decision in any number of ways, including the possibility that three humans might make excellent decoys. Certainly, in the case of Cassidy and Kim, I honestly believed this to be true, and felt no guilt over the thought. With the advantage of hindsight, however, I have to admit it was probably the look in Evelyn's eyes that motivated me to do what I did.

For long seconds, as Alaria urged me to depart, I stared back at the human woman. Finally I told her, much to my own surprise, "Very well. I will do what I can. Come on."

We rushed over the rainbow, then, the portal snapping shut behind us on that long, cold darkness.

TWO

Bright, sunless sky like a slap in the face as the dungeon's depths gave way instantly to the perpetual midday of the Golden Realm. No single point of illumination there in our own private cosmos, just a constant noontime of bluer-than-blue sky and shimmering radiance all about. Not, I reflected, the optimum conditions for a jailbreak.

Across the main square of the Golden City we raced. Now I understood why the streets were deserted and, at least for the moment, I will admit I was grateful.

In the middle of the square, the great plume of the Fountain flared up like a geyser, spouting golden sparks and stars and constellations into the too-blue sky. The column of energy towered over a hundred feet into the air before falling back down like water into the great basin surrounding its base. Frail by comparison, a gilded stairway ascended some forty feet up alongside the Fountain, topped by a ten-foot-wide platform, just within arm's reach of the current, from which various ceremonies were conducted in happier days.

The air around the Fountain fairly buzzed in harmony with the erupting shower of primal energy. Freed from the shielded interior of the dungeon, I could feel the full, invigorating effects of the Power washing over me. The clothes that have always been a part of my Aspect quickly regained their luster; my indigo shirt and pants seemed fresh and new again and my navy-blue long coat flared crisply behind me. The sapphire jewel I wore at my collar sparkled like a new star.

One thing was certain. We had to get out of the city immediately. Any planning beyond that point could wait. I led them to the main gates, but remembered my last journey on the road from Earth's plane and hesitated.

"What is it?" Cassidy demanded. "What are you waiting for? Get us out of here!"

Resisting the urge to backhand him for his impudence, I considered our options. The road I knew best—that most direct, best-mapped, and least-tasking of routes among the planes back to Earth's dimension—would surely be watched, if not by the man in black then by one of us. Perhaps by Baranak himself, once word reached him of my escape.

Anger swelled within me. I had not come all this way simply to give up and flee back to my place of exile, even were I sure it would be safe. But where else could we go? I needed information. I needed advice. I needed...

"He's right," Evelyn said, anxiety evident in her voice. "It can't be wise to stand here so long."

"Wise..." That word conjured an image from the depths of my ages-old memory. "Wisdom. Yes!"

Ignoring their further questions, I led them a short distance along the city's massive walls to another gate—a smaller one—and cautiously opened it. Seeing no signs of an attack, I motioned the humans out and closed the gate behind us. A narrow path led away from the city walls and into a wooded area down the hill, and I hurried off in that direction, the others behind me. It had been some time since I had last taken this route, and I hoped the intersection with Malachek's realm still lay in the same place.

"Where are we going?" Evelyn asked as we ran.

"To visit the god of wisdom," I replied, "and see if he can live up to his Aspect."

I strove to relax my mind as best I could, allowing my senses and my instincts to guide me as I mentally examined the texture of reality around us. It didn't take long. The point of close proximity between the City's dimension and my destination, where the barrier between those two planes was thinnest, had not moved since last I had passed this way, so many centuries earlier. Gesturing with one hand, the Power flowing through me, I pressed at the invisible wall and penetrated it easily, causing a portal to flare open. Quickly I expanded it into a ten-foot circle of blue fire that hovered before us. Smiling for the first time in quite a while, I quickly led the others through, allowing it to shrink to nothingness behind us. When we stepped out the other side, the brightness of day had been replaced by a dim world of long shadows and near twilight. The tall, straight trees from the outskirts of the city had given way to gnarly, twisted growths and thick underbrush.

Through the woods we raced, shadows descending all around. Gradually the ground sloped further down, until we found ourselves in a low area covered over completely with layers of contorted and knotty branches high above. Vast puddles of stagnant water surrounded us, leaving only mossy, narrow raised areas for walking. The sounds of swamp life buzzed and croaked and chirped all around us.

In answer to Evelyn's questioning look, I could only shrug and reply, "He likes his privacy."

On through the swamp we marched, for what seemed like hours on end. I considered opening a series of portals in and out of lower-powered adjacent planes where time ran faster, to hurry us on our way, but I feared that such actions might somehow be detected. Better to use this straightforward route to the pocket universe Malachek had found—or constructed; he was never entirely clear on this—many years before, even if it meant a depressing trek through lands he could only have chosen for their value as deterrents to visitors.

After far too long a time of trudging through muck, I sensed the texture of reality growing thin around us once more, and called a halt. This had to be the right place, the right node of intersection. I struggled for several moments, pushing with some effort against unexpected resistance, before rending the barrier enough for all of us to pass through. It snapped shut behind us instantly, leaving us in what appeared to be the same place we'd just evacuated. Frowning, I metaphorically tasted the energies around me. Ever so slightly different. Good. We had to be very close now. Perhaps only one more barrier lay before us. On we hiked.

Not long after this crossing, I felt a chill in the air. The others seemed not to notice it, which troubled me. I hesitated, raising a hand to bring them to a halt, and then I moved away quickly, my every sense alert. The air fairly crackled with electricity, something that had not been the case moments earlier. A circular glow began to coalesce in the air a few dozen yards away. Whirling, I gestured for the humans to get down, to hide themselves behind a clump of brush and fallen trees, and I followed them moments later. I held a finger to my lips to forestall any questions, and then we all peeked over the top, watching to see what developed.

The glow resolved itself into a blazing portal, and out stepped the Dark Man I'd battled earlier. Or, at least, it certainly looked like him. Black robes concealing his shape and form, face covered in a featureless mask that seemed to absorb light into its depths, he strode forward, head turning this way and that, as if searching, searching...

Seconds later, a second portal blazed open, and a nearly identical figure stepped through. *Great*, I thought to myself. *One was bad enough. How many can there be?*

I am no warrior god. I am not gifted with the cosmic flames of Vashtaar, or with the electrical abilities of Korvakh, nor even with Baranak's two good fists. Concealment, however, lies well within my talents. As we crouched there in the forest, behind our meager camouflage, I raised one hand and concentrated, encouraging a general assumption among any within range that nobody lurked behind these logs; that things were perfectly normal here, thanks for asking; that there was no one back here but us chickens.

Satisfied that I had masked our presence as best I could, I waited and watched as the two enigmatic figures in black approached one another, reaching out simultaneously to touch fingertips together. Electricity danced between them. At that moment, crimson lightning flared in the sky and struck down at them. They both lit up like red neon bulbs momentarily, then faded to dull black again. All very lovely, to be sure, but it told me nothing I didn't already know—which was little.

Apparently unhurt, the figures in black turned their backs on one another, and portals flared open ahead of each of them. Without further ado, each strode forward and vanished, the portals dwindling to bright points of light behind them, before vanishing entirely, as if they'd never been.

"Who," Cassidy was already asking me, "were they?"

"What just happened?" Kim added.

I glared at them by way of reply, then started forward again. Soon enough, they followed.

The humans had the good sense to let me be for most of the journey, my mood having transformed itself to match our surroundings. Some time later, however, Evelyn caught up with me, a question on her lips.

"The big guy—Baranak—said most of your kind had been killed. How do you know the one you seek is still alive?"

"I don't," I answered. "But we are about to find out." I pointed through the dense branches to a row of tiny lights sparkling just ahead.

Ten more minutes of tramping through slime brought us out of the dense growth and into a broad clearing, its central area dominated by an ancient stone castle complete with blazing torches along its walls and a drawbridge over a nearly dry moat. Weeping willows stood along the periphery of the clearing, doing their best to contribute to the gothic atmosphere. Somewhere to my left, predictably, a wolf howled. I made to approach the bridge, but before I'd taken half a dozen steps, a voice sounded from high above.

"From the look of you," the voice said, "you have come by the long way."

I gazed up at the figure leaning over the wall and waved once.

"It seemed wisest," I replied, deadpan.

"In these times of uncertainty, I would say you acted properly." His voice was rich and deep, with a hint of age to it—surely chosen for effect. After a moment, he added, "You didn't do it."

"Your wisdom remains undiminished," I replied. "I did not."

The rain drizzled harder, and I called back to him, "So, may we come in?"

But he was gone from the wall.

I frowned, but cheered up immensely as the broad wooden door across the bridge opened, seemingly of its own accord.

"His castle seems to be welcoming us, anyway," Evelyn noted.

"There's little difference," I replied, directing them all to cross the bridge.

The interior of the castle's main hall displayed treasures from a multitude of places and times, and the humans reacted to the sight precisely the way I'd expected. They gawked and stared. For my own part, I was somewhat disappointed; at some point in the past thousand years, Malachek had apparently grown weary of the more bizarre features of his residence and removed them. No longer did stairways and halls perform impossible right-angle turns into nowhere. It seemed his fascination with Escherian architecture had ended, though I was certain surprises aplenty remained for the unwary within his domicile.

"Greetings!"

At the top of a set of grand but quite normal stairs stood the god of wisdom in all his glory. He was, of course, just as I remembered him from so long ago: tall and slender, with an aquiline nose, and wearing the same brown tweed suit of indeterminable vintage in which I always pictured him. His silver-gray hair, long in the back, was partially covered by a hat that still dripped rainwater, but as he descended the steps he quickly removed it and bowed.

"Welcome to the house of Malachek," he said with stiff formality.

Malachek.

In the months and years before the revolt, many of the others had come to him, soliciting his views on the growing conflict. Those who had not already made up their minds one way or the other looked to him for guidance and advice. Given his Aspect, this was hardly surprising. Knowing he therefore could have a potentially significant impact on the outcome, or at least on the disposition of the factions, leading figures from both camps visited his estate, hat in hand, seeking his blessing.

He met all entreaties with stony silence.

Oh, he could hold forth on nearly any other subject for hours, if given the opportunity. His expertise in so many fields was unrivaled. But with regard to the dispute between the faction nominally led by Baranak and my own, Malachek always walked a strictly neutral path, consorting with both, favoring neither. Not once did he publicly state a position on the matter.

He might have swung the balance, but he chose instead to keep his own counsel. It was quite maddening.

When the forces of Baranak--the forces of hidebound reactionary conservatism--finally met the revolutionaries in the square of the City, there on that fateful day so many centuries ago, Malachek was nowhere to be seen. He knew precisely how the conflict would end, and knew that by not acting, he was in fact guaranteeing the outcome.

Later, when they threw me into the dungeons for the first time, I tried desperately not to hate him. He had not fought against me, and had not helped my enemies. I understood this. I should not have hated him then, and I surely could not hate him now.

Nevertheless, old slights, even those merely perceived, die hard.

Before I could utter a word, I heard the humans all gasp in surprise. I turned back to see what had startled them, but I should have known already. Malachek's ghost-guardians flickered about the room, their ethereal forms solidifying momentarily as they engaged in any number of tasks, from dusting the ancient wooden furniture to sweeping away the muddy tracks we'd left on the floor. One took Malachek's soaked hat as it passed, while another brought him his pipe.

"Do not be troubled," he reassured the humans. "Baranak has his Hosts, and I have my Ghosts. Of the two, I assure you these are much better behaved."

Smiling, he gestured them toward a side room.

"You will be provided with refreshments in there. Please make yourselves at home while I speak with Lucian."

As the humans cautiously entered the room Malachek had indicated, he gestured me toward the library.

"Come and sit. We will discuss recent events and make such sense of it all as can be made." As an aside to me, he whispered, "New minions, eh?"

"Burdens, rather," I replied, "though only until I can find a proper way of disposing of them."

His face betrayed a measure of alarm.

"Now, Lucian—do be civil. They seem perfectly harmless."

He surreptitiously looked them over, his gaze pointedly dwelling upon Evelyn.

"And not altogether unattractive."

Still wary of the flickering specters, Evelyn, Cassidy and Kim made their way into the cozy library, followed by Malachek and myself. The fireplace blazed warm and welcoming, immediately driving the chill from my bones, as did the snifter of brandy he handed over. As the humans warmed themselves and looked over the old god's collection of books and maps, Malachek directed me to a rich, leather-upholstered chair. Into this I was all too happy to collapse my lank form after a night on the cold, hard floor of the dungeon. My senses, still not fully attuned to the reawakened Power, warned me not to make myself too comfortable—to watch for any signs of betrayal. My aching body argued persuasively otherwise, however, and quickly prevailed. I sank into the cushions.

Conjuring an identical chair opposite me, he filled his delicately carved pipe with tobacco and lit it. Settling back into the cushions, he exchanged pleasantries with me briefly. Then his expression grew more somber, and he came quickly to the point.

"Let us assume," he began, "that I believe you had nothing to do with the recent deaths."

I nodded, quite happy for someone to believe this, even if only hypothetically.

"The first I heard of it was when Baranak accused me," I told him.

"So what do you intend to do?"

I laughed humorlessly.

"I have to admit, the temptation is great to secure a case of good whiskey and vanish into a pocket universe until Baranak or somebody else finds the real killer."

Malachek smiled.

"But you won't."

I inhaled deeply, looked away, exhaled slowly.

"No. I won't. Because I have very little confidence in Baranak's ability to find his ass with both hands and a set of directions; even less in his capacity to recognize the truth; and still less of a sense that he even cares to."

"You are probably right," he said.

"Think about it," I said. "Nobody has died recently. He executes me, and everyone is happy, and he remains popular. If the real killer starts up again later, all the better for Baranak—he can launch into action, bringing in another suspect. And those who remain will be cowed into obeying him, following his orders." I met Malachek's eyes again, feeling the old resentments building once more. "I do not much care for those who rule through fear and intimidation."

"Of course not," he replied. "You prefer the more subtle methods of bending your peers to your will."

I smiled. "Touché."

He puffed his pipe and regarded me silently for a time through the blue haze.

"So what can you tell me?" I finally asked.

"Many things."

"No doubt," I said. "Any of them pertinent?"

His eyes narrowed briefly, then relaxed into a smile.

"I will let you be the judge of that," he replied.

Leaning back in his chair, he gestured, conjuring a holographic representation of the central square of the City within the drifting smoke. At the heart of the image, the plume of the Fountain towered in all its glory.

"Very recently, as we judge time" he began, "the Fountain stopped flowing. Almost certainly, the murders—if murders they were—took place during that time. The only alternative would have been for the killer to drag seventy-two gods to the main square of Heaven and throw them into the Fountain, and I seriously doubt that could have been accomplished in so short a time, under Baranak's watchful eye, and with no one else noticing."

"Unless Baranak did it himself," I suggested, sipping my brandy. "Of all the gods, he is the only one who could have overpowered each of the others one-on-one."

Malachek considered this.

"I have never been particularly fond of Baranak," he said. "You know this, or you would not have come here. But I cannot imagine him capable of such an act, nor do I see any reason why he might wish to do so. Likewise, while I do not care for his personality, I have never had cause to doubt his sense of honor. If he was prepared to execute you, he was convinced of your guilt."

Reluctantly, I nodded.

"So he means well," I said. "Fine. But he is wrong."

Malachek's expression was unreadable.

"Of course," he said.

He gestured sharply, and the floating image vanished.

My mind searched quickly through all I'd seen and heard since returning to the City, and again I pondered our release from the dungeon, and my misgivings there.

"What do you know of Alaria?" I asked him.

"Alaria?" He frowned. "As much and as little as anyone, I suppose."

I described for him the events of the past few hours.

He steepled his fingers before his lips and considered.

"It could be that she was genuinely concerned for you, or for the truth, or both. But then, how often do any of us have only one single, clear motive behind anything we do?"

He smiled warmly.

"Now, for example. I help you because it serves the interests of finding the truth and of preventing an injustice. But by the same token, it also serves me personally, should you emerge from these circumstances in better position than Baranak and his friends."

I admitted to myself that I had not considered that part of the equation, and felt a measure of respect and even fondness in my heart for Malachek.

47

He stroked his chin absently, the way he always did when running up against a problem for which he did not have an immediate answer.

"You say Vorthan was with Baranak?" he asked. "Odd... It was always Rashtenn who stood at Baranak's side—but I suppose now that would be impossible. No wonder the old warrior's taking it all so hard." Malachek shook his head. "Such a waste... Eternity seventy-two times over, gone in such a brief time."

I bowed my head along with him for a moment, but then pressed on, anxious for more information and nervous about staying in one place for too long.

"So Vorthan working closely with Baranak is a new development?" I asked.

Malachek nodded.

"Oh, yes. Vorthan was never part of the inner circle."

He puffed on his pipe, a cloud of smoke floating over his head.

"It would make sense, though, at least at this time," he continued. "If the Fountain had to be repaired in some manner, our god of toil would surely be the one to turn to."

I nodded and mulled this over. Then another question—one I should have considered much earlier—came to mind.

"Why might the Fountain have stopped flowing at all? I had thought it a possibility when the Power abandoned me in exile, but there was precious little I could do about it then. For all I knew, they had found some way to cut me off, specifically. I did not discover the truth until recently."

"I've assumed it to have been a natural phenomenon," he said. "Perhaps some sort of outside interference, or something diverting it at its source, about which we know next to nothing, even after all this time."

I considered this.

"What if someone wanted to block it off intentionally? Would it be possible?"

"Intentionally?" His eyes widened, and he puffed on his pipe again, smoke now wreathing about him like a cocoon. "It would be extremely difficult to hold back the flood," Malachek said, "but not impossible, I think. But it would require very careful work and very precise engineering knowledge of the Fountain."

We looked at one another then, the same thought passing through our minds simultaneously. The same face.

"But... why?" Malachek asked, almost incredulous. "Just to allow the murder of the gods? What gain could there possibly be, from such a thing?"

I had a few ideas along those very lines, and started to reply, when all about us the flickering ghost-guardians froze in their tracks and vanished, instantly replaced by frenetically swirling lights. A loud wail echoed from every room in the castle.

I looked up, my first thoughts of the three humans who had accompanied me.

"What have they gotten into?" I asked, rising to my feet.

"No, it is an external alert," Malachek replied over the blaring noise. "Someone approaches. Someone powerful."

"That would be our cue, then."

The humans raced in from the adjoining room, Cassidy still holding a plate of food in one hand and a drink in the other, eating and imbibing as much as he could while the opportunity lasted. I had known a few men and women like him during my exile, and I found I liked him more than I had previously thought.

"What is it?" Evelyn asked.

All three humans wore questioning expressions.

"Time to go," I told them.

Malachek gestured toward a rear door and I moved to follow him.

"Thank you for sharing your wisdom and your advice," I said. "It was most welcome."

"I hope I have been of some small assistance," he replied, frowning, "though I have taken little comfort from our conversation."

He led us quickly into a small sitting room.

"Perhaps I can also help you along your way."

The wall in one area was recessed slightly. At a gesture on his part, the stone seemed to melt, falling away in liquid globs to reveal an opening.

I peered through and saw naught but darkness.

"A bolt hole," I observed. "But to where?"

Malachek smiled the most devious smile I had ever seen him attempt.

"To your own private cosmos—eventually," he replied.

"You mean...?"

I looked through again, then back at him.

"Your hideaway," he said. "Quite so."

I eyed him suspiciously.

"That would be my secret hideaway," I said, wondering which of them he meant.

"Secret to most," he replied, "but not to all."

I could not help but laugh.

"And you've known about it all this time."

"Certainly," he replied, "though I've told no one else."

He shrugged.

"I had made preparations either way when you launched your insurrection. I saw wisdom then in preparing closer ties to you as well as to Baranak and his clique. Just as I do now."

Wisdom. Yes. I nodded slowly, then smiled at him.

"Thanks. Your kindnesses will not be forgotten."

"Good luck," he replied, as I raced through the breach, the humans close behind.

The light from Malachek's castle winked out as he sealed the portal behind us. Blindly we raced into the darkness.

THREE

Blackness surrounded us, wreathed all in echoes and drenched in claustrophobia. Some of my contemporaries doubtlessly would have maintained that such an environment suited me perfectly, but I begged to disagree. At the moment, I would have given quite a lot for a simple night light—along with a hot bath, a soft bed, and a week or two of uninterrupted sleep. Not to mention that case of whiskey.

Circumstances being what they were, though, I forced such thoughts from my mind and ran on into the night. Were the three humans still behind me? I would find out in due time, and felt no particular compunction to check before then.

Part of the way along, I had risked the expenditure of a small portion of my reserves to generate a tiny ball of lightning—no great shakes, and about the best I could do at short notice on that score—and, sending it on ahead, I had managed to determine that we were in a straight, narrow, earthen tunnel that ran in an extremely straight line. After some distance, the ground beneath my feet angled up, and a short while later a faint glow appeared ahead, growing as I continued on. Soon it became obvious that the tunnel was opening out into a somewhat illuminated area. Emerging from the tunnel, I saw that I stood on a natural rise at one end of a vast, subterranean lake. The walls of the chamber that housed this lake, a weak glow radiating from them in patches, reached several hundred feet high and ran on for an indeterminate distance around the periphery and into the darkness. Waves gently lapped at the shore below me, their soft, rhythmic sounds a noticeable counterpoint to the more rapid beating of my heart. Looking around, I could not immediately determine whether this cave represented a natural or man-made feature, but I knew I had not encountered it before. Malachek may have known about my refuge, but he had found his own pathway there.

Footsteps sounded behind me as the three humans emerged from the tunnel. Pointedly ignoring them, I made my way down closer to the shore and peered out across the placid waters. I could barely make out a concentration of the greenish light emanating from a single point and radiating up from the depths, about a hundred yards out. Something about that light tugged at an old memory, albeit one that refused to dislodge from the depths of my mind and reveal itself.

As I continued to study the odd radiance, footsteps crunched behind me. Moments later, Cassidy stood to my right.

"So—where are you leading us?" he asked, almost casually.

I did not turn, preferring to continue my visual inspection of the lake.

"I don't think he knows, himself," Kim said, as he walked up on my left.

The captain, if she was even back there, remained silent.

"I think he's as lost as we are," Kim went on.

I continued to ignore them. The green glow in the water was starting to concern me. I knew now that I had encountered it before, somewhere, a long time ago.

"He's no god, he's just an Outie," Kim snorted. "This is just some kind of trick. Everything we've seen so far—

somebody's screwing with us. It's an Outie trick—they've set us up."

"You are a fool," I told him, before stepping into the water up to my knees. Bending, I ran my right hand across the surface. Cool but not cold. Not entirely unpleasant.

"Maybe we've all been drugged," Kim went on. "Maybe we're all in some Outie military prison, hooked into a brain jack and being fed all this crap."

"An interesting theory," came the voice of the captain, her boots crunching up behind us.

Ripples began to spread across the water from a point roughly corresponding to the source of the light. I watched them intently. None of this rang a bell for me so far.

"And now he wants to go for a swim!" Kim laughed harshly. "Captain, I suggest we forget this guy, forget this whole thing, and fend for ourselves from this point on. This stuff can't be real—I'm betting it can't hurt us."

"By all means," I said then, turning back to flash them a thin smile, "do fend for yourselves. I am certain you will fare quite well."

"We don't have enough information yet to make a decision like that," the captain said. She faced Kim directly, waving an arm about to indicate our strange surroundings. "Where would we go? I have no idea. Do you?" She frowned, looking at me now. "Sure, he's not the most friendly tour guide we could wish for…"

I looked back at her, wide-eyed, hand to heart.

"You wound me, lady. Truly you do."

She rolled her eyes.

"…But he's done nothing to harm us, so far. And for all we know, he could have already saved our lives once, by getting us out of the City."

"Don't tell me you're buying into this, Captain," Kim growled.

Turning back to the lake, I ran a hand through the water again. It was noticeably warmer. The greenish light had intensified; the ripples had become more violent. None of this encouraged me. I backed out of the water, leaving uneven footprints on the gray sand.

"I'm really getting sick of your attitude," Kim was saying to me, even as I backed past him and summoned up the first of several invisible defensive spheres about myself.

The ripples in the lake became waves, tossed as if by a storm. This finally got the attention of the humans, and they retreated a few steps as well, their pace quickening as they went.

It clicked for me then. Water. Green light. Of course.

"Vodina," I whispered. "Uh oh."

The lake, now blazing with green fire, erupted and spewed forth five columns of water. Instead of splashing back to the surface, the columns hovered in midair, spun about like miniature waterspouts, and then each congealed into a distinctly human shape.

"Now what?" Cassidy muttered. Wide-eyed, he backed away from the shore as well.

Each of the five water figures, female in form and wreathed in green flame, extended an arm over its head. Blazing swords formed in each of the hands. Hovering above the waters, they glared down at us like avenging angels of the apocalypse.

"You were saying you'd like to fend for yourself, Mr. Kim." I smiled a crooked smile even as I redoubled my shields. "Have at it!"

The five figures streaked forward, flames trailing in their wake, bearing down on us. They raised their swords high.

Kim gawked at them, then at me, then turned to run for the tunnel mouth.

"Wait," the captain ordered. "We stay together."

She looked at me. Her face bore an imploring look.

I sighed.

"Get behind me!" I shouted, extending my sphere to encompass them. A mere instant later, the five furies crashed against my outermost screen.

Emerald flames engulfed us there within our bubble. It lasted less than a second, and then the five furies were past us, reforming and swooping high into the air once more.

Backing up a few more steps, the humans huddling close, I positioned us so that the wall of the cavern protected our rear. This allowed me to devote more energy to the forward portion of my screens; something for which I was grateful moments later as the angelic forms swooped down again, slashing with their swords. Once again we found ourselves engulfed in flames, as the swords dissolved into sheets of green fire, surrounding us in a cocoon of light and heat. Just as quickly, the flames vanished as the water-women swooped upward to regroup for what seemed an inevitable third strike.

I will give the humans credit. For once, they had the sense to refrain from immediately pelting me with questions. Then again, perhaps they were simply too frightened. In any case, I was grateful to be able to devote all of my attention to finding a solution to our problem.

Retreat seemed the wisest course, but then I realized that whomever had been approaching Malachek's castle—likely Baranak, in pursuit of us—could very well have found our escape route, and be approaching from that direction. Malachek himself revealing the bolthole did not seem entirely out of the question, given his openly pragmatic policies. Thus I filed away the idea of going back up the tunnel as our last option.

We could not simply stand there and absorb a pummeling from the green furies until my screens collapsed. That left one direction—forward. And as I considered it, new possibilities occurred to me.

Kneeling, I sought about me on the rocky shore for a stone of sufficient size. Finding a chalky gray one with black streaks, about the size of my fist, I stood and clasped it in both hands, closing my eyes. The procedure would have been considerably easier had I not been in middle of simultaneously maintaining our defensive shields. As it was, I managed to pour what I hoped was a sufficient charge of energy into the stone before the furies attacked again.

"Here," I told Evelyn, handing her the rock, which had taken on a bluish glow.

Cassidy looked at it, frowning, then looked at me.

"We're supposed to throw rocks at them?" he asked, incredulous.

"I would not throw that rock, if I were you," I replied. "It should shield you for a time. Long enough, I hope."

"Long enough for what?" Evelyn asked, clutching the stone to her chest.

"We shall see," I replied, turning and walking back down the slope.

I could hear the furies swooping down again, behind me, toward the huddled humans, but then Evelyn shouted, "Look out!" I whirled, barely in time to raise a hand as one fury that had separated from the others struck out with her sword. The flames crashed into my hastily erected screen –probably the only thing that kept my arm from being severed—but the force of the impact hurled me backward, flailing about in midair before tumbling into the water.

Surfacing, I gasped for breath. The water was cold. Pushing my long hair out of my eyes, I looked up and saw the fury circling, about to attack again. I reached a decision then. Spinning around, I dove under the water, swimming away from the shore and downward.

Just behind me, I heard the fury plunge into the spot I had occupied seconds before. I braced for impact—for my theory to be proven wrong. It was not. The fury vanished, apparently dissolving back into the waters that had given her form. Encouraged, I swam on, deeper into the murky darkness.

After some few seconds, a greenish light became apparent ahead of me, somewhere on the bottom. I redoubled my efforts, and though I have never spent much time training as a swimmer, desperation spurred me on. Thinking back on it, I did feel confident the sword-wielding sisters up above could not reach me there, but I hardly could spend the rest of eternity holding my breath—and the humans' plight may have provided some small motivation as well, though I doubt I would have shed a tear if Cassidy or Kim had met the business end of a green-flaming sword right about then.

I seemed to be moving at some velocity, for the light grew brighter quickly. Soon I was circling over its source. Despite the glare, I could just make out a tall, slender woman, stretched out in repose on the lake's bottom, bald and naked and seemingly asleep—or dead. Every inch of her body radiated nearly blinding green luminance, as if she were a neon bulb.

As I'd had no time to prepare for such an environment, my lungs were demanding air. I had to act quickly. Swimming down to the lake's bottom, I scooped the woman up in my arms—there was no overt sensation of heat—and then pushed off, rising as fast as possible while also angling for the shore.

Breaking the surface, I gratefully breathed in the air, then rolled over and swam on my back. I clasped the lady to my chest to keep both of us above the water—though, admittedly, that did not seem like as much of a priority for her as for me. This angle also afforded me a view upward, and I could see no signs of the attackers. As we reached the shallows and my feet touched bottom, however, I heard shouts and cries from near the tunnel mouth, and knew that the humans were still alive, and still under attack.

Evelyn must have seen me then, and apparently she was not the only one, for she cried, "They're coming!"

I sensed the five furies' arrival above me, but, aside from conjuring a force sphere around the two of us, I ignored them.

Leaning over the lady's limp form, I ran my right hand down the side of her face, and spoke her name.

"Vodina?"

The furies circled about a dozen yards over my head, and I could sense their raw, primal anger. They did not attack yet, however. Glancing up, I saw them darting this way and that, clearly upset but now lacking in that single-minded drive to kill that they had appeared to possess previously.

"Vodina!" I repeated, louder, stroking her forehead and her cheeks. "Can you hear me?"

She groaned then, ever so softly. As if in response, the furies swooped down, straight for me. Their impact on my defensive screen was so fierce, it caused me to drop to my knees, but my attention remained with the lady. As they unleashed a barrage of assaults upon my shield, I felt my resistance weakening, but I continued to focus my efforts on reviving the woman.

As the situation grew serious, my reserves starting to ebb, my shields on the verge of crumbling under the pounding they were taking, Vodina finally showed signs of life. Her eyelids fluttered, and then her entire body jerked, her limbs lashing out. This lasted only a moment, and then she seemed to relax again. With a sudden gasp, her eyes came open.

The furies halted their attacks but grew even more agitated, if less focused. They thrashed about in midair like fish dropped on dry land.

Vodina's eyes met mine then, and she blinked.

"Lucian?"

"Yes. I have you."

She still hadn't entirely focused on me.

"The nightmares," she whispered.

Suddenly she looked about wildly, then back at me. "Where—where are we?"

"I will tell you all I know," I said, "but first..." And I gestured at the green furies convulsing over our heads. "You are under no threat. So...?"

Looking confused at first, her face conveyed a quick shock of recognition, and then a small frown.

"Begone," she said.

The thrashing furies high above came to a sudden halt, hovered momentarily in midair, then collapsed into five columns of water that splashed harmlessly to the ground.

Relaxing, I dropped my tattered screens. The humans, seeing the threat in abatement, made their way down to the shore. They looked on as I leaned over and called Vodina's name once more. Her eyes had lost focus again, and I feared her furies might reawaken if she slipped back into catatonia. I clasped her left hand, which had grown cold, between both of mine and rubbed it gently.

Evelyn nudged me on the shoulder, and frowned when I looked up at her.

"Your coat," she said.

I realized then that the two men behind her were attempting to take in the sight of the naked goddess while pretending to look anywhere and everywhere else.

"Right."

Shrugging out of my long navy coat, the texture of which had transformed at some point from wool to a lighter and seemingly more waterproof material, I laid it over Vodina's slender form. The goddess scarcely seemed to notice.

Evelyn knelt beside me, studying the green woman in amazement.

"Who is she?"

The goddess's eyes had focused on mine once more, and her strength seemed to be growing. I realized I had been holding my breath for some time, and exhaled in relief.

"Evelyn Colicos, meet Vodina of the Waters." I smiled. "Our Lady of the Lake."

Vodina.

Even among those so individualistic and jealous of their privacy as we, little was known of her. Seldom seen at court-- or anywhere else within the realm of the City, for that matter- -rumors always took the place of fact with regard to fair Vodina. And the rumors were not always kind.

One of Baranak's former lovers? Perhaps. Cast aside by him, and thus bitter and resentful toward him, toward all of us, toward the City itself? Probably not, given so many other things I'd heard with regard to her strength, her will, her independence. Though I had heard tales of alienation and resentment whispered from time to time about a number of the golden god's supposed conquests, contradictory stories inevitably followed. No one knew what to believe about Baranak and his love life any longer. And, aside from strategic considerations, I had never much cared.

Other rumors carried with them the virtue of at least being more colorful, if no less believable. Grenedy had once claimed, for instance, that Vodina was hiding out away off in her own pocket universe, building an army of mer-people, and dreaming up schemes to take power in the City for herself. This one in particular appealed to me, for obvious reasons; though, if it had proven true and she ever did manage such a feat, it would only mean she, instead of Baranak, would eventually fall to my next assault.

As far as I knew, though I had fully expected to have to confront her in battle, she had not been present at the time of the revolt. Baranak doubtless would have welcomed her participation, for her strength and her Furies would have served his cause well during my main, failed assault. Perhaps I would have been defeated even more quickly, though that scarcely seemed possible at the time, from my vantage point. The image of Rashtenn and the others bringing down the cosmic flame upon my supporters before we had hardly begun to fight haunts me still, and constitutes a dismal memory from which I shall never be free.

In the aftermath of the defeat, I had thought I had heard her name mentioned once as having been held in reserve by Baranak, should additional forces be required to deal with me. Perhaps. And perhaps she had only agreed to such an arrangement so that he would leave her alone, and leave her out of it.

Rumors upon rumors. The same with all of us, really. We lived in a never-ending swirl of doubtful fact and demonstrable fiction; of innuendo and gossip, layer upon layer upon layer, dragged out over millennia.

How to strip away the layers of this woman and know her heart when, for so many of us, the great fear was that peeling away so many layers might give way at last to nothing? No, I did not know her. Innumerable centuries had passed, even before the revolt, during which I had not encountered her in the City or elsewhere. Let it be, then.

Vodina. Emerging from the waters of her lake, she was as a clean slate to me.

"I do not know who it was," Vodina was saying, "but they very nearly killed me. And that is no easy task."

She was sitting up, leaning against a large rock, my coat pulled up to cover most of her torso, mainly out of deference to the expressed preferences of Evelyn. Her eyes, a radiant blue-green, flashed vividly in contrast to her pale skin and bare scalp. Out of the water, she seemed somehow less statuesque, less impressive—even the vivid green of her skin had faded to a pale imitation of itself—but she was still a being of unquestionable power and radiance. I had not seen her for many years even before my exile, and I admit I had nearly forgotten how impressive she was.

I squatted in the sand opposite her, studying her. The humans stood to my left, probably still fuming over the grudging and abbreviated introductions I had tended.

I had resolved to gain as much information from Vodina as I could, while she was still disoriented and confused. Doubtless she would become much less willing to volunteer intelligence once she was herself again.

"Where were you when you were attacked?" I asked, as casually as possible.

"The World Sea," she said, her eyes distant. "On my island. I believe whomever did it must have been waiting there for some time, as I spend most of my time beneath the waves and do not often emerge."

I nodded.

"The Sea. That is a long way down the line."

"Indeed."

"Fast time, right?"

"Somewhat. I can dwell there for months and miss little that happens in the City."

I realized then that she probably did not know about the murders. Truthfully, I was afraid to tell her. Afraid of what might happen if she were so shocked that she lapsed into a coma again—and I had no way of judging the delicacy of her condition. Perhaps more that that, I was concerned that she might instantly draw the same conclusions regarding my guilt that Baranak and the others had. I did not fancy another twelve rounds with her furies.

"Excuse me," Evelyn said then, "but I've never heard of a 'World Sea.'"

"You wouldn't have," Vodina said. "It is not within your capacity to experience. At least, not without a guide." She smiled up at the woman. "It seems that you have found one, though."

"It is in a pocket universe claimed by Vodina," I explained quickly, suddenly uncomfortable. "It lies... one might say *below* your human plane."

"Like subspace," Evelyn said, making the connection. "So time there flows slightly faster than in normal space." She frowned. "So, you're saying there are other layers to subspace?"

I did not wish to be distracted into delivering a physics lesson—nor a metaphysics lesson—while the opportunity yet remained to pump the water goddess for information. But, I reasoned, perhaps a few basics would shut them up for a bit. So, "Somewhat," I replied hastily. "Better to say that the 'subspace' you use for fast space travel is but one layer, one plane among many, both 'Above' and 'Below' your own. It lies in the Below, the faster but less powerful direction, while our Golden City lies in the slower but more powerful direction, the Above."

Cassidy leaned toward Kim.

"That does fit with some of our theories," he said. "It would sort of explain how our ship ended up where it did."

"You're not seriously listening to this guy, are you?" Kim snorted. "I still say we're jacked into some sort of Outworlder brain sim and they're just waiting for us to get comfortable and hand over everything we know."

"That should not take terribly long, I would imagine," I muttered, before returning my full attention to Vodina once more. "So, did you get any sort of a look at your attackers?"

"No," she said. "They must have been extremely good at concealing themselves both from me and from my remote defenses." She squeezed her eyes closed tightly, as one who battled a growing migraine. "Which among our number excel at concealment?" she asked.

I hastily turned the conversation away from this direction and back to the attack.

"How were you hit? What did they do to you?"

She gingerly flexed her left shoulder and winced.

"A blast in the back. It knocked me senseless. I remember little afterward."

Her luminous eyes turned upward, as if searching the cave's ceiling for answers.

"I do not know if they tried to finish me off and failed, or thought I was already dead, or simply let me crawl away to die. Somehow I escaped, though I was extremely weakened, barely alive. My subconscious mind must have driven me here, to a hidden refuge of water I had discovered long ago. I am sure it also caused the generation of my water sprites. They simply lashed out at anyone who might prove a threat to my recovery." The corner of her mouth turned up in something of a wry smile then. "I apologize for their... zealousness."

I did not like to think of the watery manifestations of Vodina's power that had nearly taken me out as "sprites." "Sprites" did not seem to me like creatures that could nearly rip your head off. "Furies" seemed a much better name for them—but I let it go. Something important occurred to me then.

"Your attack—it must have been either before the Power failed, or after the Fountain was restored," I surmised. "Otherwise you could not have escaped to this place."

She closed her eyes, as if deep in thought, then nodded.

"I know of such events only as a consequence of their impact upon me," she observed, "but I had surmised as much."

She sighed.

"When the Power first went away, I retreated to the depths of my Sea, and remained there with my court for the entire time of its absence. When I felt its renewal, my first thought was to swim to my island and make sure it was still secure, and to attempt to contact the City, to find out what had happened. No sooner had I emerged from the waters there than I was attacked."

"That was not terribly long ago," I said. "I was dwelling among the human worlds when the Power returned, and the journey back to the City took..." I attempted the math, factoring in different rates of time flow and different distances traversed within each plane along the way, then quickly gave up on that idea and settled on a rough estimate. "...perhaps two days. Another day in the Dungeon, and then the journey here. In all, your attack happened barely more than three days ago, as time flows in the City." I smiled at her. "You have made a fast recovery, especially if we are still in the Above, as I assume."

She nodded.

"Higher power, though. Closer proximity to the Fountain."

"You know, I hate to interrupt all this talk," Cassidy exclaimed at that moment, "but none of this is getting us any closer to home."

My face hardened, and I began to rise.

"At ease, Lieutenant," Evelyn said, stepping forward. "That approach clearly doesn't accomplish anything."

Cassidy stepped back and settled down with obvious reluctance. Kim started to say something undoubtedly ignorant and unhelpful, but I cleared my throat and said, "The lieutenant is quite right. We have spent enough time here. We need to be moving on."

A tinkling sound like water falling on small rocks came from behind me. I realized that Vodina was laughing.

"Lucian, your pets hold quite a sway over you. I am amused."

Anger swelled up within me, and I bit back a retort.

"Ah. I do believe that I am becoming myself again," she said then, rising to her feet.

A quick inventory of my emotions revealed to me why my reaction to her jibe had been so subdued. I was nervous. Antsy. Was Vodina about to become a problem again, or was it something else, some new threat? Whatever the cause, an extreme sensation of impending danger swept over me. It was true—it was time to move on.

Tossing my coat back to me, Vodina pranced about in a circle, stretching her arms and legs. A warm, greenish glow now radiated from her naked skin, and her very stature seemingly had increased from moments before. The humans all stared openly at her. I could not blame them.

"Okay, well, it is good to see you are feeling better," I told her hurriedly, pulling my coat back on. "We can see ourselves out—that looks like another tunnel a bit further around the shore, yes?"

Without a reply of any sort, Vodina whirled and, in three quick strides, reached the water's edge. Her leap and dive was a thing of exquisite beauty. It scared me to death.

"Go," I said to the humans. "Move."

Clearly confused, they nonetheless sensed the edge in my voice and hustled like the soldiers they were. We skirted the shoreline hurriedly, all the while keeping an eye on the placid surface of the lake. As we reached the cave mouth, I thought I heard a splashing sound behind me, but I did not look back. The humans were already racing into the tunnel ahead, and I followed on their heels with all possible haste. My immediate goal was simply to put as much distance as possible between Vodina and myself—just in case.

The glow from the lake faded quickly behind us, leaving us surrounded by total darkness. Generating a small blue globe of luminance, I set it to hover alongside us as we ran.

After a short while, Evelyn dropped back to jog along beside me.

"You didn't tell her about the murders," she said.

"I saw nothing to be gained from it," I replied.

"For you to gain, you mean."

I glanced at her as we jogged, but could not read her face.

"Vodina has already been attacked once and, now that she is recovered, is on her guard," I said. "It will be extremely difficult for anyone to take her by surprise again." I shrugged. "So I have left her in no worse a situation than I found her—and, in fact, may have hastened her recovery."

Evelyn appeared to be considering this.

"You think she was going to attack us again, anyway. Why?"

I frowned.

"Because she has probably already decided I am the most likely suspect for her attack. And why do I think so?" I shrugged again. "Just a feeling. But my feelings about these things are right more often than I would like."

"Godly insight? Some kind of omniscience?"

A wry grin crossed my face.

"I like that. Yes. I am great and mighty. Fear me."

The sound Evelyn made then is best left not described.

Ignoring her, I turned my attention to the nature of the world around us. We had run far enough; it was time to depart this plane and continue on toward my own private cosmos. My mind pushed beyond surface appearances and I reached out with my senses, examining the weave of reality around us, studying it with my mind, getting a feel, as best I could, for its strength, its density, its texture—and what lay beyond it. A portion of that same Power that radiated out from the Fountain in our City to all levels of reality flowed through me, there in the tunnel. I began the process of pushing through the barrier separating this level from an adjacent one. I envisioned within my mind's eye a portal opening for us, and in response a blue glow flared just ahead. I smiled. The barrier was surprisingly thin here. I hardly had to expend any energy at all to open the way. Perhaps we would make it after all.

The humans, startled at the sight, slowed their pace, but I urged them on towards the light.

"It's okay," I said. "That is mine."

As we neared my portal, we saw that the tunnel extended onward beyond it for only a short distance before ending abruptly in a sheer wall.

"Not to worry," I reassured them. "We're in the clear."

My blue portal blinked out of existence as if a giant had stepped on it.

I believe my chin actually hit the rocky floor, as anatomically unlikely as it might seem.

"What happened?" Cassidy shouted.

Only the dark and shallow remainder of the tunnel lay ahead of us. Shocked, I poured more energy into the space my portal had occupied, trying to reopen the way, but to no avail. Worse, I was certain now I could hear a splashing sound behind us. Some semblance of panic came over me then, I must admit, and I looked around frantically. The humans must have understood something of our plight as well, for they moved into a defensive circle and braced themselves.

At that moment another light flared, this one a bit further along in the direction we had been moving, almost to the tunnel's end. It was green in color, but a darker green than Vodina's Aspect. The humans looked at it and then back at me.

"That's not yours, is it?" Evelyn said.

"No."

I glanced back in the direction of the lake, but could see nothing that way. Cursing, I attempted to force another portal open, only to be stymied once more. The sensation was bizarre. It was nothing like the long years when the Power was gone, for I could feel the buzz flowing through me. Something simply prevented me from using it to breach the barriers between planes. My frustration was enormous.

"What should we do?" Evelyn said, her eyes moving from me to the green light and back.

"What the hell?"

I started forward. Clearly the green light had some connection with my blocked powers. Curiosity at that point became as strong as any other emotion—not to mention my growing conviction that Vodina was no longer so well disposed towards me as she had been while still in a confused daze. Such is the dark god's fate—wrongfully accused at every turn. Poor, pitiful me. For I am bound upon a wheel of fire, and like that.

"Something tells me it can't be any worse than going back the way we came," I said, and stepped up to the green circle, reaching out a hand to touch it. At that instant it flared open and a fist rocketed out, catching me in the jaw. I crumpled to the tunnel's floor, muttering something like, "Not again."

My vision swimming, I could barely make out a burly form hovering over me—though, mercifully, it did not wear golden armor. A shadowy face peered down at me. Recognition dawned as a dim star within the galaxy that currently danced across my vision.

"Turmborne," I managed, tasting blood.

"Lucian."

He nodded in greeting, his mouth a tight line.

"You're really not terribly smart," he said, "are you?"

I attempted a witty comeback, but instead found myself blacking out, even as massive hands grasped my ankles and dragged me through that green hole in the universe.

FOUR

G ood dentistry. Now that is a thing we gods have never taken for granted. Certainly we can direct a sufficient amount of the Power into any trouble spots that might occur with regard to our teeth and gums, and over time all will heal. Unfortunately, such a process tends to be long, unpleasant, and generally annoying. Therefore one thing I had a feeling I was going to miss, if I no longer dwelled among the human worlds, was good dentistry. It felt like at least two of my teeth had been loosened, between going a handful of rounds with Baranak and then taking the surprise shot from Turmborne. Idly I wondered if our wrestler-god, Fuaren, had survived. If he had, it seemed inevitable my chin would encounter his fist soon enough, too.

Coming back to my senses, I looked around and tried to take in the situation.

I sat, my back to a tree, within a small clearing in a dense forest. Judging by the substantial amount of light reaching through the thick, overhanging branches, it had to be near midday. To my right, beyond a stack of barrels and crates, the three humans were imprisoned within what looked to be a hastily constructed cage made of stout limbs bound by rope. Across from me sat Turmborne.

Turmborne, our lumberjack god. Our outdoorsman. Green of eye, red of hair, broad of jaw. He of the flannel and the beard and the broad axe. The only one of us all that might survive an extended brawl with Baranak--if he had ever shown any interest in such a thing. He had not, of course. During my time in the City, before the exile, I had scarcely seen him about. He had not even taken part in the battle in the City Square, so far as I knew. He lived for his woodlands and his hunt and his sport. I probably knew less of him than of any of the others, save perhaps Vodina--and, prior to my revolt, I had made it my business to know everything that could be known about all of them. My ignorance in regard to him irked me, and his assault on me irked me further. Plus, I remembered then, he had insulted my intelligence.

Turmborne, I felt strongly, had an ass-whipping coming.

He just sat there, watching me.

I started to rise.

"No, no," he said then, his voice deep and resonant. He motioned me back down. "Let us converse, you and I, Lucian," he continued. "The day is young yet. We have nothing but time."

"Actually, I do not," I said. "In fact, you are keeping me from important business—"

"You are being *inconvenienced*, then?" he boomed. "How unfortunate." His glare beat at me like a physical blow, and I settled back to the ground once more. "But I'm afraid you are not the *only* one being inconvenienced, these days. I have been extremely inconvenienced recently, in fact." His eyes narrowed, though he continued to glare at me. "Murder can do that. *Mass* murder, especially."

"It was not me," I said, growing tired of being seen as public enemy number one. "I was in exile. I was on the human worlds." I sighed tiredly, shaking my head. "What is so hard for everyone to grasp about that?"

A small smile played about that thin-lipped mouth. He nodded.

"I anticipated you would have a sparkling alibi," he said with a chuckle. "And it might even be true—though it would go against your nature."

"What do you know of my nature?" I demanded, suddenly fed up with all the prejudice I felt from my fellow gods. Few of them were squeaky clean—how dare they judge me so? "You don't know me! I don't even know you."

"I know you better than you might think," he said.

I gritted my teeth, angry that this big oaf already had gotten the better of me.

"What do you know, then?"

He crossed his thick arms and regarded me, his head tilted slightly to one side. I was reminded of a dog I had owned once, on Mysentia, that had looked at me that way now and then—usually when it felt that dinner was late, or that I had not fed it enough. I tried to shove that image out of my head.

"I know this," he said. "I know that the Power can be stored up. That objects can be—what was the word he used?—imbued with quantities of it." Turmborne's eyes narrowed as he peered at me. "I also know that you can do this."

I shrugged. "And?"

"And it strikes me that this would be useful... if the Fountain were to stop flowing." He smiled a thin smile. "In fact, if that happened, anybody storing up a reserve of the Power would enjoy a big advantage over all the others." He leaned closer towards me, jabbing a meaty finger into my chest. "And it did."

I will admit I had not yet considered this angle. But it begged another question, one I needed answered.

"The gods who were killed—"

"Murdered!" he growled.

"Murdered, fine. Were they all in the City when they died?"

He looked upon me with utter contempt.

"As if you don't know this."

"Humor me."

He nodded, his face registering disgust.

"Some were in the City. Many were not. Many were in their private domains, and some were among the humans."

Not what I had wanted to hear. This made his case stronger, with regard to the stored energies, though I was not certain he realized it yet. The killer had to have been able to travel among the planes without the Fountain to provide power. This also meant the perpetrator must have retained his or her abilities even as the victims had been rendered powerless. I winced. It must have been a slaughter.

This suggested another possibility, however. "Has anyone considered yet that it might not have been one of us?" I asked. "That it might have been someone not dependent upon the Fountain at all? Are we so mutually suspicious—or at least so suspicious of me—that such a possibility never even crossed anyone's mind?"

He stared at me for a moment, then leaned back, stroking his beard.

"Excellent," he laughed. "I knew the master of lies wouldn't let me down." Then, after a few seconds, "Fine. I will humor you. I suppose you have someone in mind?"

"As a matter of fact, I do," I growled, "though hardly anyone has been willing to listen to me about it."

I described the Dark Man with whom I'd had a running battle on the Road to the City, as well as the two we had seen in the bog near Malachek's place.

"The humans saw them, too," I noted.

Turmborne glanced over at them curiously, pursed his lips, and looked back at me.

"That proves nothing," he said. "I have seen many strange things on the Road. Fought with plenty of them, too.

74

Nothing like that has ever killed a god before. Much less six dozen of them."

"It proves there are other, powerful players about," I said. "It proves that way too many of us are entirely too eager to charge me with everything from murder to bad fashion sense, when there are other suspects to consider."

Turmborne laughed at that, his laughter a deep, rumbling thing that seemed to begin somewhere near his toes before spilling over his lips. I would have sworn the ground vibrated from it.

"I have to admit you're right about that," he said finally. "Not the fashion sense—though I'm hardly the best one to judge—but about your culpability for... everything... in the eyes of the others. It's true. But it's true for a reason.

"Let me be honest with you, Lucian," he said then, hunkering forward, resting his elbows on his knees. His voice was low but deep and full. "I did not know many of the dead gods well, if at all. I have never spent much time in the City. I had no interest in their perpetual parties and gatherings and ceremonies and so forth. I love my woods, and here I dwell. Sure, in principal, I'm outraged about it all. And I'll admit that there's a selfish motive for me, too—I'm pretty tough, but, given my preferences, I'd rather not have to worry about becoming a victim of some kind of clever sneak attack, myself, one day." His eyes narrowed. "And that's what it would have to be, you know. A sneak attack. A good one.

"All of that aside, though," he continued, "the main thing, as I told you before, is inconvenience. The murders have Baranak and his bunch all stirred up, and he has all but declared martial law, sealing off the City. I wouldn't go there right now if I could. I gather from some of the others it's not what you would call a very hospitable place at the moment.

"And this I blame on you," he concluded. "I really, really do not like my life to be complicated. And you've gone and complicated it."

"Well," I said. "Your honesty is… refreshing, if nothing else."

He snorted.

"And now, how about some from you?" He cocked his head in that odd way again. "You did it, didn't you? Just admit it. You killed them."

"No."

He sighed—a big, powerful sound that went on a surprisingly long time—and leaned back, resting against a particularly large tree trunk. He sat that way for several minutes, seemingly deep in thought. I let him be.

What little of the sun that could be seen in this forest dropped lower, off to my right. The temperature cooled. The insect sounds grew louder.

Finally Turmborne climbed to his feet and walked over to the cage holding the humans. He squinted at them, then looked back at me.

"What's this bunch all about?" he asked. "Why are you dragging them along on your prison break?" He grinned. "Decoys? Strange medical experiments?" He cocked an eye at Evelyn. "Don't tell me you like the girl."

The humans glared at him but, to their credit, said nothing. I knew they had to be as angry and frustrated as ever. They did not much care for me, and certainly did not trust me—yet every other god they had encountered thus far, with the exception of Malachek, seemed intent on doing them harm, or at least handing them over to Baranak. They had no better option than to stick with me, and they knew it, and they were not happy about it. For my part, I was still not sure why I had not simply abandoned them already. I assumed that if the answer ever presented itself, I would be sufficiently amazed, because it made little sense to me at the moment. Beyond that, I decided to let it alone.

"Baranak had them," I said. "That seemed reason enough to free them." Hell, it sounded as good as anything else I might have said. Maybe it would shut him up about them.

"Now that I can relate to," Turmborne said, laughing. "I've little enough love for the Golden God. But he does seem to be calling the shots, for now. If you wanted him out of the way, your efforts backfired. All your killing spree has done is to put him more securely in power."

"I would think that would serve as further evidence of my innocence," I replied. "Why would I do anything to boost his popularity? The others must be living in fear, right now," I said. "Of course they would turn to the strongman, and give him all the power and influence he claims he needs, to keep them and the City safe."

Turmborne strode about the clearing, hands like ham hocks clasped behind his back. Pausing, he scratched at his thick, red beard and eyed me curiously.

"Yeah, I'll admit that part bothers me. We've never had a single supreme leader in control in the City... And I know you wouldn't want to see anyone with that much power—other than yourself."

I looked him straight in the eye, unblinking.

"You do realize there is at least as much evidence pointing to him as to me, don't you?"

Turmborne said nothing, merely resumed pacing.

I kept quiet for a while, hoping I had sowed enough seeds of doubt at least to buy myself a little more time. I looked over at the humans from time to time; they sat in the cage, sullen but silent. Idly I wondered if Kim still thought this was all happening only in his mind.

Finally Turmborne stopped his pacing directly before me.

"I knew it was a mistake to talk this over with you. I should have done what I planned to do from the start—grab you and turn you over to Baranak and the others that minute."

He glared at me, his bushy red eyebrows bunching like storm clouds over his eyes.

"Hearing all the facts before rushing to judgment," I said. "That's never a mistake, Turmborne."

"Shut up. This conversation is over. I'm not a hundred percent sure you're guilty anymore, but if turning you over to Baranak will settle things down again, I think it's a bargain at the price."

I started to argue, but he backhanded me then, hard enough to loosen the teeth that were not already hurting.

"This is the part where you go to meet your fate in stoic silence," he growled, jabbing a finger at me. "Not another word."

I had come up with several more words for him, actually, and was about to launch them in his direction when Evelyn cried out from the cage.

"Lucian!"

We both turned our heads in her direction then, and thus failed at first to see what she had noticed: a bright white light, flaring about three feet above the ground, immediately behind Turmborne.

What I did see, as I turned back to the big hunter, was a slender figure stepping out of the white light. In one smooth action, the new arrival closed the distance between himself and Turmborne and chopped the big man in the neck with the edge of his hand.

Turmborne collapsed with precisely none of the grace or majesty of a toppled redwood. He merely fell in a sprawled heap, groaning faintly.

The light from the portal blinked out, leaving me face to face with one I had not seen in many, many years.

"Well, well," I said, by way of welcome.

He said nothing, merely raised the left corner of his mouth approximately an eighth of an inch, in what generously might have been construed to be a smile. He pushed his small, round, dark glasses a bit further up his long, straight nose.

I looked at him and immediately realized I had assumed all along he had survived. There had never been any question in my mind. Not about Arendal.

Arendal, who knows the secrets no one else knows.
Arendal, who holds the keys to long-forgotten locks.
Arendal, who watches, always watches.

He looked, of course, exactly the same as he had so many centuries before, when he had stood there in the main square of the City, aloof and above it all, refusing to get involved. I had hated him, then. I was not at all certain those feelings had changed in a mere millennium.

Thin of body, short of stature, with long, straight hair that was a negative image of my own--pale white, to match the pallor of his skin. He wore a cream-colored business suit of indeterminate vintage, and carried a silver walking stick in his left hand, the index finger of which also displayed a silver ring. A large, red stone sparkled within it.

Arendal, whom I regarded with some measure of admiration and respect.
Arendal, whom I disliked and suspected.
Arendal, whom in some small, indefinable way, I feared.

He walked past me to the cage where the humans were held, and looked them over as one might inspect puppies in a pet store. For their part, they eyed him warily, having apparently been sufficiently disappointed by everyone else they had met in my company to refrain from immediately beseeching him for assistance.

"Are they held this way for a reason?" he asked, fiddling with the lock.

"Not by me," I replied.

He nodded, then squeezed the lock carefully in his hand. The stone on his ring sparkled brighter for a second, and the lock split exactly in half. Smiling again, he opened his hand and let the pieces fall to the ground.

Kim, scowling, shoved the door open and climbed out, followed by Evelyn and Cassidy. They still said nothing. I decided that either they were in shock or had agreed among themselves to limit their conversation. Probably both.

"I think they're thirsty," Arendal said, "and hungry. Perhaps you would like to crack open some of Turmborne's supplies?"

I realized then that both of those conditions applied to me, as well. Keeping an eye on Arendal all the while, unsure of his motives, I moved to inspect the crates and barrels stacked around the clearing. Opening one of the crates, I found a variety of small food packets inside—the sort of self-contained, long-lasting military ration Turmborne would favor for his long hunts. The barrels turned out to contain drinking water, and I found a set of collapsible cups nearby. I tossed handfuls of the packets and cups to the others, and even Arendal seemed glad to have them.

Moments later, we were seated once more around the clearing, eating and drinking and all eyeing one another suspiciously. Our former captor lay where he had fallen, unmoving. Arendal kept an eye on him. For the longest time, no one said a word.

Then: "You didn't honestly believe Turmborne would help you, did you?" Arendal asked.

"He sought me out, not the other way around," I said.

He nodded. "Well, he is a good hunter, so I can't fault you overmuch for letting him capture you."

"Circumstances conspired to make the job a bit easier for him," I said.

Arendal didn't reply. He gazed at the humans, one at a time, through his tiny glasses. They glared back at him.

Cassidy could no longer restrain himself. "Who are you supposed to be?" he growled.

At that moment, a groaning sound emerged from Turmborne. He rolled slowly over onto his back, blinked his eyes twice, and ran a meaty hand over his face.

"Twelve minutes," Arendal noted. "Your constitution continues to amaze me."

Turmborne must have become aware of Arendal's presence for the first time. "Oh," he said. "You." Still dazed, he sat back against a crate, taking in the situation.

Evelyn set her food aside and stood, walking around the circle to sit next to me. Leaning over, she whispered, "Are we any closer to home?"

"Somewhat," I replied, "if we are where I think we are." I did some quick calculations in my head. "Um... still a very long way, though."

Nodding, she appeared to consider her next question for a long moment. Then, "Can you take either of these guys?"

I frowned.

"Take?"

Then I understood what she meant. Despite myself, I laughed.

She did not.

"Can you beat them, if you have to?" she said.

She was dead serious, and I understood her concern. It certainly was not concern for me, but for her crew and herself. Sad as it might be, I remained their best hope of escaping the nightmare they had found themselves in. I attributed whatever sentiment I felt for them at that moment to a desire to stick it to Baranak and his cronies by helping them escape.

Those thoughts bounced around in my mind for a few seconds, prompting me to reach a certain conclusion. Carefully, discreetly, I began to form tiny spheres of blue-tinged energy on the fingertips of my right hand, keeping my left hand in position to conceal this.

"So," Turmborne said at length, "what do you want, Arendal?"

"I have what I want," he replied.

Turmborne's brow wrinkled. "I'm sure you don't mean what I think you mean."

The pale god smiled.

"You cannot have them back," he said by way of answer.

The big man's face twisted into a frown.

"Now, just a minute!"

Hoisting his massive frame from the grass, Turmborne moved menacingly toward the rest of us.

"I captured them," he growled, "and I'll be the one to decide what happens to them next."

"Sit your ass down," Arendal said, his voice calm and even.

Turmborne hesitated, gave him that curious-dog look I was coming to think of as his trademark, and then sat down.

I heard Kim muttering something to Cassidy in reaction.

"Well, that was impressive," I said, casually spilling a handful of my tiny blue spheres onto the grass, allowing them to instantly scatter and vanish. Immediately I began to form a second set. "Can you make him do any other tricks?"

"I'll show you a good trick, Lucian," Turmborne growled, cracking his knuckles.

"Quiet, both of you," Arendal said. He faced the hunter. "I don't intend to take him back to the City," he said, indicating me with a slight gesture. "I have no desire to curry favor with Baranak or his hangers on."

"You are one of his hangers on," Turmborne said with a snort.

"I hope he believes that to be true," Arendal replied with a shrug. "But I do retain my status as an independent agent, whatever you or anyone else might think."

"Then what do you want with Lucian?"

"I am letting him go."

Turmborne looked as puzzled as I had ever seen him.

Arendal turned to face me.

"Lucian. Are you guilty?"

"Guilty? Oh, you bet."

Turmborne perked up.

Arendal sighed and shook his head in mock disgust at my sense of humor. Or maybe it was genuine disgust. I could scarcely have blamed him.

"Of the murders," he clarified.

My mouth formed an "O" shape; then, "Not in the least."

"Do you know who committed them?"

"No. I have a few ideas, though." I gave him a tight, closed-mouthed smile. "Anxious to get back to working on that."

"Yes?"

"Feverishly anxious, yes."

"There, you see?" Arendal favored Turmborne with an actual smile.

Turmborne rolled his eyes. "This is asinine."

"Where did you learn that word?" I asked.

This time the big man only sighed.

"We'd best be moving along," Arendal said then.

I blinked. "We?"

"I intend to accompany you."

I considered this for a few seconds, while Turmborne seemed to be getting worked up again.

"Can you get us back to Earth?" Cassidy demanded, getting to his feet. The others quickly stood as well.

"Eventually," Arendal replied, "but we have more pressing concerns at the moment. In fact, Lucian, I would suggest…" He was interrupted as Turmborne grasped a crate and hurled it at him. Before anyone else could react, Arendal brought his silver cane up. White lightning flared and the crate shattered in midair, sending wood chips flying and clumps of food splattering everywhere.

Turmborne hesitated, perhaps surprised by the effectiveness of Arendal's defenses. In that split-second of doubt, Arendal hurled his walking stick. The smooth, rounded grip end of the silver shaft caught the big god in the temple and he fell limply to the ground.

"Nice," I said, having scattered another set of my spheres during the action. "It definitely needed doing, anyway."

Ignoring me, Arendal retrieved his stick and then knelt down, checking Turmborne's vital signs. Satisfied, he held his cane out, parallel to his body, and bowed his head. White lightning danced up and down the silver shaft, racing up his arms and surrounding his entire body in a halo of sparkling energy.

With a loud exclamation, Arendal directed the accumulated energy outward. Thunder cracked and reality split apart, revealing a silver-rimmed portal, wreathed in white flames. Without hesitation, he grasped the big god under the arms and dragged him through the gateway, then came back through, alone, closing it after himself.

"That should keep him occupied for a while," he said. "It'll take him at least a week to figure out where he is and how to get back here." He paused. "Wait—we're talking about Turmborne here." He grinned. "Two weeks."

"Impressive," I observed. And it was. Arendal had just ripped through multiple dimensional barriers, all at once, by sheer brute force. He had used raw power to forge a direct route to his objective—a plane several layers removed from the one we currently occupied. Most of us could do it if we had to, though only through a very few layers, and at tremendous cost in terms of personal health and safety. It would merely drain most of our reserves, if we were lucky; if not, it would leave us in a coma, or perhaps as a vegetable, on the other side. Baranak had once claimed to have bulled his way through five levels in one jump, and to have walked away, perfectly healthy, on the other side. I had no idea how many barriers Arendal had ripped through, and, truth be told, I did not much want to find out.

"Time to go," he said, summoning up the Power once more.

"To where?" I asked.

He ignored me, his fingers reaching out to describe a circular motion in the air. White lightning flared in front of him, slowly spreading to form a widening circle, perpendicular to the ground.

"To where?" I repeated.

"Come on," he said.

The portal blazed a blinding white, fully formed. I tried to peer through it, but the light was too bright to make out anything on the other side.

"Not just yet," I said then.

"Why?"

"Because I trust you less even than I do Turmborne. Maybe even less than Baranak. At least both of them are straightforward and honest."

Arendal actually looked hurt. He frowned. "That's a pity," he said, "because.."

He was interrupted by a sudden humming sound, as my scattered blue spheres floated up from the grass en masse and began to spin around him. He watched them with thinly veiled interest, one eyebrow rising slightly behind his little round glasses, but made no other move in reaction. The speed of the spheres increased even as they constricted in towards him. Within a few seconds they had flattened out, blending into one another, forming a sort of disk, orbiting him like the rings of Saturn.

"Aesthetically pleasing," he noted, otherwise unperturbed. "I can't wait to see what they do next."

The rings stretched up and down vertically, blending together to form a sort of tube, spinning round and round him, from the ground to up beyond the top of his head.

"Pretty," he observed from within, his voice muffled and echoing. "Let me know when I'm supposed to be concerned, Lucian."

Quickly I traced a circle on the ground between us with the toe of my boot. It glowed a faint blue in a pencil-thin line.

"I would be happy to accept your surrender at any time," I replied.

He laughed. A silver shape emerged through the wall of the cylinder—the head of his cane. The spinning tube warped at its touch like clay on a pottery wheel. With a slashing motion, he shattered the tube, my blue energy dissipating instantly.

"If you are finished with your brave resistance," he said, "perhaps now we can be on our way."

"Come make me," I said.

Sighing, he stepped forward—and dropped through the grass, through my blue circle, vanishing. Flames roared up though the gateway, filling the space he had occupied.

Nodding in satisfaction, I snapped my fingers, closing the portal I had just set up.

"You always underestimate me, always look for the obvious from me," I said, though he was no longer there to hear. "I mean, come on—I am the deceiver, the bad guy, for crying out loud. Get a clue." I smiled. "And enjoy the barbecue."

The humans looked on wide-eyed. I think they actually might have been impressed with me.

"Let's go," I said to them. "That will occupy him for five minutes, at most, and he won't be happy when he gets out. We need to be away from here."

"You really are a master of winning friends and creating good impressions, aren't you?" Evelyn observed.

I executed a small bow to her.

"Where now?" Cassidy's voice was tired; he seemed almost resigned to his fate.

"I knew the road to your plane was dangerous," I said, "but I had no idea just how dangerous every other place had become. I am not going any further until I have armed myself properly."

The humans all frowned.

"Armed?" Evelyn shook her head. "I had sort of assumed you and your kind were beyond being hurt by weapons."

"It depends upon the weapons," I replied.

Reaching out with both hands, I felt for the shape of reality as it was woven about us. In a sense, the threads that formed the fabric of that particular space and time flowed through my fingers, and I examined them, getting my bearings. After a few seconds, I felt confident that I knew where we were— that I understood the relative flow of time there, the locations of the borders with adjacent planes, and so on. Nodding then, I sketched in the air before us with my right hand, blue lightning dancing from my fingertips and lingering there in the shape of a tall circle. I motioned towards it.

As I followed the humans out of Turmborne's game preserve and through the portal, I thought I glimpsed a white light flashing into existence behind me. I did not linger, but leapt through and slammed the gateway closed behind us, afterward to fall along with my human passengers down like cascading raindrops onto the sands of gold.

FIVE

Warm waves slurping wetly against my skull like the tongue of some giant and extremely friendly dog. An orange sun beating down, nearly blinding me. The cry of seabirds as they wheeled overhead. All seemed entirely appropriate, given the destination I had been aiming for. No, wait—the waves on the head part—that did not seem quite right. The *head*?

I realized then that I rested on my back on golden sands, my head slightly lower than my feet. As I struggled to make sense of this, a particularly large wave crashed over my face. Choking salty water, I pulled myself to my feet, my senses forcibly brought back online. Groggily I looked around.

My island. Yes. And the three humans lay nearby. A quick visual inspection revealed them to be apparently intact. Making my way over to Evelyn, I knelt in the sand beside her and lifted her hand, checking her pulse.

Cassidy had just awoken and was sitting up. He squinted and looked around curiously, then saw the rest of us and started his feet.

Evelyn groaned and opened her eyes. Kim, lying nearby, did so as well, though I scarcely noticed.

"It seems," I said, "that in my haste, I may have misjudged the precise location of the exit portal. Since you all seem to have survived, I will assume the drop was not too precipitous or harmful." I ran my hands through the sand. "At least we had something soft to break our falls."

"'Soft' may be stretching it," Cassidy said, rubbing a knot on the back of his head. "You need to work on your landings, I think." He surveyed the sandscape once more. "Where are we?"

"My tropical paradise," I announced, grinning. "Well, actually, one of my secret refuges, from before the war."

The humans looked around. They saw the surrounding blue sea stretching to the horizon in every direction. They saw the slight rise of the island behind me, with its small cluster of palm trees at the summit. They saw... well, there was not much else to see, actually. They turned to me and laughed, every one of them.

"What?"

"Lucian..." Evelyn shook her head in amusement. "This... this is like a cartoon of a tropical island. It..." She laughed again. "It doesn't seem real."

"It is real enough," I said defensively. "Besides, you have not seen all of it."

"I think we have," she replied, still laughing, "and that's pretty much the problem."

"Not at all," I said. "Follow me."

Up the sandy hillside we trudged, Kim limping slightly. The gulls called again, and I idly wondered where they had come from, since I did not recall seeing them on previous visits.

Reaching the top, I led the humans into the grove of palm trees and then into a circular clearing, about fifty yards wide, that lay at the very center of the grove, and of the island itself.

"It just gets more and more impressive," Evelyn said.

I noted that Kim had said nothing in quite a while, and filed that somewhat troubling fact away.

Walking in a tight circle, I inspected each of the trees, looking for the telltale mark. It was not there. Frowning, I walked back to the center of the clearing and, hands on hips, kicked at the sand.

"I'm not quite sure what you're up to," Cassidy remarked then, "but it doesn't seem to be helping us a great deal."

Ignoring him, I began to walk in an expanding spiral pattern, studying the sand at my feet. I had traveled about half a lap around the clearing when I saw a small, gray shape visible within a low point in the dunes. Kicking at the sand, I uncovered perhaps nine square feet of a larger, flat, metallic panel.

The others came over, looking down at it.

"Get back," I said.

As they moved away, blue lightning flashed from my fingertips, striking the panel with sufficient force to blow much of the sand away.

I had revealed what was clearly a hatch, a doorway in the sand. Folding my arms across my chest, I eyed the others.

"Now you have me intrigued," Cassidy said. He knelt beside the door, running his fingers along the edge. "So—what's under it?"

Smiling, I grasped the side and lifted up. It exhibited unexpected resistance, and I had to exert considerable strength before it came free of the remaining sand and swung upward.

The hole that was revealed contained naught but darkness. I grew more concerned; this lack of lighting, along with the lack of a guide marker among the trees, constituted two bad signs too many.

Creating a small globe of blue light, I released it over the hole, and it floated slowly down into the blackness. What it revealed—or failed to reveal—drove a wedge of fear through my heart: A sizeable chamber, enclosed by bare concrete walls, and filled with row after row of shelves and racks and tables. Very *empty* shelves and racks and tables.

Cassidy squinted at what had been revealed, then squinted at me.

"So," he said. "You've been operating some sort of used furniture warehouse, then?"

"And this is supposed to help us how?" Kim growled.

"No," I whispered. "No no no no no." Grasping the edge of the opening, I swung over and down, dangling by my fingertips for a second before releasing and dropping down to the hard slab floor.

The empty racks and shelves seemed to mock me with their pale, reflected glow. I sighed deeply. It was gone. All of it.

"What's that?" Evelyn called down, some moments later, and I turned to see where she was pointing.

On a table in the corner rested a small, smooth, black pistol. I recognized its design. It could easily be one of my favorites from my arsenal; perhaps even the one I had carried that day in the City when I had been defeated—though I had believed that one destroyed by Baranak. Why such a valuable item had been left behind when everything else here had been cleaned out, I could not fathom.

I picked it up, slid the cover back. It was loaded, so to speak. A single, small, red gem glinted inside, held in place by two metal pins. As I slid the chamber closed again, a golden glow radiated from the weapon, solidifying into burning letters floating in the air before me.

Do us all a favor.

A second later the flaming letters dissolved and vanished as if they had never been. I stood there for several seconds, grinding my teeth.

"Oh, I shall," I whispered finally.

I picked up the gun and tucked it securely into my belt, where my long coat covered it.

A couple of minutes of further searching turned up none of my beloved weapons of mass destruction. Drawing upon the Power, I spent an additional ten minutes of intense concentration in the construction of a tight grid of tiny lines of force, covering every surface of the storeroom, designed to reveal any residual energies that might indicate who had been in there since my last visit. This effort as well yielded no results. Frustrated, I sought my ladder, found it, and positioned it against the edge of the doorway above. "Someone want to secure that?" I called up.

No answer.

"Hello?" I squinted up toward the bright blue square of sky overhead, waiting. No one replied.

Growing concerned, I braced the ladder as best I could and climbed out of the storeroom, emerging back into the clearing between the palms.

The humans were not there.

Cursing their stupidity for deciding to go hiking or swimming at a time like this—and, whatever time it might have been, a good time for recreation it most assuredly was not—I trudged angrily through the trees and back onto the portion of the gently sloping beach where we had arrived.

There, in a comfortable-looking beach chair, under a large, striped umbrella, wearing sunglasses and holding a tropical drink, sat Alaria.

Alaria, she of the pale skin and the multicolored eyes and the combs of pearl and silver.

Alaria, one of my former jailers.

Alaria, who had freed me and given me the opportunity to prove my innocence.

Needless to say, I was taken aback.

"Why, hello, my lady," I called to her as I hiked down the beach in her direction.

She waved, her smile the color of the breaking waves, her long, deep-red hair flickering in the ocean breeze like a dark flame.

"Hello," she said. "Nice place you have here."

"Thanks. What did you do with my stuff?"

She slid her black-rimmed sunglasses down to the tip of her nose and gazed up at me with those remarkable rainbow eyes.

"Stuff?"

I frowned.

"Yes. My stuff. My—"

I hesitated, as her expression revealed nothing but puzzlement.

"Never mind."

I looked around, but saw no signs of my mortal charges. "How about the humans?"

"What about them?"

She sipped at her drink, her eyes never leaving mine.

Pursing my lips, I turned, searching all around. Nothing.

"Have you misplaced your companions?" she asked.

"I don't know if that's the term I would use for them," I replied absently, still looking around. "But you will forgive me if I ask you about them, seeing as how you and I seem to be the only ones currently occupying this island—or this universe."

She shrugged.

"I have not seen them, I assure you. I merely came here on the off chance you might stop by. Little did I know you were already here."

Something—some nagging voice deep in my subconscious—told me to doubt her on that score. But I did not pursue it.

"So," she said, "how are you faring with your investigation?"

I laughed.

"There hasn't been much of an investigation, so far."

In response to her questioning look, I explained, "From the moment the humans and I left the dungeons, we have been mostly on the run. Very little time for much beyond staying a step ahead of the posse. Not to mention all the others who would like to see me caught and convicted on general principles."

"Ah." She nodded once. Then she bit her lip, her prismatic eyes sparkling even more vividly than usual. "Perhaps I can be of assistance in that area. I shall see what I can do."

I bowed. "Much appreciated."

She smiled a very faint smile then, for only a second. Then, "Baranak travels all the wrong roads in search of you. As I thought he would."

I nodded.

"Good. Might I assume you had something to do with that?"

The flickering smile appeared and disappeared again, so quickly I thought I might have only imagined it.

"There is something to be said for consistency, for predictability, for the cautious and conservative approach at all times," she said, by way of answer. "In Baranak's case, that 'something' is called stubbornness, lack of imagination. Stupidity, one might even say."

I shrugged.

"So long as he keeps searching for me in places I am not."

"Even so, I would defer any extended island vacations until later, Lucian. You are probably safe here for a day or so, but I would not linger beyond that."

I nodded.

She stood and her white robes, catching the breeze, flared out from her, revealing more of her than I had expected to see. Quickly she pulled them in tighter. As always, with Alaria, I had no idea how intentional it had been.

"Until later, then," she said.

I nodded, then hesitated.

"Say—how long have you known about my little island paradise, here?"

She snapped her fingers and a sparkling white portal flared into existence, tweaked by her power and her vanity into appearing as an ornate, full-length mirror.

"Oh, Lucian. Everyone knows about your island hideaway."

Her rainbow eyes caught mine once more.

"If you are, in fact, missing some 'stuff,' as you say, then I would suggest it could have been any of two dozen different gods who took it. Or perhaps all of them."

And with that, she stepped through the looking glass and vanished.

I reeled. All of them? I could not believe it. Everyone knew about this hideaway?

I kicked the sand at my feet. I had been out of circulation for a long time, but I had never suspected the others might start uncovering all of my old secrets in the interim. Malachek knew about one, and now Alaria claimed everyone knew about another. If they had all been compromised during my exile—if my private sanctuaries were all exposed and my hidden resources were long gone—my chances of redeeming myself were decreasing by the moment.

And where in the hell were the humans?

"She's gone at last, then."

I whirled.

At the top of the rise stood Arendal.

"Must be tourist season," I muttered.

"You knew you could not long escape me," he said. "I'm not Baranak, for crying out loud."

I looked him up and down. His formerly immaculate, cream-colored suit was discolored with burn marks. One entire sleeve was nearly burned away. Dried blood covered half of his face.

"Those pilot lights can be a bitch to light, can't they?" I said.

He shifted his silver cane from one hand to the other, then exerted a small fraction of the Power. His appearance and his clothing reverted to normal.

"I simply wanted you to see one of the reasons why I have become so put out with you," he said.

I shrugged. We regarded one another in silence for a time.

"I should have known it was Alaria who let you out," he said finally. "Under normal circumstances, I would have known. These are, of course, not normal circumstances." He took a few steps down the hill towards me. "And I will say she's been much better lately at avoiding my surveillance than in the past."

I began forming tiny blue spheres on my fingertips once again.

"Maybe she did it," I said. "The big 'it,' I mean."

He snorted.

"At this point, I'm wondering if we will ever know who did it—or if that even matters," he said. "The murders seem to have stopped. And the Power flows once more, so nothing short of a plunge into the Fountain can kill any of us now. And I, for one," he added with a smirk, "have no intention of going anywhere near it."

He stopped, now about twenty paces away from me, and began to draw figures in the sand with the tip of his cane. They appeared unfamiliar to me; but then, I had never attempted to augment my abilities through technical or mystical means, as everyone suspected Arendal had.

"I find myself sympathetic with the argument Turmborne advanced some time ago," he said then. "All I really want at this point is stability; peace and quiet." He smiled. "And I think things would be very quiet if you were in the dungeon. Or in the Fountain."

I made ready to hurl my spheres.

"Before I take you back, however," he said, "there is one matter I would like resolved."

I said nothing, merely waiting.

"We've found all of your secret caches, as you have probably guessed by now."

I squeezed my eyes closed, trying to breathe evenly.

"Or so Baranak believes," he continued.

I opened my eyes again.

"I am convinced we have missed at least one."

"And why might that be?"

His eyebrows arched.

"Oh, just a hunch on my part, mostly," he said. "The evidence is circumstantial, involving a variety of small clues—not least of which is the number of weapons we have recovered, as compared to what I believe you managed to construct or acquire before your rebellion."

"Hm."

"I believe you have a storeroom hidden somewhere. The biggest one of them all."

"And this is why you did not want Turmborne taking me directly into custody," I said.

It was not a question, and he ignored it.

"Further," he said, "I believe you had weapons hidden there that Baranak has not even guessed exist."

"And you want them—these hypothetical weapons—for purely altruistic reasons."

He smiled. I really, really hated it when he smiled.

"So I am simply, obligingly going to tell you how to find this alleged hideaway."

"That would be the preferred course of events, yes."

I looked around again, frowned.

"Where are the humans, Arendal?"

"Just tending to that now," he replied.

He completed whatever it was he had drawn in the sand, and the air above it crackled and popped. With a flash, the three humans appeared, hanging in the air, immobile, each about a foot above the ground.

"I believe I have located them," he said. "Perhaps there is some finder's fee, yes? No?"

I merely waited. I had some idea where he might be going with this and, truth be told, I had no idea how I might react before the end.

"Where to begin?" He sighed, studying the humans as if he was preparing to create a work of art, and they were to be his canvas. "Where to begin."

He walked over to Kim. "Perhaps here?"

Raising his cane, he touched the shiny pommel to Kim's left foot. Silver flames erupted first from the cane, then from the man's boot. The flames raced up his shin, to stop just past his knee.

"Oh," Arendal said, gesturing with his other hand. "You may speak."

Kim screamed.

I scoffed. "Like I care."

Arendal held the cane steady, studying his work carefully, clinically. He did not even look at me.

"I believe you do care," he said, after several seconds had passed.

"You could not be more mistaken, Arendal."

I watched the silvery flames rising further up Kim's leg as the man writhed in pain.

"Do you remember who I am?" I asked.

"Oh, yes," he said, touching the cane to Kim's other leg. More flames erupted. "I believe I am actually finding this more enjoyable simply because you are... who you are."

I clenched my fists, trying to ignore Kim's cries. The other two humans seemed completely immobilized—apparently, they could neither turn their heads nor speak.

"No need to invest all of my efforts in one place, of course," Arendal said after a few more seconds.

I waited, breathing evenly, spheres of concentrated energy swelling within my clenched fists.

Arendal moved to stand beside Cassidy, raising his cane again. The silver flames lashed out. The big man managed to endure the treatment stoically for a few seconds longer than Kim had but, eventually, inevitably, the screams erupted from his throat as well.

"You are just annoying me now, Arendal," I told him. "I care nothing for these mortals, but they have done nothing to earn this treatment. It is disgraceful, and it is shameful for you to be engaged in it."

Arendal ignored me, continuing to administer the flames to Cassidy's legs. The man's screams clawed at my mind—something I found somewhat surprising.

"I ask you again, Arendal. Do you not know who I am? This is stupid and foolish. You honestly believe that torturing mortals will provoke some sort of response from the dark lord?"

He did not reply. Instead, he stepped back from Cassidy, looked at Evelyn, then looked back at me.

"One left," he said, his expression somewhere between anticipation and pleasure.

I glared at him.

He lifted the cane toward her.

Her eyes widened.

I hurled the spheres.

He jerked his cane up a split second too late, managing to deflect one of the energy globules away but allowing the other to score a direct hit. It exploded against his chest and hurtled him backwards, past the humans, where he rolled to a stop in the sand.

I was on him instantly, my fists meeting his face at least three times before he roared and shoved me back.

"You are utterly transparent," he spat at me, climbing to his feet, his glasses shattered and hanging precariously from one ear. Absently he swatted them from his face, then drew another pair from a jacket pocket and put them on. "'Dark Lord' indeed. You have become a joke! Everyone knows it."

I feinted to my right and swung out with my left boot, taking his legs out from under him. I kicked him squarely in the gut as he strove to rise.

"Who's a joke? Who?"

I kicked him in the face, sending him tumbling backward into the sand again. Blood sprayed from his nose.

He recovered more quickly than I had thought possible, and his hurled cane struck me in the chest with the force of one of Turmborne's punches. Staggering back, I shook my head to clear my vision, then grabbed for the cane, where it lay in the sand before me.

"Oh, yes, please do pick that up," he laughed.

Too late—I'd already grasped it. Electricity flared out of the cane and surged through my body. Gasping, choking, I stumbled backward. The cane slipped from my numbed fingers. I could no longer feel the middle portion of my body, and the rest of it was not in particularly great shape either. When I dropped limply to the sand, I scarcely knew it.

My pistol slipped from my belt when I hit. I watched it tumble away from me, utterly powerless to stop it.

Arendal bent over and picked up his weapon and mine. He examined the pistol for a few seconds and frowned.

"Where did you get this?"

"M—mine," I gasped.

"A thousand years ago it was yours," he barked back. "I saw Baranak take it from you after the battle, along with all the others. He destroyed all of your weapons—right there in the square, beneath the Fountain—so no one could ever use them to threaten the City again." He moved to stand over me, glaring down. "How did you come by it now?"

I groaned. It was all I could do. I cannot say which hurt worse: the pain running through my body, or the memory of Baranak gathering up all the guns I had worked so long and so hard to perfect and produce, and smashing them to pieces—over the objections of some on his side, as well as my own—in order to keep them out of anyone's hands, in the future.

"You do have a secret storehouse somewhere," he said softly, more to himself than to me.

Still frowning, he tucked the pistol into his belt. Then, wiping at the blood that streamed from his nose, he strolled leisurely back to where the three humans hung suspended in midair. Reaching up, he took hold of Evelyn's ankle and pulled. As if emerging from quicksand or molasses, she slid slowly but steadily away from the others. Still immobile, she floated along behind Arendal like a helium balloon on a string.

I watched these actions, a still greater anger building within me, but found myself quite powerless to intervene. My muscles felt as frozen as the humans' must have been, though after a few moments I could feel the numbness ever so slowly beginning to recede.

Stopping about ten yards away from me, Arendal released Evelyn's ankle and allowed her to hang there.

"Well, well. I could scarcely have imagined it." He looked down at me, a contemptuous smile spreading across his face. "You have some sort of feelings for this... human."

I wanted desperately to reply—to heap scorn upon his outlandish fantasies—but found my jaw still as limp as the rest of me.

"How long could you possibly have known her?" He snorted. "Some sort of whirlwind romance, I suppose." He looked her over, once, then turned back to me, gesturing with his cane. "This, then, is our Dark Lord now," he pronounced gravely, voice overflowing with sarcasm. "Once the scourge of the gods. Now a sad and ineffectual fraud."

Prostrate on the sand, I glared at him.

"I've had names and titles given to me over the centuries, too, you know," he said then. "Those in our City have called me quite a few things."

I noticed his voice was slightly distorted by the damage I had done to his nasal passages.

"'Hero' has never been one of those things," he continued. He smiled flatly. "Perhaps now that will change."

I tried to reply with a scornful rebuff, but only an unintelligible grunt emerged from my nearly dead lips.

"Yes, yes, well said." He brushed impatiently at the flecks of blood on his white jacket. "Your eloquence has always moved me."

Trying desperately to ignore his banter, forcing myself to concentrate, I summoned the Power and channeled it through my limbs. Pins and needles raced over nearly every surface of my body, and I gritted my teeth, willing the process to speed up. My right index finger moved, then my whole hand. I pulled in more of the Power and let it flush the lingering numbness from my system. As the seconds crawled by, ever so slowly, I felt normal sensations returning.

Arendal stood over me, leering down, kicking at one of my seemingly paralyzed legs.

"The funny thing, Lucian, is that, aside from Baranak—who is just too pig-headed to think things through—they all pretty much know you didn't kill anyone." He shrugged. "But they don't care. You have been designated as the sacrificial lamb. Lamb? No, that hardly fits, in your case." He stroked his chin for a moment. "The sacrificial black sheep, perhaps. Yes. A sacrifice to appease the gods, I suppose you could say." He glanced back at Evelyn. "Along with some degree of... unavoidable... collateral damage."

I screamed then. What I said, I do not know. It was a scream wrenched from the depths of my soul, and I believe it actually startled Arendal. Perhaps it caused him to hesitate. Perhaps it did not. In any case, I had an opening, and I knew I could move again, and I struck.

Admittedly, my first blow might not be best described as honorable; but then, we were not exactly engaged in matters of honor at the moment.

He staggered back, clutching his groin, stunned, as I struggled to my still-somewhat-leaden feet. Behind him, I saw Evelyn fall to the sand, the force he had used to hold her apparently disrupted by my attack.

Fists, boot, blue spheres—whatever I could tag him with, I used, and I aimed them at any vulnerabilities I could find. For a short while, things seemed to be going my way. Then his damned cane struck me again, this time a glancing blow to the forehead, silver fire flashing in my eyes, and I staggered back, reeling.

He had already recovered from my assault. All traces of humor were gone from his face now. He brandished the cane again, flames crackling in the air around him. I had always known him to be clever, wily, and very likely treacherous in the extreme, but nothing I had ever seen or heard about him had given me reason to think he possessed reserves of power as great as this. Had I so misjudged myself? Had I become weakened during my long exile among the humans? Or had Arendal tapped into some new power source, boosting himself beyond what he once had been? None of those possibilities struck me as positive or encouraging. For the first time, some measure of fear crept through the dark recesses of my mind.

"You have this coming, Lucian," he said then. "After what happened to Halaini."

I froze, just staring at him.

"I loved her, you know," he said.

I blinked, my mouth opening and closing, but I remained silent. I had no idea how to respond to that.

"It was your fault, after all," he continued.

He pulled himself up straight, smoothing his cream colored suit with one hand. His eyes had a wild, haunted look in them, suddenly.

"Entirely your fault. She didn't have to die. She had absolutely no business being there, in the courtyard, that day. She was only there because of you. You killed her."

With his left hand he raised the cane into a horizontal position in front of him. Grasping the other end with his right hand, he pulled. The bottom portion slid loose with a popping sound, revealing itself to be only a hollow sleeve. Where before the cane had ended with a flattened base, now it trailed down to a fine, wicked point. He tossed the sleeve aside and brandished the cane like a dagger, over his head, eyeing my chest—and then lurched suddenly forward with a grunt, sprawling face down in the sand. Evelyn stood behind him, a grimace on her face, still in the stance from which she had delivered a solid, violent kick to his back.

The pistol, knocked loose, tumbled away from him. I dived for it, grabbed at it.

He scrambled toward his cane where it had fallen. Clutching it, climbing to his feet, he looked up, only to find himself staring down the barrel of my gun.

"See," I said in an extremely soft, smooth voice, as I channeled my energies down my arm and into the specially designed weapon, and thus into the small, red crystal contained within, "that whole bit with Halaini—all it did was piss me off."

He scarcely had time to react before I fired. The weapon barely made a sound, such that one might have questioned if it had fired at all; yet, at another level, it felt overwhelming, yanking all of my nerve endings tight and shaking me to the tips of my toes. Such is the nature of the weapons of the gods. My single shot, a blue lightning bolt trailing behind it, nailed him right between the eyes, shattering his little round glasses and sending pieces flying. He stood there for a second or two, swaying, a tiny dark circle having appeared just above the bridge of his nose. Then he fell face-first to the sand.

"And now I'm really pissed. Because I didn't want to shoot anyone but Baranak."

Evelyn walked up beside me and looked down at him, frowning. I glanced at her quickly, making sure she was okay.

"Nice work," I said.

She simply nodded, then started back toward the others.

I waited there a moment, gun at the ready, in case Arendal moved again.

He did not.

I found myself somewhat surprised; one shot should have only staggered him, drained some of his energy temporarily away. I had expected more from him, given the formidable accounting he had given of himself to that point. Yet still he lay, like a mortal shot by a true firearm.

I was not about to complain, of course. Shrugging, I tucked the now-warm pistol back into my belt, silently and futilely wishing I had a few dozen more of them readily at hand. But while Arendal had been quite right in guessing that I had one last storehouse of weapons at my disposal, actually accessing it was going to be a pain. Even as the anger drained from me, though, a plan began to form itself within my mind.

"Lucian!"

I whirled. Evelyn stood a dozen feet away, her back to me, staring back up the sloping beach toward the trees.

"What—oh."

I saw it then. The other two humans were gone.

"They just disappeared," she said.

I frowned. Running to where they had been before, I asked, "Did you see any energy discharge around them?"

"No..." Panic crept into her voice. "Where did they go?"

I summoned the Power, though it was not easy, given my physical state at the moment, and searched for any telltale signs or traces of one of the others having opened a portal there. Finally, I shook my head.

"No one grabbed them, as far as I can tell."

"So what does that mean?"

I sighed. At the moment, it hurt even to think.

"It appeared as if Arendal had placed all of you within some sort of bubble, suspending you just out of synch with this plane, probably. I have seen others do it before."

I kicked at the sand under my feet, thinking.

"He pulled you out of it, but the other two were still there. Once I shot him, his connection to that plane must have snapped shut. Essentially, they were pulled back."

She just looked at me.

"Back... to where?"

I shrugged.

"Who knows?"

Evelyn rubbed at her temples with her fists for a few seconds, then stalked over to where Arendal lay.

"He does. He knows. But I assume he's dead now, right?"

"Quite to the contrary. Unfortunately."

She stepped back quickly, as if she had stumbled over a snake—which was not far from the truth.

"He's still alive?"

"The Fountain still flows. The Power surrounds us. He cannot die."

She frowned down at him, back at me.

"Then what—?"

"The weapon—or, more precisely, the crystal within it—does not kill. It merely stuns its victim, and drains some of their energies into the crystal. I added a bit of my own energy to it, as well, just to be sure, and apparently it was more effective than I could have guessed. He will recover, but from what I sense of him now, not for a while. It should give us enough time to get away from here." My mouth was a tight line. "And he will not be terribly comfortable for some time after he comes to. I see this as an added bonus."

"But he's incapacitated," she said, ignoring my dry wit. "He can't tell us where Cassidy and Kim are."

She seated herself on the sand, clearly unhappy.

I shrugged.

"Not any time soon, no." This seemed to me, in many ways, a good thing. Understandably, though, Evelyn did not see it that way.

Some length of time passed, during which the waves and the seabirds solemnly serenaded us—a god, a woman, and a near-corpse. I gazed out at the idyllic vista of my tropical paradise, yet found my thoughts arguing relentlessly, insistently in favor of a more dark and depressing attitude. I thought of freedom and of imprisonment, and of all the points in between. I considered the dubious wisdom of attempting murder, or at least inflicting grievous bodily harm, in the midst of seeking to clear my name of murder charges.

Somehow, I doubted self-defense would serve to exonerate me—but then, what was one more body on an already distressingly, depressingly large pile, with all the survivors pointing at me, the accused? At least Arendal, unlike most of the others, had deserved what he had gotten. The pity was that he, alone among them, would not stay dead.

There apparently being nothing more for either of us to say, and a powerful weariness from all of our recent travails upon us both, Evelyn and I lay down in the shade, beneath the ring of trees atop the sandy hill, and we slept.

SIX

"That I could never dream," Bronte wrote, "till Earth was lost to me."

I never dreamed, in the time before my exile. Or if I did, I never recalled the dreams afterward.

At different times in my life, I have believed different things about dreams. For instance, for the longest time I was sure they were simply the mind's way of taking out the garbage, so to speak; that, in sleep, we gather up all the negativity and hurt and fear we have temporarily filed away during the day, and we congeal those feelings and images into a not-terribly-coherent whole that has meaning only to the sleeping mind; and then we parade that odd concoction past our mind's eye, confronting and overcoming as we go. Thus in sleep we pull phantoms and devils, those things we cannot or will not confront during the day, out of the dark corners and into the light, where they may be discarded. Because I did not often dream in the Golden City, I believed I feared little, was seldom if ever hurt, and therefore possessed little metaphysical garbage that required disposal. Time and bitter experience eventually would serve to obliterate this myth. Few who have ever lived, I now know, have needed more the services of a mental janitorial service. For the lives of the gods are long, and the bad always comes with the good, and the experiences pile upwards, ever upwards, shaping and tearing down and reshaping again, leaving considerable detritus in their wakes.

Another view, one I have more recently entertained, suggests we see in dreams what we desire but might never know in waking life. As a god, little could be denied me, and my dreams, if dreams there were, always afterward seemed to be flimsy, insignificant things. The true stuff of dreams I lived every day, there in my Golden City. To what might one aspire, when one dwells forever in paradise? Conquest, yes—but that I always calculated as a real, definite goal with a specific path toward its achievement. Never did I think of it as merely a dream. With my rebellion and my defeat, however, my plans were shattered and my ambitions undone. In an instant, that which always had seemed so entirely real and possible became mere fantasy. Upon my exile, and especially after the Power vanished, I came to know fear and loss and longing beyond anything I had previously imagined. And I knew dreams, vivid and powerful and lingering dreams.

Sleeping in the sand and the shade beneath my circle of trees on my little island, I dreamed once more. Visions of hope and glory and defeat and death haunted me, and demons out of blackest darkness hunted me. Gods living and gods surely dead taunted me with assertions and accusations. I cursed them all and then begged each of them in turn for forgiveness, though for what transgressions I cannot say.

Awaking, I found myself lying on my side, wrought up and tense. The sleep had not been restful; in fact, I felt in many ways worse than when I had lain down.

Evelyn sat leaning against a tree trunk nearby, watching the sea birds where they walked in the sand, leaving small triangular tracks that circled and meandered. She glanced my way as I sat up, but said nothing. I stood and brushed the sand from my clothes, but she ignored me. For some time afterward, we only watched the birds and felt the breeze, and we kept our thoughts, such as they were, entirely to ourselves.

An interminable time later, I gave way and asked after her condition. She kept her reply to a bare minimum, and I understood that. Despite all her evident strength, she was afraid and confused and had lost the only other people to whom she felt she could turn. My treatment of her and the others up to that point, I knew then, while much of the time warranted by the attitudes of her cohorts, had contributed little to any sense of trust she might have developed towards me. Perhaps at this point I first felt some measure of shame. Such a thing I will no longer dismiss out of hand, though it still galls me to admit it.

And so I met her at least halfway, and we walked along the sands, and we talked, haltingly at first, but with increasing confidence on both our parts.

Toward dreams our conversation eventually turned, there on my beach beneath my eternally perfect sky. She listened politely but kept most of her thoughts on the matter to herself. I believed at the time she hardly listened and cared even less. I would, of course, discover otherwise later. Truth be told, I cared little for her contributions to this portion of our conversation. After all, what possible perspective could a mere mortal offer with regard to contemplations of infinite years and infinite dreams? In retrospect I see my pride and my blindness clearly and I weep now for both, though little good comes from such ruminations at this late date. Enough. Those days are done and gone and can never return. A fool is yet a fool even if he be a god, with the difference that all his foolishness is magnified a thousand fold and more.

"So, what is our next move?"

Her asking of the question broke the spell, and effectively ended the long, idyllic afternoon of our respite. On some level I understood that I had been delaying the inevitable, for a reason opaque to me then. On the surface, though, I was all business.

"My plan was to shake the trees, beat the bushes—whatever botanical expression you prefer—and try to find evidence of the true guilty party, or parties." Then I gritted my teeth, blood starting to boil again. "But Turmborne and Arendal both intimated that the others have little interest in my guilt or innocence. They don't care who is guilty—only that someone gets blamed, and the killings stop."

She nodded. "It's not terribly encouraging."

"No."

I turned away, angry, and paced a few steps in either direction, then looked back up at her again.

"I think it is time for a new plan. Or rather," I said, a glint in my eye, "an *old* plan."

She eyed me warily.

"I'm not sure I like the sound of that."

"I have no choice," I said. "Not any longer."

Her expression was ambivalent.

"So long as it doesn't make you look even more guilty."

"I scarcely imagine that is possible now," I said. "Or relevant."

Brows furrowing, she nodded once.

"So what will we do?"

"We?" My eyes met hers momentarily, and I looked away. "No. These are things I must do alone."

"What things?" she asked, though she surely had a pretty good idea before she asked.

"Raise an army," I replied. "And before that, secure arms for them."

Evelyn appeared deeply troubled. I knew the fate of her crewmen weighed upon her, and I allowed myself a moment's consideration that perhaps something else colored her thoughts, as well.

"And you're doing this alone," she said. "You're going to take me home, then?" She frowned at that. "What about the others?"

I gazed out to sea.

"Unfortunately, we cannot attempt the road to your plane now. Alaria all but admitted that Baranak's lackeys are camped out along that road, lying in wait for me. Nor can I embark on any extended search for your missing comrades, given the current political climate."

She followed after me, her voice growing strident.

"Then what—?"

"I will place you in a secure location, until I can resolve matters."

She started to object, but I turned and began to move back towards the spot where Arendal's body lay face down in the sand.

"Before we do that, though, there is one other matter to attend to."

Evelyn watched as I bent over Arendal's inexplicably still-limp body and rolled him over onto his back. She gasped in horror at what was revealed, and I found myself agreeing in spirit with her reaction.

A hole, approximately a half-inch in diameter, had been burned cleanly into his forehead. Dried blood surrounded it. The wound lay precisely where I had shot him.

After a few moments, during which neither of us moved or spoke, Evelyn whispered, "He'll survive *that*?"

I bent closer, studying the wound, shaking my head slowly.

"This—it—" I absently ran my left hand back through my hair, trying to suppress the odd sense of panic that grew within my breast. "It was not supposed to do this."

"It wasn't?"

Shaking my head again, I examined the pistol, then opened it and removed the jewel. I held it up to the sun and studied it carefully. A tiny spark danced within it.

"No," I said then. "It most assuredly was not."

Another pause, and then Evelyn asked, "So… might he actually be… dead?"

Instead of answering, I quickly began to pat him down.

"What are you doing?"

I was not seeking anything in particular, but with Arendal, it was a good bet he would have something of importance on his person. Sure enough, I felt a small, hard object inside his coat. Reaching into his inside breast pocket, I pulled forth a small, red crystal, very similar to the one from my pistol. I held it up, letting the light shine through it. It sparkled like a tiny star, flawless and empty.

"Looks like some kind of data storage crystal," Evelyn observed. "Your people use them, too?"

"No."

Out of curiosity, I tried to fit the crystal I had taken from Arendal into my gun. It slid smoothly, perfectly into place. I frowned—that could not possibly mean anything good. I resolved to test this new gem at the next opportunity, and left it in place. Stashing the old crystal in my pocket, I put my gun away and finished patting him down. Then I lifted under his arms and dragged him up the slope.

During the process of moving him, my panic evaporated and I welcomed the returning anger and resentment towards Arendal that took its place. By the time I reached the top, his fate scarcely concerned me at all. I pulled him over to the open trap door into my storage room and unceremoniously rolled him over the edge. He fell limply and hit the bottom with a satisfying smack.

Evelyn shouted up from the beach, "What if he isn't dead?"

I shrugged. "Then he wakes up. Eventually." I looked down at his unpleasantly twisted form where it lay.

"Whatever might have just broken should heal long before he recovers from that hole through his head," I replied as I slid the door closed. "But at least I got to enjoy doing it to him."

She just shook her head and turned away.

I trudged back down the hill and, when I reached her, she silently fell in step alongside me. We made our way along the beach, to the spot where we had first emerged there.

Evelyn pointed to the silver cane lying nearby.

"Aren't you going to get rid of his walking stick?"

I looked at it, took a deep breath, and shook my head.

"Screw it," I said. "I'm not touching that thing again."

She nodded.

"But isn't there some way to get rid of it?"

"There's no point," I said. "It would probably just return to him when he recovers."

She looked puzzled by that but let it pass.

I brought both hands up then, as if feeling the surface of an invisible wall in front of me. I was in fact feeling the construction of space-time around me, getting a sense of its warp and woof and detecting the areas of least resistance to penetration. Satisfied, I pushed. The air around me rippled as if I had pushed my fingers into a pond, and reality shuddered. Twisting my right hand, I exerted more of the Power, and an oval, rimmed in blue flame, irised open before us, to a height of about ten feet and a width of roughly five feet.

Taking Evelyn's hand, I led her through the portal and away from my tiny tropical paradise, idly wondering if I would ever have the opportunity or inclination to return there. A profound sadness descended on me then, though why I cannot say.

Once the portal snapped shut behind us, thick mists surrounded us on all sides. The ground underfoot was hard, red clay. I recognized our location instantly.

Evelyn looked around, eyes wide.

"We are still in the Above," I told her. "Slow time, high power."

She cocked an eyebrow at me.

"I'm still not sure I follow all of that," she said.

"It is actually quite simple," I said. "Think of your plane, containing Earth and your Terran Alliance, as well as my old Mysentia and the Outer Worlds, as a sort of middle ground. Below that, so to speak, power decreases as you go 'down' the levels. And time speeds up. Creatures in the lower levels of the Below are almost like insects—very weak, buzzing about, and living lives that, even to you, would seem quite brief. A year in parts of the Below would seem only a few hours in your plane, and only an instant in my City."

She nodded.

"And that's where subspace is located, right?"

I nodded.

"The portion of the Below that humans have accessed for centuries, for rapid space travel. Yes. Your ships move through subspace—through a level of the Below—while very little time passes back in your own plane. You still have to put your crews into stasis for very long journeys but, once back in your realm, they scarcely seem to have been gone any time at all."

"And the Above is the opposite, I take it?"

"Yes. Time moves slower than it would on Earth. And the power levels grow much greater as you go 'up.' My Golden City exists in what we believe to be the middle Above."

"The middle? There are levels higher—more powerful—than your City?"

"Very likely. We believe the source of our Fountain, of our Power, lies somewhere beyond us in the Above."

"You haven't been there, though?"

"We have great difficulty in traveling much above our City's level," I replied. "We simply lack the power to transverse such barriers."

"And are there... beings... beyond you? Those who look at you the way you look at humans? At insects?"

I glanced at her, looked away, and pursed my lips.

"Perhaps."

Despite her attempts to probe further, I would say nothing more on that score.

We walked on through the fog.

After some time, we reached an area discernable from the rest of this mist-filled realm only by a slight rise underfoot and a certain tingle in the air. It seemed right, but we would have had to be quite fortunate to have found it so quickly. I raised a hand and brought us to a halt, then kept my hand aloft and walked in a small circle, seeking the telltale signs.

"What is it?" Evelyn asked. She had not ceased to peer into the fog during our entire walk, despite the complete lack of visibility beyond about ten feet in any direction.

I found the thin patch in the dimensional barrier and pushed. Again the ripples in the air, again the blazing blue portal as I tore us a conduit from one realm of existence to another adjacent to it.

On the other side, this time, we emerged into a heavy rain under a dark, moonless sky. We descended into an arroyo, made our way carefully across its rock-strewn depths, and climbed back out again. The water pelted us relentlessly, but we pressed on.

After an hour's walk, during which time the rain finally let up to a mere trickle, we happened upon a wizened old man, his skin a peculiar shade of gray, leading an ox cart. He regarded us with little interest, until I fished in one pocket and brought out a small, blue coin, crackling with what little of the Power I could manage quickly to squeeze inside. He perked up then, accepted it, and gestured for us to climb aboard. I was quite happy to get off my feet for a time, and I could tell Evelyn, despite her military stoicism regarding such things, felt the same way.

We bounced and along at a good pace. Evelyn stretched out, napping, while I looked about, studying the surroundings, absolutely none of which proved of interest. Consequently, I turned my attention to the driver and his beast. The man mumbled something in a language I had never encountered before, apparently to his animal, and I idly wondered if the creature could actually understand him. I had seen stranger things in my travels, certainly. The ox, of course, bore little resemblance to any ox I had ever encountered in Evelyn's cosmos, but the fifth and sixth legs actually seemed to increase its efficiency, so I was not about to complain.

After a couple of hours of travel, I gently shook Evelyn awake and we hopped off the back of the wagon. The old man did not even look back.

As if on cue, the rains began to fall once more. Sighing, we pressed on.

Six more times we walked through alien landscapes, and six more times I found the weak spot I sought and opened a portal. Each time, we emerged into a world of extremely limited visibility: a light sandstorm, a solar eclipse, a thick jungle. As we emerged from a rather unpleasant snowstorm, Evelyn seemed to catch on, and finally spoke up.

"This is way too much of a coincidence," she said. "You're causing this somehow, aren't you?" She brushed the last flakes of snow from her flight suit.

I smiled.

"Not 'causing'—not precisely."

Now we walked through a dull, gray countryside, under a dull, gray sky. A nearly featureless vista stretched to the horizon in every direction.

"Then what are you doing?" she asked. "How is it happening?"

I shrugged.

"I have mapped out many paths over the centuries. I know the places where the planes intersect. I know of many planes that are likely to provide the general conditions I desire."

"So you weren't actually making it snow, then?"

"No. I cannot control these universes. I can only choose a path among the planes most likely to provide the environments I seek." I flashed a smile at her. "We have been fortunate so far—though not in this particular one, it would seem."

Her eyebrows arched.

"Fortunate? A snowstorm... a sandstorm... those are fortunate?" Barely two seconds passed, and then, "Oh. Of course. Surveillance."

"Indeed. This route is a bit longer than some of the alternate ways to where we're going, but few could spot us or track us along it. It has been good to me before."

I grimaced as a blast of icy rain smacked me in the face, and I saw Evelyn do likewise. The downpour began almost immediately afterward.

"Ah, that's more like it," I observed. We both laughed then. "Unfortunately, it is not always the most pleasant path."

"You do realize," she said, a wry smile on her face, "that after all this hardship, I'm expecting our destination to be nothing less than a four-star resort."

I laughed sharply.

"Okay," she said, "I'll settle for three stars—but the chef had better be top notch."

Passing out of the wet, gray realm and through another of my blue portals, we stepped into what seemed a vast, silvery bowl. Strange, spidery, leafless trees like bizarre aluminum sculptures twisted skyward—and what a sky it was. A vast aurora swirled overhead, filling all but the uppermost portion in a miasma of shifting rainbow colors.

"I don't know whether to be enchanted or frightened," Evelyn said, looking around. "Of course, that would apply to most of what I've encountered since the ship was captured." Her gaze lingered on a tiny object ahead of us in the distance. "What is that?"

"A landmark. An old safe-house. And a positive sign," I said, hoping all those things proved to be true.

We walked on for a time in silence, and the object ahead resolved into a small structure. From what I could see, it remained intact. I felt some amount of relief. Perhaps things would finally go my way.

Some measure of self-pity swept over me then, before I could push it away. I thought of my current troubles, and then backward to my long years in exile, on Mysentia and the other Outer Worlds, virtually powerless. I thought of the rebellion that led to that exile, and its failure, and my trial and conviction. I thought back still further, and remembered the worst moment in my long, immortal life. I remembered the last time I saw Halaini.

I remembered her golden skin, her almond eyes, and her black, spiky hair, shot through with vivid streaks of blood red and platinum blonde. I remembered her delicate hands, her slender form, and the odd, turquoise coloring above and around her eyes. I remembered the green and the gold she always wore, and the slightly rumpled appearance she affected, belied by the utter grace with which she carried herself. I recalled the air of perpetual disconcert which seemed to surround her, alternating with an equal measure of serene self-confidence, if that makes any sense—and perhaps only with her could such a thing be possible. And, for as long as I had known her, I had found her to be the most fascinating creature in this or any universe.

I remembered her as she was on that last day, beautiful and brash and utterly unafraid of anything. And I thought of her climbing high atop the platform over the Fountain, and calling down to both parties, demanding that the fighting cease, pleading for both sides to come to our senses before something tragic happened... And I thought of the shot that struck her and knocked her over the edge, falling, falling, down into the churning cauldron of energies, gone, gone.

Halaini... How I took you for granted... How I never paused to consider you, because I felt that an immortal had no cause to hurry in anything... All the time in the world, I believed... And then, just like that, the time is gone, ended forever...

I was brought back to myself when Evelyn halted, presumably for a break. I realized then that we had spent a considerable amount of time walking across that featureless concave surface. We had indeed traveled a very long way.

She stood, hands on hips, and looked around again, though there was little to see.

"Where are we now?" she asked. "Anywhere close to our destination?"

I blinked, realizing I had been lost in my memories again, my body moving along on instinct and subconscious drive—a condition I found myself falling into more and more often, lately. Idly I wondered if gods could not help but eventually go insane, from the press of memories weighing down, growing heavier each year, each millennium. Perhaps we were all fated to simply drown in that ocean of experiences. Perhaps the gods now dead had been the fortunate ones, after all.

"We are somewhere in the Above," I said. "One of the levels. One plane among many."

She considered that for a moment. Then, "How many are there?"

"How many digits are there behind the decimal point? Who knows?"

I stretched tired muscles and then leaned back against a silver tree, trying and failing once again to relax.

"Planes and levels of planes, and subdivisions of those," I muttered. "I doubt anyone will ever know the answer."

I waved a hand airily before me.

"For example, when we break through a barrier, are we truly moving from one point to the immediate next?"

She frowned.

"I thought that was what you said."

"Maybe. It is a more comforting thought. But what if we are actually skipping over layers and layers when we jump? What universes might lie hidden in the spaces in between? What wonders and horrors have we never seen, that wait just around the corner from any given reality? Who knows?" I laughed once, sharply. "Not me."

"Not an encouraging thought," she said, idly running her fingers along the trunk of another tree, apparently fascinated by it. "As interesting as I find all of this," she added, "I'd just as soon be back home and confronting problems I know how to deal with."

"I know."

"And I have no doubt Cassidy and Kim feel the same way," she said. "Wherever they are."

I regarded her. Despite my long-cultivated preconceptions and prejudices, I found I unexpectedly had come to admire her in some ways. I valued the refreshingly clear-headed manner with which she had reacted to our obstacles thus far, despite their being, for the most part, far beyond her experience. Along with this, I respected her obvious strength and determination. The others of her crew had proven severely lacking, especially with regard to the former quality.

"Are you sure you are not better off without them?" I asked.

She faced me then, clearly angry.

"I haven't been pressing the issue of the others because I'm entirely at your mercy, for the moment, and because I realize you are extremely constrained in what you can and cannot do right now. But don't think for a minute that I've forgotten about them."

She leaned closer, eyes flashing bright blue.

"We will find them. And we will get home. All of us."

A deep emotion surged up within me, a fire building in my gut and roaring out along my limbs, threatening to explode into visible reaction. I could not tell if it was outrage at her impertinence or resentment at her obvious assumption that I would happily abandon the two men to whatever fate had befallen them. The fact that this was true only made it worse. I opened my mouth, forced it closed again, and looked away, exerting all of my willpower to bring my emotions back under control. Nevertheless, something of my inner reaction must have shone through to her, for she exhibited the tiniest smile, nodded once, and walked away from me.

I stood there for long moments, looking down, glaring at nothing, softly kicking the toe of my boot against the trunk of an aluminum tree, over and over. I did not trust myself to speak. Certainly I was not going to run after her, protesting her judgment. Had I not been telling anyone who would listen lately that evil was my gig? How could I deny that now?

Evelyn had wandered a considerable distance away by the time I looked up again. I could not bring myself to follow her, just yet.

"That is not a safe thing to do," I called to her.

She ignored me.

I fumed.

I could not approach her. Not at the moment.

Idly I wondered how she had taken my words. Did she think I was referring to her wandering away, or to the manner in which she had spoken to me? And then I realized she now had me second-guessing my own words, my own intentions. Utter insanity! Yet here I was, doing just that—fretting over the possibility that I had inadvertently offended her.

The fool! In a realm such as this, she was utterly defenseless. Foolish mortal, allowing her emotions to get the better of her, to endanger her. I had to do something to protect her, whether she liked it or not.

Reaching out, I grasped the tip of the silver tree and exerted pressure. After a few seconds it snapped off, yielding a crystalline chunk of shiny stuff about the size of my fist. Holding it in both hands, I summoned the Power and channeled it into the chunk.

She turned and looked back, seeing the blue glow in my hands.

"What are you doing?"

"Providing you with some manner of protection," I called back, "as I did in the cave."

She watched as I continued to pump blue energy into the strange piece of—tree? Metal? Crystal? Whatever it was, it seemed to accommodate the influx easily enough.

"That's not necessary." She looked around. "We appear to be safe enough, for the moment."

I merely laughed. Her pride was astounding. Surely by now she had some conception of the dangers constantly surrounding us.

She shrugged and looked away again.

When the chunk had reached the point of energy absorption I desired, I sought to staunch the flow so that I might toss the newly created battery to her.

The flow continued.

Puzzled, I tried to break the circuit again, willing the flow of energy to halt.

Still the silver metal continued to pull the Power from me. It acted like a sponge—like a vacuum—insistent and insatiable, actually causing the rate of flow to increase, even as I fought to stop it. Both my hands were glued to the object's surface, and I could not release it.

"Now what?" Evelyn called to me.

"I—" I gasped, my breathing becoming ragged. I could hardly speak. My own personal reserves were being drawn upon, along with the energy I channeled from the aether, that which radiated out from our Fountain in the Golden City.

A sudden, sharp pain from the area of my hip cut through my senses then, and I looked down to see, with some surprise, a wisp of smoke coiling up from my pocket. A quivering tongue of lightning had arced out from the silvery chunk of tree in my hands and was playing along the folds of my coat. Even as I grimaced from the pain of the energy draining from me, I wondered what could possibly be happening—of course!

"The pistol," I gasped.

Even as I said the words, the gun in my pocket tumbled out, falling to the sandy ground. It lay there, glowing bright orange, the tendril of energy still reaching for it, connecting it to the silver chunk. Then, with a flash and a sharp, popping sound, the tendril vanished and the gun lay cool and dark. I had my suspicions about what had just happened, and was not at all happy about it, but I was not exactly in a position to check at the moment.

No matter what I did, I could not let go. The silver object I clutched in my hands continued to draw upon my energies, draining me rapidly. It had by this point taken on a vivid incandescent glow, blazing like a blue star in my hands.

Slowly at first, Evelyn walked back towards me. Seeing that I appeared to be in dire straits, she increased her pace.

"What's wrong?"

"I… don't know. Stay back!"

I dropped roughly to my knees, hunching over and trying to knock the silver fragment loose by smashing my hands on the ground. No luck there, either, and the pain only further reduced what little control I had left. The rate of flow had grown tremendous. I began to worry that it would either drain me entirely or burn me out as it used me as a conduit to the source of the Power. Neither fate seemed particularly appealing.

She halted, watching with a growing look of concern on her face. Evidently she had deduced a general idea of what was happening.

"Why is it doing that?" she asked.

I did not reply. In truth, I had no idea. Clearly the substance of the silvery trees contained some property that drew the Power into it—a fact I had never had cause to discover before. Over the centuries I had found or heard reports about a number of materials, scattered across the many planes, which reacted in unusual ways to the presence or energies of the gods. This one, though, jumped pretty close to the top of the "unusual" list, as far as I was concerned, trailing only one other: the red crystals I had discovered ages ago, upon which I had pinned so many of my hopes for the future.

Meanwhile a further, more ominous fear had begun to grow inside me: Even if I somehow could halt this bizarre draining effect, a greater damage might already have been done. The prodigious amount of raw power flowing through me and into this plane could serve as a beacon, a lighthouse to any who could sense it. I might well be waving a flag, blowing a horn, and otherwise loudly proclaiming to the universe, "Hey, here I am! Look at me!"

Every method of controlling the Power I had ever mastered entered my mind then, and I essayed them one by one. Going with the flow, but subtly shaping its course. Sensing the individual threads or flavors of the Power and working with each individually. Seeking to dominate the entire mass of it with sheer willpower. I tried them all. Nothing helped.

About that time the unicorn appeared.

I could not later swear to that part. I was, obviously, rather preoccupied, and somewhat delirious. But if, as I feared, this blatantly violent display of the Power could serve as an attraction to beings capable of sensing it and finding their way to it, the possibility exists.

It was pale white, and it pranced about me in a tight circle, then tossed its head once and vanished.

So too, moments later, did the red griffon and the turquoise, three-headed serpent—though my head was spinning to such a degree by that point that all of it could have been a hallucination. Evelyn later claimed to have seen none of this; though, in my defense, she was not plugged into the flow of energy, as I was, and therefore was not operating at anything like the same level of perception.

My attempts to slow the rate of the flow had proven entirely ineffectual so far, and death—in one form or another— loomed now as a very real possibility. I resolved to try a different tack. Inhaling deeply, I pulled still more of the Power into me. Yes, more of it. More even than the insatiable silver shard was demanding. I channeled it down through my arms, actually encouraging the flow to increase even more. I sought to overload the link between the piece of metal and myself—though, if it failed, this would probably result in my incineration even sooner than before.

Out of the corner of my eye I thought I detected movement, but I could not be distracted at the moment. My hands were aflame, my arms searing hot, but somehow I had to ignore it all and work through the process in careful and deliberate fashion. Taking another breath, I bore down with all my might. The air around me crackled with blue bolts of lightning, playing over the silvery trees and across my flesh. The Power flowed into and through me like a gusher. My teeth chattered, and my arms shook uncontrollably. A single crack, like thunder, sounded. The metallic object in my hands exploded, hurling me backwards.

I slid to a stop on the smooth, gray surface, small silvery pieces raining down around me. I lay there and I watched them fall, and my brain worked.

Pieces. Fragments of a larger whole, dropping out of the sky, falling into place.

I must have started to understand it all then—to subconsciously arrange fragments and pieces of the bigger picture within my mind. Distracted as I was by innumerable other thoughts and events, however, it would be some time yet before I came to know what I knew.

The silver object had disintegrated. I looked down at myself somewhat nervously, fearful of what damage I might see, but was relieved to find nothing visibly wrong. My hands were numb, while my arms tingled as if they had been asleep. Add to this the fact that my head was spinning, and I found I had some difficulty in getting to my feet. All in all, however, I felt I'd made out as well as I could have hoped.

As I struggled to rise, Evelyn rushed towards me, then stopped dead and stared past me, mouth opening soundlessly.

I looked back.

Something similar to one of my portals had opened, perhaps sixty yards away. Rather than glowing with one of the colors of the gods, however, its entirety was black, like a pool of ink turned on its edge; and it rippled like oil on water. What emerged from it was even more disturbing.

One after the other, they crossed over into our plane. Figures out of nightmare. I scrambled to my feet and backed away, toward Evelyn, picking up a few of the larger silvery fragments from the ground as I went. The beings advanced, clearly aware of our presence and coming our way. Coming entirely too rapidly.

Shadows they were, yet three-dimensional and quite solid in places. My first thought was of the Dark Men, but those silent stalkers had been clad in fully solid and substantial featureless suits, and had moved with robotic precision. These creatures appeared nothing like that. They flowed from point to point, shimmering in and out of visibility. At times it seemed their clothing consisted of tattered ebon rags, yet at other moments they appeared smooth and naked. And the faces: nothing that could truthfully be called features, yet in place of eyes and mouth, slashes in the black revealed sparkling depths: pinprick stars and twisted nebulae and blazing suns, as if offering a view into deepest space. Sprung from the purest chaos, these creatures were. There could be no doubt. Demons, some called them. Mindlessly they had roamed the many planes since the very dawn of time. Out of that dark breed these interlopers had sprung, though they appeared to be of a variety I never had encountered before.

And one thing more, deeply troubling. Demons were limited to their home planes. None I had ever encountered could open portals through the dimensional barriers. For that reason, demons had never represented a serious threat to the gods—we could always simply walk away from them. Yet these beings clearly had the ability to penetrate the barriers, to move among the planes with ease. This was not good. Not good at all.

Somewhere in our navigation of shit creek, we had misplaced our paddle.

With my left hand I reached out, trying to get a feel for the fabric of spacetime around us. Nothing. My senses were beyond numb. I could scarcely feel my fingers, much less the delicate and sublime folds of the cosmos.

Reaching down, I clutched at my pistol where it still lay in the sand, grasping it in nearly dead fingers. Sliding open the chamber, I was greeted with the sight I had feared. The crystal had disintegrated. Only dull, red dust spilled out. The metallic pins that had held the gem in place and regulated its properties were melted away. It was useless. I hurled it away.

"Damn!"

Grasping Evelyn's hand, I pressed two of the silvery fragments into it.

"Here. Doubtlessly they have been charged up far beyond what I had intended. They should provide some measure of defense."

Her eyes widened. They did not waver from the dark horde advancing upon us.

"How much is 'some?'"

I considered several comforting responses, discarded them all, and said, "Not enough."

She merely nodded.

We continued to back away, and the demons kept pace, seemingly enjoying the cat and mouse aspect of our new relationship.

"This might be a good time to open us a way out of here," Evelyn said after a few more steps.

"You may rest assured that I have tried," I told her with some annoyance. "It's not happening. I nearly burnt myself out. At the moment, I am not able to focus the Power into anything remotely as cohesive or complicated as a portal."

I laughed humorlessly.

"Not that it would do much good, probably. I'd be willing to wager these demons are perfectly capable of tracking us, now that they have our metaphysical scent."

"Great. So, what will they do—eat us?"

I shrugged.

"Your guess is as good as mine. Demons come in many varieties, and their habits vary just as widely. But if we are on the menu, I intend to provoke the most extreme case of acid reflux in history upon whichever one tries to digest me."

The dark figures started circling around us on both sides as we spoke, obviously seeking to surround us. We retreated in the direction of the building, though I doubted it would offer much in the way of cover or defense.

"I thought you couldn't die!"

"All the worse for me, then," I shot back. "I get to enjoy eternal, near-death suffering." I allowed myself a bitter smile. "But how nice of you to think of my well-being at a time like this, rather than your own."

The small, low building lay close behind us now, and I glanced back, making certain the demons had not overrun it.

"No one knows the exact fate of victims of demons, possibly because no one who was stupid enough to be captured by them has ever escaped to tell the tale. But the rumors have always included dark, hellish dimensions… endless torment… living death… that sort of thing. Experiences best avoided, I would say."

I sensed the building behind us and reached back, never taking my eyes off the nearest of the horde. Feeling the rough, splintering door, I shoved and it swung open easily. I pulled Evelyn with me through and inside.

"What is this place?"

I looked around quickly, simultaneously checking out the condition of the edifice and looking for any, oh, heavy artillery that might have been left lying around. Disappointment greeted me on both counts: the building had seriously deteriorated from the last time I had visited it, and the inside had been cleaned out, save for a few random planks lying about. It was little more than an empty, crumbling shack.

"This used to be one of my safe houses—a hideout," I told her, as I bent over and picked up the most solid-looking plank I could see. "Had to bring in all the lumber myself, from elsewhere."

I shoved the plank into position to brace the door.

"I suppose Alaria wasn't lying when she said they all had been found."

Light from the swirling aurora in the sky filtered down through cracks in the ceiling, casting eerie, ever-shifting shadows. Sounds began to reach us from outside. Scuttling, shuffling, and extremely disconcerting sounds.

Trying once more to open a portal, I managed only a smattering of blue sparks. My system was still too traumatized.

Crackling, popping sounds came from all around us, as dark hands worked their way through cracks in the walls and pushed inside. Ghastly fingers probed and grasped.

"Are they deliberately playing with us?" Evelyn asked, her voice growing strident.

"Somehow, I think they like the theatricality of it all," I replied.

"Fabulous. Murderous demons with a flair for the dramatic."

Quickly I spared a glance at Evelyn. She retained her flippant attitude even in the face of such horror, and I found this impressive. But I could tell from the tone of her voice, from her face, that she was reeling inside. I could not blame her. None of this was terribly new to me, in general, and yet it had pushed me to the limits of my physical and mental resources. I could scarcely imagine how a mortal could hold up at all.

Seconds ticked by. The weakened, crumbling walls gave way slowly but surely to the demons' insistent pressures. We waited. Evelyn made no sound, but I could feel her body tensing beside mine.

They would be upon us in an instant.

"Squeeze the silver pieces and focus on the thought of a bubble around yourself," I said, my voice hoarse.

The wall to our right gave way. Demons surged forward. A blue hemisphere blossomed around the two of us as Evelyn used the charged silver fragment to summon a shield. The demons recoiled from it at first, then approached it more confidently. They pawed at it, clawed at it. Talons raked over its surface. All too quickly, it began to rend. Again the dark fingers reached toward us. Evelyn's free hand had grasped my upper arm, and she squeezed it very hard.

And then the earth moved, the heavens opened, and crimson fire rained down, down upon our enemies, down from *somewhere...*

SEVEN

These crimson flames that cascaded down from heavy skies and smote our enemies and drove them back relentlessly—these flames I knew, and knew all too well. Most recently, a thousand years ago, they had interposed themselves between my forces and the great citadel in the square of the Golden City. They had resisted my every effort to circumvent them, and scorched coldly at my dark soul as I sought to bull my way through them. Their eldritch energies frustrated my forces and disrupted my plans, and they succeeded in holding me off until Baranak arrived with his throng to utterly crush my uprising.

Yes, these flames I knew. Their master, the great engineer of the gods, however... That was a different story.

What little time I had ever spent in the company our god of toil, in the long years prior to my rebellion, had involved exceptionally large quantities of alcohol and obscene amounts of tasty but doubtlessly unhealthy food.

The two of us had conversed at length on only three occasions that I could recall. In my memories, each carried with it a different flavor, a different mood pervasive over it. While none of the three could rightly be called grand or momentous, each remained vivid in my mind and would contribute a piece to the puzzle that emerged later.

The first time was in a dark and smoky bar in Drezas, the capital city of Tolkar. I entered with a pair of attractive young mortal women in tow, midway through an exceptionally pleasant evening of celebrating the success of one of my innumerable minor schemes. He sat alone at a small table in the back, smoke from a long, slender cigar wreathing his bald head. I had sensed his presence instantly, even before laying eyes on him, and approached him to offer greetings and to make polite inquiry as to his presence. He had feigned ignorance of the place as a known favorite of mine, and had let on just enough in the way of his darker thoughts that I had been drawn in and felt compelled to sit down and continue the conversation. The two young women were forgotten; I have no idea what became of them. But he and I spent the remainder of the evening deep in conversation, drinking the establishment dry and talking the moons out of the heavens. His mood had been black—darker even than mine on a good day—yet the words we spoke to one another that night carried a strange power. Afterward I could remember few of the particulars, which I found odd, other than a sense that he was searching for something, and having little success. For a long while I attributed this gap in my memory to the alcohol, or to my lack of attention and patience for the rambling discourses of my fellow gods. Later I would have cause to question this.

My second encounter with him came several decades later, and again took place in a bar on the mortal plane. In all the time since our first meeting, I had scarcely thought of that earlier night or dwelt on its larger implications, until by chance I passed him on a sidewalk in a city on Majondra. His mood was lighter, and he greeted me heartily and talked me into joining him for dinner at a nearby restaurant that was one of his favorites. About the time of the third course, his demeanor turned dark again, his eyes in their deeply recessed craters burned bright, and the conversation moved inexorably back to where we had left it before—his quest for knowledge in areas long beyond the ken of even the most learned of the gods. I managed to depart our dinner later with at least that much intact in my mind, though again the rest flew away with the coming of the Majondra dawn.

From these two early conversations I had decided that, far from a mediocre, mid-level god useful mainly for his technical virtuosity, he was someone to watch in the future, on many levels. I also believe we developed something of a grudging respect for one another. Perhaps, had events allowed it, we might have developed a true friendship—or as close an approximation of one as seems possible among we of the Golden City.

The third time I ran into him, our meeting lasted only minutes. I had set myself up for a period of months on a snowy world several planes removed from both the City and the human plane, living with a small retinue of servants and hangers-on in a vast, alpine lodge I had ordered constructed some years earlier. Generally I prefer warmer weather, but occasionally—as such spans are measured in the lifetimes of immortals—the desire for skiing and related activities takes hold, and must be satisfied. This encounter began with an unexpected knock at the front door. Tearing myself away from my glass of wine, bearskin rug, and lovely female companion, I opened the door and, with some degree of surprise, welcomed him into my lodge and invited him to share drinks by the fire. He would have none of it. He stood in the doorway, his goateed face twisted in a mask of anger and frustration beneath that gleaming bald scalp, and he sought to question me roughly about matters of arcane art and science for which I had little knowledge and fewer answers. Apparently dissatisfied with my responses to his little inquisition, he first intimated that I was holding out on him, attempting to deliberately mislead him. Then he grew frustrated and whirled about, stomping down the steps and flashing away in a splashing circlet of red flame. I shrugged and closed the door behind me, returning to the soft rugs and the warm fire and the warmer embrace.

Those varying incidents encapsulate our three one-on-one encounters. My fourth encounter with him was, as I have said, in the courtyard of the Golden City, during my insurrection, where he had stood with Baranak and the others against me. He had not been present afterward, at my sentencing, when Baranak's clique exiled me to the mortal plane. Our most recent meeting was in the dungeon, when he and Baranak and Alaria had visited me and listed the charges of murder against me.

From these few, brief episodes, one might well conclude that he was many things—brilliant engineer, brooding seeker of knowledge, moody loner—but neither guardian angel nor cavalryman riding to the rescue probably would make that list. Thus my great and profound surprise to discover that it was indeed Vorthan, the great engineer, the god of toil, who had arrived to rescue Evelyn and me from the demon horde.

The crimson flames flashed down from that madly shifting sky, high above my gray, bowl-shaped world, and smote the demons where they stood.

It began with a blinding flash of light from outside, from behind the massed body of demons. A split-second later, a rolling boom sounded, shaking the floor at our feet. The demons inside the shack with us whirled around, flowing like quicksilver, to see what was happening.

Again the flash and the thunder. The demons all but forgot us in their rush to investigate this new phenomenon. In mere seconds, the building was empty but for Evelyn and me.

Lowering the fist that contained the silver fragment, Evelyn frowned and looked wordlessly from the open wall to me to the opening again.

I shrugged.

Wails reached our ears then. The wailing of demons. Again the flames, again the sound and the fury. What did this signify?

We moved cautiously to the opening and peered out.

Standing on bare, muscular legs some short distance away, a bald figure clad in leather and wielding a massive hammer smashed at the ranks of demons. Red energies spilled from the weapon, lashing at the dark horde and driving them back.

Evelyn gasped.

"Who is that?"

"You've seen him before," I said, "though in somewhat less chaotic circumstances."

Before us, the scene appeared thusly: Vorthan stood on a low rise approximately thirty yards from my safe house, hammer clutched in both hands, muscles rippling. On three sides, the demons pressed towards him, thwarted each time by another swing of the hammer, another gout of flame arcing out from it. Each time he struck they fell back, then quickly pushed in again, gaining a little ground each time.

The feeling had come back into my fingers, something I took as a very good sign. I considered a number of options, some more attractive than others. Most, admittedly, involved immediate flight. Finally, I looked at Evelyn. She met my eyes and held them, her gaze solid as steel. No words were needed. My options were closed out instantly.

I could not very well humiliate myself in front of this mortal woman, could I? I had to act. Even considering who it was that needed the help.

Shrugging, I stepped through the doorway.

Vorthan glanced my way, saw me, and seemed unsurprised. He said nothing, preferring to let his hammer speak for him. This time it caved in the skull of one of the dark creatures. The others crowded forward, filling the gap.

"Thanks for the assistance," I called to him, taking a few steps in his direction. He was quite occupied, and so did not reply. I wondered if that were the only reason he said nothing.

A few seconds ticked by, as I took a couple more steps forward. Did he desire my help? Did I wish to give it?

All the while, the creatures gained more ground on him.

"Lucian," Evelyn said, concern evident in her voice.

Nodding, I started forward again, despite my decidedly mixed feelings. By this time, Vorthan had almost disappeared from view behind the wave of attackers. Just as I reached the outer periphery of the melee, he fought his way partly free, and I finally heard his gravelly voice calling to me. He sounded remarkably calm, given the situation, revealing only a hint of strain and exhaustion.

"You might consider... returning the favor... at some point," was all he said.

Frowning, I raised a hand before me and willed the Power to flow. Blue sparks erupted from my fingertips. The numbness was mostly gone; I felt close to normal.

The demons pushed in tighter, to the point that I lost all sight of him in the press of shapes, of bodies.

Vorthan is quite powerful and, from what I have heard over the years, generally unlikely to place himself in extreme jeopardy if it could be avoided. Yet I sensed he had perhaps gotten in over his head this time, figuratively and literally. I had never encountered demons like these; they seemed quite resilient and powerful. Perhaps he had underestimated them, or overestimated himself. I found that this thought somehow pleased me, despite the fact that Evelyn and I surely needed his help if we were to escape these creatures.

I raised both hands to waist level and allowed spheres of energy, weak at first, to drop from my fingertips, spilling to the ground. Even as I willed them to roll over the dull terrain, I fed them more power, increasing their size along with the intensity of their blue light. I could also feel additional power feeding into the spheres from elsewhere—from all around us—though that made no sense. All of these energies coming together, I realized, would allow for quite a powerful effect when I triggered it. Resolving to address my technical questions only after the enemy was defeated, I concentrated on charging the spheres to their utmost levels. When they reached the edge of the demon scrum, they insinuated in among the dark bodies, disappearing within the black and shifting mass. At the same moment, strange ebon energies rippled out from within the pile.

I caught Evelyn's attention and gestured with my head toward the doorway behind us.

"Get back!"

Raising both fists above my head, I gritted my teeth and exerted the full measure of my power, then brought my fists down hard. In a blinding flash of blue flames, as impressive as anything I had ever managed before, the spheres exploded. The eruption shook the ground and nearly blinded us. Best of all, it hurled shredded bits of demon all about, leaving a mound of unmoving black shapes where Vorthan and our adversaries had stood.

Evelyn whistled in appreciation. "Nice," she observed, emerging from the building. "How come you've never done that before?"

"Rarely do my opponents allow me the time to prepare something like that," I replied, blinking the spots from my eyes, moving forward rapidly. "I think I was somehow able to tap into the power I expended earlier, too. The trees here siphon it up, and I was able to draw upon it, without even realizing it. A fortunate turn of events."

I reached the periphery of the blast area and engaged in a quick inspection. Not a single living demon remained. Any that had survived the explosion must have fled. Kneeling, I examined the smooth gray ground for any residue. Nothing. After the unpleasant task of dragging several of the strangely boneless bodies out of the way and climbing over many others, I arrived near the center of the pile.

It was hollow, vacant. The formerly writhing mound of demons that had overwhelmed Vorthan now appeared like a donut, with a perfectly round, empty center. Had my blast annihilated them? Was that possible? And what of Vorthan himself?

"Well?" Evelyn called to me, after waiting for some length of time.

I crawled back out of the heap of carcasses and, grimacing, dusted myself off.

"He is not there. He must have transported himself away. Or else..."

"Or else they took him?"

"Maybe."

I sighed, pursed my lips. A number of things nagged at the corners of my mind, but they could all wait.

"I think we need to get out of here," I said.

I led her back to the safe house. She was doubtlessly puzzled. By this point, though, she apparently had come to trust that I knew what I was doing, even if things did not always work out for the best. I'd like to think so, anyway. But, in all honesty, what else could she do?

Entering a small room to the rear of the building, I felt with my right hand along the rough, paneled wall. Now that my body had recovered from its earlier strains, I could once more feel my hands, and thereby feel the texture of spacetime around me. Quickly a sensation developed as of something tugging at me.

"Ah. Here it is."

I gave the empty air a small twist, as if turning a doorknob. The wall vanished, replaced by a blue, iridescent tunnel. I was somewhat amused to notice that Evelyn exhibited no surprise at this whatsoever. She had already become a veteran of interdimensional travel.

"After you," I said.

Nodding once, she stepped through the portal, and I followed after her.

+ + +

We stood at the edge of a bronze desert, beneath a vivid, purple sky.

I looked out at it, at that desert of my dreams; at its strange, alien, shifting sands, and the depths of its overwhelming emptiness. I felt strongly that it represented a metaphor for... something. For what, I had no idea. Frankly, at the moment, I didn't much care.

Beside me, Evelyn moved through a series of stretches, extending one leg out, then the other, working out the cramps and kinks. Straightening, she ran her hand back through her hair and gazed out toward the horizon.

"We have to cross this?"

"Unfortunately, yes," I said.

Much to my surprise, Evelyn only nodded.

"Okay," she said. And then, "I think things will begin falling into place for us on the other side."

"Oh?" I looked at her, raising one eyebrow. "You know something? Something you'd like to share?"

"Of course not. Just wishful thinking."

I drew back my lips into a tight smile, shading my eyes with my hand.

"Good enough."

We started to walk.

As we traveled, I think I came to understand that desert a little better—and, perhaps, to better understand what Evelyn had meant, as well. I got a sense that if I should succeed in crossing it, and move beyond it, I would also be making some fundamental change within myself. The shape of that change, like that of the desert itself, did not immediately present itself to me. But I knew, at some fundamental, almost instinctual level, that success or failure, death or redemption—or both— lay on the far side of that sparkling expanse.

The sand shifted beneath our feet, despite the absence of wind, as if some vast creature writhed deep below the surface—or as if this world had determined to take my metaphors literally. I had visited this plane a hundred times before, and it always unnerved me, threw me off my game. Gritting my teeth, I pressed on, and Evelyn followed.

Hours passed, with only the whistling of the wind to serve as company for us. I counted the steps we had taken thus far, and worked out how much farther we had to go. Too far for my taste. Still, it beat a snowstorm or a demon horde. Resolute and determined, we pressed on.

We had made relatively good time since leaving the not-so-safe house. A brief stop at an isolated oasis I mercifully remembered revived us somewhat. We located it just as our hunger and thirst, not to mention weariness, truly caught up with us. While hardly able to partake of an ideal meal there, we did enjoy some fruits and cold, clean water, and Evelyn refilled the water bottle that was integrated into her flight suit. Then we stretched out for a brief nap. Afterward, we both felt somewhat better, and capable of continuing our journey.

Evelyn had said little since our departure from the safe house, so that when she finally spoke it startled me.

"So, what's the goal now?"

I sighed, glancing over at her.

"What?"

"I mean, I know you're thinking to leave me at an undisclosed location, and then go looking for ways to protect yourself—putting it generously."

I said nothing.

"But beyond that," she stubbornly continued, "what is the greater plan? The real goal?"

I was not certain how to answer, how much I should share with her. So:

"My original plan—-if you can call it that, generously—-was to search for evidence that indicated who framed me for the killings. But just avoiding capture—or worse—has become such an all-consuming task that we have hardly had any time to investigate. It is maddening."

She nodded. "It makes me wonder if someone wanted it that way."

I looked at her, arching my eyebrows, then nodded once and turned away.

After a few moments, she said, "You do have a plan in mind, though, right?"

I smiled. "Yes. Several, in fact."

"And they include finding Cassidy and Kim."

I nodded. "If everything works out, we should both get what we want."

"Plans with happy endings," she said. "I like that."

"Oh, most of my plans feature extremely pleasant endings. Many include Baranak on his knees, begging me not to drop him into the Fountain."

Evelyn frowned her evident disapproval.

"Oh, relax. However pleasant that scenario might be, I would probably be willing to settle for an abject apology from him. Along with a binding oath of fealty, of course."

She looked sidewise at me and laughed. I found myself smiling, though why I could not say.

We walked on in silence. The time passed quickly. After a while, she spoke again, her voice startling me again as it broke the still silence of the desert.

"So you have a short-term plan. But what are your long-term goals?"

I blinked.

"Goals?"

"What you want to accomplish. Where you're going. Does being a god—or whatever—preclude you from having goals?"

She moved to where she could look back at my face.

"Has anyone ever asked you that?"

I looked down, avoiding her gaze.

"Once," I whispered.

She backed off for a moment, obviously surprised by my response, but I could tell she was not satisfied.

We trudged on for a bit, the broken ends of the conversation hanging like tangible objects between us.

"I'm trying to come to grips with you, with all of this," she finally said, gesturing to the bronze desert around us, the bright violet sky overhead. "I think it would help if I simply understood you a little better."

I frowned, uncertain of where she was going with this, and found myself hoping she would change the subject. Instead, inevitably, she seemed to warm to it.

"I've been thinking about all of this," she said. "Does extreme longevity remove the imperative to get anything accomplished?"

I tried to wrap my weary brain around that one.

"Oh," I finally said. "You're asking if immortals procrastinate a lot."

"Right," she said. "Because there's always tomorrow, and tomorrow, and tomorrow, and you don't ever have to be in a hurry."

I shrugged.

"That depends on the individual, I think. We're all pretty different."

She considered that.

"Maybe it seems that way to you," she said at last, "but, from what I've seen, I think there are more similarities among you than you realize."

I frowned at that, and said nothing more for a time.

The desert passed beneath us, step blending into step, mile into mile. Her voice, when she spoke again, startled me out of a sort of waking dream.

"Hasn't anyone ever asked you what it is you really want from your immortal life and your immense power?"

I blinked, glancing back at her.

"Yes. But not in a very long time."

"Well then—what are your goals?"

"To rule. To conquer the Golden City and make it my own."

She stared at me, blank-faced. Absurdly, I felt somewhat uncomfortable.

"That's it?" she said.

I stared back at her, feeling at least as bewildered as she seemed.

"The Golden City," I repeated. Could she not understand that? I hadn't said I wanted to conquer the Terran Alliance, or carve out my own empire among the Outer Worlds—though those prospects had seemed quite attractive, very recently, now a lifetime ago. I was talking about the Golden City! She had seen it. She had walked its streets, albeit not under the most ideal of conditions for appreciating its beauty, its glory. But still—!

"And," she continued, "to mete out some sort of revenge against all those you feel have wronged you over the years, right?"

"Exactly!" Now she seemed to be getting it!

But instead she only shook her head.

"You're a god, you say. You have the power to do so many things. During your exile, when you say you had almost no power aside from longevity, you still managed great things. Have you forgotten all of that so quickly?"

I was overcome with frustration, and became aware that I was grinding my teeth together.

"The Golden City," I repeated yet again, this time with a weak and halting voice. Did that not answer everything? Why couldn't she understand?

"And then what?"

I frowned. "Pardon?"

"After the conquering and the vengeance? Then what will you do? I mean, this is an immortal lifespan we're talking about, right? So—what then?"

I paused, thinking. I did not want to admit to myself that I had not devoted terribly much effort to considering such a time. The pursuit of victory in the City had consumed my thoughts for longer than I cared to remember. Finally, I hit on an answer.

"I reign," I said, firmly.

"You reign."

"Yes."

"That's it."

"Yes. I reign in the Golden City, and a new age sweeps across the universes."

She frowned, bit her lip, and looked away.

For reasons entirely unknown to me, I felt more hurt by that reaction than by anything I had experienced in centuries. My stomach twisted, turned upside down. I felt nauseous. Had I caught some sort of illness? What illness could possibly affect me? My confusion and my indignation were enormous.

"That's so sad," she said then.

My determination, my utter, driving convictions, began to melt away at that precise moment. Had I been deluding myself all this time? Had all my dreams and ambitions truly been so weak and shallow? The Golden City! But as I talked of capturing and ruling that perfect, idyllic place, this woman—this mortal—looked at me as if she were embarrassed for me!

This aggravation could not stand.

"Well," I said to her then, "what are your goals? What does a mortal woman in the service of a corrupt interstellar empire seek from her life?"

She frowned, and some bit of hope swelled within me that perhaps I had turned the tables on her.

"Personal happiness... Professional fulfillment..." She shrugged. "I suppose I want to rise to the top of the ranks in the Terran Navy."

"And then you will be satisfied? Merely with the rank, the title? With the uniform on your back and the insignia on your sleeve?"

"What?"

"If you were to achieve the rank of Admiral in your fleet, but then you died before anyone ever saluted you or before you ever commanded a single vessel, would you still feel satisfied, as if you had achieved your goal?"

She gazed off into the distance.

"…No… I suppose not."

"Then your goal is not to become an admiral. Your goal is to command a fleet, to issue orders to vast numbers of intelligent, well-trained individuals—and to be obeyed. To have power and glory at your fingertips and at your command."

Her voice was soft. "That's not quite how I've ever thought about it," she said. "Power and glory have never been that big with me."

"Then your goal," I said, "is merely to drive your spacecraft around a brief while, until age and death claim you. How thrilling."

She glared at me. I looked away quickly, somewhat surprised not to feel the thrill of rhetorical victory I had expected. Far from exposing her self-delusions and conceits, it felt as if I had only rubbed her nose in some deeper truth better left quietly ignored. She could not help that she was not born one of us. What right had I to taunt her with that fact, with the knowledge of what she was being denied? And, given what she had said to me moments earlier, I felt as though I were the bigger fool, perhaps wasting a far greater opportunity on mere vanity. Damn it all, these were not thoughts I needed to be entertaining as I prepared to confront my adversaries! Who had brought this whole topic up, anyhow?

We walked on for some time, exchanging no further words, and the open hostility between us faded somewhat with the miles. The temperature around us dropped a few degrees, and the violet sky, like my mood, darkened.

At last the bronze sand gave way to sandy soil, then in rapid succession to sparse grassland and to thick, lush growth. At about that time, the hazy line on the horizon at last resolved into the edge of a forest, broad as the world.

"And thus we have crossed our desert," I said.

Evelyn nodded. "Feel any different?"

I thought about that for a few seconds, then genuinely surprised myself with my answer: "Maybe so."

Another hour's walk brought us to the forest. We stopped, drank some water from Evelyn's bottle, and surveyed this sudden and dramatic change in scenery.

"This is amazing," she said, staring at the twisted, contorted conglomeration of every type and size of tree imaginable.

I could only laugh, knowing what she had yet to see.

"Getting close now," I said, in response to her unasked question. "In we go."

I indicated a nearly invisible path leading, tunnel-like, into the forest's depths, and we started forward again.

Rich, organic smells enveloped us. Tiny insects swarmed about us once or twice, but quickly dispersed before becoming too much of an annoyance. The temperature, which had hovered well within tolerable ranges for some time, grew hotter, and the humidity increased to uncomfortable levels. Shrugging out of my long blue coat, I rolled it, tied it, and looped it over one shoulder. Within my boots, my feet felt as tired and cramped as I could ever remember. But we were getting closer, so much closer...

After a time, the woods grew so dense on either side that one scarcely could have penetrated them, making it all the easier to remain on the cleared path. Other than climbing over an occasional exposed root of gargantuan size, or skirting a standing pool of black water of indeterminate depth, we made good and steady progress.

After about three hours of walking, the path ended. It vanished at the base of a huge oak tree. Coming to a halt, I sat on a fallen log off to one side and watched with amusement as Evelyn stared upward to where the tree vanished into the thick green canopy of branches above, then looked around for any other possible path we could follow, and finally, failing that, turned to me with a look of exasperation.

Wordlessly I stood and led her around the right side of the tree, stepping carefully over the big roots, and indicated a series of small notches cunningly cut into the trunk. They had been cut in such a way as to make them extremely hard to spot from anywhere other than directly in front of them.

She studied the notches, her eyes widening as she understood what they were for.

"Your secret hideout... It's a treehouse."

I smiled.

Looking up at the tree's mammoth heights again, she emitted a long, low sigh. Then she shrugged.

"And I suppose you want me to go first, right?"

"Actually, yes—for reasons that will become apparent soon enough."

Narrowing her eyes, she studied me for a moment, then took hold of the trunk and began to climb. I followed after her, admittedly enjoying the lovely views of nature thus afforded.

Soon we had attained a fairly lofty height and were moving into the bottom of the sea of branches and leaves that resembled nothing so much as a ceiling over the lower portion of the forest. The notches in the trunk led us unerringly through what appeared to be narrow, randomly open areas amid the limbs. Evelyn was a good climber, for the most part giving me the impression that I was actually holding her back. It mattered not. We were not going far. Or, rather, not far up the tree.

After I had followed her up through the thickest portion of the limbs, wherein our route had curved around and back such that we could no longer see the ground, I called a halt to our climbing and released my right hand from the hold. Leaning out, I took hold of the threads of the Power that pulsed invisibly all around us and twisted carefully. A horizontal, blazing circle of blue flame sprang into existence about six feet out from the tree trunk, just below her and a bit above me.

149

VAN ALLEN PLEXICO

Evelyn looked at the portal, then back at me.

"No."

I nodded.

"That's our doorway," I said. "Just hop on through."

She looked down at the thick jungle of branches, with the ground a good distance below that. She glared at me.

"This is why I had to go first? So I can test it and see if it still works?"

I raised my eyebrows in mock surprise.

"Actually, I had not thought of that, but it is certainly a fine idea and an added bonus."

I laughed, then motioned with my head for her to go on.

"This is the only access point I have ever found," I said. "The only alternative is to climb back down the tree and, well, turn ourselves over to Baranak."

She muttered something unintelligible, then asked, "Where will I land? It's not this far up, on the other side, right?"

"I would roll with the impact," I said. "I'm sure you practiced that in your military training at some point."

"…Right."

"And try not to miss the portal when you jump."

She glared daggers at me.

I shrugged.

"Seemed like a reasonable enough warning."

A low growl emanating from her throat, she released her left hand and her left boot and leaned out from the tree trunk. Taking a deep breath, she leapt out and dropped through the center of the blazing circle, vanishing.

"Good job," I muttered, climbing up to the level she'd just evacuated. Gesturing again, I caused the circle to drift closer to the tree, until the flickering blue flames nearly touched my boot. Then, with the utmost dignity, I stepped gingerly off the tree and dropped through the burning hole in the sky.

EIGHT

Evelyn struggled to her feet in the midst of a thick growth of weeds as I dropped gently to the open ground nearby. She glared at me.

"You knew the exit was barely any distance above the ground here," she growled.

My expression was one of utter innocence—a look I had long ago perfected, but could never use effectively on those who truly knew me.

Her eyes narrowed as she brushed the shredded foliage from her flight suit.

"And where you landed—that's closer to where the tree was. I didn't have to jump out that far." She folded her arms and fixed me with a withering stare.

I smiled.

"Exciting, though, wasn't it?"

Before she could reply, I gestured at our new surroundings, and she halted in mid-exclamation, looking around.

We stood a the bottom of what appeared to be a narrow ravine, with rough, gray walls close in on both sides, and only a narrow opening at either end leading out. Far overhead, the sky was a deep black with no stars. A pale light flickered over us from some unseen source beyond the opening.

"This is… something else," she commented dryly. "You really know all the best places to take a lady."

Ignoring her, I walked toward the nearer opening and climbed out. There, one of the two sheer walls ended, giving way to a drop off, and leaving me standing on a narrow, stony ledge. Evelyn hesitated for a moment, perhaps still angry, then followed me through and joined me on the outcropping. She peered over the edge, gasped and involuntarily jerked backward, stumbling.

I grasped her arm and pulled her back, understanding then that the vista she gazed upon, so very old and familiar to me, was quite new to her, and extremely disconcerting.

We stood overlooking an endless drop. The world opposite the rock wall behind us could not have been emptier. A void of blankness extending beyond the mind's comprehension, it laid siege to the senses and spoke great volumes of nothingness.

Evelyn looked at me, uncomprehending.

"Bottomless," I said. "Or rather, simply empty. The difference is meaningless here."

She looked down again. The ledge protruded out over, and into, utter blackness. Not so much the blackness of a deep, dark place. More like the blackness of the ending of the universe, if such a thing can be imagined or described adequately.

"Come on," I said with a wry smile. "There are greater sights to see, yet."

Her eyes widening, she followed me as I walked a bit further around the curving ledge and then began to climb up the cliff face. A dim but growing blue light flickered from above, providing our only illumination, and soon it became apparent that we were being illuminated not by some benevolent star but by a shifting, twisting azure aurora that crackled and writhed like an angry dragon high up in the empty heavens.

The climb was not so difficult a task as it looked. We made quick progress, and the way grew easier as we went. Somewhere ahead of us, a low roar grew steadily louder. After several minutes our path up the cliff curved around to such an extent that we could no longer see our starting point below us. Some moments after that, I could finally see the shelf above us that I was headed for. From that shelf, the full extent of our locale could be viewed and appreciated. I slowed, considering just what her reaction to this next wonder might be. Then, amused at the prospect, I hoisted myself over the edge and reached back to help her up.

As she topped the edge and scrambled onto the flat, hard surface, she looked up, and her mouth opened and the blue fire sparkled in her eyes as she beheld the true glory of my most secret sanctum.

The shelf we stood upon represented only a small outcropping of a vast, floating island, hanging suspended in a black void of nothingness. To our left, very close at hand, a tremendous river disgorged its contents in the form of a mighty waterfall cascading over the island's edge, the torrent curving around and disappearing somewhere beneath us. To our right, away in the distance, perhaps directly opposite the waterfall, a continuous roar resounded from a torrent of water gushing up and over that edge. Bigger than a geyser, it looked like a waterfall turned upside down—which is precisely what it was.

Evelyn looked at the waterfall, then at the gusher. Back and forth. Finally, she turned to me.

"Is that—is that the same—?"

"Yes. The same river. It wraps around the island. If we stood on what looks like the underside to us now—and we could, gravity somehow working that way, here—you would see the same thing you see now, but reversed."

She regarded me with an odd and rather uncomfortable expression that involved one eye squinting closed and the other eyebrow arching high. I took this to mean she was attempting to come to grips with the entire concept, but had not yet fully accomplished it.

I could not blame her. For many, many years the combination of beauty and natural-law-defying physics of my private cosmos had left me in silent awe. Eventually, I had gotten used to it, or as close as one could ever come. Yet it still worked some small magic upon me, as few other locales could.

Truth be told, I had been extremely fortunate to happen upon such a place, many centuries earlier. Almond-shaped, the sky island measured approximately ten miles long and a five miles wide. Rocky hills protruded upwards at the center of both sides, sloping down past thick forests of strange blue trees to grassy slopes, followed by the cliffs that girdled the equivalent of its equator. I had never discovered how this strange flora could grow in only the light of the aurora, and I had never cared enough to find out. This was one of the more exotic realms I had ever encountered, and when it came to its botany and its physics, it kept its own counsel.

I allowed her a few moments to soak in the strange beauty, and unexpectedly found myself staring as well at the majestic waterfall to our left. Something about it spoke to me then, as it never had before. My eyes were drawn to the edge, to the point where the smooth, glassy slab of water made its ninety-degree turn and, taken by the forces of chaos, shredded into a torrent and vanished from view over the side. What a powerful metaphor for life, I thought then. We live forever in the "now," in that brief instant of the present. Trailing out behind us, the past churns and boils away from us, chaotic and turbulent but all too quickly lost from view and gone. And ahead, the future is a smooth, tranquil stream of possibilities and eventualities, all shapeless and waiting to be formed. All of life consists of that edge, that razor-thin line between the two, where hope and possibility meet reality and resolution.

Another thought presented itself then. For me, that river leading up to the edge would always flow, a never-ending stream drawing from a limitless source. For mortals such as Evelyn, though, the pool was quite finite. Sooner or later, for her, no more water would flow over that edge. This realization pressed itself upon me with considerable urgency and served to remind me once again of the absolute futility of allowing myself to grow close to a mortal. I resolved to redouble my efforts at keeping her at arm's length, despite her admittedly appealing traits.

Finally, one last troubling possibility ran through my mind. Was my pool truly bottomless, truly infinite? If three-quarters of the gods could die in only a brief span of time, how safe did that leave me? I knew then that this possibility had gnawed at me for some time, subconsciously, and eventually I would have to face it. Not now, though, I told myself. For now, I had work to do.

Leading Evelyn up the slope, through the strange, wiry blue grass, I indicated a low cave entrance set into a rocky area just ahead, and we made for it. Bending under the opening, we entered a space entirely dark until I raised my left hand and tweaked the flow of the Power around us. Torches along both walls flared to life, revealing what amounted to my living room and storeroom. Boxes, mostly, and crates. A few random doodads I had picked up here and there. Little in the way of furniture, beyond a small table and one folding chair, since I had never intended to bring anyone else there.

"I like what you've done with the place," she said, looking around, her distaste as obvious as her sarcasm.

"Its only priority has ever been secrecy, and at that it excels," I replied.

Evelyn inspected several of the crates, which were actually high-tech sealed storage devices.

"Water," she observed. "Canned food. Camping supplies. Fuel." She looked back at me. "How did you ever manage to get all this stuff here?"

"Don't ask," I replied. "It was neither quick nor easy."

Nodding idly, she returned to her inspection.

"Books. Journals."

"You should leave those be," I said flatly.

Eyeing me, she closed the lid on that box and dug around through the ones next to it.

"As you can see," I said, "there are plenty of supplies here."

She nodded, then stopped and looked at me, frowning.

"You were in exile for a thousand years, you said."

I nodded.

"So, just how old is this stuff?" She poked at the packaged contents of another box. "The food, the water?"

"We are far enough in the Above that they should still be perfectly fresh. In local terms, they have only been here a short time."

Finding a cup that didn't look too dirty, she filled it with water from a barrel. She sipped at it carefully at first, then downed it in one long swallow, sighed and smiled.

"Tastes fresh to me."

She refilled it, then refilled the bottle we had finished on the journey.

After another long drink and a sampling of the contents of a few food packets, she regarded me quizzically.

"So—here we are," she said, looking around. "Charming. And this is supposed to advance your cause… how?"

"It was our immediate destination," I said, "because it offers safety and sanctuary and a respite from our travels and troubles of late. But I do not intend simply to hide out here. I have a bit further to go yet, and then things should begin to turn in my favor."

"You?"

"What?"

"You said *you* had a bit further to go yet."

I sipped at a cup of water, set it down and regarded her.

"You might wish to stay here while I attend to my task."

She looked around at the sparse accommodations.

"Stay here?"

"I know it is not the most luxurious of accommodations, but—"

"That's not the problem at all," she said angrily, cutting me off.

I pushed on.

"It would be safer for you. There are very, very few places where this plane is congruent with anywhere else—at least, anywhere the others are ever likely to go. This is as remote as any place in the larger universe can be. No one will find you here."

I gestured at a pile of cushions lying against one wall.

"And it's comfortable enough... There are plenty of supplies... It might get a bit boring, but I am sure you could manage for as long as it took. Considering the time difference this far into the Above, you would scarcely know I had gone before I returned."

"If."

"What?"

"*If* you returned. That's the problem. *If.*"

I frowned.

"Come on," she said. "Nearly every force in the universe is out to catch you. If one of them does, you might never return."

She looked around at the interior of the cave again.

"And, as much as I would miss your sparkling wit and charming personality, the worst part seems pretty obvious: I would be trapped here for the rest of my life."

I sighed.

"Point taken. You will come with me."

She nodded.

"In fact, you might wish to remain there."

It was her turn to frown.

"There? Where?"

"Our next destination. For the moment, I will say only that it is neither your Earth, nor anywhere else in your Terran Alliance. It is, however, in your plane, your home universe."

"My…"

Her eyes widened momentarily, then she shook her head.

"No. Not without the others."

The others. Of course. How could I ever have forgotten them?

Through sheer effort, mainly.

Reluctantly, I nodded. "…Right."

And so we ate and we drank and we rested until we felt as good as we could reasonably expect to feel, given the circumstances. And then I led her to the back of the cave, and found the spot where the layer between dimensions grew thinnest, and I exerted the small amount of Power necessary in that place to open a portal. Together we stepped through the blazing circle, emerging directly into my most secret location of all.

"You're kidding," she said, upon seeing it.

"Certainly not."

Evelyn looked around, her eyes quickly adjusting to the dim lighting. We stood in a small pool of light within a vast, gray room, extending perhaps fifty feet up and as many yards away from us in every direction. It was filled with row upon row of shelves. Those shelves were covered with every size and shape of box and crate and container imaginable. The musty smell of long-stored items in a long-sealed room washed over us both. Evelyn wrinkled her nose.

"This is it?"

She fixed me with a look that spoke of surprise, bewilderment, and no small amount of disappointment.

I laughed softly, nodding.

"This is it."

"You show me the wonders of the universe, building up to this grand finale—and it's a warehouse?"

I could not help but laugh again.

Hands on hips, she waited.

Finally, "I never said it was a 'grand finale,' as you say, and I promised you no spectacular vistas. But, if all is as it should be, this warehouse should contain something quite pleasing to the eyes."

She cocked her head at me, incredulous.

I shrugged, adding, "To my eyes, anyway."

As I moved to the nearest shelf and studied the markings, getting my bearings, a light flickered our way from some distance down the aisle. Evelyn saw it first and motioned frantically at me. I whirled, just in time to see a man in gray moving through a more distant cone of illumination. He was coming toward us, his footsteps echoing off the crates and the walls, accelerating as he became aware of us.

"Who's there?" he cried. "Don't move!"

He drew a sidearm and halted a short distance away from us, studying us carefully. He was an old guy, white-haired and hunched over a bit. I had not realized I employed anyone of quite that vintage in a security capacity, but he appeared competent and alert enough. Then I recognized him, but realized it had been years—many years—since I had seen him last. I could not even remember his name.

He gave both of us a perfunctory once-over, his expression wary and nervous, then moved his hand to activate his communication link.

"Hello," I said, moving quickly but casually toward him, directly under one of the cones of light shining down. Then, "Do you not recognize me?"

His hand froze and he blinked, peering closer at me. Then he gasped, moved back a step, and said, "Lord Markos!"

Smiling, I nodded, and clapped him warmly on the shoulder.

His suspicious expression evaporated, and he grinned back at me.

"I—I apologize for.."

"No, no," I said, stopping him. "You do your job well," I squinted at his name badge. "Tony. I was scarcely here a minute before you spotted me."

He swelled with pride and bowed slightly.

"I heard some talk that you'd found a way to look young again," he said, "but I didn't believe…"

"It's true," I said.

He stared at me unabashedly, and shook his head in wonder. Then, with more formality, "My lord, we've been worried at your absence. You simply disappeared, and you've been gone for over two months."

So the many shifts among different planes high up in the Above had cost us more time, relative to this universe, than I had expected. Sighing, I nodded.

"I was called away on urgent business," I said.

He nodded, an anxious and eager-to-please look on his face. I found I liked him a great deal. In fact, I—what?

Ridiculous. He was a mortal. One of my former servants.

Shaking my head to clear what must have been a touch of temporary insanity, I continued, "It was very secret business, I'm afraid. And I am in fact still in the process of dealing with it."

It galled me to have to treat so with a common guard, but I wanted what this warehouse contained, and the alternatives all seemed likely to result in greater delays.

"It could not be helped," I added.

He nodded, taking it all in.

"I'm just glad to see you're all right," he said after a moment's silence. "No one was quite sure who should be in charge, and there have been some problems—"

He looked past me at Evelyn, seeming to take full notice of her for the first time, and he stopped in mid-sentence. His smile evaporated. He narrowed his eyes as he stared at her. It took me a moment to figure out why, and then I realized— she was wearing her flight suit, her military uniform from the Terran Alliance Navy.

Before he could act or speak, I cut him off.

"Lieutenant Colicos here is with me. She is a liaison from the Alliance, working with me on some very sensitive matters."

"Ah."

He nodded slowly, his expression still conveying suspicion. Outworlders harbored enormous dislike and hostility toward Terrans, who likewise viewed them with contempt and scorn. That mutual animosity could be traced back to well before my time of exile. Indeed, it extended as far back as the earliest days of the Second Empire, when the earliest jump ships first ventured into the great dark unknown between the stars. At its heart, though, the animosity probably was driven by simple resentment and competition—motivations as old as life itself.

"I appreciate your diligence, Tony," I told him. "But I have a few items to collect here, and then we will be out of your way."

Turning back to me, his face warmed again, and he executed another little half-bow.

"Of course, of course, sir. If I can be of any help—?"

"No, no, we have it well in hand. You may continue your rounds."

"Yes. Thank you, sir."

Bowing to me again, then giving Evelyn a cursory and half-hearted one as well, he bustled away down the aisle.

Evelyn watched him go, then chuckled.

"Your security staff is quite impressive. I'll have to tell the folks back home not to dare try an attack here—they wouldn't stand a chance against Tony."

Groaning, I shook my head dismissively and set off down the aisle.

"You were pleasant with him," Evelyn noted as she followed after me.

"Yes."

She stared at me, hands on hips, waiting for more.

"He was once one of my soldiers. He has served me faithfully all his life." I laughed. "He thinks he served my father, too."

Evelyn nodded, saying, "But he's a mortal. Where was the contempt? The scorn?"

I shrugged.

"He served a different me than the one you first met. I was powerless, and had been so for a very long time. It was a lifetime ago."

"Lucian, it was two months ago. And only days ago, to you and me."

"Yes. As I said, a lifetime ago."

Evelyn continued to regard me for a few more seconds, her expression unreadable. Sighing, I moved on, following the rows of crates and boxes that lined the shelves and walls of the dingy storage building. I examined the markings on each item, working from memory. Very soon, I found what I was seeking: a set of crates, each approximately five feet long and three feet to a side. Unlatching the fastenings of the nearest one, I pulled the cover back, and smiled.

Evelyn leaned over my shoulder and peered down into the crate. She found cold, deadly black metal there.

"Guns?"

"Oh, yes," I breathed. "Oh, yes. Guns. Most definitely guns."

Her eyes widened, and I imagined she was thinking back to the recent events on my little desert island.

"Oh. Guns."

"Lots of guns. Oh, yes."

"Arendal guns."

"Arendal guns, oh, yes."

I pulled the crate off the low shelf and let it drop the six inches down onto the floor, then rummaged through its contents, shoving the packing material aside, counting.

"All here. Five rifles per crate. Five pistols as well. And... lots of crates."

I was surely grinning maniacally now. It is a wonder Evelyn did not flee from the sight of me.

"Would you mind telling me," she said, "how these came to be here? And, for that matter, where exactly we are?"

"Mysentia," I replied. "My old capital in the Outer Worlds."

She frowned.

"Mysentia?"

"And the guns came to be here, rather than with me in the Golden City," I continued, ignoring her reaction, "because I was extremely foolish. After spending centuries accumulating these things and hiding them here, I got careless. The Fountain flowed again, the Power rushed through my veins and intoxicated me, and I raced back to the Golden City without bringing a single one of these beauties along with me."

I shrugged.

"But I was excited. It had been so long—so many years— since I had last felt the Power surging through me, through the universe. I felt invulnerable, invincible. What need had I of any weapon? I was the only weapon I needed. And, besides, if I could sense the Power again, and access it, I assumed that meant all was forgiven, and I was being allowed to come home again."

I snorted.

"Little did I dream no one else had been able to access the Power either, those past thousand years. Little did I guess I was essentially walking into a trap."

Evelyn was nodding.

"I'd have to agree, that was pretty dumb," she said.

I let her comment pass without response or reaction— something that should have struck me at the time as noteworthy. But I pushed on to the conclusion of my thoughts.

"And I wound up thrown in the dungeon because of it."

I tapped the crate and the guns.

"But now... all that is behind me. For a thousand years I sat on this rock, and gathered this collection of cosmic firepower, with no way to get it or myself to the City. Now I have the means to travel there and the means to enforce my will when I arrive. The Golden City will open its gates to me once more, and Baranak will beg my forgiveness for daring to impugn my name, or—"

The hand laid gently on my arm brought me up short, and I halted in mid-rant, mouth hanging open, and looked at Evelyn. She simply shook her head.

"Settle down," she said. "Get a grip."

My eyebrows were thunderclouds, my anger building unabated, until... it abated. Just like that. It was the strangest thing. I worked my jaw a few times, but could no longer work up the righteous indignation within which I had been reveling only moments earlier.

"You simply want to get them to listen to you, to give you a fair chance to prove your innocence in the murders," she said evenly. "And you want to help me find my friends and get us home. That's what you want to do."

I stammered a few unintelligible words, then stopped trying to speak altogether. Leaning back against the wall, I ran my hand through my hair and stared at the floor, dumbstruck.

This was simply unacceptable, if not utterly inconceivable. How dare she? I had carefully laid plans over ten centuries and, despite completely blowing it the first time, I intended to do things right this time. Who was this woman to stand in my way?

"So," she was saying, "what do we need to do with these weapons?"

My anger, godlike and terrible, flared brighter within me, and my wrath grew to a terrifying and overwhelming pitch, and I said to her then: "Um... Help me find the forklift."

Still in a daze, I roamed the aisles, alongside Evelyn. Soon enough, we found the forklift.

It was actually a gravity-defying device that could hold quite a load of crates. We managed to secure ten of them on board before the stack grew unwieldy. That totaled fifty rifles, with an equal number of pistols. A nice start, I thought. And, given the drastic reduction in the—you'll pardon the expression—manpower that Baranak would be able to bring to bear, quite possibly more than enough already.

With a grim sense of satisfaction I had not felt in quite some time, I activated the controls and steered the hovering platform down the aisle and to the warehouse exit. Unlatching the door, I slid it upward, and Evelyn and I stepped out into darkness.

Nighttime in Mysen City. For a place I had called home only days earlier, it could have been the far side of the galaxy to me. What a difference in outlook the Power made, as it moved through the body and energized the muscles and heightened the consciousness—and amplified ambitions.

Evelyn walked alongside the forklift, clearly uncomfortable. I had found her an ill-fitting but nondescript gray coat within the warehouse, to cover her bright blue flight suit with its golden Terran Alliance markings and insignias. I hoped it would prevent any further incidents and forestall uncomfortable questions from any who happened by us. Evelyn, though, could not possibly have been happy to walk the streets of a world she considered distasteful at best and rebellious at worst.

I looked at her then, studying her as her own attention was drawn to the darkened buildings and the few people moving about the streets. I had to admit I found her quite attractive. Though battered and bruised by all we had endured since our escape, she carried herself with a natural grace, an inner strength and beauty that radiated beyond the surface. And those eyes, blue to the point of luminosity, held a power of their own, subtle but distinct. Then I remembered my earlier admonition to myself about involvement with mortals, chuckled at the outrageousness of the thought that I should even need such a warning, and put the entire subject out of my mind.

Soon enough, we reached our destination. A big, square building, windowless, it boasted another broad door like the one we had just exited. By habit, I started to reach out and touch the identification pad, then laughed and exerted a tiny fraction of the Power instead. The lock cycled and the door slid upward.

We led the cargo lifter inside and I pulled the door closed behind us, then hit the lights. Evelyn gasped.

The entire space of the building's interior was hollow, and only one object sat within it: my personal spacecraft. About thirty-five meters long, and nearly as wide, it resembled a giant bird of prey, its forward cockpit section curving down, its metal wings spread in graceful, curving arcs. The overhead lights shone down, rippling over the slick, smooth surface.

I stood back, admiring my favorite toy.

"That's… that's… wow," Evelyn stammered. "That's beautiful."

Evelyn walked forward in a daze, reached out, and ran her hand along the synthetic resin and ceramic surface.

"It looks like a Viggen-12, but there shouldn't be any of those out here in the Outer Worlds."

She walked around the side, her eyes moving over the big, silvery bulk.

"And it really isn't even that, is it? It's something new…"

"Very new," I said. "One of a kind. Based on the Viggen, yes, but heavily modified by the best engineers and designers to be found on Mysentia."

"You must have found some good ones," she said, envy obvious in her voice.

"It is quite remarkable what one can accomplish, given enough time and resources," I replied.

"And power," she added.

"I had no access to the Power during much of my exile."

"I didn't mean that kind of power," she said. "If you really were close to unifying the Outer Worlds, before you abandoned it all to go running back to your City, you must have commanded a great deal of power and influence out here."

I shrugged, no longer terribly interested in discussing the political matters of this plane. When Mysentia had been my only home and refuge, I had devoted considerable effort to bettering its position and power. Yet, as concerned as I had become over the plight of the Outer Worlds at the hands of the Terran Alliance, it had all become much less important to me the moment the Power had returned. Surprisingly, I found I did still feel something of a slight attachment to and a concern for Mysentia, but I dismissed this as pure sentimentality manifesting itself upon my return. Casting such thoughts aside, I returned my attention to the huge gleaming vehicle in front of me.

My beautiful spacecraft filled almost the entire available space, but, in truth, it did not seem terribly bulky. Indeed, it appeared sleek and streamlined and ready to hurl itself into the void of its own accord. Its smooth, blue-gray flank sparkled and rippled with a light that could not entirely be accounted for by reflection of the building's own illumination. Even the four landing pads upon which it sat spoke more of sculpture than cold mechanics. How proud I was of it. To think I might have remained in the Golden City, had I been welcomed there, and never thought to revisit this grand machine again! Perhaps seeing it again represented something good to have come from my travails. I surely couldn't think of anything else that had happened so far that fit that description.

Recalling the security codes from my memory, I gestured with one hand and exerted a touch of the Power. The cargo hatch unlocked and slid open. Maneuvering the lifter around, I pushed it up into the cargo bay and closed the door.

"This may seem like a dumb question, given that you're loading your weapons onto a spacecraft, here," Evelyn said, "but: We're flying somewhere?"

"Yes."

She bit her lip, thinking.

"You don't have an army to go with your guns. Planning on doing some recruiting?"

"Soldiers are not all I need before I can assault the Golden City."

"Okay…" She waited a few seconds, until sure I would not volunteer any further information. Then, "So, what else do you need?"

"You will see soon enough. When we reach Candis."

"Candis?"

She frowned, puzzled.

"Is that rock even inhabited?"

"Your prejudices are showing again," I pointed out, only half-seriously.

She snorted.

"Some do live there," I said. "Not many, fortunately."

She nodded slowly.

"And… we can't just zap our way there?"

"You may have noticed," I replied, "that I cannot 'zap' our way everywhere, else our legs would not presently be so sore. Travel via portals requires conditions conducive to opening them, unless one wishes to exert enough overwhelming energy to bludgeon one open—something I generally prefer to avoid."

Walking around to the front, where the ship's long nose section angled down, I motioned again and another hatch opened, this one leading into the passenger cabin and from there to the cockpit.

"There are simply no good spots to open a portal on the surface of that world," I said, "or even in the vicinity of space around it."

She took all of that in, then returned to her original point.

"So what do you want there?"

She climbed through the hatch, and I followed her, closing it behind us.

"You will see soon enough," I replied.

I took my place in the cockpit and Evelyn slid easily into the seat opposite me. She took a quick inventory of the controls and indicators and seemed comfortable enough.

"It looks close enough to a Twelve that I know where everything is," she said with a tight smile. "I could fly it."

I smiled back, settling into the cushioned seat.

"By all means, then," I said.

Her eyes widened, then quickly she leaned forward and began touching control surfaces, bringing up the holo display and starting the engines.

"Not a problem," she said, taking the unified control stick in both hands.

A faint shiver ran through the deck, and then the engines started and the craft vibrated with a steady throbbing.

I waited for her to look up through the overhead window and ask the inevitable question, and she did so soon enough.

"Do I just turn the guns on the roof, or—?"

I laughed and touched a control to my left. Above us, the ceiling retracted silently, leaving a clear pathway to a starry nighttime sky.

Evelyn smiled and pulled up on the stick.

With a sudden surge, the ship lifted cleanly up and lofted out into the air above the city.

I was impressed. She confidently and comfortably manipulated the controls as if she had spent days in a simulator. Soon enough we were in orbit, then moving away from Mysentia at a brisk pace. The blue-white marble of my adopted homeworld receded to just another sparkling point in the spackled velvet curtain of space, and I reversed the viewscreen to show the path ahead.

"Very nice," I commented. "Very smooth."

"I've been flying ships like this one a long time," she replied. "Though it has some improvements I'd love to examine in closer detail."

"Maybe later," I said with a laugh.

Her hands moved to the navigational console, activating the tactical display.

"So, do you already have the course we're taking laid in? I assume you'll want to jump to subspace as soon as possible."

"No need," I said. "There are no good points for opening a portal near Candis, but I can still get us close enough for only a short trip after we arrive."

I closed my eyes and felt the Power flowing through me. Visualizing in my mind an image of our ship, I reached out ahead of us and pressed upon the delicate folds of the universe, pushing them open.

The ship lurched violently, twice.

"Hey," Evelyn shouted, clutching at her armrests.

"It's not my doing," I replied, my voice somewhat distant, my mind still largely tied up in the maneuver I had been executing.

Crimson bolts of energy flared past, disrupting the viewscreens and causing us to spin about as they crackled along the ship's electromagnetic field. The portal I had been opening snapped closed as my attention returned to the ship and to our immediate situation. Evelyn fought with the controls as I switched one of the displays to rear view.

Another bolt impacted the ship's defensive screens. Alerts screeched deafeningly. Sparks flew from the control panels, causing both of us to jerk our hands away.

"What the hell?" I shouted, furious.

"Someone's shooting at us," Evelyn replied, pointing to one of the displays. "They're behind us, closing fast."

A ship, sleek and smooth and gleaming silver, closed in on us. I could make out no identifying markings.

I ran through every curse word I knew, and invented several creative new ones.

"Can nothing ever go simply?" I all-but-shouted. "Does it always have to get complicated?"

We lurched again. Sparks flew from yet another panel, and Evelyn let loose a profanity I had not even thought of, followed by, "The screens will be gone in less than a minute, unless they're a lot better than standard."

"They're better," I replied, "but not that much better."

I ran my fingers over one of the control panels, hastily initiating what repairs I could, but mainly delaying the inevitable. We had to get away, or get rid of that other ship.

"Who are they?" Evelyn shouted as she fought to bring us back under control. "And what did you do to tick them off?"

"I have no idea," I replied, anger swelling to mighty proportions, "but I don't have time for this."

She ran us through a few more impressive maneuvers, none of which had the least effect upon our pursuers.

"They're too fast," she said. "Running's not an option."

I scoffed.

"Running is always an option. Can you give me five seconds without a violent shock?"

She looked at me, gripped the controls with both hands, and nodded. Then she proceeded to put the ship through its paces, executing a beautiful piloting display, neatly avoiding the incoming fire.

Three seconds... Four...

My mind at peace, my concentration undisturbed, I reached out and forced a circle of blazing blue light to open directly in front of us. We hurtled blindly into it and I yanked it closed and the stars blinked out and blackness descended like a wall. The universe around us went away: poof, gone.

NINE

Spiraling swirling rainbows twisting and contorting one upon the other in mad embrace until they disgorged a single spacecraft, spat out and spinning madly through strange emptiness.

We had exchanged one universe for another. Shimmering violet rather than deep black surrounded us on all sides.

Evelyn peered at the displays and frowned.

"These readings are crazy," she said. "We're not anywhere I know."

"One level up in the Above, if I did it right," I replied.

She smiled wryly and nodded. Apparently, my cursory explanations of the wider universe had made some sense to her.

"I get it," she said. "They'll have no choice but to assume we jumped to subspace. But when they look there, they won't find us." She laughed. "That'll drive them crazy—it would certainly drive me crazy. Almost as crazy as trying to figure out how a ship this small pulled that off in the first place."

I smiled.

"I'd like to know who they were, though," she said, looking at me again.

I shrugged. Innocent as ever, this dark lord. Of course.

And so we made ourselves busy inspecting the ship's components, evaluating the damage to what was obviously broken and instructing the computer to find the problems that were not so obvious. Fortunately, it seemed to be largely superficial and well within our abilities to repair.

"So," Evelyn asked after a few minutes of silent work underneath a console, "you really don't know who it was we were avoiding back there?"

She was not letting it go. Fine.

"No clue," I replied, adding, "It did not resemble any ship I have seen anywhere in the Outer Worlds."

"I agree. It could have been an Alliance ship," she said, "though not one I'm familiar with."

"There are some you are not familiar with?"

She frowned at me.

"There are plenty in secret development, I'm sure. I just fly the ones they give me."

"Of course," I said, nodding. "I forgot the deep secrecy surrounding all things Alliance."

She rolled her eyes at me.

"Please, Mr. Dictator-for-a-thousand-years."

"Touché."

She bit her lip, thinking. "If it was an Alliance craft, you'd better hope they don't conclude from this that your Outworlder ships are growing too advanced for them to keep up with. They might choose to act sooner rather than later to put a halt to something like that."

I frowned, finding myself genuinely troubled by that. I considered a number of responses before hardening my heart and simply saying, "That is of no further consequence to me."

She stared at me for a few somewhat uncomfortable moments, then crawled back under the console and returned her attention to repairing the ship.

I said nothing more, but did dwell upon her words a bit longer, and found they were not so easily dismissed from my thoughts as I would have expected, or hoped.

We worked for a while longer, neither of us speaking beyond the necessities of the job. After about an hour of work, the computer indicated that we had accomplished as much as we could, given that we had limited resources and were floating in the void. Most of the systems were back up and the indicator lights in the cabin were all green.

Evelyn crawled out from under another console and replaced the cover, then dusted her hands off, despite the fact that my ship was immaculately clean. The tension between us seemed to have ebbed once more, something for which I found myself grateful.

"So," she said. "Candis. How far is that on this route?"

She moved around to her copilot's seat and began to sit down.

"Not far," I replied. "I will drop us back down into your universe in a couple of hours."

"Hours?"

She halted in mid-sit and climbed back to her feet again. Looking back at me, she said, "I'm taking advantage of the opportunity to freshen up a little bit. A Twelve would have a decent galley, bunks, even a real shower. I assume you haven't modified those things out."

"Improved on them, actually," I replied.

Smiling wickedly, she climbed through the cockpit hatch and vanished into the ship's interior.

Not a bad idea, I thought. Far simpler for me, though. I settled back into my seat, closed my eyes and summoned the Power. It surged into my body, racing through my veins and crackling over my skin. Fatigue poisons burned away, along with grime and sweat and other pollutants. My hair stood momentarily on end, sparkling blue, then fell back to my shoulders, clean. My clothes shimmered and smoothed.

"Ah," I sighed. "Much better."

Nothing to do then but nap, as the ship drew ever nearer to my destination, and I drew ever closer to revenge and to my rightful glory.

I was awake when Evelyn returned to the cockpit and settled back into her seat. She had donned a generic, tight-fitting black flight suit. Silver lines ran along the sides of the arms and legs, and up both sides of the torso, but otherwise the outfit was unadorned. Small pouches along both legs contained a number of useful tools and other items, if I recalled correctly.

"I took the liberty of digging through your storage lockers," she told me, indicating her new wardrobe. "Fits pretty well."

Indeed it did. It and the others like it in the locker were designed to adjust to the size and shape of any of my crewmembers. Getting a good look at Evelyn's particular shape in the suit, I could find no reason whatsoever to object.

"Good," I replied, forcing my attention to the absence of insignias and rank markings on the suit. "No need to announce your loyalties and your employers to the people we are about to meet."

We had only a few minutes to wait until I felt the time was right to open another portal for the ship. I sipped at some tea and watched the shifting colors within the holo display, trying to gain a more complete sense of the texture of space around us.

"Thanks for the use of the shower," she said after a few moments.

I blinked, pulling my attention back from the swirling depths, looking over at her. The transformation was remarkable, now that I looked for it—as if her very spirit had been laundered along with her body. I suppressed such thoughts immediately and instead asked, "How was it?"

She grinned and tousled her bobbed blonde hair.

"I'm clean. Clean!" She sighed. "It was way overdue."

"Indeed."

Her grin becoming a grimace, she shot back, "Hey, I wasn't the only one doing all that hiking and climbing and stuff, you know."

She looked at me then.

"You're clean, too. When did you—?"

"I have my ways," I said.

She raised an eyebrow.

I held up a hand.

"It's time," I said.

I sat up and reached out with the Power, harnessing that mighty energy and using it to punch open a portal, ripping a passageway through from this level of the Above back down into Evelyn's native universe. Passing through that great sapphire circle in the sky, we emerged into the universe we had departed, with great haste, some hours previously. The blurred, dingy sphere of Candis, remote frontier planet of the Outer Worlds, hung in the distance, outlined against the blackness of space.

"Nice work," Evelyn noted, studying the blue-gray orb on our displays. "Now what?"

"Now we land, and we secure the other half of what I need."

"More guns?"

"Not precisely, no."

The remainder of the trip took only about fifteen minutes, given the performance capacity of my ship, and soon enough we found ourselves swooping down into the atmosphere of Candis, streaking high over icy and barren landscapes.

Evelyn peered at the displays and frowned.

"Nice place. For an uninhabited wasteland, anyhow."

"It is inhabited," I replied. "In its way."

She glanced over at me, curious.

I had turned the controls over to her again, glad to have someone else to do the piloting. I keyed in a set of coordinates and told her, "Head in that direction, and when you pick up the beacon, follow it in."

"Beacon?"

"To the settlement."

"Settlement?"

"You will see soon enough."

Shrugging, she returned her attention to the controls and to the tundra-like landscape flowing by beneath us.

As she flew us along, I closed my eyes and let my mind drift back over all that had occurred since my return to the Golden City. In our constant state of flight since our release from the dungeon, I had scarcely had time to examine the big picture; to see what patterns might emerge from the disparate clues I had discovered along the way. What did I know, and what had I guessed at, so far?

During my absence, someone had killed nearly three-quarters of all the gods of the Golden City. Perhaps a god or gods did the deed, or perhaps some other force was involved. I had dismissed the possibility that the Dark Men I had previously encountered could have been solely responsible. Those mindless automatons seemed, from my limited observations, to be only instruments at the service of some greater power. Likely one of us. And while they were powerful and dangerous and admittedly I had no idea of their numbers—I had encountered three, or perhaps only two, personally—I found it nearly impossible to believe they could have killed seventy-two gods by themselves. We are simply too smart, too wily, too experienced, for that many of us to be defeated by dumb, brute force. No, the Dark Men could not be the ultimate answer. One of us, or someone very like us, had to be behind it all, pulling the strings.

Assuming the culprit still lived, and was indeed one of the gods, that left twenty-eight suspects. I knew I was innocent, at least of those crimes, even if no one else believed it. So, twenty-seven. I still did not know the identities of the other survivors, beyond those I had recently encountered.

Turmborne, Vodina, Arendal, Baranak, Alaria, Malachek, Vorthan... I turned their faces and their Aspects over in my head, sifting through what I knew and what I suspected concerning each of them. Which of them was capable of such an act? Arendal was cold-blooded enough, but from his words and his behavior during our encounter, I doubted him. Baranak was powerful enough, and Malachek was smart enough. Yet neither had anything to gain from committing mass murder, as far as I could imagine. In fact, both had much to lose; each of them, in his own way, lived off of the impressions he created in others, of being the strongest and the wisest, even among the gods. But then, how could any of us have gained from this? What motive could there possibly have been?

A degree of technical expertise had been required, as well, I reminded myself. The Fountain had been shut off, weakening each of us to the point that death had become possible. Who could have found a way to do that? Vorthan the engineer, certainly, if anyone could have. Yet Baranak could easily enough have manipulated him or someone else to do the deed, either on a pretext or through simple threats. Was Baranak actually a monstrous puppet-master, manipulating the Dark Men and the gods alike toward his own ends, killing all who threatened his position, and using me as the scapegoat, the fall guy? A part of me wanted very much to believe this, did believe it. But doubts still gnawed at me.

Perhaps they were all guilty. Maybe all the other survivors were part of some conspiracy, and I was the only remaining god outside the cabal, expendable. Not a comforting thought, and not one I wished to dwell on for any length of time; at least, not yet.

The proximity alert squawked, bringing me back from my thoughts, just as Evelyn studied the heads-up readouts and announced, "Three sub-atmospheric craft approaching fast."

I nodded calmly.

"As expected. Stay on course."

My eyes moved to the rear display, where three small dots had grown very quickly into three formidable-looking aircraft, wings swept back and guns evident. I toggled a switch on the console.

"Hello," I said, with as much friendliness as I could muster.

"Intruder vessel," came back the terse reply, "state your business on Candis."

"I assume Buchner is still in charge around here," I said. "If so, we would like to see him."

A short pause, then one of the aircraft overtook us, its tail showing up in our forward display.

"Maintain current course. Do not alter heading or speed. Follow me into the landing bay."

"Understood," I said, then switched off the microphone.

"Jealous of their security here, aren't they?" Evelyn said, her eyes fixed on the multiple guns currently trained on us from in front and behind.

"With reason."

"You seem to be taking it in stride."

"It is expected. And they are taking us where I want to go."

Shrugging, she continued to steer us along behind the lead escort craft.

We dropped altitude steadily, until we descended through a final bank of clouds and emerged over a mountainous region covered in snow and ice. Banking about, we dropped to just a few hundred feet over the flattest portion of the landscape in view, and cruised along at high speed until we suddenly roared out over the edge of a cliff. The ground dropped away beneath us in a dizzying transition, and the lead escort arced around in a broad curve, leading us back the way we had just come. Ahead of us, the cliff face reared up like a titan's hand. The escort dropped still lower, below the level of the cliff, and Evelyn glanced at me, frowning. I gestured in an offhanded "steady as she goes" sort of way, and she sighed and followed the other craft down.

As we neared the cliff face, a broad, rectangular panel in its surface slid slowly aside, revealing a dark chamber within. Lights flared on inside, and the first escort darted through the opening.

"Of course," Evelyn sighed, slowing our velocity and aiming for the landing bay. "I knew that was coming."

We passed inside the big facility, following the flashing landing lights until we came to a halt and settled to rest near a doorway in the interior wall. Evelyn shut down the engines and we climbed out of our seats, making our way through the ship and to the hatch.

Four armed guards, clad all in dark gray with red trim, waited for us outside. I did not recognize them. General thugs—hired help—I decided upon a quick glance. But their uniforms—questionable in taste but clearly expensive—bespoke money backing them up, as one would expect. They had formidable-looking guns clutched in their beefy paws, and decidedly unfriendly looks on their faces. One of them gestured through the doorway, and we proceeded along with them through the opening and into the mountainside.

The corridor through which we marched was narrow and dark, with very few doors leading off of it. The walls were a dull, bland gray color, much like the personalities of our guards and quite similar to the landscape outside—cold, dim, and drab. It was all meant to lull us off our guard, though. I did not doubt that dozens of spy-eyes and analyzers were studying us every step of the way. The average visitor would possess few secrets after taking a walk down this hallway.

We rounded a corner and came abruptly to a dead end. The guards stood motionless, waiting for something. After a moment the wall in front of us slid soundlessly aside, bright light pouring out from the room beyond. We stepped through into a space of color and light and beauty—a change as sudden as if I had opened a portal into a pocket cosmos.

The panel slid closed behind us, leaving us standing within the large office I remembered from my previous visit. The wall to our left appeared to be a giant aquarium, complete with dozens of colorful, exotic fish flickering here and there, though I could not immediately tell if the marine life was real or a holo simulation. The wall to our right shifted colors and textures repeatedly, every few seconds, changing from dark stone to red brick to brown earth: the ultimate touch for the indecisive businessman decorating his office. At the near end of this wall stood an ancient grandfather clock, its pendulum ticking softly and rhythmically. The floor, which had first seemed to be a bright pink shag carpet, had morphed into sand, and I even found my boots sinking slightly beneath the surface as gentle waves washed over them. The ceiling above shimmered with the view of a sky seen through dense trees at twilight, as from a recording taken on some planet far more hospitable and attractive than this one. Individually, each of these design elements represented a decorating faux pas; taken together they achieved some sort of apotheosis of utterly ridiculous bad taste, a veritable morass of ugly.

At the far end of the room, as out of place as anything else, sat a large, wooden desk, filling most of the space. It seemed a thousand years old or more, and was covered with all sorts of odd knickknacks, from a sailing ship in a bottle to a small teddy bear.

Behind that desk sat the single most disconcerting element of all. He was an old, wrinkled man, ruddy of skin and sparse of hair—though what there was of it was an almost colorless gray—clad in an immaculate, dark blue suit. I noticed him amid all the distractions when he coughed a wheezy, hacking cough and made some vague motion toward one of the goons.

I knew him. Ridiculous as he was, I remembered him well, and I still felt the power he commanded.

Buchner.

The guard led us up to the desk and then stepped back. We waited. I was in no particular hurry, and felt no desire to push things unless absolutely necessary.

Buchner studied a display on his desk for a long moment, a frown cutting its way through the lines, before he finally looked up at us. His face smoothed to a placid, welcoming smile, but his eyes lost none of their intensity.

"Well, well," he said. "I had nearly decided you must be Markos the Liberator. But no, too young, too young. You have to be the son, yes? I do see a strong resemblance."

His voice was raw, a croaking sound, oddly accented, and nearly drowned out in the whoosh of the wave effect at our feet.

"No, you were right the first time," I said.

His eyes widened and he leaned forward, staring at me, seemingly caught between a dismissive laugh and a gasp of awe, unsure of which way to go.

"But—how?"

"There are ways," I said. "Given sufficient wealth or power, there are always ways. You know this."

Blinking, he nodded once, clearly mystified. "To some degree, perhaps," he muttered under his breath. "But this…"

I shrugged.

His smile returned then, broadening into a predatory, leering grin.

"Wealth… Power… These are things I possess, too," he said. "Perhaps you will tell me of these ways you mentioned."

"Perhaps," I replied, nodding. I gestured at the hulking figures around us. "Still dressing your men like bellhops, I see."

"Yes, it is you," he said with a laugh, sitting back. "Well. So good to see you again."

His eyes shifted momentarily to Evelyn, just long enough to get a sense of her, and to give both of us the creeps.

"You I do not know," he said. "Your face does not turn up, no, on any of my databases. Not on the networks, either. Which," he said, shrugging, "could be a very good thing. Or else a very bad thing. So far, I do not know which."

He turned his attention back to me.

"I do hope you know with whom you are consorting, lad, because she could easily be Terran Alliance Intelligence—"

"Navy, actually," Evelyn announced.

To Buchner's credit, he only slightly recoiled at those words, though shocked expressions flashed across the faces of his thugs in the office. I can only imagine my own face revealed a similar look. I thought she had understood that we were among very independent, anti-authoritarian people, with little love for the weak, disorganized Outer Worlds governments, much less the powerful and hated Terran Alliance. Perhaps I had not made this clear enough. Or perhaps she simply did not care. Either way, the situation had just become exponentially more complicated.

Two of the goons instinctively stepped forward, protective of their boss. The others went for their weapons.

"Twelve years of service on Alliance scows," she was saying amid the tumult of thugs brandishing their various implements of violence, "was more than enough to make me look for… other ways of making a living."

Buchner raised a hand, and the movement around him ceased instantly. He leaned forward, squinting at her more closely.

"So, you are saying, then, that you were once a naval officer for the Alliance… but are no longer in their service?"

Evelyn nodded.

"And we should be believing this why?"

"Because why else would I be here, alone—or, rather, in the company of the Liberator of the Outer Worlds, of all people? Why would I even admit my old allegiance if I hadn't already discarded it?"

"Because you know we would have found out sooner, rather than later, eh? And you wish to circumvent, yes, to get around this revelation when it appears."

He grinned his leering grin.

"I know your mind, I think."

"If the Terran Alliance were interested in you, or your operation, or in Candis in general, believe me, you wouldn't be looking at one disgruntled former Navy officer," she replied. "You would be facing an armada of battleships. Point of fact, you wouldn't even be here now. Just a big, smoking crater."

"You think so much of your former employers, then?"

"I respect their power, their abilities, even if I don't care for their internal politics and their arrogant attitudes anymore."

Buchner still looked skeptical, but his side of the conversation had already moved subtly from accusing her of lying to accepting, to some degree, that she was no longer with the Navy. For my part, I was fascinated by her performance, wondering how much—if any—of it were true, and curious as to just what she would say next.

It turned out to be, "Now, you have business with my new employer here, so I will just step aside and let you gentlemen carry on."

Buchner pursed his lips, considered for a brief moment, then turned to me. Within the space of a few seconds, he seemed to have forgotten Evelyn entirely. That was fine with me.

"So," he said as one of his underlings silently offered us drinks, "what business does the great Liberator have with me and my humble organization today, then?"

I accepted a glass of what appeared to be scotch with a polite nod, and said, "The stones. The ones we spoke about some time ago."

Buchner frowned, stroked his chin, picked up a display pad from his desktop and made a fuss of scanning through the listings, set it down again, and harrumphed, "I am not certain of which of my holdings you speak, Markos. We have discussed different items on different occasions, of course."

He smiled suddenly.

"Why, recall the diamond you acquired from me a few years ago. For a lady on... Majondra, I believe, yes? Beautiful, beautiful."

He glanced at Evelyn.

"Or perhaps we should not be so quick to recall that incident, maybe, eh?"

I ignored his banter and replied, "You know the stones I mean. Small. Reddish. Virtually worthless."

His eyes widened.

"Ah. Those. Yes. I do know."

He laughed then.

"Point of fact," he said, "you might be surprised, I think, about the level of demand for those stones. Quite surprised."

That puzzled me. Was Buchner merely trying to drive up the price? Did he honestly think I'd believe that anyone else could be interested in them? Impossible.

"I do not know what you see in them," he was saying, "those ugly red stones."

He opened a drawer in his desk and dug around in it a bit, finally withdrawing a small cloth pouch.

"Ah."

From the pouch he drew out a dark red crystal, about the size of a grape, and held it up to the light.

"Here we are, yes," he said, handing it to me.

I gazed into the crimson depths of the crystal and allowed myself to feel a measure of true happiness for the first time in quite a while. Within the particular structure and properties of this gem, and those others like it in Buchner's possession, dwelt the possibility of hope for my cause. These small stones gave me the opportunity to shake the foundations of the Golden City, and to force Baranak and the others to respect my might.

Buchner had not discovered the gems, for that was not his specialty. No, he was no discoverer or inventor. Nothing original had ever come from him or his organization. His specialty lay in the field of storage. He lived to acquire things and hoard them away. And what he kept, he kept safe and sound for as long as desired, with very few questions asked. For many in the Outer Worlds, and some in the Alliance itself, Buchner represented the best option for securing valuables and protecting them from any sort of loss—theft, disaster, invasion, or simple disappearance. It seemed that valuables kept elsewhere had a nasty tendency to disappear, but items stored on Candis—and especially within Buchner's facilities—always remained safe and secure. Few understood why this should be so, but after centuries of mysterious disappearances of valuables all across human-occupied space, the wealthy and the near-wealthy had learned it was worth the exorbitant rates charged by Buchner and his competitors to stash their most precious belongings away on Candis.

Not so coincidentally, Candis, of course, happened to be the one inhabited world where we gods could not force open portals from adjacent dimensions. As I said, things tended to remain safe on Candis that inevitably and mysteriously vanished when kept elsewhere.

"Yes," I breathed, nodding slowly as I gazed into the stone's sparkling interior. "This is the one. I believe, when we discussed them previously, you said you had a private stock of at least sixty or seventy of them on hand."

I handed the crystal back to Buchner and smiled flatly.

"We also discussed a price, should I decide to buy."

A pained expression crossed Buchner's face. Dropping the stone back into the pouch, he walked back around his desk and sat down.

"Ah, my boy, that is a problem," he said at last. "Yes, a most vexing one. For, you see, I cannot sell you those stones."

Anger flared within me instantly. My fists clenched and I forced myself to relax them. Glaring at Buchner, I managed a low, even voice.

"And why, might I ask, would that be?"

I leaned over the desk, closer to his face. My voice was nearly a whisper.

"Are you attempting to raise the price on me?"

The guards around Buchner had subtly come to greater alert during our conversation, and now they all moved a step closer. Buchner waved them off.

"My lad, I would sell you these puny rocks if I could. Believe me, I have no use for them, and they merely take up space in my vaults that could be put to more profitable use."

"Then why?"

"Because," he said, "they have already been sold."

I froze. My mouth actually hung open for an instant before I forced it closed. The ancient grandfather clock across the room ticked once, twice, three times, its sound now like thunder. I breathed in, out. Buchner's eyes met my own. The moment hung a second longer. Then I straightened myself up and stepped back from his desk. The guards, Evelyn, and Buchner himself all appeared to relax a bit.

"So, you see, I have no choice in the matter," Buchner was saying, though I was scarcely listening. "I cannot sell you what I no longer possess."

"Who?" I asked simply.

"I cannot tell you that," he said. "You know this. It is private."

"Why would you sell them when we had already—"

"We had discussed, yes, informally, a possible sale. Some time ago. But my buyer was definite, and had the money on hand. He made a very reasonable offer and I felt I had no choice but to agree. Anyone would have done the same."

I breathed slowly, in and out, again.

"Now," he said, smiling flatly, "if that is all of your business with me, I am afraid that I have other things to do, so—"

I raised a hand, cutting him off in mid-sentence.

"No one else would have wanted those stones, Buchner. There has to be more to it."

He flared. "Is no more to it! Another buyer came and offered a generous sum! They are gone! Now leave!"

The guards moved forward, some of their hands reaching for us, others reaching for sidearms.

I reached out myself, metaphysically, took hold of the Power, and drew it into myself. My hands, now raised palms-outward to shoulder level, blazed with blue flames, and a shimmering sphere formed around Evelyn and me. The guards, startled, pushed up against it and were forced back.

"What is this?" Buchner demanded. He stood behind his desk, his face flushing bright red. "Again? Some kind of weapon is brought into my office? Impossible!"

I heard every word of that exclamation, and things began to add up for me. "This is not the first time you have encountered such a display, is it? Here, in your own office, despite all your safeguards and scanners."

Buchner glared at me, saying nothing. The guards looked to him for instructions, but he ignored them. Long moments passed.

Carefully I allowed the crackling, blue energy sphere around us to expand, overturning furniture and forcing the guards back further. In front of me, the sphere pushed up against Buchner's desk, which in turn started to slide back into him, forcing him back into the wall. He cried out in surprise and sought to crawl out from behind it, to no avail.

"You have seen this sort of power before, have you not?" I asked again, my voice booming within the enclosed space of the office.

"Yes!" he cried. His face was a mask of anger and bewilderment. "Yes, from the one who bought the stones."

"Who was it?"

I forced more energy into the sphere, pressing all of the others back harder into the walls.

"Who?"

"I do not know his name," he hissed. "But he was a big man, muscular. Very rough, very tough individual."

"Baranak," I whispered. Evelyn met my eyes and nodded. "He had a beard, right?"

"Not precisely, no," Buchner replied through clinched teeth. "A—um—a goatee. Yes."

"A goatee?" I frowned. "Was he blond?"

"No… The goatee was dark. But otherwise, he was… quite bald." He gestured at the blazing sphere of energy that pushed against him. "He could do something like this, as well. What is it with you people? But it was red. Red fire."

"Red," I repeated.

"Yes."

He groaned as the desk pinned him tighter to the wall.

"Please—?"

"Oh."

I relaxed the flow of the Power and the sphere around Evelyn and myself shrunk down until it only just surrounded the two of us. My mind was racing.

Him.

What possible use could he have had for the stones?

The guards picked themselves up from the floor and glared at us, but hesitated, awaiting some definitive signal from Buchner. Angrily he gestured for them to push his desk back into place, and then climbed slowly back into his chair. He straightened his dark suit, and fixed his eyes on me.

"He took them all," I said flatly.

"Yes. Well, not all, actually."

Buchner fished the pouch out of his pocket.

"I kept three for myself. I wanted to find out what was so special, so valuable, about them."

I was eyeing the guards. They seemed to have relaxed a bit, having received no attack signal from their boss.

"And what did you find?"

He shook his head.

"Nothing."

I opened a hole in the sphere surrounding Evelyn and me and extended my hand toward him. He looked at it, glared at me again, and handed me the pouch.

"Are you robbing me, then?"

"I will transfer the funds to you when I get back to the ship," I told him. "Based on the price we discussed before."

He said nothing, merely continued to glare at me.

I turned and started for the door. My mind was filled with conflicting emotions.

So close.

I had come so very close to possessing armaments capable of enabling me to storm the City. Now, that was gone.

I looked down at the pouch, squeezed it.

Three.

Only three crystals. No more. Thus had my crates of weapons become useless junk. I wanted to scream, to rage in fury, to tear Buchner's place down around his ears.

"We have no further business here," I said, my voice tight.

Buchner glared at us, made a quick gesture, and the guards moved out of our way.

When we reached the other end of the room, the door slid open and we passed through it.

As we walked down the corridor toward the hangar area, we heard Buchner's tortured voice echoing from behind us, shouting the question that would surely haunt him the rest of his days:

"Who are you people?!"

TEN

He could have been another one of your people," Evelyn was saying as I piloted the ship up and away from Buchner's compound.

The escorts that had followed us in had emerged behind us again during our departure, but this time they kept a respectful distance, and soon enough they turned back.

"He is a powerful and well-respected man within his field, yes," I said, accelerating up through the atmosphere's edge and into space.

"No, I meant he was pretty strange," she replied. "Eccentric."

I considered this for a moment, then shrugged.

"You have a valid point."

Evelyn was reclined in the copilot's seat, a set of magnifying goggles on her head and one of my pistols disassembled in her lap. One by one, she picked up each piece, brought it close to her face, and studied the components in detail. When she was finished, she reassembled the weapon with remarkable dexterity and speed. I doubted I could have done it any faster.

"It took centuries of research and experimentation," I told her, "before I found the right combination of ammunition and firearm to do the job."

She took one of the three priceless red gems I had acquired from Buchner from the pouch and studied it with the same attention she had given to the pistol.

"And these are the key, right? The ammunition."

"Yes. They possess the unique ability to both drain the Power from a god and deal some degree of damage to him."

"Like with Arendal."

"I am not certain," I replied, after a moment's hesitation. "My pistol seemed to cause a greater injury to him than it should have, even with my own Power augmenting it somewhat. I still don't quite know what to make of that."

She nodded as she continued to examine the gem.

"What material is it?"

"I don't know. It is unique. I happened upon one of them during my many years of searching for weapons that would be effective against my colleagues, and I discovered its properties. Eventually I acquired some dozens of them, using them to equip my assault force for the rebellion. But they were taken from me after the battle. Only by luck did I later learn that quite a few of them had come into Buchner's possession on Candis."

She pulled off the goggles and glanced over at me.

"Why didn't you buy them from him then?"

I sighed.

"Because, honestly, they were safer with him than with me on Mysentia. Any of the others could have taken them from my palace with a little effort, but Candis's properties tend to prevent my brethren from stealing things there."

I shook my head, the anger still alive within me.

"I never dreamed he would sell them. I never dreamed anyone else would want them."

Evelyn continued to nod as she slid the gem into the chamber on the side of the pistol.

"And that's all there is to it, right? Just pull the trigger."

"Yes."

She looked at me, then back at the weapon.

"How many times will it fire with one crystal?"

"I don't know. Numerous times. I believe it uses the target's own energies against him, so it could conceivably last forever."

Evelyn slid the chamber closed with the gem still inside and set the pistol down on the deck next to her feet, beside a duffle bag she had retrieved from my storage.

"What are you doing?"

"I'll be keeping it, for now," she answered. "And I don't think you'll object."

I studied her face a moment, then nodded once.

"Yes. You're right. That's fine."

She hefted the pouch with the two remaining crystals, then lifted her duffle bag and dropped the pouch inside. I saw two more pistols in the bag.

"The other two we can give to Cassidy and Kim," she said.

I hesitated again.

"If you trust me with one, you'll trust them as well. They're my crew," she said.

"Alright. Fine."

She nodded, zipping the bag.

"If we find them," I said.

"When we find them," she countered. Her voice carried cold steel.

I nodded. "As you say."

We flew on a bit in silence, the gray sphere of Candis slowly shrinking behind us.

"They're not entirely unique," she said suddenly.

"What?"

"These crystals. You said they have unique properties. But that's not entirely true, is it?"

"What are you—oh."

I realized then that she had to be referring to the silvery metallic trees we had encountered in the sandy, bowl-shaped world before.

"That is true. But the effect was quite different, with the tree material. There was no controlling, no focusing the flow of the Power. Those trees are like sponges, somehow. Unlike anything I have ever seen. Very dangerous. I was fortunate to escape the effects of the piece that ensnared me."

I stroked my chin, considering.

"They might well have weapons applications in the future, yes. But I doubt they could be used as ammunition for my guns." Smiling, I added, "But it is a pleasant enough thought."

She eyed me warily.

"You have an odd idea of what makes a pleasant thought."

I snorted.

"And here," I said, "is an extremely unpleasant one: Aside from these three pistols, we are now carrying a cargo of worthless weapons. And that is a thought so exceedingly depressing as to make me want to drop a thermonuclear bomb on Buchner's headquarters."

She glared at me.

"Just a thought," I said, waving dismissively. "Just a pleasant, pleasant thought…"

The violent jolt shook us both out of our relaxed states, and nearly shattered the ship around us. Alarms wailed and lights across the console changed from green to red.

"Someone's firing on us," Evelyn said instantly, her instincts honed via years of experience on warships kicking in.

She brought up the tactical display and studied it as I executed a rapid series of evasive maneuvers.

"A ship—a larger ship—just behind us and closing fast."

We shook again as another blast deflected off the shields and armor. I grew deeply concerned—my ship was tough, but not designed for heavy combat.

"I've seen that ship before," Evelyn said suddenly. "Yes. It's the same one that attacked us on the way to Candis."

"Great."

I keyed in a string of navigational commands even as I continued to jerk the ship around in as unpredictable a course as I could manage without killing us myself.

"But who?"

The barrages of fire forced me to alter our course to such a degree that we were soon headed back in the direction of Candis. By the time I figured out what was happening, of course, it was too late.

"Can't you open us a portal out of here?"

Evelyn's voice carried considerable strain; she had studied the tactical displays and knew what I was rapidly discovering for myself: that the other vessel had us completely outgunned and overpowered.

Even as I sought to summon the Power and do precisely what Evelyn had suggested, I looked up at the forward display, saw the growing circle of Candis just ahead of us, and felt my heart sink.

"No," I said. "I cannot."

She looked up then, too, frowning, and then remembered what I'd said and understood our situation. She groaned. For Candis, and the space surrounding it, held no access points for those such as me. We were reduced to what the ship could do for us.

The communicator crackled to life.

"Lucian," the voice said, deep and rich but very feminine. "I know you are there. You cannot escape. Do not attempt to do so."

Evelyn looked up at me as another volley of fire rattled off the hull; not a full barrage, but just enough to remind us that we were in the gun sights.

"Who was that?"

"That was… not good," I replied. "Give me all the power you can spare to the engines."

Evelyn manipulated controls on her console and I punched the acceleration. My ship roared forward. Immediately, vastly increased weapons fire from the other ship hammered on our hull, shaking us violently.

"So," Evelyn said, "I take it your relationship with Ms. Not Good is... not good."

I executed another torturous series of maneuvers, dodging most of the fire, but not nearly enough of it.

"I will take it as a very positive commentary on the state of my relationship with her," I said then, "if she does not completely riddle us with energy blasts within the next few moments."

She riddled my ship with energy blasts. Try as I might—and try I did—I could not avoid even a fraction of the barrage that came our way. Though it seemed like hours, surely only scant seconds passed before every warning light on the display boards flashed red, flames sprung up from under the consoles, and finally whole pieces of equipment broke lose and tumbled to the deck. My ship did not have much life remaining to it, and that fact saddened me—though not as much as the possibility that Evelyn and I might share that condition with it.

"Hold together!" I begged, struggling to work the nearly powerless controls, fighting to steer us away from Candis—and knowing we were not nearly far enough away yet.

"Where's the escape pod?" Evelyn cried, clutching the duffle bag containing the weapons.

"There is no escape pod," I replied, smashing a fist down on the console in frustration.

She gaped at me. "What?"

The ship disintegrated around us and we were flung into the void.

At previous points in my life, I had generally enjoyed the vantage of open, empty space. To stand in, say, an observation dome aboard one of my larger vessels, leaning back in a cushioned chair and gazing out at the infinite blackness… losing myself in it, feeling at once godlike and yet tiny to the point of insignificance… for whatever reason, always this appealed to me.

Until now. Now I hung weightless in space, a miniscule speck adrift in the void. Beside me floated the human woman who had followed me this far. She still clutched the duffle bag, something I was glad to see, at least for her sake. With each of us experiencing some degree of shock, we both breathed rapidly, which was not good, considering we had a very limited amount of air to work with. Surrounding us, at a distance of about twenty feet in any direction, a blue sphere of energy blazed, keeping the scant atmosphere in and the vacuum out. My outstretched fist clenched from the effort, I willed the sphere to remain strong and solid, and hoped beyond hope that nothing distracted me from that effort.

Nothing such as, say, a massive gunship, swooping in to stop a mere hundred yards away from us, ports open and weapons ready to fire.

Evelyn glanced at me, at a momentary loss for words, then blinked and reached down to her belt, the belt of the flight suit she had borrowed from my ship's locker. She activated the small, mobile communications unit attached to it. It crackled to life, and a voice emerged from it.

"Lucian. I believe I have never seen you in such a state."

The voice was forceful, but not as mocking as it might have been.

"Not even that day in the City," she went on, "when you lay down your arms to Baranak."

My teeth ground together nearly to the point of shattering.

"I would tend to agree, Karilyne," I replied, very quietly.

The big ship just hung there, unmoving, those awful guns staring us down.

"So," I said. "What is this all about?"

"Please. You know exactly what it's about."

"I know you attacked me—twice!—when we did nothing to provoke you."

"You are comical," she answered back. "You have already been tried, Lucian. I am merely carrying out the sentence."

The guns powered up, flame-red energies churning and spilling out of the barrels in preparation for firing. It would not kill me, not precisely—though Evelyn would be vaporized. But blasting away my protective sphere would leave me drifting in space, probably putting me into a coma, very near unto death. I would be hanging to life by the narrowest thread imaginable, and only for as long as the Fountain in the City flowed, radiating out the Power through all the planes of the universe, just barely sustaining my life. If it ever stopped again, I would instantly die. These thoughts passed through my mind in a mere instant, but what I said was simply, "Karilyne!"

The ship hung there still, not moving.

"Karilyne, why would you do this? This is beyond cruel and unusual. And you have not even heard my side of the story."

Nothing.

"Because, you know, I do have a side to the story, and one you surely have not heard from Baranak or anyone else."

Nothing. The guns glowed brighter.

"What do you have to lose? It is not as if I could escape you, here."

The ship moved closer, the guns a hellish row of infernos poised to engulf us.

"It is as you say, Lucian," Karilyne said then. "You cannot escape me. And you might prove to be amusing, with your wild fairy tales and the humiliation of your frantic begging for mercy."

Evelyn looked at me again. Her expression was surprisingly firm, even angry.

"Nice lady," she hissed.

"You will remain my… *guest*, Lucian, for as long as I desire it. You will make no efforts at escape, you will open no portals unless at my express order, and you will not threaten me, nor anyone in my service. In exchange, I will guarantee your safety and security from any outside threats. Will you agree to these terms?"

I looked at Evelyn, at her comparably frail and fragile form, and at the huge battle cruiser poised to obliterate my little bubble and everything inside.

"Yes," I whispered.

"Excellent."

She laughed sharply then.

"How things have changed. The Lucian I once knew would never, ever have agreed to such terms."

She paused, and the ship moved closer, the weapons ports sliding closed.

Evelyn looked at me again. If there was sympathy in her expression, I did not want to see it. I looked away.

A hatch on the side of the ship spiraled open and a remote pod moved out and toward us.

"This could prove very interesting," Karilyne was saying, though I was scarcely listening to her anymore. "Very interesting indeed."

Far too many of my kind had always placed undue emphasis on their appearances. This was true of the males as well as the females, for vanity among the gods knew no gender bias.

But for all the concessions the others made to that vanity, for all the time and effort sacrificed on the altar of beauty and glamour, I never much found the bulk of them, in truth, particularly attractive. No, of all the gods, only a relative handful ever struck me as truly worthy of high regard purely on aesthetic grounds. Many adored Alaria, of course, and she reveled in it. I could understand this, though she never moved me to poetry or song myself. I had my wonderful Halaini, of whom I have spoken before and who will have her long sleep disturbed by me no more. But of all the women, the most striking and awe-inspiring had to be Karilyne.

Karilyne, lady of silver and black. Lady of shining plate mail and broad battle-axe. Like some time-lost titan; like a glorious and terrible vision from a realm utterly removed even from our own glorious City; like a counterpart in power and glory to our golden god of battle, for whom I knew she carried a not-so-secret torch; like all these things and more, our lady Karilyne inspired loyalty and fear in roughly equal measures. For centuries she strode across the realms of the Above like a Jove, sweeping kingdoms and empires aside, dealing justice and retribution with an iron-mailed fist, and leaving worshippers and enemies by the thousands in her wake. Karilyne. A one-woman social revolution she was, embodying the best---and sometimes the worst---of us all. I respected her, and I feared her, and, curse it all, I even liked her. A little. Sometimes.

We stood together on the bridge of the vast starship, three islands of icy calm as crewmembers scuttled here and there around us, carrying out the myriad functions required on a ship so much larger than my own; than the one I had loved and that had been obliterated around me. I resolved that, should I survive this entire ordeal and come out free and whole on the other side of it, I would present Karilyne with a sizeable bill for restitution.

In the meantime, Evelyn and I faced the considerable task of remaining free and staying whole. The silver warrior goddess who stood next to me, for all that I felt little animosity toward her in general, had made herself obstacle number one, and my mind had already worked through numerous plans to deal with her. The fact that none of them seemed remotely practical scarcely deterred me. I would find a way.

An officer approached, carrying a silver tray laden with three tall, slender glasses containing something sparkling and clear. Karilyne took one and gestured for Evelyn and myself to do likewise. We did.

I sipped the drink and smiled.

"Vintage Amarec, yes?"

She nodded.

"From high up in the Above," I said, in reply to Evelyn's questioning look. "Difficult to acquire."

"But worth it," Karilyne said. Then she laughed softly. "I would guess you have not tasted it in… a thousand years, perhaps?"

Vintage Karilyne. With her, the verbal barb almost always came wrapped in silk and velvet.

Evelyn sipped it and said nothing, but I could tell she was holding back her true reaction. Amarec was not a product of her universe, and it had to be throwing her for a loop, despite her cool demeanor. Despite this, she was casually looking around the bridge, absorbing everything there was to see. No doubt she was mentally comparing it to the ships of her Terran Alliance Navy, memorizing features and components as best she could. I left her to her work and turned back to Karilyne.

"So, what are you doing out here?" I asked.

"In the Below?"

I frowned, saying, "I would not necessarily call this 'the Below.' We are scarcely down in the weak, fast areas." I pursed my lips. "This is more the in-between, so to speak."

"Perhaps it is, for her," Karilyne said, nodding her head in Evelyn's direction. "But not for us. We are well below the City. Ah, but I forget. You have lived in this realm for quite some time, haven't you? I suppose you have become defensive of it. Gone native, so to speak."

I was starting to remember how frustrating it could be to converse with this woman. I said nothing, contenting myself with watching the starfield slowly shift in the massive viewscreen before us. It appeared as though we were still somewhere near Candis, but I suspected that would change shortly. If only I had not been compelled to agree to her terms—I could open a portal and have myself and Evelyn a million miles and seven dimensions away in a heartbeat. But I could not do it. I would not. It galled me, but there it was. I would have to find some other way.

"To answer your original question," Karilyne said finally, "I have been patrolling the space adjacent to Candis and a few of the other Outer Worlds for some time now."

This puzzled me. "Why?"

"For... various reasons."

"Ah. Baranak wanted you to."

"*No*," she flared, her icy calm shattered. She restored it instantly, but we both knew I had hit a tender spot.

"I care not what Baranak wants," she said firmly. "I chose this area to observe in the hopes that one of several targets might happen by."

Her mouth tightened into what I assumed was a smile as she added, "One did."

I bowed my head in acknowledgement of having been bested in that regard.

After a few minutes of silence had passed, broken only by the low-level murmur of the crew at their tasks, I asked, as casually as possible, "So, where are we going now?"

Karilyne waited for the space of several heartbeats before answering. When she did, her words chilled me to the bone.

"Home," she said.

ELEVEN

Fortunately, "home" turned out to be her personal refuge among the Outer Worlds. I was quite right to be chilled, however—her adopted homeworld was none other than Stopholod, planet of ice and snow and little else. When the opportunity had arisen, years earlier, for my own forces on Mysentia to annex it, I had decided against it, for the simple reason that it was scarcely worth the trouble.

Leaving her massive battle cruiser in orbit, we took a shuttle down through dense clouds and out over icy, windswept plains. I could not imagine where on this world she might have found an acceptable place for a dwelling, but I awaited that revelation with some degree of anticipation.

As we rocketed over a ridge of gray mountains capped in white, a broad valley opened out before us. A mostly frozen river curved along the bottom of it, but what truly caught the eye lay just beyond. On a massive rock outcropping over the valley, a huge structure had been constructed, apparently all of ice. A palace, I saw then. A palace of ice. It gleamed in the weak sunshine, its domes and minarets sparkling like stars brought down to earth. Not as large as the central citadel in our Golden City, but close. I was impressed.

Karilyne watched Evelyn and me as we gazed at her home. She smiled.

"That is the reaction I usually get," she said. "And it never gets old."

The shuttle curved down and landed smoothly in an enclosed hangar beneath the palace. The door slid closed behind it, sealing us off from the vicious winds whipping outside, and Karilyne's pilot opened the hatch for us. I braced myself for the inevitable wave of cold that would surely hit us as soon as we stepped out.

It did not.

I blinked, as did Evelyn.

As we moved out of the shuttle and into the big hangar space, its walls crystal-white and frozen solid, we felt no change in temperature from the comfortable level of heat the shuttle had provided. I turned back to Karilyne, puzzled, the question unnecessary.

She laughed this time.

"Give me a little credit, all right?"

She looked around at her handiwork, clearly proud of it.

"I like the cold, but I would not wish to dwell in sub-freezing temperatures all the time."

She moved to the nearest wall and ran her hand over it. Evelyn followed her and did the same.

"Such a thing is no great feat, if one combines the achievements of science and technology with the Power of the Fountain."

I nodded slowly, appreciatively.

"Exceptional," I said. And it was a good thing, too, as this place held the potential of being my home, and Evelyn's, for some time to come. "I believe I am warming up to you, Karilyne."

It was to both their credits that they rolled their eyes at me at the same time.

+ + +

Any further conversation of a serious nature we reserved for dinner, which Karilyne promised would be memorable. With that understanding, she assigned two of her household staff to escort us to our new accommodations.

I was pleased to see that, once she had agreed to take me into her custody rather than turning me in, she seemed to have transitioned smoothly from an adversarial attitude to one of, shall we say, professional courtesy. My dealings with the silver goddess had never been as cordial as they could have been, but we had never had a falling out, either, as best I could remember. For whatever reason, she had not even been present in the City on the day of my rebellion and defeat, an occasion that had soured my relationships with so many of the others.

Up a broad, grand staircase we climbed, following an older man and woman clad in the house staff's immaculate, silver and black uniforms. They showed Evelyn to her room first, the woman leading her inside, and then the man gestured to the door across the hall. Nodding my thanks, I opened the door and entered.

The walls, appearing to have been carved directly from the ice, sparkled all around—though, upon checking, turned out to be as warm as wood. A large double bed filled one end of the room, along with a wardrobe and dresser, both made of wood so light in color as to be almost white. I could see a door leading to a bathroom at the far end. Removing my long coat, I hung it on a peg beside the door.

I followed the servant back out into the hall and walked through Evelyn's open door. She had dropped onto her bed, which was identical to mine, and lay spread-eagled, sighing.

"I see you're making yourself at home," I said.

Her eyes opened but she didn't otherwise move.

"You'd better believe it," she said. "I don't think I've hiked as much as we have the last few days since basic training. I'm overdue for some rest and relaxation."

I moved across from the doorway to a large, black leather chair and sat down, sinking appreciatively into it.

"I never expected I would turn to Karilyne, of all people, for rest and relaxation," I said, shaking my head. "Things get stranger and stranger."

Evelyn sat up, scooting back to lean against the headboard.

"You know, this place really is a lot like her," Evelyn said. "Grand. Imposing. Intimidating. Statuesque, even."

"Indeed."

She frowned.

"Sad somehow, though. Bleak, almost. Like something is missing—something is keeping it from being complete."

"I believe there is more truth to that than you know," I said.

She nodded.

"But it's not as cold as you'd first think."

I smiled at that.

"Let us hope it continues to be so."

She looked at me sideways.

"You must be pretty sure things are going to stay warm around here. You took off your coat."

"I think we are safe at least through dinner," I replied. "She has bragged enough about the food that I cannot imagine she will do something rash before we get the chance to experience it."

"I hope you're right," Evelyn said. "I'm starving."

Dinner met every boast Karilyne had made about it beforehand, and exceeded most of them.

The servants came for us after about an hour, and we were led back down the grand staircase and into a vast dining room, at the center of which stood a long, dark wood table, impeccably turned out with the finest linens and silverware. Tall candelabras stood at intervals along the length of the table, and high-backed chairs surrounded it. Karilyne stood at the head, awaiting us. The servants led us to the seats on the end, to either side.

"Your hospitality is overwhelming," I told her. "Far better than I would have expected, given the poor footing we got off on."

She nodded graciously.

"You are now my guests, and will be treated as such, for so long as you remain here."

"And how long do you anticipate that will be?" Evelyn asked diplomatically.

Karilyne turned to her as if she had just become aware Evelyn was there.

"That remains to be seen, does it not?"

She smiled.

"And it depends, in part, on the answers I receive to a number of pertinent questions."

I sat forward, surprised that she would broach the topic so soon but knowing it had been coming eventually.

"Such as?"

But she smiled again, raising a hand as if to hold off that line of conversation.

"In due course. And speaking of courses, the first is served now."

The servants had moved silently up behind us and set wide, silver plates on the table before us, each presented beautifully, each with a wildly different theme, each based around a completely different main ingredient, yet all somehow blending together visually and—I was certain before I had even tasted any of it—gastronomically, as well. I had experienced something like this before, on Majondra, at a grand banquet for the planetary governor, and I shared this recollection with Karilyne.

"Yes, I have dined there, as well. My chef, though, is superior to that one."

"I do not doubt it."

More courses followed, and Evelyn and I ate more food in that one meal than we had consumed over the entire course of our travels together, it seemed. The Amarec flowed, as well; it turned out Karilyne owned a large and well-appointed cellar. The drink had never been one of my favorites, but I hardly let that stop me. Eating, drinking, and generally unwinding—if the silver goddess's plan was to loosen my tongue, I can only conclude she knew the right avenue of approach.

During most of dinner, however, the conversation remained light. Not until dessert arrived—an odd, brownish concoction, partly liquid, partly solid, and entirely delicious—did she skillfully turn the conversation toward the things I was certain she really wanted to discuss.

"Lucian," she began, "what business did you have on Candis?"

I shrugged, sipping the Amarec and then watching a servant once again refill my glass the instant I set it down.

"Buchner is an old friend. I wanted to see if he had any bargains."

Karilyne frowned at me, the first sign of unhappiness from her in quite some time.

"Lucian. Please. I scanned your ship's wreckage. I saw the guns. I know that design—I've seen it before. I've had one pointed at me before. By you, in fact."

I grinned sheepishly.

"Karilyne, that was a long time ago."

She ignored me.

"You intended to assault the City again, did you not? It would fit in perfectly with everything else that has happened recently. The murders, for instance. Kill the excess population, reduce the opposition to a manageable size, then attack."

"No. No! That is not true."

I leaned forward, my forearms resting on the table. The Amarec had my head buzzing, and I thought to summon the

Power and try to burn some of it away, but first I wanted to refute what our host was suggesting. I gestured toward Evelyn.

"Those weapons were for the humans, for defense."

"Humans?" she repeated, turning to look at Evelyn. "More than one?"

"There were three, originally," I replied, annoyed I had already given her something for free.

"We were in the process of searching for my friends when you attacked us," Evelyn said, her eyes flashing.

"You thought they were on Candis?"

"No," I said, running my hand back through my hair. "Well, the visit to Candis was just part of the overall operation, you see."

"Operation? I have witnessed your 'operations' before, you know. I do not like the sound of that."

"Not an operation as such," I quickly backtracked, growing exasperated. This was not going the way I had thought it would. Talk some sense to her, I had told myself earlier. Get her to see the big picture—how I had nothing to gain from killing anyone, while someone else out there clearly did. But something—the Amarec, the food, something—clouded my thoughts. I sought to regroup and start over.

Karilyne cut me off before I could.

"And from whom did you feel the humans needed this protection? From our brothers and sisters? You would have humans assault us? You would arm them with weapons far beyond their ken? You would actually enable them to harm us?"

"Not necessarily protection from them," I said quickly. "The Dark Men, the demons… all sorts of dangers are lurking on the Road, and on all the other byways, these days."

"Demons. Dark men. I have heard others speak of your claims in this regard. Tell me: Why have I never encountered any of these, aside from the usual low-powered demons of the Below?"

"I… I do not know. But they are out there. Powerful, mindless beings lurking in the shadows. Demons that appear through portals, attacking suddenly and viciously."

Karilyne waved a dismissive hand.

"Impossible. They are incapable of that."

"Yet they did it. Or someone helped them." I recalled the rest of our encounter with the demons and added, "In fact, one group of them attacked Vorthan, and apparently carried him away."

She frowned at this.

"Vorthan? You have seen him recently?"

I nodded.

"He tried to help us against those very demons."

I told her of the outcome of that incident. She listened but said nothing afterward. I could see she was taking it all in, though—whether or not she believed it in the least.

"In regard to the guns I had with me," I said then, "you will note I did not have any ammunition for them with me. Difficult to gun down my fellow gods without anything to actually put in the weapons' chambers." I spread my hands out before me, asking, "Did you see any ammunition in your scans?"

She pursed her lips, looked away.

"…No. But that could mean many things."

"Certainly it could. But one of those things is, 'Lucian had some empty weapons and no ammo.' Another of those things is, 'Lucian has yet to be seen hurting anyone.'"

I thought of Arendal then, but kept that to myself. I refused to feel the least bit of guilt over the outcome of our conflict. He had brought that entirely upon himself. And if he turned up later, recovered and with still more accusations against me, well, what were a few more charges added to the list?

Karilyne appeared to consider my words for a few moments, something I felt good about. Then, she asked, "What of these 'Dark Men' to which you keep referring. Assuming, for the moment, they do exist, what do you believe they are? Where did they come from?"

I shook my head.

"I don't know. But they are powerful. And dangerous. One assaulted me on the Road as I returned to the Golden City, and I have no doubt he would have done me serious bodily harm had I allowed him to catch me."

I motioned toward Evelyn.

"She was with me when I encountered two more of them later, on the outskirts of Malachek's domain."

I described what we had seen, and Evelyn verified it.

"Have you not seen them at all?" I asked.

"No…" She hesitated, as if searching for the right words. "But I have heard stories from some of the others."

She shrugged.

"Baranak, of course, does not believe it. If they exist at all, he is sure they are something you yourself cooked up, to distract attention from yourself and your activities."

"Including having one nearly kill me." I sighed. "Sure."

Karilyne nodded.

"Yet, if they are as prolific as you say, but the rest of us never see them, what else can we believe?"

I shook my head, having no answer for her. She stared at me for long seconds, clearly thinking through what had been said. I held my tongue. For the most part, she had all the information I had to offer now. The rest would simply come down to how believable she found me. Not the ideal situation, no, but what else could I say?

Evelyn leaned forward then, unexpectedly, and met Karilyne's gaze.

"I would simply like to say this: A few days ago, I had never met any of you people. I knew nothing about your existence, your powers, or your feuds. In the time I've spent in Lucian's company, he has been an irritant, a nuisance, and an arrogant, boorish jerk."

My eyes widened at this as she paused for breath, and I wondered just where she was going with this, and how she could possibly think that saying it was a good idea. Even if it happened to be somewhat true.

Karilyne smiled and gestured for her to continue.

"However, he has also saved my life on numerous occasions, protected me to the best of his abilities, and continued to try to find some way to reunite me with my lost crewmen, despite the fact that I know he doesn't care for either of them."

Evelyn sat back, arms crossed.

"So you can criticize him and suspect him of all sorts of bad things, based on what you knew of him back in the day. But from what I've seen of him up close, hour after hour, day after day, during exceptionally trying circumstances, I can tell you that he's not what you think. Not anymore. And you would do well to listen to him—to heed his warnings. Because those creatures are out there—I've seen them!—and I think one of your people is controlling them. And that's who you need to be rounding up—not this man, who has done nothing other than try to help some poor, weak mortals, and to clear his own name."

Karilyne just stared at her, open mouthed, for a long moment. And so did I. No one said a word, until at last the servants stepped forward and removed our plates.

"Well," the silver goddess said finally, "I believe that is the first time in more than a thousand years I have heard anyone speak well of Lucian. Not since Halaini…"

Still the boot to the gut, with the mere mention of that name. I said nothing.

Karilyne trailed off, looking away; I knew the two of them had been close. She stood then, and we did likewise.

"Thank you for the company and for a most… interesting conversation. We shall continue it on the morrow."

Thanking her for as fine a meal as I had ever had, I bowed, somewhat unsteadily, and then Evelyn and I followed the servants back up the stairs. Evelyn disappeared into her room, and I followed after her, once the servants had retreated back down the hall.

"Where did all that come from?" I demanded, closing her door behind me.

She sat on the edge of the bed and laughed.

"It needed saying."

"I suppose it did," I replied, still somewhat in shock from her words. "The liquor," I concluded. "It had to be the liquor."

"It helped, but I was being honest. When we first met, I thought you were an absolutely terrible person. But, after being around some of the others, I have to admit, you're one of the better ones."

"Thanks... I think," I said.

She shrugged.

"I've just gotten frustrated, really," she said. "Here we sit, in the lap of luxury, but unable to do anything to help Cassidy and Kim." Her face betrayed her deep concern for them. "If they are in a place with no food, no water—they may have been dead for days! It may already be too late to save them."

"Not necessarily," I replied, searching for the right thing to say, but utterly lost. Consoling and cheering upset humans had never registered among the many things at which I excelled. Truth be told, during all the time of my exile on Mysentia, I had probably never attempted it once. I had surrounded myself with followers and soldiers and advisors, but never with friends. The women had come and gone, yes, but never had I allowed myself to become emotionally connected with any of them. If Evelyn needed a sympathetic ear and a skilled hand at the art of comforting loved ones, then she had, in me, come to just about the least appropriate person I could imagine.

As if sensing my thoughts, she scooted away, pulling her legs up in front of her.

"Don't worry about me," she said. "You have enough concerns."

"I—"

Infuriating! Why could I not engage in a simple conversation with this woman? Was I so far removed from dealing with anyone other than servants and subordinates that I lacked the capacity entirely? Surely it was the Amarec. Surely.

"I suppose it's bedtime, anyway," she was saying. "We could use the rest, and I think we'll probably both sleep pretty well, given that meal."

Blast it all, I refused to fail at the simple act of expressing compassion for a fellow being. If I chose to do something, I would do the best job I could at it. War? Conquest? Simple! Create an army, an overwhelming force of devoted followers, pull them completely under your sway, and march out. Push forward to absolute victory. Nothing to it. I had done it numerous times as master of Mysentia, during my exile— hence the nickname, "Liberator," partly for my efforts at overthrowing petty tyrants and bringing their worlds under my own sway. And now, if I chose to be a friend and confidant, surely I would make myself the most effective one the universe had ever seen!

Amarec still flowing through me, my head swimming, my odd rationale making perfect sense to me, I sat on the edge of the bed next to Evelyn and leaned toward her, attempting to summon as much sympathy as I could muster.

But before I could speak, she looked at me and said, "You don't have to say anything else, Lucian. I appreciate your just being here, talking with me. But we'll get 'em. We'll do what we have to do. We'll get out of here and get back on the trail soon enough. I have no doubts."

I blinked, taken aback. She was cheering me up now?

"Yes," I said then. "Of course we will."

She leaned forward then, quickly, and kissed me.

Time froze.

We separated simultaneously, and I stood quickly, part of me as drunk as ever, another part now utterly sober.

"I will—um—time for bed, I suppose."

"Yes."

She looked away, reddening, and ran her hand back through her short, blonde hair.

"I'll talk to you in the morning," she said, now sounding entirely sober as well.

"Um. Yes. The morning."

I turned and strode quickly through her door, closing it behind me, my thoughts a blur. To this day, I have no recollection of stumbling back to my room, collapsing on the bed, and passing out instantly. But that is what I did. Strange that those waking memories should be lost, considering what happened next, and what I remember of it.

Sleep descended like a black shroud over my consciousness, and I was dead to the world. And into my head strange thoughts and sensations came, unbidden, to haunt my fevered mind.

Within that blackness, time seemed to pass in sudden surges and random, awkward halts. In some ways I felt I lay there only minutes; in others, the night went on for an eternity. And during that night, within that shroud of black and fitful sleep, images appeared and danced within my mind's eye, taunting me with just enough familiarity to stir my deeper thought processes, but without the certainty, the clarity, to become anything like understandable to my waking mind. Often, dreams will make perfect sense to the dreamer, only to crumble into absurdity upon reflection in the light of day. These, however, mystified even my sleeping mind, and I somehow knew that they contained shards of some larger truth, long denied to me.

I saw a city. A massive, majestic city of the mortal realm, spread across a vast, rocky prominence. Surely this was the greatest city in existence, the greatest city of its age. The capital of some interstellar empire it must have been. I knew this even as I gazed upon it in mystified wonder.

At the center of the city, a towering dome pierced the sky. Banners fluttered all around it. Down, down, my vision spiraled, until I looked upon broad marble steps leading up to the grand entrance of this facility. On those steps stood a number of figures, all dressed impeccably, all moving with purpose and studious concentration from one point to another, within and without. Closer my perspective drew, until I could make out the individuals standing on the steps. And there, at the top of those steps, stood a man clad in a long, blue coat, insignias of office adorning his lapels. His black hair was long but tied in a ponytail behind his head. He looked about himself, gazing out at this imperial capital, and he smiled a broad, warm smile of utter confidence and contentment. And then he looked at me, and the vision exploded in a shower of fragments that caused me to jerk upright in bed, suddenly wide awake.

The dream-images were gone. I knew I had seen something, and something important, but what it had been I could not say. Sinking back into the sheets, I managed to fall asleep once more, after a while, and if more dreams came they did not make a big enough impression to rouse me again.

The next morning, as I exited my room, my clothing and coat cleaned and fresh again, I ran headlong into Evelyn coming through her own door. We scarcely spoke to one another, a ridiculous state of affairs that I should have been able to overcome easily, yet found I could not. I discovered that this bothered me intensely, for whatever reason, though I did not fully understand why. Our actions of the previous evening, and the feelings within each of us that may or may not have been aroused or exposed then, did hang in the air between us, invisible yet all too present, for the few moments that we made our way down the broad staircase to the grand hall. What we saw when we arrived there, however, drove all other thoughts from our minds in an instant.

In a leather armchair before the roaring fire sat a big, muscular figure in black leather, his bald pate gleaming and his dark eyes glittering. He watched us as we entered, stroking his goatee, but made no move and said nothing.

I stopped in mid-stride, uncertain of the situation we had literally walked into, of precisely how to react. Evelyn came up behind me and froze, as well, a slight gasp escaping her lips.

"Well, well," I said finally, bowing my head slightly. "You yet live."

"Indeed," replied Vorthan, nodding slowly. "Though, soon, the same cannot be said for you."

TWELVE

Neither Vorthan nor I moved a muscle. Unbearable tension hung in the air, a palpable, tangible thing separating us. Long seconds ticked by, stretching out like eons.

Then Karilyne stepped out of the anteroom. Her long, thick, black hair was bundled up in a ponytail—a sight that gave me pause momentarily, nagging at my mind somehow, though for what reason I could not guess. A silvery, silken robe was wrapped about her in place of her usual armor. She carried a brown mug in one hand, sipping something steamy. Seeing us, she nodded toward her new guest.

"We have company," she said. "He arrived during the night. You can probably guess why he has come."

I took in Karilyne's wardrobe and the fact that Evelyn and myself had not been awoken earlier, and allowed myself a moment's idle speculation about what else had been happening during the night. But I dismissed those thoughts quickly—I simply did not want to know.

Vorthan did not move or speak. He sat there, a dark statue, waiting.

"You called him?" I demanded. "You're selling us out? Going back on your word?"

"I did not call him," Karilyne replied softly.

"Then how—?"

Karilyne gave me a look, shaking her head slightly.

I started to say something else, but thought better of it, and instead paused, considering. If Karilyne had not told Vorthan, or presumably Baranak, of our presence on her world, then someone else…

Seconds crawled past. Karilyne turned and walked to the table, lifted a spoon and added something to her drink. Evelyn looked from one of us to the other, surely wondering what this new development could mean for us, for her friends, for herself. Vorthan merely continued to watch me, silent and menacing as all hell.

"I am glad to see you survived the demon attack," I said finally, growing weary of these games.

Vorthan nodded once. Then, without a word to me, he stood and turned to face Karilyne. The fire blazed brighter behind him.

"You will of course turn them over to me now," he said.

Karilyne frowned, looked away from both of us.

My face twisted with the disgust I felt for Vorthan and for Baranak.

"So you are an errand boy, now?" I laughed. "The golden god cannot be bothered to do his own dirty work?"

Vorthan shot me a withering look but addressed Karilyne instead.

"I could ask you why you have not reported their presence to Baranak."

She said nothing, merely continued to stir her drink.

"I could even present a case whereby you might be considered an accomplice, should it come to that," he added.

"This is pathetic," I said then, anger rushing through me. "I know you and your master back in the City are desperate to gain custody of me, but—"

"He is not my master," Vorthan growled.

"—But leave Karilyne's reputation out of it. She captured me—and pretty handily, I might add; something you and your cohorts have been singularly unable to accomplish."

"Enough of this," Vorthan boomed.

He looked at Karilyne, his eyes cold and deadly.

"I shall be taking them back with me now."

He took something small from a pouch at his side and held it up. It was one of the red gemstones.

"Lucian, I have developed a method using these stones of yours for containing and limiting one's access to the Power. I will require that you submit to this procedure, so that I may safely convey you to the City without concern for any attempts at escape."

He smiled.

"It is not, I am afraid, entirely painless, but it is quite effective, and the effect lasts for some hours. That should be more than sufficient to secure you inside the dungeon once more."

I glared at him, furious, and prepared to summon the Power. If I had to fight both of them, I would certainly lose—hell, I might well lose to either of them, individually. But I would most assuredly go down fighting.

Vorthan strode towards me.

"Time to go now."

To my left, Karilyne flexed her arms, then stretched them out over her head. Her silken robe shimmered, vanished. In its place, she was now clad in her imposing armor. In her left hand she carried her axe, and in her right her sword stretched out, in Vorthan's general direction.

"I think not," she said.

Vorthan looked at her, incredulous.

"What?"

"They are my guests. I have given them my protection, and sworn not to hand them over to anyone else, so long as they obey my rules, until I deem the time has come to do so."

Her eyes narrowed, focused sharply on Vorthan.

"And, given the conflicting stories I have heard from various parties in recent days," she added, "I do not yet feel that time has come."

Vorthan's complexion darkened.

"This is outrageous," he growled, his calm demeanor evaporating, his voice becoming like rocks scraping together in a well. "Baranak has ordered—"

"I care not what Baranak has ordered," she replied quickly. "Do I dwell in the City? Do I hang upon his every word, bend to his every decree—as some do?"

Vorthan blanched at this, his fists clenching.

"Woman, you—"

Karilyne breathed in deeply and exhaled, a look of pain moving quickly across her face before she reflexively banished it.

"I have ultimate authority in this house. I say again: Lucian and his friend are my guests. I will decide if and when they are handed over, and to whom."

Vorthan just stared at her, his mouth opening and closing soundlessly. Karilyne had instantly moved up in my estimation by leaps and bounds. This from a woman I had felt certain was about to kill Evelyn and me a mere day earlier.

"I would say the matter is settled, for now," I added.

Karilyne glanced at me; I could tell she was still not on firm footing with her actions, but was growing in confidence by the moment.

"Unless you have other business here?"

The engineer god scowled at both of us, visibly shaken by this unexpected resistance.

"Baranak will not look upon this insolence of yours with favor, Karilyne," he seethed. "You had better think twice before—"

"You had better think twice before threatening me in my own home, god of toil," she shot back sharply, "whether in Baranak's name or your own."

"This is far from settled," he barked, moving brusquely toward the front door. By custom and good manners, we had always observed the courtesy of opening our travel portals out of doors, rather than appearing and disappearing in the midst of one another's homes. Vorthan's anger overcame him, though, and he halted short of the door, gestured angrily with his left hand, and ripped open a blazing red portal. Without a look back, he stomped through it and was gone.

"Good riddance," Evelyn said. "That guy gives me the creeps."

Karilyne favored her with a smile.

"I have always thought so, too."

She turned her attention to me then, and the smile vanished.

"Lucian, let none of what just transpired and what was said cause you to think that I have taken your side in this dispute, or that I believe your story over that of Baranak and the others. I merely know them well enough to understand that if you are handed over to them now, you will never have the opportunity to prove that what you say is true."

She leaned closer towards me, her eyes flashing.

"And if you, prince of lies, have been lying to me now, then my retribution will be swift and terrible. Far worse than anything the golden god has planned for you. That I can assure you."

"I believe you," I replied—and I did.

We sat on a broad terrace overlooking the valley, far below. The sky, streaked with gray clouds, was not terribly bright for midday, but with the additional glare from the snowy slopes behind us, it provided ample light for a picnic lunch.

Around a small table cut from the ice we sat, various sandwiches and other snack foods arrayed before us. The ladies both ate, but I had no appetite. In truth, I had yielded to Karilyne's suggestion of an elaborate, alfresco meal with great reluctance. Time now seemed of the essence, yet with my oath to the silver goddess still in place, I could not flee, and could think of no other action I might take, while remaining in her custody, to protect myself. Evelyn and I were completely at her mercy, and she surely liked it that way. The problem was, she could not seem to understand that she was, in turn, now at Vorthan's mercy, and therefore at Baranak's. I had tried to explain this to her as soon as the god of toil had stormed out, but her legendary stubbornness, as I saw it, prevented her from fully accepting the facts. So here I sat, on the terrace, cool winds blowing around me, watching Karilyne as she behaved as if she had not a care in the world. And, for my part, I leaned back some distance from the table, hands folded before me, fingertips steepled at my lips. And I brooded.

The most buoyant vessel must, at some point, notice a heavy anchor that has been tossed over the side, dragging at its progress. Karilyne finished a small sandwich, set her palms down flat on the table, and turned to me.

"Lucian," she said. "Relax. Eat."

"Relax?"

I regarded her with equal measures of surprise and bewilderment.

"Do you not understand, Karilyne? They know where I am, now. Vorthan will be back. Or perhaps a contingent from the City. Maybe even Baranak and his Hosts."

I spread my hands wide.

"Do you wish to have them knocking at your gates? Perhaps even storming in here directly?"

She nibbled at another sandwich, then shook her head.

"You exaggerate the situation, Lucian. None of them would dare such an action. Not here. Not in my refuge, with my own honor pledged to your safekeeping."

"Once, that may well have been true," I replied, as calmly as I could manage. "But not any longer, I fear. You do not fully appreciate the intensity of their animosity toward me, nor the level of their desire to recapture me, and to lay the blame for every ill that has ever plagued the City upon me."

I breathed in and out deeply, forcing my taut muscles to unwind somewhat.

"With me here," I concluded, "you and your people are not safe."

"That is just what Vorthan told me this morning," she said with a wry smile.

"In that, he was correct. But the source of the danger was not what he surely intimated."

Karilyne nodded her head once, then motioned for a servant to pour more water for each of us.

"I understand all of this, Lucian. Frankly, I am somewhat offended that you would suggest I do not."

"Then why—"

"Nevertheless," she continued, raising her hand, "I must continue to observe the forms of conduct in such matters. I have pledged your safety here, and the others must respect that, until I have made my decision regarding your disposition, and that of your friend. And you, in turn, must continue to abide by the terms of your oath to me. That is the beginning and the end of it, for now."

I ground my molars together till I feared they would rupture.

"Were these normal times, my lady, I would stand in full agreement. These are, however, anything but normal times. Seventy-two of us—at last count—are dead. Someone—not me—killed them, and probably also engineered the shutting down of the Fountain during that time. How can we expect anyone to abide by ancient rules at a time such as this?"

"I expect you to, and that is all you need concern yourself with at the moment."

She stood and walked briskly away from the table, out to the railing overlooking the valley, and she would hear no more from me on the subject.

In the few seconds between that exchange and the moment the black star appeared in our midst and opened, I formulated a dozen new arguments on the subject. They instantly became meaningless. Sirens shrilled from all around as the sensors arrayed about Karilyne's palace detected the ripple in space-time, but the warning came far too late to do any good.

In the center of the terrace, a crystalline star flared from nothingness to blinding intensity over the space of a heartbeat. It expanded outward in every direction, forming a blazing oval, the center of which filled with darkness, as if the light had been sucked violently out of it. From that void emerged a horde of demons—the same sort Evelyn and I had encountered earlier, in the bowl-shaped world. Skin blackened as if burned by some other-worldly flame, clothing hanging from their twisted frames in tatters, deepest space reflected in their gaping mouths and fearsome eyes—these nightmare figures grew no less unsettling upon repeated encounters. They charged out of the dark depths and swarmed across the terrace, making no sound yet filling everyone who saw them with fear and dread.

To her credit, Karilyne reacted before anyone else, her silvery robes transforming in an instant into hard plate mail, her axe and her sword in each hand, at the ready. Even her stature appeared to increase, and she rushed to confront the hellish intruders, her long, raven hair flaring out behind her, like some beautiful and awful force of nature.

Pushing Evelyn behind me, I summoned up the Power and created a strong defensive sphere around both of us. Personal safety thereby seen to, as best it could be, I moved forward to assist Karilyne, even as the doors leading out from the palace crashed open to my left and a cadre of her personal guard charged out, weapons brandished. To their credit, the soldiers hesitated only briefly at the sight of the attackers, before quickly moving to confront them.

"Here they are again," I called to Karilyne. "Those demons that do not exist, doing things that are impossible."

"Indeed," she called back, from the center of the fray. "Someone is using them as pawns, as catspaws."

"You think?"

Shaking my head in frustration that it had taken something like this to get through her thick skull, I drew upon the Power and prepared to unleash what few offensive capabilities I possessed. Raising both arms, palms facing outward, I spilled small, blue orbs that rolled across the terrace to explode upon reaching the attackers' flanks.

In response, the demons redoubled their assault—but not in my direction. They seemed intent upon one target—the silver lady. Karilyne roared, her sword and her axe singing their own songs of destruction in a swath all around her. The horde broke upon her like a wave upon the rocks, and I stood back momentarily, watching her in awe. Only Baranak, I imagined, could have equaled or excelled her skills at massive, devastating violence. Then, as a renewed attack by the demons pressed at her, I moved forward again, lending what little I could in terms of offensive firepower.

Another battalion of guards arrived then and opened up with their firearms, for what little good it did. The demons shrugged off the energy beams and solid projectiles with ease, and continued to focus most of their attention and their murderous efforts on Karilyne. She beat them back, hacking at them savagely, yet I saw no bodies anywhere around her. Either they were carrying their dead and wounded away as they fought, or the bodies left no trace after death. I had no idea which of those might be the case, but it scarcely mattered at the moment. Hurling exploding blue spheres of energy, I chipped away at the flanks of the enemy, opposite the side where the guards did the same.

Not enough. Our efforts were not enough. I had seen it happen before, with Vorthan, and now it was happening again with Karilyne. The silver warrior vanished beneath the press of twisted, grotesque bodies, and within moments only the tip of her sword and the occasional swing of her axe appeared above the fray. Seconds later, neither of those weapons could be seen at all, and the horde had grown noticeably smaller.

This time, I understood. They had some sort of escape portal at the center of their crowd, and surely Karilyne had already been carried through. She was gone—at least for the moment, though Vorthan's own apparent escape gave me some reason for hope concerning her fate.

The crowd of demons had dwindled down by this time to a relatively small clump, heatedly battling with the palace guards. Neither group seemed terribly interested in Evelyn or me. I turned back to her, and saw that she had drawn one of the pistols from her duffle bag and was preparing to fire.

"No," I said. "Save it. There is nothing more to be done here."

She looked at me wonderingly, but replaced the gun in the bag.

"Then what—?"

I watched the last of the demons fighting what must have been a holding action, keeping the guards away while the majority of their brethren spirited Karilyne away. Only a few of the guards appeared injured; Karilyne had trained them well. Turning away from the scene of combat, I motioned for Evelyn to follow me, and we moved to the far side of the terrace, away from the commotion.

"The pact I swore with Karilyne is dissolved," I said. "Whether of her own volition or not, she has departed this plane. She is no longer serving as my guarantor and protector. The terms were clear. I am free to go."

Evelyn thought about that for a second and nodded.

"An interesting interpretation, but I would tend to agree with it, given the circumstances."

She pointed back past me.

"Especially since they seem to have taken notice of us, finally."

I glanced back, saw that the last of the demons had vanished and that now the household guards were coming our way. They moved uncertainly at first, unsure of my current standing in their house, and what with their mistress not being present to give them orders. Quickly, though, they gathered their confidence and advanced.

"Hm. Yes," I said, "I would definitely say that it is time to go."

Raising both hands, I willed a portal to open between the troopers and us. They stopped short, then regained their nerve and charged. I stepped forward, into the blue, and Evelyn moved with me, reaching back to wave goodbye to Karilyne's crack forces just before the doorway to elsewhere slammed shut in their faces.

THIRTEEN

My plans now in ruins, perhaps the only god willing to listen to me now in the clutches of the demons, and my mood black as night, I led Evelyn on a silent, circuitous, roundabout journey back toward Mysentia. I had little to say and, in truth, nowhere else to go. Mysentia had been my power base during the period of my exile, and it held a quick route to my only hideaway that remained a secret, the floating island. It was therefore as good as any other place, and better than most. That did not change the fact that my only avenue of redress against Baranak and the others had been lost, when my weapons had been destroyed and I had failed to secure the gemstones that powered them. Finding safety and solitude and time to regroup, to create a new plan… my thoughts did not range far beyond those parameters as we made our way from Karilyne's ice world, through jungle and valley and meadow and forest, back toward my adopted home.

"That's twice," Evelyn said at some point.

"Twice?"

"Vorthan and Karilyne. Both abducted by the demons. Both times with you present. And this time it even helped you. If I didn't know better, I might think you were behind it all, too."

"But you do know better."

Fortunately, she nodded.

"There has to be a connection, though," she said.

"…I know."

On we marched along the path. One path among so many I knew; so many I had walked over my centuries and centuries of life. So many footsteps. Enough footsteps to circumnavigate the universe, surely. All of them leading me ultimately, inevitably… where? Here? Trudging through some lost forest on some remote world important only because it lay along the dimension-hopping road I had mapped back to Mysentia. Millennia spent in the effort to acquire power and glory and the mastery of the Golden City and its inhabitants—and here I walked through brush and vine and thorn and mud. Had I truly fallen so low? Misery dropped upon me like some giant's boot crushing down on my head, and I may have even groaned softly in my throat. I must have, for Evelyn looked over at me as we walked, concern etched clearly on her face.

"Are you all right?"

I made a dismissive gesture and kept walking.

"You don't seem all right," she said.

I stopped, turned to look at her, frowning.

"At least we're free again," she pointed out.

"Wonderful."

She looked away.

"It's better than waiting for the others to come and take you back to the City."

I shrugged. At the moment, nothing seemed particularly "better" to me.

She watched me for several moments, as if waiting for something, but saying nothing.

I glared at her.

"This is insipid," I growled.

She pointed at a nearby fallen log, moss covering one side.

"Sit," she said firmly.

"What?"

She pointed again.

Grudgingly, I sat. I could not truly object. At that point, I felt I had nothing better to do. Misery surrounded me like a cloud.

We faced one another, neither speaking. The only sounds were those of the forest around us, gently swelling.

"You feel as if you've failed, don't you?"

I said nothing, staring at my boots, planted in the dark earth.

"You're not the only one who feels that way, who's lost something, you know," she said. "I'm still no closer to finding my crewmen. Honestly, I'm beginning to think it may be too late."

"We don't know that," I replied. "Arendal is not stupid. Unless he specifically wanted to kill them, he would have made arrangements to keep them alive in case he was detained."

I laughed sharply then, the first moment of anything other than depression I had experienced since the demons carried Karilyne away.

"And we certainly detained him, did we not?"

Evelyn smiled at that.

"We did."

I eyed her with surprise.

"I was under the impression you felt I was perhaps too rough on him."

She scoffed.

"Hardly. The jerk had it coming."

I leaned back, my eyes moving along the thick, twisted vines hanging down from the towering trees all around us. Sunlight trickled though branches high above to lie in dappled patterns here and there about us, but the overall effect was one of being within a small, darkened room, or perhaps a cave. I closed my eyes and tried to think of my

235

long, lost Halaini, but her face was not the one that came to me. Disconcerted in the extreme, I opened my eyes, stood, and began pacing in the mud.

"Maybe you can find more of the gems," Evelyn was saying. "There have to be more, somewhere, right?"

I looked back at her, forcing my thoughts back under control.

"I don't know. And what good would it do, with the weapons they power currently floating in pieces above Candis?"

She nodded sadly.

"Not all of them, though," she said after a moment, patting her duffle bag. "I still have my three."

"And that is all we may ever have, I fear."

Sitting again beside her, I thought about what we had learned from Buchner.

"I should have asked Vorthan about the gems when I had the chance, back at Karilyne's. But I had other things on my mind then, obviously. He would have lied, in any case."

I chewed at a fingernail absently.

"I suppose he and Baranak are assembling an armory to reinforce their group's claim to power in the City."

"But they destroyed all your weapons the last time, didn't they?"

"So they claimed. Perhaps it was a trick. Perhaps they have stockpiles of the things."

"Then maybe they're overconfident." She shrugged. "They've surely struck me that way, every time I've met them."

I nodded once but said nothing. My thoughts were moving across everything I knew, everything I had learned, wrestling with each facet, searching for connections. Something connected with Vorthan had rung a bell, just then, and an unexpected one. He had appeared to us the first time as we were being attacked by demons. His removal from the scene then could have convinced anyone that he was as good as dead, or at least in imminent danger of being seriously injured. Instead, he showed up again later, none the worse for wear, with no desire to even discuss what had happened. Then, after that appearance, more demons. And just as I had someone important, someone powerful, beginning to listen to me. As if he knew. As if he were watching all along, and waiting. But if his goal were to capture me, to return me to custody in the City—as surely Baranak had instructed him to do—then why not come for me earlier? Why wait until I was besieged by attackers, on the bowl-shaped world? Or, if Baranak's clique had already decided my fate, why not leave me to the tender mercies of the demons?

Another line from Bronte occurred to me then, I knew not why: "Like a false guard, false watch keeping." Saying it to myself, I laughed out loud, for no particular reason. Clearly, my time in exile had resulted in my having far too much time on my hands, to be reading that stuff.

Evelyn looked up at me, startled by my laughter.

"You seem a little bit less miserable now, anyway," she said.

Looking at her, I felt a slight smile working its way across one corner of my mouth, and I fought it down ferociously.

"Perhaps," I said. "Perhaps you have been of some help in that regard."

"Isn't this sweet?"

The voice had sounded from behind me. I whirled, the Power rushing through me, ready to erect a force shield around Evelyn and myself in an instant.

Across the clearing, seated on a low branch, a tall, slender woman gazed down at us like the Cheshire Cat. Her thick, red hair sat in a bundle, held atop her head by pearl combs. Her long, black dress draped over the limb and fluttered lazily in the breeze. She wore a mischievous smile as she watched us.

Evelyn had jumped to her feet but, seeing who it was, she relaxed somewhat. I kept the Power within easy reach as I rested my hands on my hips and called up to her, "What are you doing here, Alaria?"

"Enjoying the show, obviously," she replied. "You two are very amusing."

Anger welled inside me. She may have been the one who first released us from captivity, but I trusted Alaria no more than any of the others, and I had never taken to her teasing.

"I am pleased we could provide you with some entertainment," I said. "Now, let me ask again. Why are you here?"

She frowned.

"You are no fun, Lucian."

She hopped from the branch and landed easily on the ground before me. She turned toward Evelyn.

"Is he?"

Evelyn said nothing, but I noticed she had picked up her duffle bag. Good. Despite the fact that Alaria had only ever assisted us thus far, I wanted Evelyn to understand that none of the others could be entirely trusted—and it looked as though she had grasped that concept well enough.

"I heard through the grapevine that you had visited Karilyne's world, so I worked my way up the path you seemed likely to take away from there."

Cold panic gripped my heart. Word had reached the City already? And—if Alaria could accurately guess my route, why couldn't Baranak?

"Relax," she said, reading my mood. "I said nothing to the others. The golden god seeks you in fields far remote from these. Or, rather, he sends others to do the seeking."

She laughed.

"He has holed himself up in the City, surrounded by those few he feels are most loyal, drawing up his plans."

"Do those few not include you?" I asked her, for several reasons.

If she visibly reacted, it was very brief.

"He trusts me," she said.

"More the fool, he," Evelyn said.

Alaria glared at her, then recovered smoothly.

"Perhaps," she said, looking back at me. "In this matter, anyway. I have nothing against him otherwise, and believe he administers the City wisely and fairly."

She reached out, a pale white hand stroking my cheek.

"I simply do not want to see my friend Lucian wronged without opportunity to exonerate himself."

"A sentiment with which I think we can all agree," I said. "Now: What brings you here?"

She clasped her hands behind her back and strode across the clearing, then turned theatrically and said, "Several things, actually. Where to begin? I have seen the 'Dark Men' of whom you earlier spoke."

"Finally," I breathed. "It was starting to seem as if I were imagining them."

"No, they are quite real, and quite deadly. I was fortunate to avoid their notice."

"How many did you see?"

"That is just it," she replied. "I saw only one at a time, but in several locations. But I got the sense, for whatever reason, that it was not the same one each time." She paused, chewing her lower lip, then continued. "They appear to be on the move, perhaps proliferating, moving all along the main roads leading out from the City."

Sighing, I shook my head. "I was holding onto the hope that there might only be two or three of them at most. I should have known we could not be so fortunate."

"I wonder," Alaria said, "if, in fact, they could be the parties responsible for the murders."

"I think not."

She looked at me with some surprise.

"Truly? I had expected them to constitute your prime alibi—to be your main suspects," she said.

I told her of the reasoning I had worked out earlier, and added, "A significant factor in the killings was that the

Fountain had stopped flowing. How could these creatures, mindless as they seem to be, have engineered something like that?"

She shrugged.

"The second bit of information for you is this. Demons have begun to appear on some of the human worlds."

Evelyn and I both reacted with shocked expressions.

"Explain," I demanded.

"I cannot explain it, Lucian—and do not take such a tone with me."

I took a deep breath and nodded. Beside me, Evelyn anxiously looked from one of us to the other, waiting to learn more.

Alaria moved closer, her hands spread before her in what I took to be a gesture of openness.

"All I know is this: Two worlds of the Terran Alliance, and one or two among the Outer Worlds, as well, have fallen prey to invasion. At first, we thought the attackers were some variety of aliens from within the humans' universe, but that turns out not to be the case. Though many of them have been arriving at their target worlds in vast spacecraft, others have simply sprung up planetside. In every case, they attack anyone nearby with murderous fury. Thousands are dead already, and the Alliance and Outer Worlds governments have both declared a state of high alert."

I simply stared at her, then at Evelyn.

"Can this be true?" Evelyn demanded. "How?"

She was distraught, and I could scarcely blame her. She stumbled backward and seated herself roughly on the log, staring up at us.

"What can we do?"

I shook my head.

"There is precious little *we* can do," I replied. "At least, for now. But I am beginning to suspect there is much more to all of this than I first believed. The murders, the Dark Men, these demons appearing everywhere lately—it all fits together somehow. If we can get to the bottom of it..."

Evelyn's eyes, reflecting shock and confusion, met mine, and after a moment she seemed to pull herself together.

"Yes."

Her jaw now set, her uncertainty evaporated from about her.

I looked back at Alaria. "What are your plans now, if I may ask?"

She shrugged.

"I had not thought about it, beyond finding you and giving you this information."

Frowning, she cast her gaze all around the clearing. "What became of your other two companions?"

"Arendal," Evelyn stated succinctly.

"He abducted them," I explained. "We do not know where they might be."

"Ah," she said, nodding. "And where is he now? I have not seen him in some time."

"You just missed him, the last time I saw you, actually," I said, weighing the consequences of telling her what had happened on the island, and deciding to share most of it—though keeping a few of the details to myself.

"Typical of him," she said when I was finished. "I do not blame you for what you did."

She thought for a few moments.

"Perhaps I can be of further assistance."

"How so?"

She smiled.

"I have talents of which you know nothing, Lucian," she said. "Where is his body now?"

"Still on the island, last time I saw it."

"Then let us be off for your tropical paradise," she replied. "And, as I am in no mood for a long hike, allow me to do the honors of opening the way. If I do so, my energy signature should mask yours—we should be able to take the shortest, most direct route, without arousing any suspicions from anyone watching."

Anything that meant less walking for Evelyn and me was welcome indeed. "By all means," I said, "lead on."

She swirled her hands before her. A sparkling crystalline oval appeared, taking the form of an elegant, full-length mirror. It hovered in midair, and stretched out to the size of a broad doorway, touching the ground. The "glass" rippled as she passed through it. Then her hand reappeared, gesturing for us to follow her, and follow her we did.

We stood on those familiar warm sands, beneath the perpetually shining sun, the waves crashing behind us and the gulls squawking overhead. My once-secret island. Up the hill we walked, in silence, at last reaching the partially hidden hatchway in the grove of palms. I pulled the door open and pointed down.

"I left him down there," I said.

Alaria gazed down into the darkness, then at me.

"And how did he get down there, pray tell?"

"It is… complicated," I replied. Evelyn unsuccessfully tried to suppress a laugh.

"Well, I am not climbing down there. Bring him up."

Sighing, I grasped the edge and swung down, landing with a thud on the hard floor. My eyes quickly adjusted, and I saw Arendal lying just where I had dropped him. His condition was unchanged—something that puzzled me, since I had half-expected him to have recovered entirely and departed by now, or at least to have healed the obvious wound in his forehead, even if he were still comatose. Frowning in puzzlement but not terribly concerned for his health, I moved the ladder into place, and lifted him easily over my shoulder. Grasping the rungs, I started climbing back up again, and hefted him over the edge.

Alaria reacted with visible surprise and distaste to his appearance—or, more precisely, to the burn mark between his eyes where my shot had struck him. From where she knelt over his prone form, she looked up at me, frowning.

"It has been some time since I last saw the effects of your weapons, Lucian. A thousand years, in fact. I still do not approve of them."

"I do not doubt that, lady," I replied. "But there are times, unfortunately, when one has no other choice."

"And I presume you felt you had no other choice, that day in the City, than to shoot down some dozen or more of your fellow gods? To harm so many, before you were restrained—before Halaini…"

"I will not speak further of it," I shot back angrily. "What is past is past."

I pointed at Arendal.

"Here he is. You said you could do something useful with him. Please do so."

She gave me a withering look, but then turned her attention back to the body lying before her in the sand. Reaching down with both hands, she touched the sides of his head, and closed her eyes. Sparkles of light like tiny stars flickered around both of them, and she groaned. For several long seconds this continued, until finally she released him, sat back, and opened her eyes.

"No," she said. "It is not all here."

"What do you mean?"

She looked up at me, biting her lip.

"Perhaps you still have the weapon that dealt this damage to him?"

"No. It was ruined, some time later, along with the jewel inside it. I threw it away."

She frowned, clearly upset—more upset than I would have expected. I did not think she and Arendal had ever been particularly close.

"Wait," I said then. "The gem—I actually do still have the one that was in the pistol when I shot him. I forgot that I had swapped it out with another I found on him."

Her expression brightened considerably, and she reached out to take the gemstone I produced from a pocket. Clutching it tightly in one hand, she leaned over him again, her other hand moving to touch his face. She squeezed her eyes closed again, and mumbled something unintelligible. Seconds passed, during which Evelyn and I exchanged puzzled expressions but said nothing, waiting. Then, after nearly a minute of this, Alaria grunted sharply and jerked backward, stumbling in the sand and falling on her backside. Smoke curled from within her still-clenched fist, and from the wound in Arendal's forehead.

Evelyn and I helped her to her feet, and she dusted the sand from her black, silken robes. She looked down at her hand as she opened it, seeing the jewel sparkling there like a tiny sun. She nodded slowly.

"I have it," she said, looking up at Evelyn. "I know where your friends are."

Evelyn restrained herself, but her excitement was more than evident in her eyes, in her barely contained energy.

"Then let's go," she said softly, and she clutched the duffle bag tighter to her side.

"First things first," I said, hefting Arendal's body once more. I started to toss it over the edge again, but thought of Alaria's probable reaction and stopped myself. Instead, I climbed back down the ladder and lay him on his back on the floor.

"That is better than you deserve," I whispered. "And I shed no tears for your condition, Arendal, whatever its cause. As far as I am concerned, you can sleep here for the rest of eternity."

Once out of the hole again, I swung the door closed and turned to Alaria.

"I didn't know you could do that—whatever that was."

"There is much you still do not know, Lucian," she said softly.

"True. But I am starting to believe that situation may be changing. And changing rapidly."

She glanced over at me, then away into the distance. When she spoke, her tone was not a pleasant one.

"I would agree," she said. "For all the good, and the bad, that implies."

The three of us walked in silence down the sloping hillside to the beach. We stopped there as Alaria shaded her eyes with one hand and pointed off to the left and closer toward the water.

"What is that?"

I turned to see where she was looking.

"What?"

She was moving that way quickly already, her delicate white feet churning the sand as she ran. Evelyn and I stood there, waiting. She stooped down and I realized at that moment what she had seen. She reached out and grasped the object in the sand—

"No, wait!" I called, but it was too late.

—and she lifted it easily, holding it up before her as she stood: a slender, silver rod with an ornate grip on one end.

"Arendal's cane," she said. She looked at me, puzzled. "You just left it here?"

"It—seemed wisest at the time," I replied, puzzled but glad she had not been attacked by it. "The thing is dangerous—I had no desire to handle it. Besides, we were in something of a hurry."

Her expression portrayed the dubious reception with which she greeted my reasoning. She studied the cane for a few moments, then raised her free hand and gestured. A small portal shimmered open in the air beside her. Carefully she reached out and placed the cane through the opening in the fabric of the world, then withdrew her empty hand and sealed the portal closed.

"There. It will remain safe in a pocket universe until things have settled down a bit."

I had no objections—I would have left it where it had lain until time and tide and the sands had buried it forever. If she wanted it, she was welcome to it. She made a better custodian than most of the others, in my estimation.

Returning to where we stood, Alaria gestured again, this time opening a person-sized portal.

"Time to move along," she told us, then stepped through. The opening remained, sparkling in the air where she had stood.

Evelyn was sipping water from a container she had evidently stashed in her duffle bag. Screwing the lid back on, she dropped it back inside and slung the bag over her shoulder.

"So," she said.

I motioned toward the portal.

"After you."

With a polite nod, she turned and followed Alaria through.

Bringing up the rear, I stepped through and emerged into a dense, dark forest. Earthy smells washed over me, and the sound of insects vibrated like the motor driving the world. It was overwhelming, especially after coming directly there from a desert island. It took a few moments to regain my equilibrium.

Evelyn and Alaria were tromping along through the brush, so I gathered my senses and set out after them. I had a suspicion then where we might be, but I wasn't sure. Had I known for certain, I might have been watching more carefully for the two, tiny red eyes, hidden in the foliage, that doubtlessly followed our every move.

"May I ask," I called out finally, "just where we are going?"

Alaria paused and looked back at me. She pointed to her forehead.

"I have it all in here now," she said.

"Wonderful," I replied. Then, "All of what?"

"Arendal."

"Ah." I considered. "Sorry to hear that. Oh!" It dawned on me then. "You know where it is."

"Precisely."

We started moving again. Evelyn looked from one of us to the other as we marched. After a few seconds, she came out with it: "You know where what is?"

"Arendal's private sanctum," she replied.

"No one has ever found it before," I added, "as far as we know. We have always been sure he has all sorts of interesting and useful things stashed away there, given the interesting and useful things he has shown up with in the City, from time to time."

"And even more while you were away," Alaria said. "Some of it he might invent, though we are not terribly sure of that, and he has never said; other things he acquires in various locales throughout the infinite planes. But, somehow, he has always had a knack for finding the best items. The most useful gadgets."

"That would not be my reason for visiting," I said. "I believe there are answers to be found there. I think he knew far more about what is happening right now than he let on."

"Perhaps it will be a profitable and beneficial visit for all concerned, then," Alaria said.

I started to voice my agreement, when suddenly I felt my feet leaving the ground. Stars swam about my head, gravity did a flip-flop, and the trees flew by, sideways. Then someone turned out the lights and the troubles of the world just drifted away. Big time.

FOURTEEN

I opened my eyes carefully and looked up at the ground; at the green, green grass and the occasional patches of sand and mud, spinning lazily above me. Trees, growing from their leafy limbs down below, all the way up to their winding roots, far up in the sky, whirled past in a circle. My left leg, or as much of it as I could feel—and something about that fact struck me as odd, but I was not sure exactly how, at the moment—dangled out beside me. My right leg, in a similar state of numbness, save for a strange, tugging sensation, extended straight down toward the blue, blue sky, far below.

I dwelt on all of this sensory input, considered it carefully, and concluded one thing: I was about to be sick.

Squeezing my eyes tightly shut again, I waited, and the wave of nausea passed, mercifully, without becoming productive. I breathed in and out, slowly and deliberately. Something nagged at me. Something was wrong, beyond an upset stomach. The world—something about the world was not right. But what?

Carefully I eased one eye open, peeking out, afraid the sickness would hit me again. This time I found myself staring into another eye, all sparkly with a thousand different colors. Recoiling momentarily, I calmed myself when I realized that I knew that eye. There was only one—or, rather, two—of them in the entire universe.

"Alaria?" I whispered through lips I realized were as numb as my legs.

"Mrgghhhh."

Not the reaction I was hoping for. I closed my eyes again, struggling to think, to kick my mostly dead brain into gear. Blue ground. Green sky. Gravity... *wrong!*

Upside down. I was upside down. But why? The nausea returned, but I forced it away through sheer force of will. My mind was working now, after a fashion, and I focused on the situation with all my determination.

Hanging. I was hanging upside down, and so was Alaria. And even more than that: we had been... drugged?

Back through memories I pushed, striving to remember... But it was like walking through molasses. I had to jump all the way back to a time I somehow knew was a good bit earlier, when Alaria had first joined us and we had set off for... for Arendal's sanctum.

We.

We?

I opened my eyes again, watching the world spin around me slowly, until Alaria's own spinning, upside-down form passed by. And then: trees, trees, trees... Alaria again.

Who was missing? Someone...

Evelyn!

But where...

"Alaria."

I said her name louder, but this time she made not even another gurgling sound. Her mouth hung open, seemingly lifeless.

"Alaria!"

"So. Awake. Good."

The words were twisted, bitten off, and oddly pronounced; they sounded as though they were spoken with vocal cords not meant to carry speech. They came from somewhere above me—below me—wherever. From the ground, off to one side. I waited patiently till my slow spin pointed me in that direction, and I leaned up as best I could, striving to see who had spoken. Soon enough, I saw, and my memories received another jolt, and things became clearer.

A tall, extremely thin being stood at the edge of the clearing we occupied. His skin, brown mottled with green here and there, resembled tree bark in texture. His bare feet splayed out at the ends like roots. A long, narrow nose dominated his smallish face, along with two beady red eyes. He wore no clothes. As I looked at him, and as he became aware I was looking at him, he hopped back and forth from one foot to the other.

"Yassili," I said.

Possibly the most reclusive of us all, Yassili claimed dominion over the plant kingdom, and generally despised interaction with anything that did not sprout from the soil. Rarely had I encountered him in all the years past, but still I knew him. He was one of us, yet not one of us, and I had never made the slightest effort to recruit him or even get to know him. And now here he was, in the—flesh? Fiber? Chlorophyll? —and I had cause to regret that earlier neglect.

"You... are enjoying... view... of my forest, yes?" he asked in his maddening, halting way. "Unique per-perspective... you have now... I think."

Ignoring him, I sought the hum of the Power flowing through me. It was not there. Had the Fountain been shut off again? No, somehow I knew it had not; I could feel, just below the surface, the usual buzzing of the Fountain's energies radiating outward through all the planes. It was still there; I simply could not access it.

Drugs. It had to be drugs. Somehow, Yassili had drugged me; apparently, he had done the same to Alaria. As she swept past again, I could see the thick vines that bound her, wrapped tightly around most of her body, suspending her about ten feet above the ground from their connections high up in the trees. I could feel them around me, too, though one of my legs dangled free.

Yassili's upside-down form approached us slowly, circling warily about the clearing in which we hung. One long, wiry arm, knobby and branchlike, folded out and prodded at Alaria, producing a delirious moan from her. He greeted the sound with a broad, repulsive, toothy grin. His hair, ratty and dangling like moss from one side of his head, shook back and forth as he trotted around to me and repeated the poking, prodding procedure.

I glared at him, searching my contorted thoughts for the right approach, still not feeling completely myself or entirely confident in my potential actions.

"You... disappoint... me," he said then, his face somehow even more hideous upside-down. "You... are... prince... of lies. Master...of deception. And yet..." He grinned again, even wider. "...And yet Yassili capture you... so easy." He dragged the next-to-last syllable out to the point that I wanted to punch him, and would have, had my arms not been bound tightly to my side by ropelike vines. I became aware at that moment, of course, that my nose itched terribly. What a surprise.

Shaking my head in a vain attempt to clear it further, I focused my attention on him as he continued to circle about us. I needed to buy time until I could regain my wits, perhaps give Alaria a chance to wake up, too, and generally figure out some sort of strategy for dealing with this annoying, walking foliage.

"What is it you want, Yassili?" I asked, as politely as I could manage.

"Hah. From you? Nothing."

He wagged a bony, sticklike finger at me.

"From the others, though..."

The grin again.

"I... will... negotiate... with... Baranak..."

He snorted a bizarre sort of laugh.

"And then we... shall... see!"

"You have to be kidding me," I said, as much to myself as to him. After everything I had survived to this point, the walking houseplant of the gods was going to turn me in?

I started to say something else to him, possibly antagonistic, probably insulting, when I felt the drug seeping into my system again. Yassili had not approached any closer; it had to be the vines. The same vines that held us secure and dangled us from the trees also administered some sort of sedative. My thoughts were swimming again, blurred and fuzzy as rational thought slipped slowly, steadily away...

Smoke. The sudden, pungent smell of smoke pierced through the veil clouding over my mind, and revived me somewhat. I definitely smelled something, somewhere, burning.

Yassili must have smelled it, too, for at that moment he leaped back from Alaria and me and whirled around in a circle, his face contorting with rage and fear, frantically dancing from one foot to the other, looking, looking...

From out of the underbrush across the clearing charged a figure in black. I fought against the sedative and stared, trying to make out who or what it was. One of the Dark Men? Here? Had things just gone from very, very bad to exponentially worse?

But no, it was not a Dark Man—or, at least, like no Dark Man I had yet encountered. This person, though clad in black, sported a short, bobbed blonde hairdo. I blinked, fighting against the returning mental haze, recognizing who it was.

"Evvvlnnn..."

She did not pause to acknowledge my slurred reaction. She simply rushed forward, brandishing something in her right hand.

As Yassili saw her coming and moved to face her, the vines and bushes all around the clearing sprang to life, crowding in toward him protectively, moving to interpose themselves between him and his attacker.

Evelyn raised her hand, which I could see now held... a gun? Yes, a pistol. She fired; it made a soft, popping sound. Yassili stumbled forward and fell, tumbling over the grass and dirt.

"Staaaaaa... baaaackkk..." was all I could manage by way of warning to her, but she advanced anyway, the weapon still pointed at Yassili.

Sure enough, he started to rise again, indecipherable words sounding from his twisted throat. He made it to his knees, reaching out for her, before she fired the weapon again. Pop. He fell, and this time he did not move.

Instantly the vines holding Alaria and myself released their grip, and we fell. Fortunately, the thick grass cushioned our impact somewhat, as we had virtually no control over our muscles. The vines over our heads now dangled limp and lifeless; the attacking plants around the perimeter collapsed back into their normal, vegetative state.

Managing to roll over onto my back, I raised my head somewhat and looked around. Alaria was awake now, but barely able to move. She lay nearby, both hands pressed to her eyes. Evelyn stood over me, a big smile on her face, her duffle bag slung over one shoulder, one of my pistols gripped in her hand. She indicated the gun: "This seemed like a good time to try it out," she said.

I found I could smile back.

"Yes—I think it was a good decision," I said, my words only slightly slurred.

I tried to stand, failed, and sat back on the ground, barely sitting up. Pins and needles assailed my extremities.

"Yassili... attacked us?"

It was Alaria, finding her voice again. I nodded, then said, "Yes," when I realized she still had not uncovered her eyes.

"I do not recall that," she said. "What happened?"

"I'm... not sure, myself," I replied.

"He jumped us as we were passing through this clearing," Evelyn said. "He hit both of you with something big and solid—I didn't see exactly what. In the confusion, I managed to slip into the bushes."

"Good work," I said, and Alaria, somewhat reluctantly, echoed me.

Evelyn gazed down at me, looking quite pleased with herself.

"We must have been out for a little while," I said then. "What kept you?"

She scowled at me, then patted the bag that hung from her shoulder. "I got separated from the guns when we were attacked. Something grabbed them away before I knew what was happening." She shrugged. "Afterward, the green guy never seemed to pay me any attention—he was totally absorbed in you two—so I went looking for them. Found them, finally. But then two very animated fern trees wanted to play 'keep-away' with the bag."

I nodded. It sounded no more fantastical than just about anything else I had experienced recently.

"So, how did you get it back from them?"

She smiled and patted a small bulging pocket on the hip of the black flight suit she wore—the one she had borrowed from my ship's stores.

"Fortunately, you keep an emergency kit in your suits, and it included an igniter." The smile became a grin. "You would be surprised how accommodating a giant, killer plant can become when you set fire to it."

I laughed, and so did Alaria. I glanced over at the flame-haired goddess, and saw that she was regarding Evelyn with newfound respect—which, for Alaria, in relation to mortals, basically meant with any respect at all.

Gingerly stretching my legs out before me, I kneaded them, trying to work some feeling back into them. After a few minutes, I found I could stand, and so I made my way, stumblingly, over to Yassili. He lay in a twisted heap, his long, gangly arms and legs splayed out around him. I contemplated his unconscious form, thinking of the few times I had encountered him before. None of those incidents registered as a particularly pleasant memory. Idly I wondered if I had wronged him at some point in the distant past. Then again, no one else had ever much cared for him, either. He had never been terribly social. For many years, he preferred to spend his time in his large garden outside the City. Eventually, he abandoned even that, and moved out into the wild. Over time he had grown more "wild" himself, his body changing along with his voice, and with his mind. Rumor had it he had used the Power to bring this about willingly, along with gaining some mastery over plant life itself. Evidently this was all true. I shook my head, thinking of his clumsy attack on us, and how it had nearly succeeded. How he would have sold us to Baranak for something as pitiful as slightly better treatment in his rare dealings with the City. Had he simply come to me for help, in normal times, I would have aided him, I believe. Certainly I would have sided with him against Baranak and his minions, and would have treated him far better than they ever did, had the Golden City been mine to rule. Now, though, I looked down at him and felt nothing but anger and revulsion and disgust.

"I believe I have come up with the ultimate proof that I am not guilty of the murders," I said then.

"Oh, indeed?" Alaria looked over at me, interested. "And what might that be?"

"The survivors," I replied.

She raised an eyebrow, waiting.

"Because most of those still around are not the ones I would have chosen to leave alive."

Her expression soured. "Present company excepted, of course," she said.

"Oh, quite so," I replied with a small bow. Evelyn laughed.

I bent down and examined Yassili's head and neck, where Evelyn's first shot had struck him, and found no wounds whatsoever.

"What is it?" she asked, leaning down beside me.

Alaria came up behind her, peering over her shoulder to see.

"It did exactly what it was supposed to do—what all my weapons are supposed to do," I replied, continuing to examine Yassili's body for wounds like the one Arendal received. "It stunned him and drained his energy. The second shot knocked him out completely; he will probably sleep for a day or more."

Evelyn kneeled down beside me and studied him carefully.

"No burn mark. No hole."

"Right." I frowned. "That is a good thing, but still—"

"Why did it affect Arendal the way it did?"

I bit my lip, thinking.

"The gun I shot him with. I've been thinking it was one of mine, one from my original production run, before the rebellion. It certainly looked like one of them. But—"

"You didn't have it when we first met," Evelyn said. "Where did you get it?"

I told them both about finding it on the table in the otherwise empty storeroom on the island. I did not mention the "note" that had accompanied it.

"Someone left it for you?" Evelyn asked, surprised.

She frowned, thinking, then said, "Someone wanted you to have a more deadly version of your own weapons? That doesn't sound like any of the gods I've met so far. Quite the opposite."

I looked from Evelyn to Alaria, who had said nothing during this conversation. She merely shrugged, shaking her head.

"I suppose we will find out soon enough," I said, finally. "There are other mysteries that require answers before that one."

We started forward again, and then Evelyn asked, "What about him? Yassili? Do we just leave him there?"

"He should be fine," I said. "Better than he deserves, anyway."

Apparently Alaria concurred, for she never even looked back. On she led us through the forest, until we came to a spot, unremarkable from most any other spot we had passed through, where she raised her hand and brought us to a halt. Extending that hand out from her body, she made a slight twisting motion, and another portal sparkled into existence before us.

"Only a couple more jumps after this, I think," she said, and we followed after her.

Her pace was quite good, and Evelyn and I pushed ourselves to keep up. The remainder of our journey carried us through a strange set of locales—a rocky canyon, done all in oranges and purples, was my favorite—though not much stranger than any I usually choose when I map out a new path. One generally seeks routes that contain mostly clement environments—not too hot, not too cold, not too little oxygen in the air, no acid rain, and so forth. Scenic routes are nice, and are generally appreciated by guests when we choose not to travel alone, even if they take a little longer to traverse. For our purposes now, however, I was hoping Alaria would skip the sights and concentrate on the most direct path to—to wherever we were going.

She must have done this, for at the end of only two or three hours of hiking we emerged from a sparse clump of dying trees and found ourselves walking along the edge of a steep cliff, and there she signaled a halt.

I looked around, now that we were out in the open, trying to get a sense of where we were. Dusky mountains towered behind us, the sun dropping below them even as I looked. Their ragged slopes did not level out to flat, boulder-strewn land until just a few dozen yards from where we stood. In the other direction, the cliff dropped off dramatically, giving the overall impression that we occupied a narrow strip of horizontal land in an otherwise nearly vertical world. There was little else to see; the bottom of the cliff lay far below, obscured in fog, and while there appeared to be another, matching cliff face, it had to be nearly a mile away from us, across what must have been a vast ravine. As nightfall crept over us, the wind picked up, tugging at my long coat with surprising force. It was getting cooler, and there was no shelter to be found, that I could see, anywhere.

"Alaria," I said then, only half-sarcastically, "is Arendal's place invisible?"

Ignoring me entirely, she walked to the cliff's edge and peered down for a few seconds, then stooped down and hopped off the edge.

My eyes widening, I rushed to see where she had gone. Evelyn did the same.

Alaria gazed up at us from a narrow ledge about ten feet below where we stood. Motioning for us to join her, she moved quickly but with remarkable agility and grace along the ledge.

I hopped down myself and then helped Evelyn, and then we were rushing along, as quickly as we dared, following the redheaded goddess's lead. I noticed soon that the ledge inclined slightly down, and after a couple of minutes looked up and realized we had curved back under the cliff to such a degree that I could no longer see the top. The world had become rock wall on one side and blank emptiness on the other, and the fog rolled in thicker to obscure what little there was to see. Lightning flared in the distance, followed by thunder several seconds later, low and rumbling. The wind grew stronger, and a few scattered raindrops smacked on the ledge around me. A storm was setting in.

"Come on," Alaria called back. "We are nearly there."

I grew a tad nervous. This was not a situation I wanted to be in: no visibility, exposed against a uniform background. I followed her advice and moved as rapidly as I dared, short of running over Evelyn, who occupied the middle spot in our procession.

After a while, the ledge curved around to the right and opened up into a much wider shelf that had been hidden from sight. We continued across it and at last Alaria stopped, standing in front of a narrow, rectangular groove that seemed to have been cut into the rock of the cliff face.

"Ah, this must be the front door," I observed.

Ignoring me, Alaria brought both of her pale hands up, her long, black sleeves hanging down. The golden rings she wore on three of her fingers glittered dimly in the pale light. Stepping forward, she pressed her hands to the rock wall. We waited—

—and nothing happened.

Glancing back at me, puzzled, she repeated the attempt at whatever it was she was doing. Again, nothing came of it.

"Did you try knocking?" I asked, but she was already drawing her hands back in toward her body, clenching her fists. I felt the Power surge through the area, buzzing through me but clearly building up in Alaria. Then she reached out again, touching her now-sparkling hands to the rock wall.

The shrieking sound that resulted I first attributed to Alaria, but I quickly realized it was not being produced by a throat. Some sort of alarm had been triggered, and I took that as a cue to back up and summon a blue sphere of protection around Evelyn and myself. Alaria I left to her own devices. The last thing any god ever wanted was a knee-jerk protective gesture from another of us. Even so, I stood ready to extend the sphere if she looked to be in danger.

The danger hit soon enough. As she stepped back, surprised by the sound, two small, heretofore invisible panels slid open above her head and metallic, snaking tubes extended outward, small spheres at the tips glowing bright green. Like insect eyes on stalks, they waved about, looking this way and that before focusing on the three of us. The tubes retracted back inside the panels with a snapping sound and another pair of cylinders, these not so flexible, protruded out from below them. I knew a gun when I saw it, and called out a warning. Alaria, though, was slow to react, focused as she was, I presumed, on trying to open the door.

Instantly I reached out with my left hand, the one not currently engaged in channeling the protective sphere, and willed the creation of a smaller sphere just in front of the barrel of the weapon. A brilliant emerald beam of energy speared out, met my new sphere, and deflected just enough to miss its target.

"Dammit!" I yelled at Alaria, just as the other weapon fired a shot that struck my larger sphere but failed to penetrate it. "Get in the game!"

Alaria looked back at me and blinked, as if only just noticing what was happening around her. In her defense, it had all transpired within a couple of seconds, but still I expected better from her—-there was no telling how powerful these weapons were, or what they could do, even to us. Especially since they were, presumably, Arendal's creations. Moving into action now, she reached up and grasped one of the gun barrels. The Power flooded through her and sparkling light rippled down her arms. As I watched in amazement, she exerted her strength upon the barrel and it twisted in her hand, then came entirely free in a shower of sparks and metal fragments. Repeating this with the other weapon, she had them both disabled before they could fire again.

I waited for a few more seconds, just to be sure we were safe, and then dropped the defensive sphere.

Behind me, Evelyn clapped her hands slowly and said, "Nice job."

I nodded and said, "Yes. Nice." Alaria continued to surprise me with her resourcefulness and her abilities.

Bestowing a half-smile upon us, Alaria turned back to what I was sure now was a door, pushing and poking and prodding it. Minutes passed, during which her mood grew blacker and her language coarser. Finally she whirled and glared at us.

"The defenses are entirely disabled," she growled, "but I cannot find a way to open the locks. And they are... formidable."

Before I could make a suggestion, Evelyn said, "What about the cane?"

Alaria's eyes widened.

"Yes," I agreed, somewhat annoyed it hadn't occurred to me, either.

Alaria rubbed at her eyes with her left hand, muttered a few more choice phrases, then raised her right hand to chest level and exerted the Power.

"We have traveled a great distance from your island, Lucian. I will have to approach the pocket universe from a different direction, obviously," she said, reaching inside.

She fished around for a few seconds, with no success, then leaned further toward the hole she had torn in reality, reaching deeper.

"But," she said, "I believe I can—ah."

And she drew forth the silver cane with a flourish.

"Simplicity."

Holding it up before her, she studied the instrument with a mixture of awe and curiosity, tracing the fine lines engraved along its length with a finger. Then, apparently satisfied, she turned and raised it high, pressing it against the door.

"No guarantees," she said. Though the manifestation of their energies took similar form in terms of color and effect, I could tell that Alaria was suppressing her own power and encouraging the emergence of that which Arendal had infused within his cane. A field of sparkling white light fell upon the door, and as we all watched, the stone slab slid slowly, soundlessly to one side, revealing an opening into the cliff side.

Alaria ceased channeling the cane's power and the light faded. With a satisfied nod, and not even a look back, she stepped through the doorway. Evelyn and I followed.

The interior was so dark that I could not get a sense of just how big it was, how high, or how deep it extended into the mountainside. A flash of lightning outside provided a quick glimpse of a huge chamber ahead of us, stretching for at least two hundred yards. Alaria and I both raised a hand at the same time, generating twin spheres of light above us, one clear and one blue, revealing a bit more of what lay ahead. And this is what we saw:

Banks of exotic machinery more than forty feet tall lined the nearest side wall, all of it dark and apparently deactivated. Rows of large metal worktables in orderly rows, some covered in odd mechanical components, filled much of the floor space. Light fixtures dangled a few feet above eye level here and there, suspended from chains and cables that disappeared high overhead into darkness. The place had the air of some mad scientist's lair, abandoned yet not entirely safe. Cautiously, the three of us moved into the chamber, extremely wary of any sounds or movements not our own, but detecting none.

"Do you see a way to turn on the lights?" Evelyn asked.

"Not yet," I replied, and Alaria shook her head as well.

The darkness seemed somehow fitting, though. For as long as I could remember, the location of Arendal's secret sanctum—his refuge, his lab, his hideaway—had been shrouded in metaphorical darkness and mystery, as one of the better-guarded secrets among the gods. Never reluctant to show off his latest discoveries and inventions, he never felt the desire to discuss their origins, leading to all sorts of speculation as to whether he was creating the stuff himself or had found it somewhere. Hence a great desire on the part of many to find this place—and ransack it. Part of the reason he had caught me so unprepared in our earlier confrontation was my surprise at his lack of weapons and gadgets, other than his cane. Apparently he had internalized some of the components he had created, and incorporated others into his cane, making himself quite formidable. I already considered myself somewhat fortunate that our clash had resolved in the manner it had; now I grew positively grateful.

Evelyn, standing a few feet behind me, produced a small but powerful flashlight from a pocket in her flight suit and moved off to the left, clearly anxious and excited at the prospect of finding her compatriots, surely believing she was closer to them now than at any time during our travels. Meanwhile, Alaria made her way among the tables to my right, pausing briefly here and there to examine interesting pieces of equipment as she passed it. And I, my blue light shining above me, strode over to the banks of machinery covering the near wall and leaned in close, studying it.

For several minutes, nothing of note occurred, and I began to wonder why we were wasting our time hunting about in a dark and abandoned workshop. Then a metallic, sliding sound came from Evelyn's direction, and I turned to see what was happening.

She had pulled back a panel in the side of one of the bigger worktables.

"Look at this," she called, then began pulling items out and setting them on the tabletop.

Moving around the table, I looked at her find and felt the shock of awful recognition.

"Those…"

Alaria joined us.

"What?"

She peered at the matte black objects now sitting atop the table and frowned.

"You have seen them before," I told her. "We all have."

She shook her head, waiting.

"The Dark Men," Evelyn explained, holding up a glove and turning it over and over in her hands. "These are parts of what they wear."

Alaria's eyes widened. "I—I did not recognize them. But—yes, I see it…"

Boots, more gloves, and smooth faceplates lay where Evelyn had put them; all so dark the light from our spheres of illumination seemed to disappear into their ebon surfaces.

"But why would Arendal have such things?" Alaria asked softly.

"I am afraid I know why," I said.

"Perhaps he defeated one of them, and dissected it for research purposes," she suggested, the tone of her voice indicating she scarcely believed it and doubted I would, either.

I shook my head, stunned.

"Arendal was not my main suspect," I said. "This surprises me."

"Maybe someone is framing him," Evelyn suggested.

"Are we certain this is his facility?" I asked Alaria.

"Yes," she whispered. "I took the location directly from his mind, from his memories."

I looked at her then, startled.

"His memories? Did you see anything else there? Anything that would explain what he was doing?"

She looked at me, started to reply, and suddenly the room shook violently, metal tables rattling and dust falling from high above. Crimson lightning flared within the room, and with a ripping of the fabric of reality, a glowing red portal gaped open wide. Through it charged two of the nightmare figures that had seared themselves in my mind at our earlier meetings. They had found us. In the blink of an eye, the Dark Men were upon us.

FIFTEEN

More than one of my colleagues in the god business had, at some point or other, described me as a deceiver—a title I must admit had held some degree of legitimacy, at least in the old days. Now, however, I found good reason to question whether the one person I had best deceived in all my life was myself. For I had actually begun to allow myself to believe that things were looking up, that the whole sordid mess in which I had been embroiled since my return from exile might soon be resolved. More the fool, me, the ebon engines of destruction seemed to say as they reintroduced themselves to my already overly complicated life.

Crimson lightning flared about, filling the chamber with jagged, flickering shadows. The two Dark Men emerged from the portal and looked around, their bodies stiff and their motions jerky, robotic.

"Get down!" I shouted, pushing Evelyn back and reaching for Alaria. I felt that in this case she might actually appreciate my help. She had already moved to her right, away from us, though, so I made the snap decision to allow her to fend for herself and to concentrate on Evelyn and myself.

"Stay low," I hissed at Evelyn. "Use the tables for cover. Head toward the exit."

The Dark Men crackled with power, rivulets of blood-red energy coruscating down their arms and legs and sparkling in the air around them, giving them the appearance of voids at the center of crimson suns. First one, then the other became aware of our presence and our location and started toward us silently.

I considered every option at my disposal, from a quick offensive to the strongest defensive measures I could employ. None seemed likely to be effective. I had only escaped unscathed from the first one I had encountered because we had been out in the open, where I could outrun and outmaneuver him. And still I had been forced to employ every element of our surroundings to my advantage, use every trick in my book, just to make it to the gates of the City. Here, in a closed room, and against two of them at once, I did not fancy our chances at all. Our best bet was to get outside, quickly, and run for it.

As if reading my thoughts, one of the Dark Men moved around to position himself near the door. The other advanced on us smoothly.

Risking a quick look back over my shoulder, I saw another doorway further along the wall. I had no idea where it led, but at this point I was in no position to be picky. Grasping Evelyn by the wrist, I dashed for the other door, pulling her behind me.

The door looked to be made of a heavy, gray metal, and I found myself hoping it was heavy enough to withstand what was surely about to happen to it. It was surrounded by a broad frame and had a small, transparent window in the center. I searched around it but could find no way to open it. Anger and frustration grew inside me, along with other feelings I chose to ignore as best I could.

"He's coming," Evelyn said, her voice nearly cracking from anxiety.

I heard her rummaging in her bag and pulling out one of the guns.

"Would now be a good time?" she asked.

"Now would be an excellent time," I replied, just before I spotted a small red square lower down on the left side of the door framing. I pressed it and the door slid open. Behind me, Evelyn pulled the trigger of her pistol twice.

"Nothing. They're blocking it or something," she said. "We need to get out of here!"

Unceremoniously I yanked her through the open doorway and into what turned out to be a much smaller storeroom of some sort. Crates and boxes and jumbled piles of of equipment lay everywhere. Whirling around, I realized the nearest Dark Man stood only a few steps away. His hands, wreathed in burning energy, reached out.

"Alaria! Where are you?"

No reply. She was nowhere in sight.

I shrugged, felt bad for her for only a second or two, and pressed the button, sealing the door closed. Keeping my finger on it, I surged the Power through the door's circuitry, feeling the internal controls shorting out even as sparks sprayed out in my face.

"Where is she?" Evelyn asked, the gun still in her hand.

"I don't know," I replied, straightening up again and cautiously attempting to peer through the window in the door, looking for signs of either Alaria or our attackers, and seeing neither. "What happened when you shot them?"

"Nothing—except that the aura around them flared up both times I fired. Could they deflect it?"

"How should I know?" If my super-guns could not bring them down, what chance did we have at all?

A dark shape moved suddenly on the other side of the door, and I tried to see—and then jumped backward just as a black-gloved fist smashed into the window. The clear material cracked but did not shatter. A second blow, an instant later, impacted the door just below where the first had landed. The door shuddered and no longer appeared to fit properly; it now had a distinctive curve inward towards us.

"They will be through this thing any second now," I breathed.

"Can you get us out of here?"

I had not tried yet, for a number of reasons: It takes a few seconds to complete the procedure, even when one is not facing cold, merciless death, mere feet away. Worse, I had never been here before, and Alaria had done the navigating on our journey, meaning I would be starting from scratch, with no clue as to our exact location or what planes lay close by. Moving too hastily, I could easily tear through the wrong barrier and drop us into a volcano or cause us to step out into an airless vacuum. And, on top of all this, Alaria might still be out there in the other room somewhere, injured and unable to escape. Dark lord I was, yes, but I could not simply run away and leave her at the mercy of these... things.

Another blow of a black fist and I started to reassess that last thought. Just then, though, something caught my attention—something about the Dark Man who stood mere inches and a single metal door away. As he drew back his fist to strike again, I noticed that the energies flowing all about his arm, while crimson in color, appeared to congeal into fiery globules where they came closest to touching his form. The pattern of the globules, the way they flowed about him and down his body, like thick liquid more than energy—this seemed extremely familiar to me. I had seen it before, somewhere... and the memory made me think, perversely, of beautiful women and laughter and...

The fist struck again and I stumbled back, away from the door, but not before I noticed a flash of white through the glass, moving quickly. I leaned as close as I dared—the glass could shatter in my face at any moment—and saw Alaria leaping onto one of the tables, fending off the other Dark Man with Arendal's cane. The Dark Man leapt onto the table in front of her, a blinding white flash lit both that room and our own—

—and Alaria was gone.

It took me a couple more seconds to realize that both of the Dark Men were missing, as well.

I waited.

Nothing.

I glanced back at Evelyn; she looked from me to the window to me again.

"What—?"

"I have no idea."

We waited some more.

Nothing continued to happen.

"Do you think they're really gone?"

I shrugged. "Alaria certainly is."

"Did they... kill her?"

"I wish I knew."

Bending down to inspect the lock mechanism, I saw that my efforts had hopelessly ruined it. It scarcely mattered, though—the Dark Man had done the work for us. Grasping the twisted door by its now-exposed edges, I easily pushed it aside. It came off its track and fell to the floor with a clang. Ah, well. If we were attacked again, we would have to look elsewhere for sanctuary.

I moved out first, the Power at the ready for attack or defense as needed. Evelyn followed me, shining her flashlight back and forth across the big room.

Nothing.

I allowed myself to exhale; it felt as if I had been holding my breath for five minutes, though the conflict had not lasted nearly that long.

"Alaria!"

My shouted call brought forth no reply. Evelyn joined in, but a few seconds of this gave us reason to believe she was no longer in the vicinity, if even on this plane.

Raising my hand to generate a sphere of light again, I moved carefully toward the exit. Evelyn met me there, coming around from the direction where we had last seen Alaria. We stood just inside the main doorway, looking back inside, lightning flashing at our backs and rain pounding down to splatter around our feet.

"What do we do now?" Evelyn asked, still dazed from the shock and the adrenalin.

And then the thoughts that had been dancing just beyond the reach of my consciousness for several minutes solidified, snapping into focus. And I remembered.

It had been more than two thousand years earlier—no wonder it took me so long to recall the incident. We were spending time on a plane in the Below, Jarren and I, carousing in bars and romancing the women and generally behaving like boorish idiots who still had a few centuries of growing up to do. And at one bar, as Jarren and I were speaking to two particularly comely young things, Jarren had summoned the Power and allowed some of it to manifest about himself. Showing off, essentially. No one else had seen it but the women and myself, and I quickly passed it off with them as some kind of novelty device he was using to impress people. Embarrassed with himself and angry with me, he had stormed out of the bar and I had never seen him again. Things had worked out well, though, at least from my perspective—I had ended up with both of the girls. A singularly pleasant memory, at the time, though I had not dwelt upon it in years.

What brought it back to me now, however, was something other than the outcome of the evening's socializing.

When Jarren had summoned his energies about him, bringing forth his own particular manifestation of the Power, as each of us could do, those energies had flowed about his arms in rivulets, and congealed in the spots closest to his body in tiny, spherical clumps, running downward.

How had this creature, this Dark Man, come to steal the power of a god?

I breathed in and out a couple more times, clearing my head. "Lucian?"

I blinked and came back to the present. Looking at Evelyn, I forced something of a smile. "We have good evidence now," I replied. "Much better than I first thought. We need to get it to the City."

"The City?" She stared at me in amazement. "You think anyone will listen to you there?"

I shook my head tiredly. "I don't know. But I am not running from them any longer. These Dark Men are too powerful. Others have seen them now. The others can scarcely blame me for every trouble that besets them now."

The ground and walls around us shook as thunder from the most recent lightning strike rumbled past, followed almost immediately by another bolt that hit just outside the doorway. As Evelyn and I stumbled back into the chamber, stunned, the electricity raced along a thick metal pipe bolted to the wall ahead of us and thereby gained entry to a bank of computer equipment, which in turn exploded in a shower of sparks and flame. As the electricity dissipated, some small portion of it continued on beyond the ruined equipment and traced out the sparkling contours of a sphere, about ten feet in diameter, apparently hovering in midair. The entire effect lasted barely a second, and then was gone again. Quickly I ran to where the sphere had appeared, waving my hands through the space.

"What are you doing?" Evelyn said, coming up behind me.

"Did you see it?"

"See what? All I saw was the lightning, and now I'm mainly seeing spots."

Nothing. There was nothing there. But I had seen it. Walking in an arc around the area, I continued to wave my hands about, through thin air.

Evelyn had moved quickly from puzzled to bemused. "Did it strike you in the head?" she asked.

"Maybe."

Raising both hands, I released the Power in the form of a broad, weak current that saturated the area in front of me. Ever so faintly, the shape of a sphere formed again, this time outlined in blue.

"Hey!" she said. "What's that?"

"I'm very glad you see it too, now," I noted, as I expended more energy, seeking to grasp hold of the shape. It was tricky; this was a construct made entirely from the Power, channeled by someone other than myself, along lines with which I was unfamiliar. After several instances of the shape slipping from my extended grasp, I finally managed to snag it. And I pulled. With a deep, resonating sound that vibrated the tables and equipment throughout the chamber, the sphere slid out of its pocket universe and into the one we currently occupied, there to hover in midair, glowing bright white.

Evelyn gasped.

After advising her to take cover, I sized up the artifact. Without question it was a vessel, containing something its owner wanted kept safe.

"Just what have you been hiding, Arendal?" I muttered as I prepared to assault the shell of energy before me. I had to be careful about this, just in case my hunch proved correct. Allowing my own energies to flow over every millimeter of its surface, I found the weakest spot in the weave and exerted as much strength as I dared on that one spot. For a moment, nothing happened. Then, with an ear-splitting CRACK, the sphere split open and dissolved away to nothing. From its interior dropped two figures in blue, falling the short distance to the chamber floor and lying still.

Evelyn rushed past me as I sought to rein in my energies.

"It's them!" she shouted, bending over what I could see were her two misplaced crewmen. "They're alive."

In a few moments, both of the humans had regained consciousness and were sitting up, coughing and trying to regain the feeling in their limbs. Both were terribly

274

disoriented. Evelyn had the small medkit from her black flight suit out, just in case, but neither appeared to have suffered any serious wounds.

"I'm fine, fine," Cassidy growled, pushing the diagnostic tool away. "Just feels like I've been asleep a long time," he said.

"Yeah," Kim agreed, attempting to stand up and failing. "How long were we out?"

"That would depend on a number of factors," I replied. "We are not in the best position to judge at the moment."

"You've been missing for several days, as far as we're concerned," Evelyn told them. "But, as I understand it, time may have moved differently where you were." Then, blinking, she looked up at me. "Where were they?"

"A pocket universe Arendal had set up," I said. "I couldn't get a sense of exactly where it was, though— in the Above or the Below. He is very talented, and his constructions are always very complex."

The two crewmen looked around, taking in their surroundings for the first time, squinting at the dark interior of Arendal's sanctum.

"I think I liked the beach better," Cassidy said.

"I think I dreamed," Kim said, his voice distant.

"Of castles in the sky, or of taking out the trash?" I asked.

He looked at me curiously but did not reply.

Anxious to leave this place and get moving again, this time with a definite destination—the Golden City—in mind, I urged the humans to their feet. As they struggled to get their legs back under them again, Evelyn filled them in quickly on some of what had transpired in their absence.

"Let me get this straight, Captain," Cassidy said, interrupting early on. "You've put up with this guy for *days* now?"

"Just the two of you?" Kim added, eyeing me suspiciously.

"He's been a gentleman," Evelyn told them firmly.

"This guy? Right," Cassidy said with a snort. But he looked at me with something other than the usual contempt and distaste, for once.

Evelyn gave each of them one of the pistols she had carried in her duffle bag. After she had explained a bit about them, and what they could do, Cassidy and Kim seemed to perk up tremendously. Kim, cradling the gun in both hands, eyed me in such a way as to cause me to rethink the idea of giving him such a weapon.

Then she got to the part about the human worlds being under attack by a horde of demons.

"What are you talking about?" Cassidy demanded.

"Demons?" Kim looked from her captain to me to Cassidy. "You have to be kidding."

Evelyn shook her head.

"We have no reason to doubt the information. And I've seen them—the demons. They're real."

Kim looked at her as if she had grown a second head.

"It must be some kind of alien invasion," he finally said. "We need to get back."

He turned to me, reddening.

"You hear that? Our worlds are under attack. No more stalling, no more delays. You have to get us back there now."

"To do what?" I asked. "What can three more humans do in a war surely now covering a dozen worlds or more?"

I shook my head.

"No, the answer to it all, the key to both our problems, lies in the Golden City. I am sure of it."

"But—"

I gestured at Evelyn.

"Your captain understands. Returning to Earth now would do you no good at all."

I looked at all three of them, and spoke the most difficult words I had ever attempted to say.

"I need you here, with me."

The three of them gawked at me, silently, for what seemed like an eternity.

At last, Evelyn broke the silence. "You need us?"

"Someone in the City is behind all of this," I said. "Maybe Baranak, attempting to extend his domain. Maybe Vorthan. Enough circumstantial evidence points his way, but you can imagine that I am not fond of accusations based on weak evidence, at the moment. Perhaps both of them together are responsible. I don't know. But I am firmly convinced that all of this—all of it—will not end until we discover the source of it all, and stop it *there*."

Cassidy and Kim glanced at one another, then back at me. "And you want us to come along," Cassidy said.

"You are now armed. You have had some experience in dealing with my kind. You have a personal stake in it, now, as well. Also, to some degree, you are in my debt. And…"

I looked down, extremely uncomfortable, and thought of the words Evelyn had spoken to me, in the dungeon, just after we had first met.

"You are all I have."

All three of the humans visibly reacted to that. I turned and strode across the chamber, hands clasped behind my back, long coat flaring behind me, waiting.

The two men looked at their captain, waiting for her to speak. After a second, she nodded.

"There's no question we can do more good with him, out here, than we can do on our own, back home," she said.

Somewhat reluctantly, Cassidy nodded.

Kim frowned but, outnumbered and outranked and unable to defeat our reasoning, he agreed as well.

As the two crewmen turned back to the task of familiarizing themselves with the pistols, Evelyn walked over to where I stood.

"We're with you," she said. "Don't let me down."

I looked at her, my first, instinctual reaction quickly squashed by all I had learned in the time since I had first met her and her crew. Soberly, I nodded.

"You could have just ordered them to obey, though, right?"

She frowned at me.

"Lucian, I didn't hike halfway across the universe and risk death in a dozen different extremely bizarre ways in order to rescue my crew, just to treat them like tools, like robots, afterward. I value their knowledge, their opinions."

She shrugged.

"Of course, if they had disagreed, then I would have ordered them to obey my decision."

She grinned, and I could not help but do likewise.

The crewmen's conversation caught my attention then, and I walked back across the room to listen.

"Demons," Kim was muttering. "Crazy."

"It's not the first time, though," Cassidy said, scratching his chin. "The Second Empire was overrun by them. That's what brought it down—or at least, my grandma used to say so."

"Oh, please. The Second Empire collapsed because of economic failure and internal revolt," Kim asserted loudly, as if reciting a line learned in grade school.

Cassidy shrugged. "My granddad always said it was because the imperial government got too big, too involved in everyone's business."

"Whatever." Kim waved a dismissive hand. "The point is, it wasn't some supernatural plague of demons that brought it down. All those thousand year old myths about devils coming out of the earth and swallowing up whole planets—ridiculous."

"They did not swallow whole planets," I said, stepping between them, "but they certainly laid waste to cities, and they slew humans by the millions."

I shook my head.

"Amazing how, in only a few dozen generations, humans can forget even something like that."

"There's never been any evidence found of it," Evelyn pointed out. "You would think we would find the remains of bodies, artifacts of some sort, scattered all over the worlds of the old Empire."

"They brought little with them and took everything when they retreated," I said.

"What do you know of it?" Kim said, facing me, frowning. "Some psycho from the Outer Worlds. You expect us to believe you know anything about the fall of the Empire?"

"I was there," I said. "I fought them."

They stared at me. Evelyn started to smile and turned away; she understood enough now, had seen enough, to know the truth. The other two probably never would believe it. I shrugged.

"Where?" Kim demanded.

"Mysentia. Argos. Chronos. I led the resistance there, and in other places. The invasion was not confined just to the Seven Worlds, the future Alliance worlds, you know."

"Markos the Liberator," Evelyn said, nodding. "Yes."

Kim stared at her, then back at me.

I smiled.

"Did you think I earned that title just by leading a revolt against the Terran Alliance?"

My mouth drew into a tight line as I thought back across the centuries.

"I helped liberate half a dozen worlds from the demons, a thousand years ago."

"Why?" Kim shook his head. "What did you care?"

"It was my home," I replied. "My exile had just begun. I fully intended to dwell on Mysentia for centuries, or longer. And, as it turned out, I did."

Cassidy and Kim both appeared to be taking all of this in. Finally Kim waved a hand in the air.

"It doesn't really matter now," he said. "We're all in agreement to follow you, to see this matter through to the end."

"Whatever end that might be," Evelyn said, zipping up the duffle bag she had stuffed with pieces of the Dark Man armor we had found—our evidence.

Cassidy nodded.

"Then let us be on our way," I said, heading for the doorway.

With a cracking and a shuddering like the birth pangs of the world, the night before us flared far brighter than any lightning strike could ever cause. Racing to the door, we looked out in wonder, and saw a fiery wound opening in the sky. Out of that wound golden light poured. As we watched, the opening expanded into a broad oval, perpendicular to the ground, about thirty feet above it. Through that oval a giant strode, radiant in blazing glory, beautiful and terrible.

I took this spectacle in and summed up my feelings about it succinctly.

"Aw, crap," I said.

Baranak: In his left hand rode war, and his right held back the thunderbolts. Time, which never diminished our kind, seemed only to magnify his power and his glory, and again, as I had for uncounted millennia before, I looked upon him and I knew true fear.

Baranak. At last. The confrontation I had hoped for and dreaded since the beginning. While this was neither the time nor the place I had planned for it, I had little choice. I could not flee him; he was at least as fast as me, and could punch through dimensional barriers I could not. But he would probably not listen to reason, either. Resigning myself to my fate, whatever it might be, I prepared my arguments on the one hand and my attacks and defenses on the other. Though I knew I had little hope of even surviving the clash, if it came to that, I set my jaw, summoned up all the Power I could pour into my thin frame, and strode forward to face the master of the Golden City, my nemesis.

Thus I was completely unprepared when he collapsed at my feet.

SIXTEEN

As the portal through which Baranak had emerged moments earlier dwindled down to a tiny pinprick of light and then vanished, I managed to get a sense of just how many barriers, how many layers of reality, he had torn through in order to reach this place. Seven. The knowledge staggered me. Never had I heard of such a feat. No wonder he had collapsed; the effort of forcing himself through that many different planes, all in one leap—that alone should have all but killed any of our kind. Looking down at his smoldering form, though, I saw that the jump alone had not left him in his present condition. His gleaming golden armor was dented in places, and scorch marks streaked his arms, as if he had been wrestling with a flamethrower. He had been in a fight, and had taken a considerable pounding.

All the more amazing, then, when he struggled up to one knee and gazed up at me, very much alive.

"Impressive," was all I could say.

He lunged at me.

Backpedaling quickly, I released the energy I had stored within myself, aiming a barrage at him. I am no offensive juggernaut, but with my life on the line, and a bit of time to prepare, I can conjure up a few methods of attack. I had hoped not to have to employ them against the god of battle, of course. I had had other plans for dealing with him. But here we were, and my options had grown extremely limited.

Surprisingly, the column of blue-tinted energy I directed into his midsection rattled him, and he staggered backward, grunting. I repeated the effort as soon as I was able, and this time he crashed to his knees again, gasping, his golden plate mail clanking on the hard floor.

Now, this was just silly. I could never hope to reduce Baranak to such a condition by myself. He had to have been much more seriously hurt than I had first suspected. Half of me relished the completely unexpected opportunity to finish him off forever. The other half of me——a half I had scarcely suspected existed until this moment——held me back somehow.

Once again Baranak attempted to rise and attack me. If nothing else, I admired his determination. Again I smashed him to the ground, this time leaving him flat on his back, his breathing ragged.

Baranak lay on the verge of defeat. I had him. He was beaten, though I had not been the one to do the bulk of the work, by any means. Nevertheless, all that remained was to administer the coup de gras. Summoning up the Power, taking aim at his prone form, I looked inside myself for the elation I thought I should be feeling at such a moment... and found nothing.

I risked a quick glance at the humans. They all hung back, at the far side of the room. They had seen Baranak before, and understood to some degree the power and the danger he carried with him.

"Finish him off," Cassidy called. "For God's sake, man—— you may not get another chance!"

Cautiously, my energies at the ready, I approached the big, armored form, peering down at his still body. His eyes were closed, but they flickered open again as I watched. I braced myself.

He regarded me with what looked to be genuine surprise, then scowled. "Enough," he said in a voice as weak as I had ever heard from him, though still carrying tremendous force of command. Slowly, painfully, he attempted to pull himself up to one knee.

He seemed sincere about ending the fight, and treachery had never been something associated with him, so I waited. Unsure of whether to help him up or kick him back down, I merely stood there, staring at him. After a few seconds he sought to stand, and reflexively I bent down, helping him up, terribly worried that he might strike again at any moment.

"What are you doing?" Kim demanded.

"You can't be serious," Cassidy added.

"Quiet," Evelyn ordered, and the other two shut up.

Baranak coughed roughly, then looked at me, unsteady.

"Lucian. Well."

Leaning on my arm, he actually managed a sharp laugh.

"How ironic."

He pulled away, then swayed unsteadily for a second before seeming to regain his equilibrium.

"What did this to you?" I asked, stepping away again quickly, just in case he renewed hostilities.

He tried to move, all but staggering forward, then halted again and stood like a giant redwood, swaying in the breeze.

"I can... no longer... dispute your account of these... Dark Men," he wheezed. "Four of them... beset me... on the Road."

"Four?"

I stepped back another step, as quickly as if he'd said he brought them along with him.

"You were attacked by *four* of them?"

"Yes," he huffed, his breathing labored.

"And yet here you are," I said, shaking my head in wonder. "At least you managed to get away from them—"

He glared at me with enough force to knock a lesser man through a wall.

"Get away? No! I fought them!"

"Of course, you fought them," I amended. "That much is obvious. But..." And I summoned up the Power to full force again, preparing to unleash it upon him, "...you then decided to come straight here, after me?"

"Not... after you," he said, slowly regaining his composure. "I had no idea... you were here. I came looking for Arendal."

He grasped his helmet in both hands and wrested it off his head. His thick blond beard dripped with sweat; his piercing blue eyes showed no signs of defeat.

"I sought his help," he said, "or perhaps a weapon of his, that I could use against them."

I blinked. "You came here looking for Arendal?" Somehow, that thought had not even occurred to me.

Then I started to laugh.

He glared at me, waiting.

"Of course you did," I said. "But I'm afraid I have some unpleasant news. Well," I added, "unpleasant for you, anyway." I thought of Arendal lying in the sand with a hole in his forehead. "Sort of pleasant for me, actually."

His eyes bored into mine, and I could feel his patience evaporating. Quickly I gave him a very brief synopsis of the clash between Arendal and myself on the beach. After I finished, he continued to glare at me, his anger now almost palpable.

"Then you may have doomed us all," he growled, "even if you did not kill the others, before."

His words struck me like a physical blow, and I almost stumbled. *What?* Had he just conceded my innocence in the matter of the murders—or at least admitted that some degree of doubt existed in his mind? What had changed? As much as I wanted to pursue that topic further, I also wanted to know how my settling of matters with Arendal could possibly result in any sort of calamity, so I reluctantly bit my tongue and waited for him to continue.

"We needed Arendal," Baranak hissed.

He shifted his gaze to the ground, then, and his voice grew as quiet, as troubled, as I had ever heard it.

"The City itself is under siege," he said. "We are beset by an army of these Dark Men!"

I swayed on my feet, shocked.

"What? An army?"

"Yes. And there are more of them than there are gods remaining to defend the City. Many more. They have taken up positions outside the walls."

His eyes narrowed.

"I was convinced it was your doing."

I glared back at him.

"I was convinced it was yours, all along," I growled.

"Murderer."

"Tyrant."

We stared one another down for a long moment, broken finally by Evelyn, who had approached us from the side, saying, "Your city! Under attack. Remember? Not to mention our worlds..."

Both Baranak and I blinked and glanced at her, then quickly turned back to one another.

"Let us not forget that part of it," Baranak said. "The demons have returned to the human worlds. You deny involvement in that?"

"Oh, sure...I unleashed demons against my own adopted homeworld."

I rolled my eyes.

"How far do you intend to push this absurdity, Baranak?" I demanded. "Can you not see there is more going on here than just me up to my old tricks?"

Sullen now, Baranak said nothing. Seconds ticked past, as I waited to see if he would press the matter or even attack again. It appeared, though, that he had come to some sort of acceptance, whether he would admit it or not.

Then I became aware of something that had nagged at my thoughts since his arrival.

"Your Hosts, Baranak. Where are they?"

He looked away.

"Dead. Or near death, anyway."

He exhaled, long and slow. He looked more worn down, more beaten, than I had ever seen him—than I could have ever imagined him.

"They fell defending me, providing a chance for... escape." The words came hard to him; the thought of leaving a battle before it was entirely over had to gall him. "But I—-we—needed help. The welfare of the City had to be put first. I—I had to come here."

I did not know whether to feel hatred toward him for all of the harassment he had given me for so long, or sympathy for his current plight. The errand he was now on was for the good of our City, though, and I owed him honesty in that regard.

"Arendal surely would not have been of any help to us," I said, "even were he here."

Baranak frowned.

"What? Why?"

Taking the bag from Evelyn, I unzipped it and dumped out the contents.

"We found these here, in Arendal's sanctum," I said. "He had to have been involved."

Baranak stared at the black pieces of armor, then looked back at me, his expression bleak. Breathing deeply, he drew off one of his mail gauntlets and ran his hand over his face. The swagger, the arrogance with which I had always associated him, was gone.

"This is grave news," he said.

He lifted one of the dark faceplates, studied it, and tossed it aside in disgust.

"If these... things... were never controlled by you, and if Arendal is out of the picture now... then who...?"

"I don't know," I replied. "But I have my suspicions." Best to wait for more evidence before accusing his recent right-hand man, I reasoned.

"Whatever the things are," he growled, "they are powerful. Remarkably powerful."

"From my own experiences, I would tend to agree with that."

"They possess abilities similar to our own."

I nodded. "Remarkably similar, I would say."

He looked at me, frowning.

And it clicked.

"Tell me, Baranak—-how can I be a murderer, when no one is dead?"

His frown deepened.

"What?"

"Did you see the bodies?"

"Of course! At least, the ones who were killed in or around the City, while the Fountain was not flowing. Others I saw after it was restored, when their bodies were brought back to the City, just before you arrived. All were quite dead."

"And what became of them?"

"What?" he repeated.

"Were they disposed of in the Fountain?"

"I assume so."

"You assume?"

His frown, impossibly, became still deeper yet. He wiped the sweat from his face again, thinking.

"There were so many... We held funeral ceremonies in mass, in the main courtyard. The bodies themselves were turned over to Vorthan as part of the investigation. He was to dispose of them afterward."

I nodded slowly.

"And where is Vorthan now?"

"I... I left him in charge of the defense of the City, while I sought help." His expression had become unreadable. "We thought that only I... could break through their lines..."

"Probably true," I said, "but leaving Vorthan there, in charge, was not a good idea, I think."

"You would turn me against him, as well as against Arendal?" Baranak growled.

Ignoring that, I motioned for the humans to join us outside the doorway, on the broad shelf. The sky was brightening a bit, as whatever passed for daybreak in the place attempted to assert itself. The storm appeared to have blown over, I thought to myself, scarcely guessing the half of it.

"The only thing we can do now," I said, "is get to the Golden City as quickly as we can, and hope it is not already too late." I met his eyes evenly. "There we will find the truth, once and for all."

"Perhaps," Baranak was saying, "perhaps that…"

He never got to finish the thought.

Crimson lightning flared and split the sky in half, accompanied by a deep, rolling boom.

"They are upon us!" Baranak shouted, pulling his gauntlets and helmet back on.

With a cry, golden energy trailing from his fists as he moved, he rushed forward, just as a crimson portal shimmered open across from us and two Dark Men charged through it. The collision shook the foundations of the world, and all three of the big figures sprawled across the ground, dangerously close to the ledge.

Motioning for the humans to retreat inside the chamber once more, I summoned as much of the Power as I dared, flooding my body with its essence. Then, a shield of my blue energy firmly in place around me, I strode forward, a part of me shocked at the very notion that I was going into battle alongside Baranak.

The Golden God climbed to his feet quickly, roaring. His fists, glowing now like suns, smashed against the Dark Man nearest to him. The ebon figure, deathly silent, shuddered from the blows, but recovered and initiated its own attack, hurling crimson lightning bolts back at him. Baranak staggered, but advanced again.

The other Dark Man turned to face me, and I redoubled my shields even as I rushed into the fray. We met halfway across the rocky shelf, and I managed to elude two blows while striking my opponent with a series of quickly-hurled blue spheres, each of which sent him stumbling back a bit but none of which did any real damage.

Meanwhile, his anger and outrage only recharged, Baranak advanced on the other Dark Man once more. His fists moved like twin hammers, and the figure in black became the nail. The Golden God delivered such a beating then that our City would speak of it in hushed and reverent terms for millennia afterward, if any remained alive to do so.

On we fought, for what felt like hours, and the rains came again during that time.

Drenched and muddy and above all bone-weary, I fought on as best I could. All too soon, my strength flagged; I am not, after all, the god of battle.

Some part of me watched the clash from outside myself, and wondered at the very fact of it. Diving into battle is not a thing I have traditionally done often, or willingly, or well. Yet I found that something drove me on, spurred me to action, pushed me to go all out against our foes. As most of my attention remained focused on the Dark Men, a small sliver of my mind diverted itself to understanding just why that might be; what could be urging me to violence.

Hate?

How long had I hated Baranak? Forever. He represented everything I despised in a leader: the arrogance, the simplicity of thought, the belligerence against anyone espousing different views.

Hate, then. Hate for Baranak, though? How could that be pushing me to battle, when I was fighting alongside him?

Even as I thought it, I knew it wasn't so. I did not hate Baranak—-not any longer. I disliked his stubbornness and his arrogance, yes, but among our kind he hardly held the monopoly on those traits. I wanted to convince him of my innocence, or at least to end his pursuit, but in the depths of my once-black heart I could find no more evil designs directed at him.

The hate that drove me into the battle and pushed me to pursue it to its end could only be hate of those who had brought all of this upon us; upon the Golden City, upon the gods themselves, and most especially upon me!

There, then, lay the true targets of my hatred: those who would harm the City. I loved that City even as I, dark lord that I was, loved myself—and, as I have said, the City always reflects in its beauty and its glory the esteem its inhabitants hold for it.

Perhaps the sharp blows my skull absorbed from the Dark Men contributed to my revelation, but in any event I became convinced then of a possibility I had suspected since first leaving exile: our natures and our Aspects might actually be able to diverge. Was it conceivable? Could we grow beyond our old simplistic restrictions and definitions? I had always found it odd that we gods were so much more than mortal, yet so confined within Aspects staked out for us in the unknowable depths of the past. Maybe the potential had always been there. Maybe something inside us changed when the Fountain was stopped and restarted. And maybe it simply took immortals a long time to grow up and out of our selfish, petty preoccupations. Whatever the case, I felt with certainty that my world was broader now than it had been before.

All of this passed through my mind in the time it took Baranak to drive one of the Dark Men to its knees and the other to force me back toward the cliff's edge, about to strike. All of this and one thing more: If we could become more that we had been, if our natures were not encompassed entirely by our godly Aspects, then perhaps the outcome of my long quarrel with Baranak was not a foregone conclusion after all.

Perhaps it did not have to be one or the other of us. Perhaps we could coexist, somehow.

Finding encouragement where none had existed, I moved. The black fists descended but the blows missed their mark. I rolled quickly to my right and scrambled to my feet, energized by something of which I'd known precious little, lately: hope.

We clashed again, and I actually managed to hold my own for a while. It would be a lie to say I bested the creature in any real sense, in a straight-up fight, but I gave a decent enough accounting of myself to retain some shreds of self-respect, and to cause Baranak an expression of surprise, once or twice, as he snuck an occasional look at how I fared. Nevertheless, the Dark Man surely would have beaten me had not fate intervened. Fate took the form of a shattering blow dealt by Baranak to his own foe, who in turn stumbled backward and into mine. The two sprawled out on their backs, limbs entangled. This was all the opening Baranak needed. Lightning crackled all around as the god of battle pounced upon them, his eyes burning with rage. His huge fists, two golden blurs, pistoned up and down, delivering thunderous blows that smashed them into the ground and took the last of the fight out of them both.

As the humans approached, surely awed by the display, I picked myself up and dusted off my clothes.

"Nice job," I managed, my breathing still labored.

Baranak did not even look back at us. He straddled one of the still figures, his armored form crushing it down, and pried at the featureless faceplate. With a popping sound, the dark, glassy oval came loose, and Baranak actually gasped. Looking over his shoulder, I did the same.

A once-familiar face, now all pale and gaunt, stared back at us through vacant eyes. Half embedded in the center of the forehead, a small, ruby-colored jewel flickered with internal light. As we watched, the flicker changed to a steady pulse, and the Dark Man attempted to sit up.

As I kept an eye on that one, Baranak whirled and grasped the faceplate of the other, wrenching it loose. A different face greeted us, but in a similar condition, complete with throbbing jewel in the forehead. The surprise was gone by then, though our sense of shock and outrage felt just as profound.

Baranak stood slowly and uncertainly, a look of great confusion masking his features.

"This is what you suspected," he said flatly.

I nodded.

Evelyn approached, gazing down at the black-clad bodies, seeing the faces.

"I take it you know them."

"Ferrik, our mischief-maker," I said, indicating the one I had fought. "And Kravak, god of the current." Regarding Baranak, I asked, "Both were believed dead, yes?"

His silence was all the confirmation I needed.

"It seems the reports of their demise were slightly exaggerated," I said, probably needlessly.

Baranak glared at me for a long moment.

"I felt their lights extinguished, all of them, within the aether," he said at last. "Having seen them now, are you so convinced I was wrong?"

I looked again at those bleak, blank faces, and could not argue.

Someone had not murdered the gods, but done something nearly as bad, or perhaps worse: transformed them into automatons. Into mindless slaves.

Baranak looked from one to the other of our former foes, his face now revealing not fury but disgust.

"Kravak was no weakling. Someone brought him to this state... made him into this. To humble him so..."

Something else caught my attention then; something at the very edge of perception, like the buzzing of a tiny insect. "There's a signal," I said. "It's pulsing to match the gems."

Baranak nodded once. "I feel it."

I gazed at their blank faces and knew unexpected grief. "They have been reduced to nothing more than puppets," I muttered.

He frowned. "There's something else. The Power…"

"Yes…"

I could feel it happening even as he spoke. The Power was fading. This could be no coincidence. Someone was tampering with the Fountain, just as they had before. And I was certain I knew whom.

"Yes," Baranak said, nodding. "Just in the past few seconds, it has diminished…"

"It's going away," I said, the thought chilling me. "They're shutting down the Fountain again."

Baranak's face grew ashen.

"We will be trapped," I said. "Powerless."

"The Golden City," he barked. "Now!"

"How far away are we?"

"Too far," he said softly. Then, with greater force, "But we have no other choice."

Understanding what he was about to do, I stepped back a pace, watching. And I was awed.

Baranak raised both his mighty, gauntleted hands before his chest, arms extended outward, fists clenched tightly, knuckles almost touching. Closing his eyes, he emitted a deep, resounding groan, and then slowly moved the fists apart. In the widening space between them, the fabric of reality itself rippled and twisted and tore itself apart. How many layers, how many barriers he broke through simultaneously at that moment I do not know; but it represented a titanic effort, an act of sheer power and will, and on a scale I would never witness again.

He shuddered from head to toe, but still he stood, his arms stretched out wide to either side. A blazing golden portal stood open before us.

The humans rushing along behind us, we committed our bodies to the void.

SEVENTEEN

We ran along the Road to the City: that main, best-mapped, most-traveled thoroughfare that leads among the planes closest to home, and then right up to the City's gates themselves.

The last time I had traversed this route, one of the Dark Men had hounded my steps the entire way. Taken by surprise on that occasion, I had nearly been demolished by the savage attack. I found myself wondering now which god that had been, evidently brainwashed and hidden away beneath layers of ebon armor, and how much damage I had done to him. I truly hoped it had not been a former friend. Given my level of popularity, the chances of that were slim.

Baranak ran just ahead of me, and the three humans trailed only a short way behind. The Golden God had made no objection to their accompanying us, and I felt they deserved to see things through to the end. Their worlds, too, were at stake in this conflict, and besides, I had gotten used to having them around. Evelyn, at least.

For now, I had advised them quietly to keep the pistols hidden away. Baranak's reaction to discovering such weapons still existed at all, much less seeing them in the hands of mortals, was impossible to predict. Better, I felt, to wait until absolutely necessary before revealing their presence.

On we raced. Trying to gain some sense of our whereabouts, I found myself frustrated continuously. Baranak was navigating now, and before him, we'd been following Alaria. Consequently, I will admit that, aside from recognizing the Road itself, I had no idea where we were. I was not entirely sure just how close Baranak had been able to bring us to the City, with that one jump. Despite his heroic efforts, clearly we still had some distance to cover.

The area we moved through now consisted of rolling, grassy hills under a bright, yellow sun. The place seemed familiar. If so, it would mean we were getting close, and the City would soon witness a homecoming no one could have expected: Lucian and Baranak, entering together, as allies. Unthinkable. Yet here we were.

The Road could not possibly be wide open to us, all the way, though. Obstacles seemed inevitable. Soon enough, the first arose.

The air just ahead of us sparkled and twisted in upon itself, a gaping, blood red wound ripping open. From out of it poured demons—demons by the bushel, demons by the barrel. Their tattered, dark clothes fluttered madly around them as they looked this way and that, saw us, and rushed forward madly. Their void-like mouths gaped, slashed eyes sparkling with unearthly hunger.

Baranak hardly slowed. He plowed into the first wave, moving right through them, sending them sprawling. On he ran.

Hastily I erected a blue dome of protection over the humans and myself—just in time, as the demons fell upon us next, pounding at the barrier's sides, scratching and clawing at its coruscating surface. I heard shocked questions from the two men behind me, as well as quick explanations from Evelyn, who had seen more than a mortal's share of such creatures. I remembered then that more of these things—many more—

now lay siege to her people's worlds. Cassidy and Kim might well have been the last humans of their generation to lay eyes on the demons, rather than among the first.

More of the foul creatures appeared further along our path, and this time attacked in sufficient numbers to halt Baranak's progress. Coming up behind him, I unleashed what Power I could, driving some of them back, keeping them away from the humans who, behind my shield, had their pistols in hand, ready.

As the crowd around us thickened to the point that not an open space remained in any direction, my hopes faltered somewhat. Baranak raged and pounded straight ahead, pushing a portion of the attackers back, but always they closed ranks again and struck back. Many lay incapacitated around us, yet the bodies vanished within seconds, even as reinforcements poured out to replace them. Soon a much larger wave of demons surged forward, and this time Baranak was swept from his feet and buried under the deluge.

No longer able to see him, I whirled around, checking to be sure the humans were still safe. To my horror, I saw that the rising tide of creatures had nearly engulfed my blue dome, assailing it from all sides. While simultaneously maintaining the defenses around myself to hold them off, I directed what energy I could to reinforcing the shield.

Not good. Not good at all.

My capacity in no way matched Baranak's, even in his weakened state. With him swept beneath the onslaught, I knew I surely could not hold out much longer—especially while keeping the others safe, too. Panic sought my heart, found it. I faltered.

They were upon me then. Crawling, flailing, beating with their fists, they overcame my personal defenses and drove me down, beating me to the ground. Their weight, their stink, their overpowering wrongness—all these things pressed down on me, suffocating me, driving me toward despair. The sunlight was gone, and darkness closed in, crushing, crushing...

And then it lifted, if only a tiny bit. For whatever reason, they had ceased to concentrate on bashing at me and were squirming and wriggling away; only a few, at first, but soon in sufficient numbers that I forced myself to my feet again and blasted them away in a small circle around me.

Gasping, able to move again, I looked around frantically for the humans. The shield I had constructed for them was gone, as I had feared it would be, and for a long moment I could not find them. Then, I saw, and was amazed. And proud.

The humans stood in a triangle, each facing outward, and blasted away at the demons with their pistols. While not dealing a tremendous amount of damage, they had managed to drive the attackers back and hold them at bay. Surely they had also distracted the demons enough to enable me to break free.

Striking at the demons with my hurled spheres of blue energy, I attempted to make my way toward the humans, all the while scanning about for any sign of Baranak. A conspicuously large and dense conglomeration of demons some distance away seemed the best indication of his whereabouts. The fact that the occasional demon came flying out of that scrum, tumbling head over heels, also indicated Baranak yet lived and fought. Finding myself surprisingly happy for his success, I trudged toward my three mortal charges.

Just before I could reach them, a renewed wave of attackers—the largest yet—crashed into all of us. Seemingly limitless in number, the demons carried me under again, sweeping me along like a child caught in a riptide. I fought them hard and well, and scarcely a minute had passed before I regained my footing and pushed them away. Looking back to where I had been standing, however, I saw that the humans had vanished.

Striking down attackers as I moved, I raced as quickly as possible for that spot. Reaching it, I could find no signs of Evelyn or the others. I called their names, turning in a slow circle, still dealing death and destruction upon my foes as I moved. Nothing.

An explosion of demon bodies behind me caused me to whirl about then, and I beheld Baranak forcing his way out of a crowd, golden energies flaring around him, fists flailing. Quickly he carved out a circle of relative safety around himself, as I had done.

"The humans," I called to him. "Do you see them?"

He cast his gaze about quickly. "No."

On we fought, pressed from all sides. Still the numbers against us grew, and we could not help but wear down. I found myself wondering what would become of us if we were defeated by this unholy crew.

The huge silver axe that slashed its way through the crowd at that moment thus became one of the more welcome sights I have ever beheld.

As many of the demons before us whirled to see what new enemy had struck them, Baranak renewed his offensive and surged into the main bulk of their forces. For my part, I moved toward him and attempted to shield the other attackers away from the group he fought, preventing reinforcements from entering the battle and overpowering him. Together we created an opening in the wall of bodies ahead of us, even as the silver axe appeared again, rising and falling, sending demons and demon parts spinning away.

"Karilyne!" I shouted.

The tall goddess in silver and black roared to match Baranak, and her axe and her sword rose and fell about her, bringing in a harvest of destruction.

"Did you lose something?" she called to me.

I saw then the humans grouped closely behind her.

"Yes!" I cried, overcome with joy. "Yes!"

Fighting his way to her first, Baranak stood back-to-back with her, the humans in between, and together they carved a circle of bodies out of the horde.

I arrived some moments later, and saw that the humans had apparently lost their pistols. The weapons were no longer needed here, though; Baranak, Karilyne and I authored a tale of devastation upon the demons then, and soon the survivors lost their nerve, backing away or vanishing entirely, as their fallen comrades had already done.

And thus, moments later, we stood alone on the Road, our adversaries and our victims all gone.

Gasping, panting, leaning forward, hands on our knees, we sought to catch our breath and recover from our wounds and exertions. Once we could speak again, I thanked Karilyne for the timely aid and for rescuing the humans.

"I do not know these other two," she said, indicating the men, "but I could not abandon my new friend, Captain Colicos, to such a hideous fate."

Evelyn smiled at her, and they shook hands.

Cassidy and Kim just looked at one another, still struggling to comprehend all they were seeing, learning, experiencing.

"Those things—the demons," Cassidy said, "They stripped away our guns. I tried to hang onto mine, but…"

"They knew what they were doing," I replied. "Or whoever directed them did."

Baranak nodded. He had come to the party late, but now he was a believer.

Sufficiently recovered, we caught Karilyne up on what was happening.

"I felt it, too," Karilyne said after we described the sudden drop-off in the Power that had spurred us to this course. "Just as it felt before, when the Fountain stopped. Heading to the City seemed the best thing to do."

"It is no accident," I said. "We go to remedy the situation, no matter the cost, once and for all."

Karilyne required no convincing. She was with us.

Onward we raced, toward the City.

With three of us acting together, the transitions through the various planes proceeded very smoothly, barriers yielding easily as our combined power and vision brushed one after another of the veils aside. One could hardly tell we were jumping from universe to universe as we ran.

Soon, the grasslands gave way to a rocky topography, with smooth hills replaced by rough and jagged outcroppings. As we picked our way along this more difficult route, the violet sky overhead darkened to indigo and rain began to splatter down in big drops around us. Disturbed by us or by the weather or both, unseen creatures among the rocks chirruped an insistent, tuneless call. We came then upon a narrow stream that meandered its way through the jagged countryside. Following along beside it, we came to a small waterfall, emptying down from a high outcropping into a broad, circular pool of a peculiar shade of green, before continuing to flow past us.

Something about the water troubled me, but I could not say what, precisely. Then, it became all too obvious.

"Look out!" I cried, again summoning a shield from the greatly diminished Power now available.

Baranak and Karilyne whirled, uncertain of what we faced. Then they, too, saw it.

From out of the waterfall emerged five forms, all female, each carrying a flaming sword. Behind them strode their mistress, Vodina.

"Not again," I muttered, preparing for the worst.

Then I realized that Vodina looked, if possible, even worse than when I had first rescued her from the lake bottom in the cave. Her eyes were dim, vacant. Her skin had none of its vibrant, green color to it. And, in the center of her forehead, a small, crimson jewel pulsed.

"They've gotten to her," I yelled, even as Baranak and Karilyne stood still, uncomprehending.

The Furies struck then, knifing instantly across the distance from the pool and swinging their swords in broad arcs, the green flames lashing at the two warrior gods and staggering them back.

Struggling to his feet, Baranak saw the jewel then and, understanding, attempted to rush Vodina, but the Furies swung around and beat down at him with flame and sword. He staggered backward a few steps and glared, defiant.

Karilyne must have gotten the gist of the situation by then, too, for she unsheathed her sword with her right hand and hefted her axe in her left, and brought both to bear on the Furies. They grouped into a shimmering wall of violence in front of her and, raising their swords high, they advanced.

With an ear-splitting roar of defiance, Karilyne leapt forward, into and through the Furies, splitting their line easily. Tumbling past them and then regaining her footing with remarkable skill, she spun her sword and her axe in a dexterous, complex maneuver. Then she rushed ahead, colliding violently with Vodina. The two crashed to the ground, each seeking to grasp the other as they rolled along the rocky surface, back toward the pool. The Furies, apparently taken aback, unsure whether to press the attack on us or move to defend Vodina, hesitated momentarily. Then they whirled and rocketed back toward their mistress, swooping down toward the spot where the two goddesses grappled.

As Baranak and I pressed forward, Karilyne got to her feet once more, gained a bit of distance from her foe, and hurled her axe. The big weapon struck Vodina a titanic blow just below her chin and flipped her backwards. Racing toward her, sword held high, Karilyne called back to us, "Go! The City! The Fountain!"

Baranak and I exchanged glances momentarily. Neither of us fancied the idea of leaving Karilyne in the middle of a fight, no matter how tough she might be. As Baranak started to shout a reply, though, the silver goddess reached out and grappled again with Vodina, and the two of them tumbled backwards into the water.

"Karilyne!" we both shouted as one, starting to move forward.

She surfaced momentarily, a green hand grasping at her face, her own fist striking down repeatedly into the water. "I have her," she cried. "Go!"

The Power fluctuated again, then dropped further. It had become dangerously low. We had to act, and now.

Suppressing further debate, Baranak and I abandoned our lady of silver and black and raced along the Road once more, the humans in tow. We told one another that Karilyne could best Vodina, even in the water. We told ourselves it was for the greater good. And we cursed the entire situation from top to bottom.

The situation, of course, only grew worse.

Emerging from what had turned out to be a long valley, we topped a rise and faced an open plain, flat and dusty, with no end in sight. What looked like an asphalt-paved highway out of antiquity ran like ribbon across it, just ahead of us. As we neared it, a portal shimmered open, its energy halo sparkling white, with traces of red lightning forking through it. From out of the circle stepped another Dark Man.

Immediately Baranak and I took up defensive stances, both of us cursing this additional delay.

Instead of attacking, though, the Dark Man stumbled sideways, moaning softly. This possibly constituted the first sound I had heard one of them make. The moan was followed immediately by a much louder wail, as of someone in great pain. The Dark Man reached up to his own head with both black-gloved hands, clutching at himself.

"What do you make of this, Lucian?" Baranak growled.

I merely shook my head, waiting to see what would happen next.

We did not have long to wait. With a sudden cry, the Dark Man tore at the blank mask covering his face, managing after a few seconds to pull it away. For a moment the face was obscured, as the dark figure kept ripping and tugging on the hood and other garments covering its upper body. Then, pulling the last shreds of black fabric and armor away, he stood revealed to us.

Arendal, his white suit rumpled and torn, scorch marks streaked across his skin, stumbled forward. His glasses were missing, his clawlike hands empty.

Baranak wasted not a second; he rushed forward, his voice shaking with fury.

"Are you the traitor?" he cried. "Are you?"

Arendal looked at us, eyes blank, and I could see that he was not himself. More even than Vodina, he seemed a zombie, animated by an outside force.

"Watch out," I called to Baranak—as if he needed protection from anyone or anything.

The God of Battle ignored me and seized Arendal by the collar, lifting him up. Golden energies flooded along his arms as he shook the slender god roughly.

"Speak!" he commanded. "Confess!"

Then Baranak gasped and recoiled, hurling the other god to the ground.

"His forehead," he said, pointing.

Coming up beside him, I looked down at Arendal where he stiffly struggled to rise.

From a distance, I had not seen a jewel on his forehead, like those that had been so prominently attached to Vodina and to the Dark Men. Now, though, I could tell that he, too, wore one. His, though, had been barely visible, so deeply was it implanted in a small, round hole in his forehead.

The hole created days earlier by my pistol.

Arendal still fought to rise, one hand reaching out in a jerky motion toward us. Baranak and I both tensed, preparing for attack. Instead, he opened his mouth and gagged, seemingly attempting to speak, his words choking in his throat.

Crimson energies flared from the sky then, one tendril striking Arendal and connecting with the jewel. Crying out, he fell backwards to the dusty ground. Then, before either of us could react, he leapt up and charged at us.

Baranak stood impassively and waited until Arendal got within an arm's length away, then swung his huge, golden fist out in an almost casual motion, striking him against the side of the head.

The slender god tumbled away, arms and legs flailing, until he rolled to an eventual stop in what looked to be a very painful position. His suit, now filthy, hung from him in tatters as he once again attempted to rise.

Baranak and I moved to stand over him, ready for further action.

"Noooo..." he gasped, his mouth forming a distorted "O" as he brought up both hands before him in an almost pleading gesture. "Not... meeeee..."

Baranak eyed him warily, waiting.

"We do not have time for this," he growled. "Some resolution must come, now."

"If this is what has become of him," I said, looking down at him, "I think he's gotten only what he deserved. He was a part of this from the start, I'm certain."

Arendal, or what was left of him, slumped forward, looking down at the ground.

"Yessss..." he managed to gasp through deadened lips. "I... thought I was... the mastermind..." He sobbed then, once. "But I was... played... was the biggest pawn... of all..."

He looked up at me then, calmness and clarity coming over his features for the first time.

"The biggest pawn..." he gasped, "...except for you, Lucian."

I only nodded. This was scarcely news to me, anymore.

Baranak glanced at me, then, and I could tell that, probably for the first time, he had begun to realize I truly had been framed. Then he returned his attention to Arendal.

"Who?" he demanded. "Who was your partner?"

"I did not know…" he said, his voice now very rough, very ragged. "Did not know he would kill them… Kill so many…"

Interesting, I thought. If Arendal actually believed the gods were dead, perhaps he spoke the truth.

"Who was it?" Baranak yelled, reaching to grasp Arendal by the throat. "WHO?"

"Vor—"

He gasped, choked, and the jewel popped from his forehead, landing at my feet. A tiny tendril of red energy trailed from it, back to the wound in his forehead. The air seemed to go out of Arendal then, and he collapsed limply. Baranak released him and he fell to the ground, unmoving.

The tendril of energy vanished.

I lifted the jewel and looked into its depths. Inside, a tiny spark of light swam, just as it had in the jewel I had taken from the pistol with which I had shot Arendal before—the jewel I had given to Alaria, I recalled. This, I knew beyond question, was that same jewel.

As I watched, the light flickered, died. The jewel grew dark in my hand.

Arendal seemed to sigh, once, softly, and then his body crumbled to dust, disintegrating before our eyes.

Startled, Baranak stepped backwards, nearly stumbling.

We looked at one another, wordlessly. There was nothing to say.

Again the Power shifted around us, dropped.

We had very little time remaining to reach the City.

We ran.

+   +   +

At last the gates of the City loomed before us.

"The Dark Men are gone," Baranak said as we approached. "They had surrounded this area, laying siege."

"I fear I know exactly where they are now," I replied.

His face hardening into quite possibly the most fearsome and intimidating expression I have ever beheld, Baranak strode forward.

We gathered before the gates, all five of us, we improbable rescuers of the eternal realm: three humans, hurled out of their universe and their depths; the golden god of battle, my eternal foe and constant tormenter, now my only trusted ally; and me, the erstwhile dark lord, home again at last to save the City he loved, or die trying.

The gates were closed. Each of us who called that place home, however, carried the key within ourselves.

Leaning forward, resting both massive, armored hands upon the golden surface, Baranak pushed.

The doors resisted.

He groaned, redoubling his efforts.

Still they did not budge.

Louder he groaned, and I knew he had bent all of his will, as well as his strength, to overcoming the resistance. Moving up beside him, I lent my own efforts to the job.

Those gates could hold back an army, but they could never withstand the force and determination of the master of the City. With a shudder, they parted slightly, the light from inside spilling out. And then, as if some invisible barricade had been removed, they gave way and swung easily open.

We strode onto the gilded streets of our Heaven, our eternal realm. Palaces and towers lined the broad avenue ahead of us, jewels glinting from every surface, but I saw no one on the terraces or balconies, no faces in the windows. Once again I experienced a visceral reaction to the sheer emptiness of the place, but I shoved the feeling down through force of will and buried it.

"Beware," Baranak growled, "for the Power ebbs low. We are extremely vulnerable."

At the far end of the avenue lay the great basin, a circular bowl of white stone perhaps a hundred yards wide, set into the ground, its lip raised up about four feet above street level. It contained the pool from which the Fountain sprang. One look at it confirmed his words and my fears. In place of the usual towering geyser of cosmic energies at its center, roaring up from none-knew-where, instead existed a mere sputtering trickle. What little remained of the Fountain could be seen bubbling just above the top of the ceremonial stairway and platform that extended out over the basin.

The state of the Fountain was not what caught my attention, however. As the five of us raced along toward the main square in which it lay, we saw that the basin had been surrounded by figures in black. More of the "murdered" gods, I was certain; their bodies perverted into mindless servitude. From high up on the platform extended myriad forking tongues of red lightning, each reaching down to touch one of the Dark Men below. The creatures writhed at the touch of the current, almost basking in it.

If what I suspected was true, the violation was even worse than I had believed. Not only had he bent them to his will, but he had made them utterly dependent upon him, upon his channeling of the Fountain's Power to them via himself. Anger swelled within me, and I started forward again.

The golden god of battle arrived first. He fairly shook with rage, and his voice echoed off the walls of the deserted city. "Who dares?" he roared. "Who dares pervert the golden realm so?"

"Show yourself, Vorthan," I yelled, and Baranak looked back at me. I'll give him credit; stubborn as he was, he no longer seemed surprised.

A figure moved into view at the head of the stairs, atop the platform. Neither his rich red robes nor his uncharacteristic wearing of gold and jewelry could disguise him from us. We knew his face quite well. Mottled bald scalp, black goatee, eyes burning red; our rugged, powerful god of toil had seemingly joined me in moving beyond the limitations of our Aspects—a proposition I found more than troubling.

"I have no more reason to conceal my activities or myself," Vorthan said, granting us a mock salute.

Reaching into his robes with his left hand, he gestured with the other, and the horde of Dark Men parted before us, allowing us a pathway to the foot of the stairs. When we had moved past them and reached that position, he bade us halt.

"You no longer present a threat," he gloated. "Only a bare few remain to oppose me. The rest now comprise my dark army." He raised his bare arms, blacksmith's muscles bulging, and crimson energies flowed from his clenched fists. I could only guess he had devised some way to channel much of the remaining Power from the Fountain directly to himself, or perhaps even to store it up when the flow ceased entirely. That tracked with what I had already theorized—that he had attacked the others when they were powerless and he himself was not.

So Vorthan most likely retained all his energies, all his potency. Meanwhile, Baranak and I existed as little more than mortals. At that moment I believed our predicament could scarcely grow worse.

"All of the City is mine," Vorthan crowed.

"Ours," a melodious voice corrected from behind him.

"You!" Evelyn gasped, moving between us to gaze up at the new figure on the platform.

Baranak and I watched in stunned silence as our lady Alaria strode to the edge and stood beside Vorthan. Alaria, as beautiful as before, her thick, auburn hair a halo about her, her black dress shimmering in the light. Now, though, she carried with her an air of danger and terrible power, enticing yet utterly deadly, that radiated outward as a palpable, tangible force. Alaria, who had released me from the dungeon and had provided clues along my journey of discovery and self-discovery. Alaria, who had used me, I saw now, as a pawn, with which to distract and misdirect Baranak every step of the way. I couldn't have done it better myself.

"A pawn," I whispered then, and remembered where I had just recently heard that word spoken, through dying lips. I knew beyond a shadow of a doubt that she had used Arendal just as thoroughly as she had used me. For different ends, of course—him, for his weapons and his knowledge; me, for my reputation and my usefulness as a decoy—but to equal effect. She and Vorthan had played us all for fools. And I had been so blinded by my anger toward Baranak and Vorthan that I had never seen it, never suspected.

"Why?" Baranak whispered, his carefully ordered world collapsing around him.

"This is beyond understanding," I snapped before either of them could reply. Truth be told, I did not want to hear their justifications. It all struck too close to home for me, in more ways than one. Even I, the dark lord, had never conceived of going so far as to render my fellow gods into mindless slaves.

"What I want to know," I said, "is how."

Vorthan's lips parted in a cruel grin.

"You would," he laughed.

He drew a large red jewel from his robes—surely what he had been clutching there before—and held it aloft. It was similar in appearance to the smaller ones we had encountered so often of late, but much bigger.

"All the gods," he cackled. "They're all in here."

He held the gem before him, leering at it, madness dancing in his eyes.

"So very efficient," he continued. "One of my finest works. It took but a few centuries to construct—a synthetic gem replicating the properties of the very jewels that powered your weapons, Lucian." Looking at me, he chuckled. "The gems that, in your weapons, merely stunned... but, given a few modifications of my own, grew capable of drawing out a god's life force, imprisoning it within, and leaving the body a perfect, empty vessel... possessing some degree of power, and needing only... control."

I thought of Arendal, and how I must have done the same thing to him, back on my island, that Vorthan had done to... to so many of us. I shivered. At least the three gems in the humans' guns had been acquired directly from Buchner; they could never have done the damage Vorthan's gem had. For this, if for little else at the moment, I was grateful—I did not need anything more on my conscience.

Baranak glared at me, once, surely for my unintentional contributions to Vorthan's dark accomplishments. Then he returned his attention to the lunatic before us.

Vorthan gazed into the gem's dark depths, and from my vantage below I thought I could see flecks of color swimming within.

"All the souls of the gods—if such is your preferred term—held within, and their bodies mine to command. Though capturing them drained away most of their individual Aspects and abilities, they remain powerful soldiers in my army. Powerful... and *obedient*."

At that, the row of Dark Men snapped to attention and all turned toward us. There were dozens of them.

My mind worked frantically, searching for a way to turn this to our advantage. I took a few steps up the stairway, Baranak automatically following. I focused on Alaria, trying somehow to know her mind, to understand what dark desires and motivations had driven her to this end. Unexpectedly, I found she was already staring at me, seeking my own thoughts. I met her eyes and knew then what she wanted. I do not know what she saw in mine, nor do I want to know, but she must have felt it was enough.

"Thank you, Vorthan," she said then. "Your expertise has been most useful, and your assistance most appreciated."

He frowned, but was not able to look back at her in time.

The silver cane of Arendal appeared in Alaria's hand, white lightning flaring about it. She raised it high. Then, with a cry, she planted its sharp, pointed tip squarely between Vorthan's shoulders.

The god of toil gasped once, his eyes wide, then fell to his knees, his crimson energies gushing out through the wound opened by that mighty weapon. He toppled forward, the large gem spilling from his fingers and bouncing just past Alaria's outstretched, grasping hands to tumble down the stairs.

It skittered to a stop at the feet of the human, Cassidy. He picked it up and peered into its shimmering depths, oblivious to all else around him.

Baranak rushed up the stairs, apparently thinking Alaria an easy mark now, or perhaps believing it had all been a ruse, to defeat Vorthan. Betrayed by his chivalry and his condescension, at the end.

Even as Alaria noted that one of the human men had caught the jewel, she drew the cane from Vorthan's back and held it at her side. "Oh, Baranak," she greeted him. "You muscle-bound fool. You think Vorthan had the cunning to mastermind all of this?"

He recoiled, but too late. The deadly weapon struck again, piercing his golden armor and biting deep into his chest.

Shoving Baranak's gasping form aside, she fixed her gaze on Cassidy. "Give me the stone!"

The human captain raised his pistol but could not fire. She had virtually hypnotized him. I had seen it so many times before, when she would venture to the mortal realm. Men could rarely withstand her Aspect and her will, manifested as overpowering beauty and desire. Cassidy found himself walking up the stairs, the jewel proffered in one hand.

Evelyn and Kim raced after him and tackled his legs. I imagine they fought to save their colleague and friend rather than to save the souls of the gods, but in any event, they delayed him long enough to infuriate Alaria. With a cry, she brought down the lightning—yet another ability I'd not known she possessed—hard upon Cassidy, and white flames consumed him before he could make a sound.

As Kim, stunned, bent over the smoking remains of their fallen friend, Evelyn gathered herself and had the presence of mind to dive for the jewel. Snatching it up, she began to climb the stairs toward me. Then she cried out as Alaria, coming down to meet us, gestured once more. The lightning flared again, and both Kim and I leapt to shove Evelyn out of the way. I didn't get there fast enough, though in my own defense I was much farther away. Kim, devoted as ever to a woman who did not possess the same feelings for him, shoved her aside and took the brunt of the blast. He met the same end as Cassidy. Evelyn, having received a glancing blow, lay still, unmoving but still breathing, now the only human left alive.

A sick feeling crept over me then. Part of it was for Kim, yes. He had not deserved such a fate, nor had Cassidy. Part of it, though, was for myself.

Again I had failed to save a woman from the wrath of the gods. This time, though, someone else had given his all to cover for my shortcomings. And thus I felt guilt. Guilt over my own failure to save either of them. Guilt that a mere mortal, Kim, had proven himself my better by making his sacrifice. And guilt over my complete unworthiness in regard to either Halaini or Evelyn.

Guilt, I knew then, was not new to me. It had resided within my heart for a thousand years, ever since Halaini's death. Guilt—that tiny seed I had unwittingly allowed through the cracks of my soul, there to work its gradual evil; or rather, in my case, the opposite. And once that seed of guilt took root, could other strange spiritual flora not be far behind?

Kim's sacrifice, and all the thoughts it unleashed, passed through my mind even as I watched the jewel tumble from Evelyn's fingers and skitter across the steps. I leapt for it, but Alaria got there first.

"Ah. My gracious dark lord," she said to me, a gleam in her eye. "Someone I can do business with, perhaps."

Hatred and fury held tightly within, I raised my eyebrows in mock surprise, knowing all too well what she meant. "How so?"

"I know these creatures meant nothing to you," she said in her purring voice. "I know your Aspect." She smiled wickedly. "I have always loved you, you know." She shrugged. "And hated you."

I frowned. "What—?"

"I left the gun for you, there on your island, and the note with it. 'Do us all a favor,' it said. I was never entirely sure, myself, what I meant by that. Kill yourself. Or kill Baranak. Or Vorthan. Any of them would have been fine with me. Any would have made my choices easier." She laughed once, sharply. "I didn't expect Arendal to be your choice—I didn't want him interfering so soon—but, in the end, it all worked out."

My teeth clenched, I sought some reply, some powerful rejoinder, and found nothing. To buy time, I nodded slowly, my mind racing.

"What fun would it be," she asked, "to spend eternity with no one for company but faceless automatons?"

"I can see where that might be a problem," I replied, as my internal debate raged on. I moved closer to her, forcing my disposition to appear pleasant.

"I knew it," came the croaking voice of Baranak, still lying where he had fallen, a couple of steps below. "I knew you were truly evil, Lucian."

I looked from Baranak's dying eyes to Alaria's, full of fire and beauty and life. Was there ever really any choice? Any doubt? I met Alaria's eyes levelly. "Evil is my Aspect, but it is not necessarily my nature," I told her. The words felt so familiar, yet in many respects they felt fresh and new. "And naivety even less so. Give me the jewel, Alaria."

She screamed wordless fury at me, then turned and raced to the top of the platform.

"It was me, you know," she said then, glaring down, anger lacing her every word. "I was the one who engineered Halaini's death."

My voice was a near-whisper, my heart falling from my chest. "What?"

"Arendal pulled the trigger, but it was my plan. It tested his loyalty to me, and he passed with flying colors. He loved her, too, I know—but he loved power more. The power I offered him."

"No," I gasped, my mind reeling.

"I hated that witch from the dawn of time until the day she fell into the Fountain," she continued. "The way you doted over her, while scarcely giving the time of day to anyone else in the City. I knew that removing her would remove all your restraints, turn you into a wild card—which was precisely what we needed." She smiled again. "And it worked to perfection."

My head reeled. I could not handle this now. No way. I had to set it aside, to deal with it later. So much, so much… I forced it down, into a compartment, and nailed it shut inside my soul. Then I glared back up at her, murder in my eyes.

She had turned away, back toward the Fountain. Extending one hand out near the weak, bubbling jet that was all that remained of it, she seemed to be warming her fingers, as over a fire. I thought I knew what she was actually doing, though—absorbing all the energy she could hold, for one last effort. Against me.

As I started forward, to settle matters one way or the other, I felt Baranak grasping at my leg. I looked down.

His eyes, meeting mine, burned with golden fire. He had heard. He understood at last. His gauntlet removed, he reached up with a bare hand that faintly crackled with his remaining energy.

"Take it," he gasped. "All of it. You will need it."

"No! I—"

"Look!"

He pointed beyond me, and I turned. The Fountain grew larger again as I watched. The bubbling stars and constellations fairly danced—but only for her. Alaria controlled it now, and she had nearly restored it to its full force, but its energies flowed only into her, even as the rest of us diminished. Nothing reached the rest of us now. It was as if the Fountain had ceased to exist. All of us were completely vulnerable, completely mortal. Death looked on from above, hungry, watching, waiting.

"Take it!" Baranak cried. "I was wrong about you! Now take it!"

I grasped his hand and felt the last of his energy flowing into me. Then the hand went limp, the great hand of the golden god of battle, and I could only watch him die.

Filled with fury, I charged up the steps to the platform overlooking the great basin. Preparing to strike, I grasped and focused the mass of golden power that surged within my breast.

Then I saw Alaria. She stood with one hand still outstretched over the churning Fountain. In the other hand she clutched the big red gem—the jewel that held the souls of so many gods.

"You will be my slave, Lucian," she said then, "or the jewel goes into the Fountain."

I visibly deflated. Any attack would only send the jewel into the torrent, annihilating it.

"Swear the binding oath," she demanded. "The oath even the dark lord dares not forswear. Swear to serve me for all of eternity!"

"I—"

She held the jewel at arm's length over the torrent. "Swear!"

This could not be. It could not. Even my own black conscience could not bear such a burden—the death of so many, truly dead this time—across all of eternity. I had no choice.

"Very well—to save these gods, I—"

"Traitorous, lying bitch!"

A dark figure lurched past me, thin red contrails of energy trailing out in its wake, as it lunged toward Alaria. Her eyes still locked onto mine, taking my oath, she didn't become aware of him until it was too late.

With the last of his fading strength, the dying Vorthan crashed into Alaria. She cried out, once, and then they both tumbled over the edge, and down, down, down into the surging, churning Fountain.

I raced to the edge, looked over, despaired.

They were gone. Consumed. And the jewel with them. Not a trace remained.

Behind me, the army of Dark Men collapsed like marionettes, their strings all cut at once.

The Fountain dwindled suddenly, sputtered, and the ground beneath us shook. The world held its breath, gathering up, gathering, growing… and then the Fountain erupted at full force. The Power flooded out, washing over me, surging out through the aether, reinvigorating the universes.

It was glorious, incredible. A sight for the ages.

I cared not a whit.

I knelt there, on the edge, for how long I cannot say. Even later, when a battered and bruised Evelyn, the only other survivor, hobbled to my side and laid a hand on my shoulder, I could do nothing more than weep. Tears cast into the cosmic whirlpool.

EIGHTEEN

Some indeterminate time later, I stumbled down the stairs and stood, shaking, in the courtyard. Evelyn leaned against me, herself scarcely able to stand.

We examined the remains of the Dark Men, and discovered what we had feared to be the case. They had, all of them, turned to dust. Their animating spirits ripped out by Vorthan, then dropped into the Fountain, it had become as if they had never been.

I had no tears left to give them. I stood there, in the courtyard, the Fountain roaring behind me, and I came as close as I ever have to utter despair.

There silver Karilyne came to me. Whether she had defeated Vodina outright or simply benefited from the destruction of the large, controlling jewel, I never discovered. It scarcely mattered. She, too, lived, and she had come looking for me.

She knew what had happened. She knew Baranak had died at my feet, his last energies going into me. How she knew this, too, I never discovered, though many of us possessed rudimentary telepathic abilities that manifested from time to time. Those two warriors, so alike, surely had shared a greater link, in life, than most of the rest of us.

And so I faced her, waiting for the blow to fall, for the chop of her axe or the swing of her sword. Baranak was dead, and I had no doubt she somehow blamed me for this. Blaming me had practically been our national pastime, after all. In this, though, I had to admit to myself, she was not entirely wrong. I was the only one still alive who shared any culpability; who had, in any way, contributed to his death. She surely wanted vengeance and, at that moment, I felt no strong urge to resist her.

Squaring up before me, she drew forth a sword. It was not silver, though, but golden, and much broader than the sword she usually carried.

I fought through the anger and sadness and depression, and I looked at her questioningly.

"This was Baranak's blade," she said flatly, "though he rarely carried it. He rarely needed it. He felt few—including you—were worthy of being struck by it."

I nodded. That much was true, without question.

"It would only work for him—only conduct his unique form of the Power. But, in his hands, it was… formidable."

I nodded again, wondering why she was telling me this.

She held it out to me, point down, offering the pommel.

"Perhaps, one day, you will find a use for it."

She looked about, then back at me.

"Until then, let it serve as a reminder to you of Baranak's sacrifice this day."

I did not know what to say. Numbly I reached out, accepted it.

She nodded, then looked around again at the City.

"I am finished with this place," she said. "I have no more love for it. None at all." She paused then, meeting my eyes. "Nor for anyone in it."

Turning about sharply on her heel, she strode away.

And that was the last time I ever saw Karilyne, the silver warrior goddess, late of the Golden City.

+ + +

The human worlds survived their ordeal, not terribly worse for the wear. The demons assailing them all vanished as suddenly as they had appeared, once the events at the Fountain had concluded. I had suspected they might. Notes I found later led me to believe that Vorthan had summoned them—that he had believed all along that he could control them. He never could, though he continued to employ them till the very end. He had set them, and the Dark Men, upon us at different stages of our journey for various reasons—to herd us along, to remove us from Karilyne's custody and put us back on the game board, to spirit Alaria away when we asked her too many questions about Arendal's memories. He had even fought them himself, when they had gotten free of his control and looked to actually kill us, back in the bowl-shaped world.

Control. That was what he wanted. Control over demons. Control over the gods.

His creation of the Dark Men had come from that, from his work in controlling beings of power. He wanted an army strong enough to accomplish his aims, but completely obedient to him. If he could not get that from creatures from the Below, he would manufacture them in the Above, from his fellow gods. What monstrous evil. Arendal had claimed he had not known the full scope of it all, and I believed him. The same could not be said for Alaria. She had played upon the greed for power, the vanity, of both of them, from the start. Fools, all of them. Damn them to hell forever.

Evelyn was hurt more than either of us had known, there at the battle before the Fountain. I kept her with me in the City for some time and we both healed from our various wounds, visible and hidden. I would like to believe we grew closer during that time, but I know she regarded me with suspicion and distrust, even after all I had done and tried to do to make amends. She had lost so much, though scarcely more than I.

At the time of our parting, I was still unsure of her feelings. At least, I told myself that was the case. Perhaps at that time I believed it. I took her home, finally, to her mortal Earth, and left her there.

I visited Malachek some time later and sought his wisdom, but he had little to offer beyond, "Follow your heart."

Yes, Malachek survived, as did twenty-one others who had possessed the good sense to stay away and let someone else— me—clean up the mess. The others, now including Baranak, Vorthan, Alaria, Vodina, and Arendal, were all gone, all of them, forever.

Irony of ironies: I followed my younger heart, and lived my fondest dream. I ruled in the Golden City. And served as its entire population. The others dispersed, as Malachek had done long ago, and as Karilyne had done more recently, for more exotic locales. I doubted I would see many of them again.

I reigned. At last, at long last, I reigned.

Hooray for me.

I reigned over a ghost town. Had any subjects been present to look upon the new lord of the realm, they would have been woefully disappointed. Filling the seat of power, I became a solitary and forgotten figure, who might as well have hurled himself into the Fountain along with the others.

In the end, I did the unthinkable. I abandoned my throne and my lonely outpost. Willingly I walked away from it.

I would like to believe I had matured beyond the desire to possess such a place, but the truth is not so clear-cut, or so flattering. The City, as I have said, reflected in its nature the esteem its inhabitants felt for it. With one lonely and discontented god as its only inhabitant, how glorious could it have been? And if its nature seemed cold and dismal, what did that say about the esteem I felt for it then? What did it say about me?

Thus did I come to turn out the lights and lock the gates behind me, and embark upon the long journey back down the winding Road. With the gods and Dark Men gone, the passage would be forevermore uneventful, and for that fact I found myself both relieved and disappointed. But I had no further doubts. I turned my back on my former Heaven and followed my new heart, my crisply laundered soul.

All along, when pressed, I would admit the possibility that we gods had not always held the form we now did. What we had been before, where we had come from, I did not then know. Perhaps I had known once, millennia ago, and simply forgot. Perhaps something greater, or more insidious, was to blame. But if we had indeed once been something different, something closer to human, then perhaps we were not as trapped by fate and by the great cosmic forces surrounding us as I had once believed. Perhaps other... *career options*... yet lay before us, if we could only allow ourselves the luxury, the agony, of change.

And so I became Markos again.

Thus, six months after my return to Mysentia, my flagship rendezvoused with the Terran Alliance fleet on the fringes of Alliance space, near Trinity, just as arranged. At the appointed time, the peace delegation from the Alliance walked across the docking link and entered my ship, to a stately and formal reception. A dozen immaculately dressed diplomats and officers led the way, with more entering behind them, and I greeted each of them in turn, introducing each to his or her counterpart on my own staff. The entire time, however, my true attentions lay elsewhere. My eyes looked past faces and over shoulders, searching the crowd, looking, looking...

There.

Bowing courteously and making quick excuses, I maneuvered around to the rear of the delegation, at last finding the person I sought.

I found I had gotten used to her wearing the black flight suit from my own ship. Now, though, she looked very different. Resplendent in her dress uniform, navy blue with polished gold buttons and red trim, the Terran flagship's captain greeted me formally. Then she smiled.

"So, the Mysentians were willing to believe you were their leader." Her mouth twisted in a wry grin. "And that despite your extended absence and your... remarkable physical rejuvenation."

"It took some time to convince them all," I replied, "but eventually they all came around."

Taking a couple of drinks from a passing tray, I offered one to Evelyn.

"Some cling to the notion that I am Markos's son. Others figure I discovered a fountain of youth, some restorative drug or procedure, and they hope I will one day introduce them to it. Many of my subjects have dreamed up even more bizarre explanations. Given recent events, they are not so terribly unbelievable." I shrugged.

"In any event," she said, "Mysentia is yours once more."

I nodded.

"And you are... satisfied? You have personal fulfillment?"

I started to nod again, then remembered our earlier conversation, during our long journey together. A touch of anger flared within me, but I quashed it with surprising ease, and merely smiled.

"Somewhat," I said.

A knowing smile playing about her lips, she looked away for a moment, then turned back to me, her eyes moving toward the knot of officers gathered about the tables.

"The admirals were a bit nervous about your demand that I captain this mission," she said.

"If I have to spend time in the company of Terrans," I replied, "the least they can do is to make one of them an old friend."

She smiled, then looked around the room at the array of bigwigs and muckety-mucks filling most of the space.

"So, you're going to make a truce with us, then. With the Alliance."

"It seems prudent." I shrugged. "And perhaps, as well, I have found some... deeply *personal* motivations... to work toward better relations between the Outer Worlds and your government."

"Until the time comes to launch your next attack, either on one of your neighbors or against us," she suggested, only half-playfully. "I know how you think."

I placed a hand over my heart. "You wound me, lady. Surely you see that I have become a man of peace."

She leaned in closer, looking at my hand.

"You're not fooling me," she said, shaking her head. "I already know there's nothing under there."

Then she laughed, and I deflated a bit and joined her.

"I would hate to think that were so," I said then.

She paused, looking around the room again, and I waited. Part of me once again looked on from above in shock that a human could so disconcert me. Another part of me—now the greater part—rejoiced in her company once more. Yet it was all so awkward, so different from before. Perhaps we had both moved on, I reasoned. Perhaps I should have just been grateful for the time I had spent with her, and for what I had learned about myself during that time, and left it at that.

Turning back to me then, she bowed slightly and started to move away.

"I have to get back to running the ship," she said.

"Of course..."

I frowned, attempting to turn my thoughts back to diplomacy and business. Behind me, the two groups of delegates were seating themselves around a large conference table.

Then she poked me in the stomach with a finger, and I looked back at her, startled.

"When this session has adjourned," she said quietly, "we should catch up on things."

She pressed a small chip into my hand.

"This will grant you access to the living quarters of my ship, and will register you as a welcome guest on our security monitors."

I nodded dumbly.

"Maybe that way," she said, "no one among my crew will try to earn a reputation by capturing the dreaded Markos the Liberator, in the act of breaking and entering."

She smiled again, then turned and started back toward her ship.

"It couldn't be easier," she added, looking back. "No jumping out of trees, no ripping holes in the fabric of the universe."

She smiled, and that smile warmed me as nothing else had in months.

"Just follow the signs," she said.

And now five hours have passed; five long, dull hours of diplomatic wrangling and military arguments and map drawing and re-drawing, during which I could scarcely pay attention at all.

And now the meeting stands at recess, and I stand before the hatch to the captain's quarters; and I, who have ruled worlds and commanded armies and slain gods and emperors, fairly shake with nerves and fear. I summon up some of the forcefulness of my younger days and bring my hand up high, and I knock.

Abandon all hope, I once told a crew of explorers lost on unfriendly shores. As Lucian, the dark lord, I believed those words, or thought I did. I surely believed in power and glory and victory above all.

I have known power and glory, and I have known defeat and loss and bitter guilt that dogged me down through the centuries. And now, I believe I can know peace, and happiness, and love; or as much of those things as an erstwhile dark god is entitled to know.

Amazing, I think to myself as the door opens before me and I see her sparkling eyes once more. Amazing that I could have been *alive* so very many years and, until now, never really known how to *live*.

THE END
OF
LUCIAN: DARK GOD'S HOMECOMING

THE STORY OF THE ORIGIN OF THE GODS
AND THE GOLDEN CITY
IS TOLD IN
BARANAK: STORMING THE GATES

THE SAGA OF THE SHATTERED GALAXY BEGINS IN
HAWK: HAND OF THE MACHINE

THE FUTURE OF THE GALAXY
AND ITS INTERACTIONS
WITH THE SURVIVING GODS
IS TOLD IN THE LEGIONS TRILOGY,
BEGINNING WITH
LEGION I: LORDS OF FIRE

Thanks and appreciation this time around to:

Roger Zelazny, for this one above all others. This book is dedicated to him and most strongly reflects his influence upon me. Though we never met, I will forever think of him as my cosmic mentor.

Ami, Maddie and Mira, as always.

Mark Williams, for his continued artistic brilliance.

Ron Fortier, Rob Davis and everyone at Airship 27 for taking a chance on this novel back in 2009.

And of course all of my readers. I hope you enjoy this series even a tenth as much as I have enjoyed telling the tales.

The Shattering saga will return!
Next up: THE LEGION CHRONICLES 2: RED COLOSSUS!

ABOUT THE AUTHOR

Van Allen Plexico writes and edits New Pulp, science fiction, fantasy, and nonfiction analysis and commentary for a variety of print and online publishers. He won the 2015 Pulp Factory Award for "Novel of the Year" for *Legion III: Kings of Oblivion,* the 2015 Pulp Factory Award for "Anthology of the Year" for *Pride of the Mohicans,* and the 2012 PulpArk Award for "Best New Pulp Character." The first volume in this series, *Legion I: Lords of Fire*, was a finalist for Novel of the Year in the 2014 Pulp Factory Awards and the New Pulp Awards. His best-known works include *Lucian, Hawk,* the *Assembled!* books, and the groundbreaking and #1 New Pulp Best-Selling *Sentinels* series—the first ongoing, multi-volume cosmic superhero saga in prose form. In his spare time he serves as a professor of political science and history. He has lived in Atlanta, Singapore, Alabama, and Washington, DC, and now resides in the St. Louis area along with his wife, two daughters and assorted river otters.

Van Allen Plexico's Sentinels
Super-hero action illustrated by Chris Kohler
The Grand Design Trilogy
Alternate Visions (Anthology)
The Rivals Trilogy
The Order Above All Trilogy

TheShattering
Lucian: Dark God's Homecoming
Baranak: Storming the Gates
Hawk: Hand of the Machine
The Shattering/Legions Trilogy

Other Great Novels and Anthologies
Gideon Cain: Demon Hunter
Blackthorn: Thunder on Mars
Blackthorn: Dynasty of Mars
By Ian Watson
My Brother's Keeper
By David Wright

Nonfiction:
Assembled! Five Decades of Earth's Mightiest
Assembled! 2
Super-Comics Trivia
Season of Our Dreams &
Decades of Dominance (Van Allen Plexico and John Ringer)

All are available wherever books
are sold, or visit
WWW.WHITEROCKETBOOKS.COM

79186304R00202

Made in the USA
Lexington, KY
19 January 2018